PERFECT NATURE

ELIZABETH KNIGHT

CREATIVE WONDER PUBLISHING

Knight, Elizabeth

Perfect Nature

Editing: Swish Editing Services

Cover artist: Ruxandra Tudorica | Methyss Art

www.methyss-art.com

Formatting: Creative Wonder Publishing

ISBN: 979-8-88958-030-0 (ebook) / 9979-8-88958-031-7 (print)

"What lies behind us and what lies before us are tiny matters compared to what lies within us."

—Ralph Waldo Emerson

Authors Note

Dear Readers,

Perfect Nature is a book that contains quite a bit of darkness, that could be triggering to some people.

If you feel like this could be a problem for you, please protect yourself.

No work of fiction is worth your mental health.

Elizabeth Knight

The full list of content warnings is available on my website.

Link found here: https://www.elizabethknightbooks.com/omega-assassin

CONTENTS

ONE

FINLEY

After our conversation with Ayla, I sat alone in the back of the SUV as we drove back to the pack lands. So much had happened in one afternoon that I craved the chance to just sort through things in my mind. When we left, Ayla was going to return to her current clan and inform them she was leaving and moving to our pack. How the pack would take finding out I was an elf and we'd be home to more as time went on, I have no idea, but that was a problem for a later day.

What was hitting me the hardest was knowing my father was alive. Staring down at the photo in my hands, I couldn't wrap my mind around the fact he knew I existed and never once said anything to me. I'd grown up believing I was well and truly alone in the world.

Was my mother still alive?

Did my father not want me?

Was he even an elf?

Just when I didn't think the world could throw another bomb at me that would blow up my entire view on life, it did just that. I'd thought things were starting to settle. My men were figuring out how to manage with Rath in the group. All but Zander were in the mental bond where I could feel them all reaching out to check on me, but

I had it closed off. I loved them and knew they were worried, but I needed time to understand how *I* felt about what I had learned.

Turning the picture over in my lap, I gazed out the window as we entered our forest. The trees called out their greeting, happy to have me back. I got visions of things that happened with the pack or hikers out in the mountains while I was gone. Having an entire national forest as my eyes and ears would come in handy with the fight we were about to pick.

The sun was well on its downward journey and was just peeking over the mountains as if to do a final check on everything before it called it a night.

When we pulled up to our home, I let out a sigh of relief. All I wanted right now was to curl up with all my mates, watch a movie, and eat junk food. If Zander allowed it. The health nut he was always worried about me eating *real* food. I bet if I sent the twins to the pack house, they might have a stash somewhere.

As the guys unloaded out of the SUV, Rath stood near the car door, eyes trained on me. I knew he hated it when I blocked him out, but I was still adjusting to all my men having the ability to read my emotions.

"*Nin mel,*" he called, reaching out a hand to me. "We've let you sulk in the back long enough. Now it's time to let your mates help you." I grasped the offered lifeline and let him pull me from the vehicle and into a hug. "I know your assassin side urges you to hide away but don't forget you are an omega on top of that. Your softer nature, including your elf, needs the comfort of a pack, not to be isolated."

"Not everyone likes a know-it-all," I murmured. "I just needed time to accept what I learned today, but I was done for now."

Rath kissed my temple before guiding me toward the house with his arm still around my shoulders. "What can we do to help?"

"I was just thinking a night in with all of you together would be nice. We've been going from one problem to another and haven't just had time to be. Once Ayla returns and I start digging into whatever the laptop holds, I don't think there will be another chance," I answered, feeling the truth of my words. "Things like this tend to overtake your life, chew you up, and spit you out."

"Not if we don't let it, *nin mel*," Rath countered as we walked into the living room. "Although I agree it will be good to have a night together as a *Nos*, building trust and comradery."

"What are you talking about, elf? I think we've all done well to adapt to all the changes," Colt interjected, clearly having been listening to our conversation.

Rath nodded, giving me another kiss before releasing me. "There was a bit of a rocky start, but I agree we are learning our places and roles within our *Nos*. Finley has a great need for us in this upcoming fight and the universe chose well for her. I am honored to call you all my *gwanur,* and I hope you feel the same, but there is more for us to learn about each other, I think."

Lane leaned against the couch, listening and nodding his head in agreement. "Packs are only as strong as the trust they have in each other. Rath has a point."

"So, in the name of bonding, I vote for junk food and movie night," I announced, looking at the others.

Mason let out a whoop and pumped his fist in excitement. "Snuggles, you have some of the best damn ideas! Alright, Z-man, where's the popcorn? Do you have any Twizzlers?" He paused, seeing the look on Zander's face. "You know what? I think the twin and I might need to run to the pack house for the right supplies."

I couldn't help but smile to myself, knowing they wouldn't fail me when it came to fun.

"Why would I keep that shit in my house?" Zander grumbled as the twins jogged back out to the SUV. "If it can survive a nuclear blast, it's not food."

I walked over to him and wrapped my arm around him, placing the other on his chest as I looked up at him. "Then tell me, what do you do for fun? I'm not sure I've ever seen you do something just because you enjoy it."

"Oh, I can think of one thing I *do* just for fun," he said, his voice tinged with a growl.

Rolling my eyes at him, I slapped his chest. "Sorry, but I don't count. I'm serious. Everyone is always getting after me for not having hobbies or things I do just because. Now it's your turn."

My demanding alpha paused to think. His silver eyes narrowed in concentration. "Ah!" he blurted. "I play video games. The whole setup on the second floor was so I could play this one game that came out last year. Then I figured why not also make it a movie room?"

Elias looked at the alpha and cocked his head. "Did you ever beat the game?"

"No..." Zander hedged. "I only had about a month before I was back on tour."

"When you were on the tour bus, what did you do to relax?" I pressed, feeling like he had to have something he did that was just for him.

"Sweetheart, maybe you don't want to know that answer," Lane warned.

I knew what he was referring to but what happened between my mates and others before they met me wasn't anything I could hold against them. "I've had others before I slept with all of you. I'm sure you all have. What does that matter?"

All my alphas started to growl, eyes glowing as their wolves pushed for control.

Rath cleared his throat loudly, drawing everyone's attention. "Maybe it's best we don't talk about past experiences when it comes to sexual acts. Not all of us are proud of our past and what we had to do to survive."

Everyone fidgeted as they understood what Rath was saying. I knew what the Dark Ring was like, saw it with my own eyes, and it broke my heart to think my sweet, assured mate had experienced any of it.

"Reading," Zander admitted with a sigh. "I love to read about the history of other supernaturals. My hope is that by understanding the world and the people in it, we can find a better way to live. I don't just do music to make money or to be famous. You all heard my mother. I'm the wolf to beat all wolves in pedigree and power."

Colt walked past Zander on his way to the stairs. "Don't let that go to your head, alright? The ego you have is more than enough to deal with already."

"Fuck you," Zander shot back.

Colt turned and gave him a wink. "Sorry, you're not my type, but I'm always willing to share something we both enjoy. Rath seemed to think it was quite the experience when he did."

While I was in no way a prude or embarrassed about my sexual nature, which had been much more demanding since I became an omega, my cheeks heated. I think it was the fact they were openly discussing our intimate moments with each other when I wasn't around. Granted, we had all seen everything of each other being shifters, so I shouldn't be shocked they compared notes. I never came away unhappy, so I guess I should leave it as it is.

"Let's go pick out a movie before the twins come back and take over," Elias suggested, following after Colt.

"Smart plan, those two, when it comes to movie nights, can get way out of hand," Lane agreed with a sigh.

Zander and the guys modified the couch, turning it into a giant padded square we could lay on comfortably. I was instructed to sit in the middle and things would branch out from there. The guys duked it out over what movies to watch because apparently, there was no way only one could be agreed upon.

"Okay, Rath, you get to be the tie-breaker here. We are split fifty-fifty between *Alien vs. Predator* or *Men in Black*," Lane said, holding out both movies.

"I've never seen either, but I think *Men in Black*. I do rather enjoy Tommy Lee Jones. *The Fugitive* is one of my favorites," Rath shared, taking the DVD.

Colt grinned with approval. "Now that is a damn good movie."

"Another night," I interjected. If I let them pick more than the three they settled on, we'd be up all night. "We could make this a normal thing for us, you know. Have a movie night once a week, a way to ensure we all get time together with how busy life can be."

Before they could say anything, there was a door slamming open and the sound of a scuffle.

"The twins are back," Elias commented, confirming what we already guessed.

Feet thundered up the stairs, and Mason appeared with arms full of snacks. He paused, taking in the couch, and smiled. "Nice. I was worried we would be fighting over space next to snuggles, but this solves that problem," he said as he deposited his armful on the coffee table. "Oh, and I'm assuming we're moving out of the pack house for real now that the elf is going to be moving in."

"I guess we didn't really think that far ahead, did we?" Lane mused, rubbing his chin in thought. "It makes sense. We were going to move in here officially at some point. I guess now is as good a time as any."

"*Nin mel* did say that she hoped one day to have an intermixed pack of elves and wolves. Converting the pack house to an elf lodge might be a good way to do it," Rath pointed out.

Noah finally made it up the steps with five black trash bags stuffed with things. "We might have gotten a head start on bringing stuff over." He shared as I gaped at him. He trudged down the hall to the bedroom he shared with Mason, unbothered at our shock.

The twins had always been confident men from what I'd gathered, even more so now that we were mated and found their place in our mate pack, or as the elves called it, a *Nos*. Noah was my Companion, the mate who would always be by my side, helping me through life or, eventually, kids. Mason was my Hunter, a mate who provided and had a strange obsession with making sure I ate. While Zander cared what I consumed, Mason just wanted me full. I had a terrible habit of forgetting to keep up with a shifter metabolism and ended up starving at random moments of the day. Even though Mason was my Hunter, he was also a Companion as well. It worked out nicely since he didn't like to do things without his brother.

Zander started to sort through what Mason brought. "This is nothing but shit food," Zander grumbled. "Funyuns? What the fuck is that!"

Mason snatched it out of his hand, holding it protectively. "An American staple of snack food, that's what. Don't you start bashing my shit until you've tried it. Maybe that's why you're such an uptight asshole. Your mom never let you have shit like this."

"Drinks," Lane blurted. "Who wants what?"

"Are we making this a drinking party or keeping it PG?" Noah asked as he joined us.

"We're werewolves. It would take a gallon of something strong to even feel it," Elias said, shaking his head. "I'm not looking to try that hard. Why don't we just stick to soda and call it good enough?"

Mason slung an arm around Elias's shoulder, halting him from heading downstairs. "You and I need to go out sometime. I know a fox shifter that makes a brew that will knock you on your ass."

"When all this is over, and we don't need to be ready for anything at a moment's notice, I'll take you up on that," he agreed, slipping out of Mason's hold. "Until then, help me grab stuff."

"That's what we need up here, a mini-fridge," Mason said as they headed for the kitchen.

Smiling, I couldn't help but laugh at just how normal this whole moment felt. Here I was, a light elf-omega-werewolf with seven mates, one of whom was an elf himself, arguing about junk food and talking about getting drunk. Never did I think my life would take this turn, but I'm so glad it had. It would make ending this all that much sweeter.

Lane climbed onto the couch island and crawled over to me. "What's got you smirking like that?" he asked, pressing a kiss to my lips. Then, drawing back, he settled behind me and pulled me against his chest.

Looking up at him from my spot, I kissed his neck, earning myself a purr of approval. "It just struck me that this is normal life for us now. The eight of us all together, fighting over junk food, negotiating movies, battling for who gets to sit next to me, and I didn't ever think I'd have it."

"If you told me I would one day be sharing one mate with five wolves and an elf, I'd have thought they were insane," Lane admitted. "Now that it's actually happening, I don't think I'd want it to change. It takes some adjusting here and there, having to consider other people's feelings and needs, but that is what a pack does. As alphas, it's in our nature to lead but also to care for those we look after. Some might not be as gentle about it as others, but it's there."

"All of you put others first most of the time," I said, with a lingering caveat.

Lane chuckled. "But..."

"When it comes to me," I added. "You will do anything for your pack, but if it put me in danger or were disrespectful, then you wouldn't stand for it."

"Abso-fucking-lutly," Colt butted in. "There is nothing more valuable to us than you. If we had to drop everything and live on the run to keep you out of the Dark Ring's clutches, you bet your pretty ass we would. This is why we are taking down the Senate, isn't it? You agreed to help Morwyn because, in the end, it helps us too."

"It helps everyone," Rath countered. "While we will benefit, the government has been corrupt since the start and has to be done away with. I don't know the answer of how to fix it, but I know this isn't it."

"Whoa, whoa, whoa," Mason bellowed when he and Elias rejoined. "This is movie night. All other worries are to be left until tomorrow. Snuggles wanted a night to relax and enjoy time with her mates. That is what we are doing. Leave the world domination talk for later. It will still be there when we wake up."

"Couldn't have said it better," I said, motioning for him to toss me a drink. "Now, what are we starting with?"

"Let's see..." Zander started as he walked over to the three DVDs laid out. "*Men in Black, Die Hard,* and *Jurassic Park.* Little dove, what haven't you seen?"

"Ah, all of them," I shared, waiting for the reaction I knew I was going to get. "Look, I didn't have much downtime, and what little I did was spent sleeping or training. You don't stay the best at what you do without working at it."

Noah shook his head. "We have so much to cover."

"Good thing she wants to make this a weekly date night with all of us," Zander informed them. "Keeping that in mind, all of these are series… Do we pick one of these three and keep going?"

"*Jurassic Park.*" All the wolves agreed.

Zander nodded and got to work setting everything up while snacks and drinks were distributed. Elias handed out plates and napkins for us, much to Mason's disapproval.

"You just take handfuls of what you want and shove it in your mouth," he argued.

"That's what she said," Noah yelled, making everyone laugh, even Rath.

Once the lights were out, the next trick was to get everyone settled as the movie started. Lane, pleased with himself for getting to his spot early, purred up a storm behind me. Colt ended up between my legs, his head on my stomach, making his head a perfect table for my plate. Zander was on my right, Rath on my left, while the betas sprawled out. We agreed for each movie, we would change places because I was not going to have them fighting.

I made it through two movies before I was curled up in Elias's arms with Mason's head on my ass, and I was fighting to keep my eyes open. My wolf lay on her back, grinning like a fool loving the attention and time with our mates.

She and I had been a little off-kilter since my elf magic came into play. It all but tried to shove her out, but that wasn't going to work since she was as much a part of me as my own heartbeat. Bonding to our mates both as a wolf and an elf had made a big shift allowing me to spread out my magic so it wasn't all bottled up inside me.

It would take more work to be at a point where I trusted my magic to do as I needed, not what it wanted, but as Mason said, that problem would still be there tomorrow.

TWO

FINLEY

There were many things that would wake me up in an instant but having your own magical forest sounding alarm bells in your brain wasn't one I planned on ever experiencing. I sat bolt upright, looking around the space, realizing we never left the couch nest we had made. The dim glow of the sun starting to rise told me it was early, and I'd managed to get some sleep.

The urgency that my magic was pushing at me reminded me why I was awake. Climbing over the back of the couch, I quietly padded down the stairs using all my senses to keep alert.

Something was coming.

I walked to the back door that opened to the deck and slipped outside, down the steps until my feet landed on the grass. Closing my eyes, I let my magic surge into the ground. It felt like a pack of wolves on the hunt tracking down their prey. Someone had dared to enter our lands without my approval, and the forest was not happy.

The forest sent me flashes of images from animals in the area, but nothing was making sense. It was all blurry, like whoever they were moved too fast. Elias had mentioned there was a vampire that came looking for me. Was it returning? Why would a vampire come looking for me in the first place? I'd never interacted with them other than the moments before I killed them. There's no way they could be tied to the vampires we killed back in Florida... *could they?* No, that definitely didn't make sense.

It was more likely the Senate or Dark Ring sent an assassin after me. There was no secret to me being here, and I'm sure they thought being in Zander's big house with no pack around to save me would be an easy target. If that was their logic, they would be sadly mistaken. I was even more deadly than I was, just as a normal assassin.

"*Nin mel*, what's wrong? I can feel your magic everywhere," Rath said in a soft voice as he came to stand beside me. He didn't reach out to touch me or try to press into my mind, which I was glad for because I didn't know what my magic would do right now.

"Someone's here," I murmured.

"Is it Ayla?" he asked.

I shook my head. "No, my magic and the forest would recognize her as one of us. Whatever is coming isn't an elf." I heard more footsteps on the deck as my mates joined us. "Please stay up there," I requested, opening my eyes to look back at them. "I'm not sure what's coming, but my magic is flooding the earth around me, and I don't want it to risk hurting you."

"Why would your magic hurt us? We are your mates and carry part of you inside us from when we created the soul bond," Elias asked.

Part of me was ashamed to say it, but I refused to lie to them. "I don't trust it just yet. Like our wolves, my magic had a mind of its own, and right now, I never know what it's going to do."

"That will come with time," Rath said, trying to soothe my emotions. "How close is it?"

Letting my eyes fall closed, I could tell my magic was closing in on them. Branches of trees started to reach out, blocking the intruder from advancing as quickly, herding it in the direction I wanted.

Then it stopped.

"I know what you're doing!" they yelled, keeping themselves hidden in shadow. "I'm not here to harm you. I want to talk to the Light Elf Queen."

My eyes snapped open at that. *How could he have known anything about that? Could word have traveled so fast already? Ayla said she and only two other people in her clan knew what I might become.*

"It stopped," I shared. "They want to talk to the Elf Queen."

"The fuck they're going to talk to you. We don't even know who or what this goddamn *thing* is!" Zander shouted, his words echoing with a growl.

"I'm with him. It could be a trap," Mason added. "They could say anything to draw you out, then more would come and attack."

Checking in with the forest, it confirmed what I guessed. "There is only one thing on our land that shouldn't be here. The forest is on high alert right now and would notice the smallest misstep."

"My heart, you're not going," Elias stated, his arms crossed, immovable in his opinion. "*We* will go see who's dared to enter our lands, assuming they can talk to our mate while *you* stay here."

While I understood where he was coming from, I didn't appreciate the tone he was using. I knew his wolf was in charge right now with how his eyes glowed and the emotions I could feel coming off him. Off them all now that I opened myself back up to that part of my senses. With my magic running rampant, I'd instinctively closed off everything else to control what was happening.

"I believe it might be best if we all go," Lane suggested. "Finley isn't going to remain behind, and we won't let her do this alone, so we all go."

Zander snarled, his hands balling into fists as he started to pace. "You know this was so much easier when you would listen to us when we gave an order."

"I'm going to take the asinine words you just said and chalk it up to your wolf speaking instead of you," I snapped. "I understand you all want to keep me safe, but let us not forget I made a contract with *your* mother to take down the Senate, kill her mate, and destroy the Dark Ring once and for all. There is no way you can stop me because if you do, then the magically bound deal I made will kill me." I flashed him my wrist where the mark I shared with Morwyn sat until we'd both held up our ends of the contract.

Zander paused, his eyes zeroing in on my wrist like he'd forgotten about that part of all this. "You will let us speak to this trespasser alone. You will remain hidden with Rath, Elias, Mason, and Noah until we say otherwise. As alphas of this pack, we have every right to deal with this interloper. He's on our pack lands."

"That's fair," I agreed. "While I might be something important to the elves, it doesn't change that these are your pack lands first and foremost. What happens on pack land or with the pack itself should be handled by their alphas."

"Now that we have that settled, I don't think it's wise to leave whatever's come to pay us a visit alone on our lands much longer," Colt pointed out. "Little one, can you lead us there?"

"I can," I answered with a nod. "But you don't need me to. If you follow the pull of the magic you have within you, it will lead you where you need to go."

Zander walked up to me, holding my face with both his large hands. "I'm sorry, little dove, I shouldn't have said that to you. My anger got the better of me, and I lashed out, which is no way for a man to treat his mate."

"I forgive you," I said, settling my hands over his. "Fear makes us act out irrationally, and the more we care about someone, the worse that fear gets if they are in danger. While we are quickly becoming a strong group, there are still going to be growing pains."

He caught my lips in a deep kiss, his tongue delving into my mouth as if he could steal the breath from my lungs. Zander always seemed more comfortable showing his feelings through actions or gifts rather than words. Knowing he was the last of my mates to build a soul bond with, I took this opportunity to rectify that problem.

My magic was more than eager to claim this final mate of mine, drawing them into a deeper connection. It dragged me along our mate bond as wolves until I was shoved into Zander's soul, where his wolf nearly bit off my face. I could feel Zander try to jerk back from me, but I held on tightly.

"Easy there, it's just me," I murmured to his wolf.

Once he heard my voice and picked up on my scent, he relaxed and butted his snowy-colored head against my hip. Smiling, I scratched behind his ears for a moment, then hunched down so we were eye level.

"I'm going to bring you with me for a moment. We're going to see my wolf. Think you can give up control long enough to let me lead?"

His wolf sneezed, shaking his head, and took a step back, clearly uncertain about my request.

"Trust me, as your mate, as the woman who loves you more than anyone else ever could. I don't want to take your power away from you. I want to be your partner. My dream is for us all to build this new life together, using all our strengths to support those around us. Please, I want us to be in this together, not always fighting for who's in control."

The large white wolf with the silver eyes that match those I saw in both his forms studied me. He seemed to be weighing my words, but I knew he understood what I'd said. Now, I just needed him to take a leap of faith.

Which he did.

Moving so he stood next to me, he nudged my shoulder as if I were the one holding things up. Grinning, I stood and let my hand sink into his thick, coarse fur down to the soft undercoat. Then, wrapping us both in my magic, I pulled us back to where my wolf lived alongside the well of magic. Each time I did this, the space here became more blended and at peace. My elf magic at one point scared my wolf off to the corner to hide, but now she wasn't as scared. In fact, as we arrived, there she was, sleeping next to the bubbling fountain that calmly represented my magic.

Seeing her, Zander's wolf gave a yip of excitement and rushed off, licking her face to wake her up. When she realized who was there, she rolled onto her back, pawing at his face playfully. Her tail wagged nonstop as she enjoyed the attention of her mate, who'd taken so long to come and see her.

"I hate to break up this moment for you two, but I need to bring him back. There is a problem in our woods, and I need him to help me protect us," I explained.

They both appeared incredibly put out about this, but Zander's wolf gave her a few more licks and trotted over to me. I created a lasso of magic and secured it around his neck, giving him a good scratch before I opened the door for him to return. He gave me one more appraising look, then dove into the darkness to make his way back to where he belonged. As soon as I felt the bond snap into place, I returned to the surface and the world around me.

"What did you do, little dove?" Zander asked, his breath coming in quick pants like he'd been running.

I placed my hand over his heart and met his gaze. "I placed my mark on your soul. We are now bonded deeper than any being could possibly understand. You have access to my thoughts, emotions, and many other things."

He grasped my hand and pressed the palm of it to his lips. "I do trust you, Finley. With all that I am, I trust you, but it's not always easy to trust others with you."

"Then good thing you can now check on us whenever or wherever you are," Rath said, joining us all into one mental conversation. *"Welcome, gwanur, to the true connection of an elven nos."*

Zander's head whipped around to look at all the others as we could hear them chuckling at his surprise and amazement.

"Trust me, when they started talking to me in my head, that was some weird shit. She pulled that stunt on me at the zoo right after we figured out someone was following us. Give it time, and it becomes a little less weird."

Mason grinned and clapped Colt on the back. "Just think of all the conversations we can have with no one realizing it."

"Might I suggest we do that now as we deal with our current issue," Elias commented, reminding us about the stranger in our woods. "For me, the most beneficial thing is the ability to talk to each other as wolves. No more hoping the other person figures out what we're trying to say. We can just say it."

"No way," Zander blurted, then turned to me and planted a kiss on my lips. "Little dove, you are truly amazing. This is going to change everything. Just think how well we can move as a team now that we can talk silently no matter what form we're in."

I laughed, pulling back from him, yanking my shirt over my head. "Why do you think I did this now? We have an enemy to deal with, and you couldn't be the only one left out of the conversation."

"Man, I wish we didn't have something important to do," Lane said with a sigh, his eyes lingering over me as I shimmied out of my pants.

"If we hurry up and deal with this, then who's to say we won't have time for some fun?" I teased, then pulled my wolf to the forefront, dropping onto four feet and shaking out my fur.

In no time, I was surrounded by six massive wolves, all wagging and sniffing me over. Zander let out a commanding bark followed by a snarl.

"*Use your words, alpha,*" Mason teased.

Colt looked over at Rath and cocked his head to the side. "*You gonna be able to keep up, elf?*"

"*Don't you worry about me,*" Rath assured him as he sprinted into the forest.

Zander let out a howl the others picked up, and off we went to hunt whoever intruded on our woods. I reached out with my magic, checking in with the nature around me that they were still where they stopped and hadn't moved. Seconds later, I got a literal bird's-eye view as an owl sat guard up in the trees. While they were still cloaked in shadow, I got the sense they were most likely male. The other creatures said he smelled like death, and they didn't want to go any closer than they had to.

I sent out my assurances we were on our way and would deal with this situation, ensuring the forest got my thanks for the warning. The trees resulted with delight at my praise as we raced through the woods.

It was so odd to communicate with nature as if it were another human, but everyone always said that the world was full of surprises. Of course, many thought people who believed nature was a living, breathing thing were crazy, but now, it made me wonder if they had a bit of elf blood in them.

As if Rath knew I'd been thinking about elves, he dashed in front of us, giving me a wink as he pulled Colt's tail and disappeared into the forest. He moved like a streak of light, but the more I watched, it was like he blinked in and out of existence—appearing in one place, then darting off to appear somewhere else. It had to be his magic. There was no other explanation for it. If that were the case, I absolutely needed him to teach me how to do that.

"Nin mel, I will teach you anything you want to know. Not only because I am your Guide but because you deserve to understand the full scope of your abilities," Rath's voice said, obviously having picked up on my thoughts. *"Did you know it's much easier to pick up on what you're thinking in your wolf form?"*

"Then I will have to be careful not to think of anything I don't want you to hear," I quipped, knowing he would never intrude or disclose something he shouldn't.

Rath appeared next to me and ran a hand down the length of my back as we ran. *"You're right, I would never betray your trust, and to prove it, I will tell you I'm the only one who can pick up on your thoughts as clearly. The others are soul bonded to you, but as we are both elves, it is a much different connection."*

Zander let out another howl as he picked up on the scent of the intruder, and it did indeed reek of death. It was almost as if the person themselves was dying, rotting away from the inside out. Could this be why they came here? Did they know I could heal?

"Rath, how common is it that elves are gifted healers?" I asked, slowing down a bit to lag slightly behind the others but letting them hear what I was asking.

"It is common that in every clan, there would be a group of healers of various levels. In some more prominent clans, there would even be a guild or school for gifted healers that people could call on if they needed help," Rath answered.

"Betas stay with Finley," Colt ordered. *"Even if this person is just looking to be healed, they didn't go about coming onto our lands the right way. We will investigate first, then decide what to do next. Rath, can you help us keep communication open so you can hear what's being said?"*

"Certainly, once this matter is settled, we should start working on these types of things so everyone feels comfortable doing it," Rath suggested.

Everyone grunted their agreement as we stopped and let the alphas go ahead of us. My wolf was on edge, not at all liking that they were putting themselves in danger. I tried to soothe her but couldn't do much since I felt the same way. It would give me more comfort to be able to guard their backs, but I would stay here and respect their authority as alphas of this pack.

THREE

LANE

It wasn't hard to follow the scent of rotting putrid flesh now that we were close enough. How had this thing even managed to get here while staying in one piece?

On second thought, who knew if it was in one piece?

Colt took the lead, and Zander and I flanked him as we arrived at the shadowed clearing where the scent was almost unbearable. There, sitting with his back to a large oak tree, was a man... or at least what used to be a man at some point. If I thought zombies could ever be real, this was what I would imagine one would look like. With the overwhelming stench, it was so hard to tell what it was. The speed he'd moved at didn't make sense for anything human, and I'm not sure a human could survive an illness like this.

"So you've finally come," the man said, his voice raspy, and his breathing rattled like his lungs were full of fluid.

Having been an EMT in my past life, combined with the sensitive awareness I had now as a werewolf, I could pick up on things easier. Although I don't think anyone would need to use a stethoscope to tell he was drowning in fluid from his own lungs.

"Guys, this man is practically a corpse that hasn't given up yet. There is no reason he should be alive right now," I informed everyone.

"So what, we just give the guy a pass because he's dying?" Zander demanded.

"I can feel the hum of your connection. If you're going to talk about me, I would prefer it to be to my face instead of silently behind my back," the man grumbled. "I also know that none of you are the one I'm looking for, so please don't waste what little time I have left in this world with your alpha macho bullshit."

Colt snarled, snapping his teeth at him for such disrespect while he was on our territory. Knowing we wouldn't get anywhere with those two running the show, I shifted back and slowly stood.

"Why have you come onto our lands without bothering to follow the rules? If you want our help, you'd think not pissing us off would be a wiser choice," I said, crossing my arms as Colt and Zander stood on either side of me.

The man was suddenly attacked with a coughing fit, his whole body convulsing as blood trickled out of his mouth and down his chin. "What's it matter if I piss you off? I'm dying a slow, painful death that no one but the Elf Queen could heal. It tends to make you realize what rules matter and which don't. I needed to get to her quickly and didn't have time to petition for an invite to your lands. Besides, it got you to come to me rather quickly, didn't it? I never planned on harming anyone. I just needed your attention."

"Well, you have it now," I stated. "What makes you think that there is even an elven queen? Elves have been gone for centuries. Besides all that, why would a person of such status be here in a wolf pack?"

Using the tree for support, the man slowly made it to his feet. "Don't play dumb with me. The secret is out, and it's spreading like wildfire in the underground network. She freed an entire group of supers from the Dark Ring for the second time. Hundreds, including myself, witnessed this with their own eyes."

"How did you end up like this?" I questioned now that I could see more of him through gaps in his shredded clothes.

"Ever wonder what happens when you put silver into a vampire's bloodstream? This is what it looks like as it burns through my body at a slow, agonizing rate," he shared. "Everyone left that night, scattered to the four winds, and disappeared into thin air, taking the freedom they were given to heart. Not me. I wanted revenge for what they did to my Blood Bond and me. I was foolish and went after my old master, who'd killed my Marissa when she no longer pleased him in his bed. Only all the members were on high alert after the attack, and I was caught. They tortured me for days, slowly introducing tiny drops of silver into my veins until I started to rot."

"Then what, they just let you go?" I asked with a huff of laughter. "You expect me to believe that they just tossed you aside because you were rotting?"

"No, they thought I died, and when they tossed me out into the pile of garbage to be burned, I escaped. The only good thing is that with the silver in my blood, the sun doesn't affect me as much. Or I'm in so much pain that I don't notice. Either way, I've been on the search for the Elf Queen because I know she can heal me," he concluded. Another coughing fit sent him crashing to the ground in a heap of blood, bones, and ruined flesh.

"*Rath, do you recognize him from being at that location?*" I asked.

His response wasn't immediate, which had me thinking his answer would be no, only to be surprised that it was yes.

"His name is Derven, and he was held by the same man who owned me last. Derven is a wildly impulsive vampire with a temper, but what he's said so far is all true. We didn't speak to each other much, but I trust he has no love for the Dark Ring whatsoever," Rath informed me.

"What's your name?" I demanded, wanting to see if he would be truthful.

Derven gave a harsh laugh. "What name would you like? My real name, pet name, the ones my masters called me? I've had so many names in my lifetime I don't know the answer to that anymore."

"What name do you want to be called?" I countered. "The name you would give to the Elf Queen."

"Ah, the name that matters," Derven nodded with understanding. "Many know me as Derven, but the name I would give to the Elf Queen would be Matei Derven Nistor the Third, first son of the oldest living vampire, Remus Serban Nistor the Second."

"That can't be possible!" Rath's voice said, cutting through our minds like a knife. *"Remus hasn't been seen or heard of in centuries. There's no way his son would be foolish enough to be caught by the Dark Ring."*

"Care to fill us in on why that matters?" Zander snapped.

"Remus was basically the father of vampires in Europe. Some say he was one of the first and created some of the strongest lines that still exist to this day. If that is his son, he is hundreds of years old, if not a thousand, and I know the Dark Ring has been holding him for at least fifty years. It doesn't make sense," Rath explained.

"Maybe you should join us since you know so much. That way, we aren't flying blind," Colt suggested.

"If Rath is joining, then the rest of us are," Finley cut in. *"Clearly, this man isn't much of a danger to me in his current state, and who knows what we might be able to get from him if we earn his trust."*

Colt and Zander growled at her request, but I agreed with her. Knowing who he was and that by giving us this name, he revealed how important of a person he was. Clearly, he wanted to prove he was worth saving and exposing Finley's power.

"I agree," I said, looking down at the other two. *"This man could be incredibly valuable to us."*

"Fine," Zander snapped. *"Just know if he makes one wrong move, I'll finish him off for good."*

With Zander's agreement, Colt gave in as well, and moments later, the others arrived in the clearing. Finley didn't slow until she was a few paces away from the decaying vampire. She sat on her haunches and inspected him with her quizzical gaze, the expression she always wore when trying to figure something out. Derven took her observation well and didn't back down at all when her magic reached out to investigate him further. He grunted in pain at something she did but seemed to breathe a little easier with less rattling in his lungs.

"Rath, would you please make something for me to wear when I shift back," Finley requested. *"I wouldn't want any of you killing him before we get a chance to hear him out because he saw me naked."*

"Wise of you, nin mel," Rath agreed as he gathered a few leaves off the ground and cupped them in his hands. We all watched in amazement as his hands started to glow green as fabric the same color as the leaves started to spill out from his grasp. When he was finished, he shook out a simple robe with a tie around the waist.

"I see you haven't lost your touch, Rathal," Derven commented. "It's been a long time since I've seen you use magic so freely. Has finding your *nos* helped you regain what you've lost over the years?"

"Just how well do you know each other?" I demanded. Rath made it seem like they knew each other in passing, but Derven talked as if they were much closer.

Finley trotted over to Rath, and he placed the robe over her as she shifted back. As she adjusted the robe, Rath met my gaze, and I could see shadows of his past threatening to take over. "How well does anyone know someone they were captive with? None of us were our true selves, doing what we must to survive, shutting ourselves off in the hopes we could one day return to who we once were unscathed. Sadly, that was something none of us could achieve."

Our mate wrapped her arms around Rath and placed her head on his chest, holding him as tightly as she could. I didn't need her gift with emotions to pick up on the pain and self-loathing pouring out of Rath. While I'd never had to experience anything close to what he went through, I understood what he was saying about being unable to return to who and what you once were.

My life forever changed when Colt bit me, changing me into a were-wolf, having my family reject me, and everything stripped from me all at once. No one wants an EMT that, with a scratch of a nail, could turn you into a monster.

"I apologize, my friend," Derven said with a sigh. "I haven't been out of captivity for what seems like a lifetime, and I don't always know how to interact with others correctly."

"That doesn't make sense. The Dark Ring has only been around for the past sixty years and has only become a threat to supers in the past twenty or so years," I argued.

"Before we delve into my bleak past, I would like to know that I have a future," Derven rebuffed, his gaze turning to Finley. "Will the queen finish what she started?"

"What is he talking about?" Elias demanded. *"She hasn't done any-thing."*

"Pretty sure she helped him breathe a little easier when she first joined us," I shared.

At that, everyone shifted back, sensing that being wolves right now was putting them at a disadvantage when it came to corralling our mate's actions.

"What reason do we have to save your life?" Zander asked, stepping in front of Finley so she was blocked from Derven's sight.

"You already know the answer to that, but if you must have me say it for your own reassurances, then so be it. If you heal me, I will give you the power of the Nestor coven of vampires at your back as you dismantle the Dark Ring," Derven announced. "My father will be happy to reward you for freeing me, and it would only add to his joy to destroy what took his favorite son from him."

"That's a hefty promise. You sure dear old dad will allow it at your request?" Mason challenged. "Seems that people don't believe he's still alive and running things."

I tried to hide my shock as Mason used the information that Rath gave to us and twisted it to make it sound like what he knew was common knowledge.

"The truly powerful don't need the world to remember them to control it. Manipulating in the shadows allows him to move among his people unnoticed. Trust me, my father is alive as much as one can be as a vampire, and he's been looking for me. The Dark Ring was wise and kept me locked away deep underground where it was hard for anyone to find me," he informed us, the bitterness in his voice clear. "It was only by happenstance I found my Blood Bond in those same dungeons, only to lose her far too soon, the bastard."

"If I heal you, I need your word you won't speak of what happens here to others. The Senate and the Dark Ring have eyes and ears everywhere, and I can't afford for them to know more about my powers than they must. From this moment on, you will never refer to me as the queen of anything or share that elves still walk the earth," Finley instructed. "Like your father, I want the world to believe rumors about me are just that, rumors. Information is a weapon, and I refuse to give anymore to those against us."

"You would make me swear to this?" Derven asked, surprised. "The humans might have forgotten about the elves, but we supernaturals have long memories. We know the balance they bring to the world, the hope that can be stoked from a mere whisper of their return."

"That time is not now," she snapped. "Until the world has been broken and brought to its knees, it doesn't deserve hope. When there is an outcry for change from humans and supers alike, we will stay silent and wait. The elves sacrificed themselves for the world once, and I refuse to let it happen again only to be forgotten."

Rath looked at our mate as if she'd just rewritten history and the elves never vanished. The awe and admiration practically glowed off him as he listened to her. I couldn't blame him. When Finley became passionate about something or someone, she put her whole self into it. None of this dipping your toe into the water. No, not my mate. For a woman who was only just learning the depth of her emotions, she wielded them as deftly as she did her daggers. It was incredible to watch, and with time, she would only become more powerful. That scared me as much as it excited me.

"You speak wisely and with foresight into the future, but I will caution you from hardening yourself to the plight of the world around you. They have been like the frog in a pot of water, slowly heated to a boil until it's too late for them to get themselves out of danger. Humans are young and live short-sided lives while we supers have long lives and choose not to notice the signs when we see them," Derven cautioned as he slumped against the tree, clearly running out of energy. "The sun is getting higher, and I am losing what little strength I have, leaving me no choice but to agree to your terms, Finley."

Her brows snapped together in confusion. "How did you know my name?"

Derven gave her what I think was a smile, but without much flesh left, it looked more like he was baring his teeth. "Once you heal me, I will be happy to answer all of your questions, but let's just say we all have our talents."

All of us converged on Derven, sensing the threat he had just made toward our mate.

"Stop," Finley ordered, our bodies freezing in place.

"*Finley,*" Zander growled.

None of us enjoyed this new trick she'd learned, but Zander hated it the most. They fell into an argument about it every time she did it.

Clearly, this wasn't going to be any different if the vein popping out of his forehead was any sign.

Finley walked over to Derven and kneeled, holding out her hands to him. "With how much damage your body has taken, I truly don't know how badly this will hurt."

"I doubt it can be worse than the pain I'm in now," he grumbled as he placed both hands in hers.

Closing her eyes, Finley took a deep breath, releasing it as I felt her gathering magic from the forest around her.

"*Rath, how do I keep from healing him to the point of being human again?*" she asked.

The elf frowned and rubbed his chin as he thought. "*Tell your magic exactly what you want from it, and don't allow it to do more than that. It needs to heal the damage to his body, remove the silver, and restore his energy. If it tries to go above and beyond that, call it back.*"

I saw her head nod before her hands started to glow a vibrant cobalt blue that matched the color of her eyes. Watching the process, I couldn't help but gasp as, before my eyes, his skin was knitting itself back together. The scent of death was clearing from the air and was replaced by the copper scent of blood that always seemed to linger on vampires. The features of his face returned, and I could finally distinguish him as a person.

Derven's skin became more pigmented as if he were actually alive, his scraggly dark hair thickened and filled out, the beard on his face was fuller and his eyes, unlike most vampires, weren't red. Instead, they were a deep brown with flecks of green that seemed as shocked as all of us were at what was going on. If the scent wasn't the same, I would one hundred percent believe he was human. This must be what he looked like before becoming a vampire. When she told her magic to heal him, it healed it back to his original DNA.

When she opened her eyes, Finley smiled and clasped his hands in her. "It's nice to finally meet you, Derven."

FOUR

FINLEY

By the looks on my mates' faces, I'd done something wrong when I healed him. While I've been educated in vampires and had a few interactions with them, outside of killing them, that is, I didn't *know* vampires. The first sign something was wrong was that his eyes looked human when they should look like blood-red rubies. His scent was definitely vampire, but yet in the same token, it wasn't.

Listening carefully, I didn't hear a heartbeat or anything that would make me believe he was alive. Derven was still a vampire, but yet not completely.

"It's nice to meet you as well, Finley," he answered as he stood, pulling me up with him. "You are even more stunning than I remember." The air was filled with warning growls, and Rath came to stand behind me, making his claim clear. "Goodness, they are a serious bunch, aren't they?"

Derven, now that he wasn't falling apart or in horrendous pain, came across as being rather cocky. I suppose it had something to do with being as old as he was and probably fairly powerful. How the Dark Ring kept him for so long didn't make sense.

"If you hadn't gotten away that night, would you have left Rathal to save yourself?" Derven asked, cocking his head to the side. "Once I found Marissa, there was no way I could leave her, and they quickly discovered we were a Blood Bond when I couldn't drink from anyone else."

My shock at him knowing what I was thinking was put aside by my curiosity about what he was saying. "I'm sorry, I don't know anything about Blood Bonds or what that means for you. It sounds like how I would talk about my mates, but there obviously is something on a deeper level between you and that person."

"Marissa was a human, but her blood sang to me in a way that only happens when that person was born for you. The moment her blood met my lips, we created a bond that tied her to my life, and as long as I remained alive, so would she. Together we would live, love, and share everything together... or so I thought. My old master slept with her once he found out we were Blood Bonded, and when she refused to stop fighting him, he killed her," Derven said, his voice becoming harsher as his rage was ignited, telling the story.

"While it makes the partner stronger, it doesn't make them immortal if their head is removed. The pain from our bond breaking almost destroyed me, but the flame of revenge is what's kept me going. I knew there had to be someone else who was as pissed off as I was about all this, and the first name that came to mind was Rathal. Seems the universe decided to grant your wish and mated you to the one person who can topple this whole empire down," Derven continued, shifting his gaze to Rath's behind me. "So tell me, *friend*, are we in this fight together, or have you lost your edge in the hands of those bastards?"

Colt stepped forward, grabbed my hand, and pulled me back behind him and Rath. "That isn't his choice alone," he stated, a growl rumbling in his chest. "We are a pack, a *nos*, and we do this as a team."

Derven cocked his head as he looked at my other mates, all standing in a semi-circle behind me. "I see, so then let me pose the same question to all of you. Are we in this fight together, or do I need to go elsewhere to bring down the Dark Ring and that farce of a government, the United Senate?"

Knowing Colt was trying to establish dominance in this situation, I kept quiet, but it would be foolish to let any ally walk away from us. This battle was going to be brutal, and there was no way the eight of us could pull it off without help. Derven's connections ran deep if what Rath said about his lineage was true and could change everything.

"What guarantee do we have you aren't just a puppet of the Dark Ring coming here to find out just how powerful Finley is? You might have all the rage in the world, but I've also seen what the Dark Ring can do to anyone kept in their clutches for so long. The only reason we believed Rath is because Finley, as his mate, can read him like a book," Colt challenged, making a valid argument.

"If a guarantee is what you want, then I'll open up my mind to her willingly," Derven said with a shrug. "She can take a stroll down memory lane and see all the horrors that have happened in my time with them. I'm sure being an assassin, she's seen worse and will be able to tell there is no love or loyalty that could come of it."

Colt turned to look at me. *"Can you do that?"*

"Honestly, I don't know, but something tells me he can read some of what I'm thinking. He seems to know the answers to things I've been wondering but never divulged," I explained. *"It's possible there is a way I might be able to look in his mind, but I've only ever done that with those I've been mated to."*

"Rath, what do you think? Is this a trap, or could this be the real deal?" Zander demanded. *"I don't want her going into his mind if it will harm her or if it's some kind of vampire mind trap."*

My elven mate walked up to Derven and reached out, placing his pointer finger over Derven's temple. Rath closed his eyes, and I could feel his magic flowing around us for a few moments, and then he stepped back. "I do not sense any ill intentions from him or spells that might have been placed on him by a witch."

Derven hissed. "You think I would let a filthy witch touch me! Those low-breed humans who dabble in things they don't really understand and turn their souls black with the dark magic they pull from? I would rip out their throats before I would ever let them lay a hand on me, let alone a spell."

Mason let out a whistle. "Damn, someone's got some anger issues when it comes to witches."

"If you had the history we've had with them, then you'd understand. In Romania, where I'm from, the gypsies are a nuisance, but the witches, those cunts will sell us out in a heartbeat to save themselves. Yes, the monster hunters will overlook a witch if a vampire is the alternative," Derven explained, his disgust plain for us all to see as he spit on the ground.

"Look, I know you're old as dirt, but times have changed, and they don't hunt supernatural creatures the same way," Mason argued. Everyone turned to look at him, and he realized what he had just said. "Ah fuck, that's exactly what the Dark Ring is doing in a far more fucked-up way, isn't it?"

Noah took pity on his brother and clapped him on the back. "Nothing new under the sun, twin, just gets more sick and twisted."

"So are we having your lovely mate riffle through my memories here, or should we go someplace that won't have me burning up the moment sunlight touches me?" Derven suggested, winking at me. "That would be a pity after all the hard work of putting me back together."

"Pack house?" Lane offered. "How protected from the sun do you need to be? I don't think any of our houses have basements. There's a vegetable cellar, but it's not big enough to fit us all down there."

"While I appreciate the thought, a home with black-out curtains would be just fine," he assured. "I'll meet you all there, don't worry if the doors are locked. I can let myself in."

Then like a streak, he was gone, only the rustling of the leaves to show he'd gone.

"What did he mean he could let himself in?" Noah blurted. "Doesn't he have to be invited?"

I shook my head as I slipped the robe off and folded it up to take with me. "No, that is just a myth. Vampires can enter anywhere, even churches. Best not to keep him waiting, or he might start poking around the house."

Noah looked like his world had just been turned upside down with what I'd just told him. "What else is a lie? Do crosses work? What about holy water? Clearly, silver is a problem, so that's reassuring."

"Let's go. You can ask the bloodsucker himself," Elias muttered, shifting back into his wolf.

Rath took the robe from me. "I'll hang on to it, although I'm sure the others can find you clothes to wear back at the house."

Peering at Rath, I could sense something was bothering him, but he wasn't sharing what it was. "Do I need to worry about what you're keeping to yourself?"

"No." He sighed. "When I was in his mind, I could tell how much he likes you, how attractive you are to him, and that your blood smells like the finest of wines."

"Should we find another way to check the truth of his claims? I don't want to make any of you uneasy or feel like I'm not considering your feelings," I said, placing a hand over his heart. "You are my mate, and it's my job to take care of you as much as you all look after me."

Rath cupped my face and kissed me, taking his time enjoying our lips and tongues connecting. "I will be fine, *nin mel*. We need to know if we can trust him, and you are the best chance we have at this."

"If you feel something is going too far, you say the word, and I will end it," I assured him, pressing another quick kiss to his lips before shifting into my wolf.

With a quick shake to adjust to being back on four legs, I darted off to join the others, with Rath bringing up the rear, ensuring no surprises followed. My wolf was not at all thrilled with having a vampire in our territory, but she was curious about him. I had to agree, nothing about him seemed to make sense, and it felt like I was missing something, which was a feeling I'd never liked. If I felt that way during a job, it meant I hadn't done enough research or taken a close enough look at the layout. Now that I knew I was an elf, it made me wonder if there was some kind of intuition I got because when I went back to look things over, I would always spot what I missed. That didn't really apply to this situation, though, and I didn't know how to shake this feeling.

Then it hit me, Ayla was supposed to be arriving at some point today, and I didn't want this vampire to know about her or that there were far more elves alive than people assumed. He might already know some elves survived since the Dark Ring liked to collect them, but no one knew about the clans scattered in small pockets all over the world. This information getting into the wrong hands before the Senate and the Dark Ring were destroyed could cost many lives. Elves nowadays were conditioned to hide, not to fight. They wouldn't be prepared if an attack happened.

"We need to get this over with quickly," I called out to everyone. *"Ayla is coming today, and ally or not, he can't know about her."* I got various yips and snarls in reply, but they all agreed it was best to keep our cards close to our chest.

As we broke from the forest into the main pack area, the sun was over the mountains warming up the earth from the cool evening air. Spring was coming, but the nights and mornings were still quite brisk, not that I noticed much anymore being a werewolf. What I did realize, though, was I was hungry, and when a rabbit darted out of the underbrush, my mouth watered.

I let out a yip of excitement which caused the rabbit to race off back into the woods. Just as I was about to chase after my prey, Zander cut me off with a snarl. My wolf realized what we'd been about to do and dropped to the ground with a whine of apology. As the lowest wolf of the pack, it would have been a slight to my alpha if I'd hunted only for myself. Zander closed the distance between us and snuffled my face, licking my snout reassuringly.

"I'm sorry, I didn't mean to come on so strong. We just couldn't risk you running off by yourself. Who knows what else might be hiding out there waiting for the moment you're alone," he explained, rubbing his head against mine affectionately. *"Once in the house, I'll make you some breakfast if Mason left any food there for us to eat after last night."*

"No, I see why you all harp on me so much about not making sure to eat enough. I can't believe how easily I was distracted by a rabbit," I said as I stood and followed after him up the porch steps into the house.

"Finley, go up and put some clothes on, please," Colt directed as he stood in the middle of the living room, staring down at the vampire sitting in the armchair. *"Take anything you need from mine or Lane's room. We haven't moved as much over to the other house."*

I left them to deal with things as I bounded up the stairs to Colt's room directly at the top. Shifting back, I walked over to the dresser and grabbed a T-shirt and sweatpants. Feeling a little gross, having not really taken the time to pull myself together, I stepped into the room that was originally supposed to be mine to brush my teeth and wash my face. I pulled open the medicine cabinet to see if, on an off chance, there might be a hair tie, but there wasn't. When I turned the light switch off to the bathroom, my finger got cut on a nail sticking slightly out of the wood paneling on the wall.

"Shit," I muttered at the bite of pain. Looking at the damage, it didn't seem like anything to be concerned about. I was sure that with my shifter healing, it would be gone in a minute or two. When I looked up, I came face to face with Derven, his eyes glowing red as he stared at my finger.

"This can't be," he whispered, reaching out to gently grasp my wrist. "It doesn't make any sense. I know they're all gone."

"Derven?" I questioned, trying not to react to how much his eyes freaked out my wolf. She was begging me to run away from the predator before us, but I just had the gut feeling that if I ran, it would make things so much worse.

Ignoring the fact I'd spoken to him, he lifted my hand and took a deep breath. He groaned, and before I could stop him, he popped my finger into his mouth and licked the blood off my finger. A tether snapped into place, almost like when my wolf mates marked me. My blood sang in my body as if it rejoiced at finding something that had been lost to it. Derven didn't let my finger go. Instead, he scraped his fang along the pad, cutting the flesh open, making it bleed for him. Instead of pain, it felt as if he was sucking on my clit instead of my finger, causing my knees to go out from under me.

Derven caught me around the waist, holding me to him as he sucked and lapped at my finger. Each draw of blood had me twitching, my core clenching as if it knew something should be inside us to get this type of reaction. His eyes opened and locked onto mine as he took one last pull at my finger long and hard, causing me to explode in an orgasm unlike any other I'd experienced before. I let out a cry of pleasure as I became boneless against his body, only the steel band of his arm keeping me upright.

"What," I panted as he released my finger. "What did you just do to me?"

"*Sângele meu*, I should be asking you that." Derven purred as he picked me up and sat on the end of the bed. "This should be interesting."

Before I could ask what he was talking about, Colt, Zander, Lane, and Rath were standing in the room, faces alight with rage.

"What did you just do!" Rath bellowed.

Never would I have guessed my composed elven mate could respond with such violence in this tone.

"You did something. I can feel it in our soul bond." He snarled as he stalked forward, acting just like any wolf would with his mate in danger. "Tell me what you did right now before I rip out your heart!"

"I would advise against that, seeing as you'll kill her," Derven answered as if he didn't have an elf and three wolves waiting to tear him to pieces.

Zander narrowed his eyes as a growl seeped from his lips. "What did you just say?"

"It would appear that Finley and I are Blood Bonded," he explained, glancing down at me as I gasped. "I'm sorry, the moment the scent of your blood hit the air, I was unable to fight against the call. For us, it's as powerful as any mate bond between elves or wolves. It's not a choice you can fight when it is fated to happen."

"I don't understand. You had a Blood Bond already," Colt challenged. "Was that a lie? Something to soften our hearts toward you or something?"

"Marissa was taken from me forty years ago," Derven shared. "It might seem like a long time for most people, but I'm a thousand years old. Forty years is like blinking. No one knows how Blood Bonds work, but what is known is that if you have one, you can't feed from anyone else but that one person. I can feed on others, but it won't nourish me or keep me alive, so what would be the point? If the blood donor dies, then the bond is broken, and the vampire starts to feed on others again."

"So you're saying you could have many Blood Bonds out there but only one you are actually bonded to at a time?" I asked, trying to navigate through what he was saying. "So the only way to break this bond is with my death because if you die, I will too."

"Yes, *sângele meu*, that is the simple version of things as I understand them," Derven murmured, resting his head against mine. "I'm so sorry. I didn't mean for this to happen. The last thing I would want for my bonded partner is to make their life more complicated and that, I fear, is what I've done."

FIVE

FINLEY

As the glow of my Blood Bond-induced orgasm faded, I almost felt a little awkward being held in Derven's arms as my other mates looked on. My brain told me I betrayed them, but my heart told me this was always meant to happen. Our blood had been created to give Derven life. It didn't really help make me feel all that much better, but there really wasn't anything I could do about it now.

Zander held out a hand to me. "Come on, little dove. I promised you breakfast."

Derven helped me to my feet and watched me with such sad eyes as I walked away with Zander. I let him lead me down the stairs, but when we reached the kitchen, I pulled him to a stop, then wrapped my arms around his waist letting my face nestle into the middle of his back. I needed to know that we were okay. He was shutting me out of his mind, but even when he did that, I could read his emotions. They were shifting rapidly—anger, hurt, and uncertainty warred inside him.

"I'm so sorry," I whispered, tears pooling in my eyes. "Please know that I didn't mean to betray you or the others. I had no idea that something like that could even happen."

Zander grabbed my arm, pulled me forward, lifted me, and set me on the kitchen island. He cupped my face in his hands and let our foreheads rest against each other. "This is not your fault, Finley. You are my mate, I love you with every fiber of my being, and nothing will ever change that. Is this a shock? Yes. I'm more furious at the vampire doing what he did without even saying a word. He bound you to him without even a *by-your-leave*. It was wrong and completely unfair to you."

"You're not mad at me?" I asked, the tears finally spilling from my eyes.

"No, little dove, I'm not mad at you and neither are any of the others," he assured me as he leaned back to wipe my tears from my eyes. "We will get through this together as a pack and a *nos* should."

The sound of fist hitting flesh could be heard upstairs, followed by a grunt and muffled swearing. I tensed, taking an educated guess that Derven wasn't being as warmly welcomed as Rath had been into the family. Just when I thought things were settling between all of us now that I'd soul bonded everyone. Elias and I still had to solidify his mate bond with me, but I knew he wanted the moment to be special, for the two of us without anyone else around. He was a man who couldn't be rushed, and I was happy to do what made him happy.

"Should I stop them?" I questioned, peering up at the stairs.

Zander kissed my forehead and stepped back, heading over to the fridge. "No, let them work things out. Not all matters can be solved with words alone when it comes to men and shifters. Actions speak louder than words, and what he did was as disrespectful to you as it was to us. Now it looks like we can make omelets with all the eggs and vegetables they have stocked up." I made a face having been spoiled with all the yummy sweet breakfasts we'd been having. Zander just chuckled and started to pull ingredients out of the refrigerator. "Guess that's the one nice thing about this pack being so self-sufficient you never run out of food. Chickens for eggs, garden for vegetables, cows for milk, the only thing they are missing is a mill to make their own grain for bread, and we'd be able to weather anything that came our way."

"Don't say that too loudly around Milly, or it will happen. She wants us to be detached from the rest of the world and run this as a closed commune, but we argued that wasn't what was best for the pack," Noah interjected as he joined us in the kitchen and wiggled his way between my legs to pull me into a hug. "It's all good, Finley. No matter what happens, we are your family, and we won't leave you. Now take a deep breath and tell your wolf she's fine so you can stop worrying your pretty head."

I clung to him as my wolf pushed forward, peering out of my eyes as if she needed him to say it directly to her. A hand gripped my hair and pulled my head all the way back until I was looking at Zander upside down.

His wolf caused his eyes to glow as he spoke with all the authority given to him as a superior alpha male of his kind. "Finley, you are *ours*. End of discussion."

"Yes, alpha," I murmured, my body lighting up with heat at his words. My wolf wanted nothing more than to show him just how much those words meant to us. "Who else can make breakfast?"

Before I even got an answer, I was tossed over Noah's shoulder and carried out of the kitchen and into a bedroom. It was half empty, making me guess it was either his or Mason's, but the scent of warm chocolate and hazelnuts told me it was his room. I was tossed on the large bed that took up most of the room, and I bounced once before Noah was caging me in with his body over mine.

"You can't say things like that while your need is thick in the air, Finley," Noah warned. "Not when you are in our house with all your mates around you. Who knows, maybe the others will come join us once Zander and I get you screaming."

This was the side of Noah I only ever saw when we were intimate. In every other part of his life, he went with the flow, offering support when and where he could, but when it came to sex, he knew exactly what he wanted and let me know it.

"Are you sure that's what you want?" I challenged, letting a finger trace down his shirt-covered chest. "Right now, you could keep it between the three of us."

"What would the fun be in that?" Zander countered, his chest rumbling with a possessive growl as he crawled across the bed toward me. "We know you are with the others, and sometimes, there may be a need for you to be with us one-on-one, but none of us are under the illusion we aren't sharing this perfect body between us all. To watch you come undone at the hands of another is an amazing sight to see."

Noah slipped his hands under the shirt I'd put on and let them glide up my ribs, pushing the fabric up, revealing my stomach inch by inch. When he reached my breasts, he cupped them both, kneading them gently, making me moan.

"Louder, babe, I know you can do it," Noah whispered in my ear, nipping at it before moving down to my neck. His tongue brushed over his mate mark, sending a shockwave of pleasure through me, making me shout as my back arched. "That's better. Remember, we want them to know what's happening in here."

Zander shifted Noah to the side so he could slide my sweatpants off. I knew he would find me soaked after that moment with Derven, and part of me was ashamed of it. Lifting my legs so he could place them over his shoulders as he army-crawled right up to my aching pussy.

"Did that vampire get your motor running?" he asked as he swiped a finger through my center, then brought it to his lips as he licked it clean. "You taste just like you smell, vanilla with spice."

With that declaration, he slid his hands under my ass and dove in like I was the best dessert he'd ever tasted. His tongue was pressed flat as he took long strokes from bottom to top, taking a moment to suck on my clit, making me thrash at how good it felt. I'd never been one to shy away from sex, but it hadn't been something I needed. Now, as an omega, it was almost as if it was part of my DNA. My desire for my mate was always set at a low simmer that, but in the flick of a switch, could boil over into desperation. Thank God, though, because I'm not sure how else I would manage seven... well, I guess eight men now and their needs.

Noah yanked my shirt over my head, revealing my breasts to him. He took a moment to admire, not at all bothered by Zander, who was lost in his work between my legs, making me gasp and moan with need. Noah stepped off the bed and shed his clothes before straddling my face, his thick cock bobbing in anticipation.

"I want your hot, pretty mouth on me as Zander eats your soul from your pussy," Noah instructed, letting the back of his fingers brush along my cheek. Reaching out, I tried to grab the base, but he stopped me. "No, babe, mouth only. I'll help you out if you need it."

Which he did as he pushed it down for me to get my lips around it, tongue flicking over the crown, tasting the bitterness of his pre-cum. His hand slid into my hair, offering me support as I took him as deep as I could manage before it hit the back of my throat.

"God, I love that sound," Mason's voice said somewhere in the room. "Our mate sucking on my twin's cock as one of her alphas eats her out. It's not even my birthday."

Zander paused in his efforts, making me whimper around Noah's cock. "Are you gonna join us or not?"

"Now that is a stupid question," Mason said with a laugh as he jumped on the bed, already naked. To be honest, I'm not sure if he ever got dressed. "You think I can borrow a pretty hand from you, snuggles, while you're otherwise occupied?"

I held out a hand for him and felt a blob of lube squirted onto my palm. "Don't want to get dick burn from a dry hand. Learned that real fast at age fifteen. Are you gonna join in or just sit and watch, Elias?"

Having Noah's body blocking my view of the room, I had no idea how long Elias had been in here. I reached out to him in our bond, and he assured me he was quite content to watch as he stroked himself.

"Don't worry about me, my heart. When it comes time for me to mark you, I don't want any distractions. I want your eyes on me and me alone," he whispered in my mind.

Noah decided that I was getting far too distracted and used both hands to hold my head still as he started to fuck my mouth. Zander seemed to be of the same mind since he slid two fingers in me at the same time, triggering an orgasm and making me gag on Noah as I screamed, setting off his climax as well. Zander finger fucked me through the climax, drawing it out as long as possible as he sucked on my clit. I was seeing stars as the waves of euphoria flowed over me, and I gulped down everything Noah gave.

"I say we switch things up," Mason announced. "I want her pretty peach of an ass in my hands as I fuck her."

Noah moved off me, letting me gasp for air as I tried to slow my heartbeat. He bent down and nuzzled against my cheek. "I wasn't too rough, was I? Sometimes I get carried away, and you were making such sexy noises I couldn't hold back."

"No," I answered, pulling him into a kiss, showing him just how hot I found it that I could turn him on enough to lose control. "It was amazing," I added when I broke the kiss.

Now that he wasn't on top of me, I pushed up to lean against the backboard and found Elias in the office chair, naked, eyes glowing, abs clenched as he tried to hold back, cock dripping with pre-cum. Everything about him called to me, and I couldn't resist, so I went.

Dropping to my knees, I gripped the base and removed his hand. I held his gaze as I took him as deep as I could, struggling with his length as he entered deep down my throat. This was a better angle to take all of him versus how Noah had me. Then I used my other hand to caress his balls, stroking them in time with my movements. I pulled back enough to take a few deep breaths, then went back at it, knowing he was close.

Someone came up behind me and urged me to lift my hips. Two fingers slipped inside me to check, then seconds later, I was rammed balls deep by a dick I knew belonged to one of my alphas. As I worked Elias deep and slow, the alpha matched me, stroking a hand down my back, caressing me. Then the fresh, clean scent of Lane reached my nose, and I knew who was behind me. Seems they were finished with whatever they had to say with Derven.

"Do you want me to knot you? Lock you in good and tight against me, sweetheart?" Lane purred as he leaned over my back, his bare skin caressing mine as he moved, holding my hips tightly as he thrust into me.

I pulled off Elias and looked back at him. "Please, alpha, knot me, fill me with your cum so everyone knows who I belong to."

"Good girl, now finish what you started with Elias. We don't want to leave him like that, now do we?" Lane instructed as he sped up his moments.

This time as I took my strong and silent mate's cock in my mouth, I moved faster, using my hand to double the sensation. He groaned, tossing back his head, making me feel elated that I could give him so much pleasure. Then with a good steady squeeze on his balls, Elias roared his release, shooting his cum down my throat, and I swallowed every drop. Letting his dick pop from my lips, I licked up his shaft, drawing moans out of him as he crushed the armrest of the chair with his grip.

"My heart, I can't take any more," he ground out between clenched teeth.

I released him with one last kiss to the tip of his cock, and Lane pulled me upright against his chest. He lifted me off him and spun me around so I was now facing him. Lane, my sweet, gentle alpha, who kept us grounded as a pack, never losing his temper and keeping a level head in tough situations. His warm brown eyes with flecks of gold looked at me with such love I couldn't help but melt into him.

Picking me up, he walked back over to the bed where he placed us on our side, hiking my left leg up over his hip as he slid back in me. One arm wrapped around my back while the other gripped the side of my face as he caught my lips in a languid kiss that matched his deep thrusts. This was more his speed, he could match the energy of the others when sharing, but Lane was a man who *made love*.

A hand caressed my ass, making me think it would be Mason, but the sparks I felt, and the tingles along my skin, changed my mind. "*Nin mel*, may I join you and your alpha as he worships your body?"

Rath, the romantic of the pack. It made sense he would be one of the only other people who would match Lane's energy. "You are always welcome, Rath. My body is yours as is my soul," I answered, turning from Lane as he moved to my neck and wrapped an arm around Rath's neck, pulling him to me.

My elf let his fingers glide between my cheeks, probing at my ass before letting one slip in. He was always amazed that being an omega, I didn't need much prep, especially not after all that had been going on. I was more than ready to take any mate in any hole they desired to use. Once Rath was confident he wouldn't hurt me, he slid his cock deep inside, making me moan, but he stole it off my lips, drinking it down for himself.

Lane caught up one of my nipples, teasing it with his teeth as the two men found a rhythm that had me unable to focus on anything but them. My body burned as they stoked the fire of another climax, gently fanning the flames with each thrust, caress, and kiss along my skin until I exploded, clamping down on them tightly. Lane's knot began to swell, filling me in a way that only an alpha could, the bulge pressing on every sensitive part until it was locked in place. His head nestled in, right above my breast where his mate mark was, nibbling at it, pushing my climax higher.

Rath had his arms wrapped around my waist as he rammed his cock into my ass as he neared his finish. He didn't use any magic this time, just letting us be as we were, and it was perfect. With the swell of Lane's knot, it made everything tighter, causing Rath's movements to be so much more enhanced. He came, clinging to me, whispering elven words I didn't understand, but the meaning was obvious as he kissed along my spine, easing himself out.

That's when Lane got a second wind and started rocking his knot, knowing it would send me headlong into another orgasm. My body convulsed around him, and my cries filled the air as wave after wave of ecstasy hit me. Eventually, he took mercy on me and relaxed, cuddling me close as I drifted off into a dozing state. I could hear the others talking as Lane's knot receded, and he slipped from me.

"Do you need some rest, sweetheart, or do you want more?" Lane asked as he pressed soft kisses all over my face.

"I'll never have enough," I murmured. "Mason and Zander at least need to come after being teased for so long, but I wouldn't leave Colt out either."

"Sounds to me like the perfect number of people," Mason pointed out. "One in the pussy, I called her luscious ass, and another her mouth. Then she can nap as long as she wants, not at all worried about leaving one of us with blue balls."

Rolling on my back, I laughed, looking at the one man who could always brighten my mood no matter what was going on. Then I caught sight of Derven leaning on the back wall watching everything, his eyes glowing red. They should scare me, the eyes of a predator known to kill without remorse, taking life as they pleased. Vampires were the perfect representation of gluttony, gorging themselves on blood and sex. Yet, when I looked into those eyes now fixated on mine, I could only see the man I saved from dying. He wasn't a monster. He was a person to me. One I didn't know well, but that would change over time, seeing as I was now connected to his life force.

Even though he knew I was watching him, he didn't move, perfectly content to be in the room. Before, I had trouble sensing his emotions, but now, I could catch glimpses of them. While he was confused and still trying to understand what happened when he looked at me, all

I got was hope. With his previous Blood Bond taken from him, he didn't see the point of living, but now, he had everything to live for.

"I might regret how things happened between us, Finley, but I do not for a second wish for things to change. It will be my highest honor to have the woman who is going to change the world as a Blood Bond. You have my undying loyalty, and everything that is mine to own or command is yours for as long as our lives might be," Derven whispered to me as phantom fingers caressed over my skin, making me shiver.

SIX

DERVEN

Knowing I certainly wasn't going to be invited into the orgy, I left the room. Although I felt like they should be thanking me because if I hadn't made them feel so insecure with their mate, they wouldn't feel the need to mark their territory quite so thoroughly. Spying the remnants of what looked like someone making breakfast, I sighed.

They didn't even feed her before ravaging her. Poor thing must be starving and cum, as far as I knew, wasn't a real food group.

I decided to take this as an opportunity to make myself useful and keep my new bond healthy. While vampires did not need to eat human food to survive, we still enjoyed the taste every hundred years or so. Also, when you had been alive as long as I had, you found things to do to fill your time, and cooking had been a favorite of mine.

Setting to work chopping up the vegetables, I scanned the kitchen for some herbs or spices to add. I hated to think of forcing her to eat bland food, a heinous crime that was. Opening the refrigerator, I spotted a few things but not much. It seemed these men kept it pretty basic. But then again, if this wasn't their main residence, that could explain a thing or two. Spotting the pantry door ajar, I peeked in there to see if they at least had the dried store-bought kind of spices and found myself equally disappointed.

Upon exiting, I came face to face with a strange woman with large aqua-colored eyes. Glancing down, I found a blade resting against my tattered shirt, just where my heart would be. "I would suggest against harming me if you wish your queen to also remain unharmed. It would be rather rude to interrupt their activities with her screaming out in agony."

"Why should I believe the words of a blood-sucking liar?" She snarled, pressing the blade more firmly to my skin.

Her voice was light and musical for how threatening the words were. Elves tended to be just as beautiful as they were deadly, much the same as people say of vampires. Slowly, I reached up and grabbed her wrist, crushing it in my grip hard enough that the blade clattered to the floor.

"If you didn't believe me, I'd already be dead, but you really can't be sure, can you?" I mused, moving her to the side as I returned to making breakfast.

"I pledged my life to protect our queen, and I would never do something to cause her harm, but one has to wonder when you come to a wolf pack to find the real big bad wolf in the house," the female elf said, walking around the other side of the island to stand across from me.

Pointing my knife down the hall, I flashed her a smile. "You are free to ask her if you wish. I'm not sure what this generation of elves is like. Back in the day before the battle, they were just as free with their bodies as vampires are."

"Among our own kind," she countered. "You walking carcasses will poke anything that lets you while high from the feel of you drinking from the vein."

"Didn't you hear the Senate outlawed us from drinking from the source? We must drink from a cup or blood bag. Such a tragedy. Blood is like fine wine, but when you drink out of a can, it ruins the taste," I shared with a sigh as I tossed the vegetables into a frying pan. "Lucky for me, I found myself a Blood Bond."

"I pity the person who has to be your personal blood bag," she muttered, grabbing her bag of things and heading upstairs.

"One moment, elf," I called, stepping back from the stove to keep her in view. "While I might not have the authority to stop you, I'm sure my bond partner would like to know why you feel so at home in her alphas' house?"

In the blink of an eye, the elf was back in my face, teeth bared like a wild animal. "What did you just say?"

"Oh, catch that, did you," I said with a smirk. "Surprise of all surprises, Finley is my Blood Bond. Tragically it happened all wrong, but what's done is done."

"I could kill you, then we will see if you are telling the truth," she taunted, pulling another dagger from a hip sheath and tapping me on the nose with it.

"Ayla," Rathal snapped. "Do not touch a hair on that vampire's head if you value your life. He told you he was Blood Bonded to Finley, yet you still raise a blade to him?"

The female elf... Ayla, sighed and put away her knife. "You had to take all the fun out of it, cousin. I wasn't really going to hurt him... promise. I could smell her blood on him and a hint of it upstairs." She eyed Rath up and down. "Seems everyone needed a little reassurance after the surprise."

My elven friend stood there in just his pants, eyes flashing with irritation at Ayla's words. Seeing him like that, I needed to remind myself that anything that happened between us while in the clutches of the Dark Ring was to survive. He didn't see me as anything but a reminder of the hell we both survived, even if, for a time, we were all each other had while locked away in that underground dungeon. If he wanted to act like there was nothing between us now, I would accept that. Elves who were mated were committed to their female above anything else, and I knew how badly Rathal had wanted to find his mate.

Sharing her with me would be one thing, elves knew they wouldn't be the only male, but she would be it for him. No other being in Heaven, Hell, or Earth would ever make him stray from her, and I would have to adjust. We'd always been friends. More came when we became so lonely it saved us from going mad. My hope was we could once again be in each other's lives as companions who could lean on one another during hard times.

If they truly were going to take down the Senate and the Dark Ring, all of them were going to need to lean on each other.

The scent of the ingredients getting cooked a little too well pulled me out of the past and back to what was happening now. I slid the frying pan over to an unlit burner as I cracked eggs to add into a bowl and whisked them, trying to keep out of the elven matters happening a few feet away. Although, I was incredibly curious as to why she was here and seemed to think she was part of this pack. Elves didn't mix with others of the supernatural species. Rathal was in a highly unusual situation.

"Ven," Rathal called.

I paused, surprised to hear him call me that, then peered over my shoulder at him. "Yes?"

"When you're done cooking that for Finley, I was asked to help get you settled with clothes and a shower. You still reek of rot," Rathal informed me, his tone lacking any sort of emotion.

"Do the others not want to eat? I was planning on making enough from them all," I said, looking at the pan.

Rathal walked over and looked at what I had on the stove, then flicked his gaze up to me. "That will be enough to feed Finley and maybe one other. These wolves eat more food than I've ever witnessed. Although I'm thankful they don't shy away from vegetables, I feared it would only be meat."

"Then I'll finish this up, and you may lead on," I answered, flipping the large round sheet of egg. "Shouldn't take but a few moments."

"Where am I staying?" Ayla inquired.

"I believe the plan is to move all the personal items out of this house and into the other one on the edge of the pack lands. Finley likes that one better and is more suited to what we need... although we seem to be running out of rooms quickly," he shared, his shoulders sagging with frustration. "I believe if you put your things in the room that was meant for Finley, it would be best. Once things are moved, you can choose whichever room you like."

"That's good because there will be three more elves joining me tomorrow. They heard I was going to serve the queen, and they jumped at the chance," Ayla said, flashing a bright smile. "I warned her that once word got out about there being a queen, her people would come flocking to her."

Feeling the omelet was cooked well, I turned the oven on low to keep it warm and slipped the frypan inside. "Ayla, correct?" I asked, approaching where she stood in front of Rathal.

She nodded, eyes narrowing at me slightly, her face tattoos adding to her fierceness with such a simple expression.

"If we are to be living in the same pack, I figured it would be best for me to properly introduce myself," I bowed with a flourish, then stood once more. "I'm Derven Nistor of the Romanian Nistors."

When she didn't so much as bat an eye at the last name, I made a mental note that while Father liked to work in the shadows, it might be putting us at a disadvantage with the younger generation. No press for four hundred years seems to have wiped us off the map.

"Come on," Rathal said, waving for me to follow him upstairs. "None of these men like fine clothes as much as you do, so you'll have to settle for something simple until you can go shopping for yourself. Colt, I think, is the closest to your size in height, but he has a bit more bulk to him."

"Yes, well, living in captivity has slimmed me down some," I commented as we entered the alpha's room.

Rathal didn't really acknowledge my commentary, so I let it be. "Bathroom is through there. Colt said to help yourself to what you need. There should even be clippers in the closet if you wish to do something about your beard and hair."

Taking a chance, I stepped in front of Rathal and stopped him from exiting. "What do you think? You've seen my hair short. Which do you think looks better?" I knew I was playing with fire, but I refused to let him ignore me when neither of us was going anywhere.

His eyes finally met mine, and I could see so many emotions going on in them. "I have a mate. You and I will never be anything but past acquaintances."

I would be lying if that didn't hurt more than it should have. I'd already known that, but to have him throw it in my face was worse. "That isn't what I want," I bit out.

"We were friends, good loyal friends, who protected each other during our time in the dungeon. If anyone knows how much you longed for a mate, it's *me*. I care for you, yes, but as a brother, for us to be a family with Finley and the others. Nothing more. I'd never ask you for more because it would only hurt you to do so. Elves are not like vampires, where we all openly share and share alike. Neither are wolves, so I will adjust because I'd rather have a family than indulge my vapid needs," I explained, trying to make him understand I wouldn't ruin this for him or myself. "Please, can we try to be friends again?"

Rathal closed his eyes, took a deep breath, and raised a hand to my temple. Knowing what he wanted, I pulled down my shield, allowing him to see my thoughts and emotions. I wouldn't lie to him, never to him, or Finley now that she was a part of my soul. This was her family, and that made it mine, which I would protect from everything, including myself.

"Ven," Rathal said before pulling me into a hug. "I would be lying to you if I didn't tell you I've missed you, my friend." He pulled back, dropping his arms back to his side. "When I saw them bring you into the holding area for the action, I couldn't believe it. I thought about making sure you got out, but it was too dangerous for Finley, and she is forever going to be my first priority."

"As she should be," I agreed. "Even if she wasn't my Blood Bond, she is one amazing woman whose side I wanted to be on in this fight. I already told her this, but whatever is mine to rule or that I own is now hers as well. If she wants the whole Nistor army, then she shall have it, Father be damned."

"Have you spoken to him at all?" Rathal asked.

I shook my head. "No, I was arrogant and wanted my pound of flesh, fat lot of good that did me."

"It brought you here," he offered, giving me a glimmer of hope our friendship could be renewed. "Go get cleaned up. You look like a caveman. Finley might have brought you back to life, but you need to pull it all together."

With a clap on the shoulder, he left me to enjoy, for the first time in what felt like forever, a hot shower with no fear of what might come after. After I'd washed all the filth off my body, I rummaged through the drawers until I found a decent pair of jeans and a simple black T-shirt. It wasn't at all my taste, but as Rathal said, there would be plenty of time for me to acquire what I needed. Leaving the shirt off, I looked at my face in the mirror, and he wasn't wrong. I did look like a caveman with shaggy hair and a beard that many would be envious of with how full it was.

Too bad I wasn't a fan of facial hair at all, so I shaved it down and found a razor to make my skin smooth as silk. Whatever Finley had done to me was remarkable. Seeing my human eyes took some getting used to, but it was a pleasant adjustment to make. For my hair, I took the sides short and left the top longer so I could style it back away from my face. It wasn't the best haircut in the world, but it was better than looking like Cousin Itt.

Finally feeling like a free man for once in my life, I cleaned everything up and returned downstairs to find Finley digging into the omelet I had made her. One of the twins was eating the mushrooms that ended up on the side and made a mental note not to use them again. They both looked up as I reached the kitchen, and she gave me a soft smile.

Everything about her glowed with the just-fucked look. I couldn't tear my eyes away. I felt her eyes drift over me, probably thankful I was a rather attractive man under all that hair and filth.

"Not a fan of mushrooms, I see," I commented, nodding to the plate.

She looked down as if she didn't know one of her mates was eating off her plate. "Mason, if you wanted them, you just had to ask."

"Why would I do that when this is much more fun? I wasn't sure how long it was going to take you to notice," he teased, kissing the side of her head. "We wore you out good, didn't we?"

"Hmm," she sighed, nuzzling into the beta's neck before pressing a kiss to his skin. "I can have a nap after eating, right?"

"Babe, if you can hold out a little longer, we are gonna pack some stuff up and load it into one of the trucks. When we get back to the main house, we can tuck you into your nest while we deal with things," Noah, the other half of the twins, said, coming into the kitchen, pulling on a shirt.

Finley nodded her head but didn't pick it back up from Mason's shoulder. "Come on, snuggles, you need to eat. I know you're tired, but it's really not good for you to get too hungry. It doesn't go over well with your wolf."

"I'll sit with her while you collect what you need," I offered.

The brothers looked at each other, and I could feel the hum of them talking to each other mentally. I knew this could happen with twins, but I'd felt it between all of them at one point. As a vampire, all forms of mind control, speaking, and manipulation were standard. Being as old as I was, I was quite skilled in many areas. Currently, I only had the ability to mentality speak to Finley, being my bond.

"You might want to move into one of the bedrooms since we'll be opening the door. We wouldn't want you to get extra crispy," Mason suggested.

I smiled and nodded my head. "Thank you for your concern, but it seems what Finley did to me has made me more resistant to the sun. It's still uncomfortable to be in it, but I don't start to smoke either."

They both looked at me, surprised, and this information seemed to pull Finley's attention as well. "I knew I did too much when I healed you."

"Too much?" I asked, not understanding.

She nodded, looking me dead in the eye when she said something I never knew was possible. "I can heal a person from vampirism and return them to being human."

"You know this for a fact?" I blurted.

"I've done it once by accident," she shared. "When I was healing you, I tried to keep my magic in check and only heal what was damaged, to restore what was original without making you human. Seems I left you somewhere in between."

SEVEN

FINLEY

Derven looked at me in awe, his eyes wide, mouth hanging open, as I explained my healing abilities. I'd hoped my magic had only changed his appearance and not anything else, but making him a little tougher to kill might not be all that bad. If he got burned up in the sunlight, then I would be in trouble as well. What I didn't know was if this would last or was it just an aftereffect of having been healed so recently.

"You could make me human?" he asked, seeming unsure about the whole idea.

"All I know is that I've done it before when my magic was out of control. It was that same night I rescued you all and my magic appeared. We got into a fight with a coven of vampires that fed on druggies in Miami. Then one thing led to another…" I trailed off, not really sure how to explain what actually happened.

Derven shook his head slowly, never taking his eyes off me, then paused. "Wait, so you're telling me that at some point, I might be able to have you turn me back into a human, maybe have kids, grow old with you, and die like people should?"

Hearing him ask that surprised me. Most vampires lorded over humans and supernaturals alike that they could live forever. Then again, I've never met someone who was a thousand years old and watched the world change time and time again. "I truly have no idea what the aftereffects would or could be. The one I changed, we killed to ensure my secret wouldn't get out. There is no way to know what could happen long term."

His face turned serious as he dropped his eyes to look at his hands. I could only imagine what might be going through his head right now, but I understood what it felt like to have your whole world turned upside down.

"Finley!" Ayla's voice chimed. I looked past Derven and found her sliding down the railing. "I'm so glad to see you again, and I hope you don't mind I took your old room for now. Rathal suggested it was the best place for me right now as you move into the other house."

A genuine smile pulled up my lips as I turned to greet her with a hug. While I'd never been one to have friends, I felt she and I could understand each other a little better than most. Her also being an elf would be invaluable to questions I didn't necessarily want to ask Rath.

"I heard you are bringing more to join you?" I asked, then paused in surprise when a forkful of omelet appeared in front of my face. Derven clearly was taking his task of making sure I ate seriously and wasn't going to allow me to be distracted.

While still unsettled with our new addition, my wolf was pleased to have been offered food from his own hand. Obediently, I accepted the bite, and my wolf purred with delight at being looked after this way. Plus, she was incredibly hungry and upset with me for it happening.

"There are three others who are going to come," Ayla shared. "They heard me talking to the elders and decided they, too, were tired of hiding in the shadows. Once the Dark Ring is gone and we have a queen to lead our people, there is no need for us to remain silent. Our people fought to protect the human world, and now we would like to take our place back among them. While many of the elders who lived through the war disagree, it's no longer up to them with you here."

Derven kept feeding me bites as I listened, my brain whirling from everything Ayla was telling me. If more elves were going to come, then my plan to eventually ease the wolves into the idea wasn't going to work. I hadn't planned to bring our pack into the matters with the Dark Ring, but it seemed the universe had other plans. With the addition of Derven as well, the alphas had a lot to cover in the next pack meeting. It seemed we were going to need a gathering sooner than later.

"Do you think it will just be the three, or will there be more?" Derven asked, handing me a glass of water. I smiled at him gratefully and gulped down the cool refreshing liquid, not noticing how thirsty I was.

Ayla shrugged. "There could be more, but the ones who are coming are not fighters like myself. They are craftsmen. The elders were upset because they are invaluable to a clan, but they will be what we need to help build a new village for us to live in." She then directed her attention to me. "Would you ask the forest if it is willing to become our home? It would require sacrifice from it at first, but we always replace what we take, and with your magic helping it to thrive, that will happen much sooner."

"Can I do that?" I reached out to Rath, who was helping the others pack, but I knew they were all listening in through our connection.

"Yes, nin mel, the forest has accepted you and allowed you to claim this land as your own. Asking for this will only endear you to them as it's a sign of respect to the nature you protect and nurture," he answered. *"This is how things were done before the war. Those who made a deal with the*

forest they wished to dwell in worked together to create the village the elves lived in. It's a symbiotic relationship that benefits all."

As he explained it, I could see how that made sense but the reality that the forest all around me was sentient enough to care was still so new to wrap my mind around. "I will ask," I said, unsure what else to say on the matter.

The guys trudged back and forth with baskets, trash bags, and boxes full of things. It seemed they were emptying the betas' room first, which made sense since they didn't have to deal with the stairs.

"Come, *sângele meu*, let's move into the living room so I'm not in the direct path of the sun when they open the door. While I believe I would be fine, I'm sure you can appreciate my caution," Derven suggested.

Glancing at my plate, I realized I'd eaten everything. My wolf wouldn't mind a little more food, but it would be fine until we got back to the house. We sat on the couch together, but I curled up in the corner bend, watching Derven. I had so many questions about this man I was now bound to.

Now that he'd cleaned up, I could see the attractive man he was and how it must have made it easy to find people to feed from. Then the realization of why I was bound to him and what that meant had me sitting up straight.

"You have to feed from me and only me from now on, right?" I stated bluntly.

Derven gave a slight nod as he watched me intently. It was almost as if he was sifting through my thoughts as I thought them.

"Not all your thoughts, just ones you think about me," he corrected. "I can't listen in on the conversations you have with the others, but I'm aware when they happen. It's like a hum in the air, the same as an electric current through major power lines. When you think of me specifically, it pulls me into your thoughts. It's supposed to allow me to understand what you're feeling and thinking to better care for you. Unfortunately, I can't prevent it from happening, but I believe you are strong enough in your mental abilities to block me out with practice."

"You were doing that in the clearing before you bonded with me," I pointed out.

"Noticed that, did you," he said with a sigh. "It was my first inclination you might be someone who could be a Blood Bond. I just didn't think the pull would be that strong. It wasn't at all like this with Marissa. While I craved her and cared for her, our connection was nothing as deep as ours appears to be. Maybe she was a match but not a perfect match which you happen to be. The taste of your blood was like pure sunshine mixed with cayenne pepper. Bright and packs a major hit, running like fire through my veins."

"So, how does this work?" I asked, leaning back into the sofa's soft leather. "Do you feed daily? Will it need to be from the vein? Are there side effects I should know about other than possibly orgasming every time you drink?"

"My age is to your benefit, along with how potent your blood is. That taste I got from your finger will keep me going for days," he shared. "Under normal circumstances, I should say, right now, I am still weak from the silver and not having been able to feed as deeply as I need for fifty-odd years. Wouldn't want an ancient vampire to be too strong and destroy everyone in the house, now would they," he said with a dark chuckle.

Running a hand through his hair, he paused to watch the guys haul out another load before he continued, "While in a Blood Bond situation, it is more enjoyable for both parties if I drink from the source. It is not a requirement. If you would prefer to put it in a cup for me to drink, it is perfectly fine. I know this isn't at all what you wanted for your life. We might be bonded for life, but we are strangers to each other. While I hope that changes quickly, I am an incredibly patient man when I need to be."

It gave me a sense of relief to know I didn't have to offer up my vein for this to work. Derven was right, we were strangers, but it had been the same thing for the others as well. It seemed the universe knew I was never going to open up easily on my own, so it forced me.

"As for other side effects, I don't know the answer to that," he shared, his voice soft as if he hoped the others wouldn't hear. "While I was able to feed from Marissa, they didn't let us stay close. I was attached to her to feel her emotions and some thoughts, but as you know, being bonded to someone automatically makes you closer to the other. It was my duty as her vampire to care, protect, and provide for my bond, and I failed to do all those things. It cut deep into my already unstable mental state, turning me into a wild, vicious beast. Like I said before, things between us are already so different, I'm not sure what to expect."

Not knowing what to expect was a feeling I understood well. Since the moment I got bit, nothing had been how I expected my life to turn out, yet I wouldn't change a thing. Now I had a family, people who loved me, and I loved them. Yes, Derven was a twist, but if I could love and care for seven men, how hard could it be to add in another? From now on, I was going to be extra careful around other supernaturals, seeing as I ended up mating or bonding to each new species I came across. There were only so many times I could ask my men to accept this sort of thing.

My eyes drifted close as I listened to my mates talking, laughing, and moving about the house. It was warm and comforting, knowing I was part of this pack, and I belonged when I'm not sure I ever felt that way before. Ayla seemed to have joined in to help, her musical voice adding to the others in a way that made sense. Our future was quickly changing into something new, but I was thankful for moments like this where the dangers of what was to come could be put on hold.

A body shifted to sit behind me and pulled me into their arms, running their fingers through my hair. I nuzzled into their chest. The metal tang of blood mixed with the heady, rich scent of sandalwood told me it was Derven.

His scent reminded me of a hit where the man was a collector of ancient texts and artifacts. The room he kept them in had that rich scent of incense, old money, and the bite of age. It seemed to fit my newest mate since he'd aged through the centuries but still held onto that core scent of when he was human.

"Will you be alright to travel to the other house with this much daylight, or do you need to stay here?" Rath asked from somewhere over my head.

Arms gathered me up, and I was lifted and cradled against his chest. "I should manage making my way through the forest," Derven said as he handed me over to Rath. "I'll meet you there, *sângele meu*," he whispered, pressing a kiss to my head.

The only sound he made as he darted out the door was a soft whoosh of wind. Even with my supernatural hearing, I couldn't make out any footfalls. Cracking open an eye, I looked up at Rath. "How is he that silent?"

"I'm sure he didn't end up living to a thousand without learning a few tricks. Who knows, maybe he can teach us," Rath mused as he carried me out of the house.

The pickup truck was overflowing with their things, and it seems they filled a second one as well. "Is that everything?"

"Most of it. I think with one more trip, it should be done. It's far easier since they don't have to move the furniture unless they want to switch something out. Zander had it all set up, almost as if he knew he'd have a house full of people living with him one day," Rath shared, caressing his cheek against my hair absently.

I reached up and cupped his cheek, making him pull back slightly to see my face. "Are you alright? I can tell you're unsettled, but I assumed it was because of Derven. Now I think it might be something else."

"Seeing him again had brought back many memories of my time with the Dark Ring. Few, if any, were good," he answered. "I thought leaving everything behind and working toward taking them down would help me move past things, but now I realize it won't be that simple."

I kissed him, letting my love and reassurance melt into him. "If you need an ear to listen, I'm happy to do that for you whenever you decide. Also, know that if you never want to tell me what happened, I'm okay with that too. Sometimes our past isn't something we want others to be influenced by."

"*Nin mel*, you are a gift from God, and I am blessed beyond measure to have you as a mate," he said, returning my kiss before heading to one of the trucks and setting me inside. "Colt will drive you back. I'm riding behind to make sure we don't lose anything along the way."

Seconds later, Colt hopped in, and we were off with the other truck following the rest of the guys and their things.

"Where are we going to put Derven?" I asked, leaning my head on Colt's shoulder. "Zander made his home to allow for as much light as possible in this dense forest."

"We were talking about that, and he actually has a music room he built to record his own stuff on the first floor. He's been going on and off tour so much he never got around to putting it together. It's got no windows, and once we remove the soundproofing from the walls, get some furniture, and see if we can connect the bathroom next to it, all should be good," Colt shared.

"Isn't that a stroke of luck," I mused, peering up at him. "Are we okay? I know Zander said everyone was fine and didn't hold me responsible for this, but I just feel like I've betrayed you all or duped you into adding another person into our family."

"Little one, listen to me carefully," Colt said, his voice stern. "There is nothing you could have done to prevent what happened. If life with you so far has taught me anything, it's that there will be twists and turns, but we need to deal with them as they come. Some will be harder than others to deal with, but so far, everything has happened for a reason. You needed Rath. Without him, we wouldn't have known the first thing about how to help you when your magic presented itself. Maybe Derven has something to teach you or offer you that wouldn't have happened otherwise. No matter what comes of this, it is not your fault and changes nothing with you and me or any of your other mates."

I thought about what he said and what Derven might have to offer. Then I remembered what he said in the bedroom before he left. "He gives us an army," I said, sitting up straight. "Everything he owns or commands is now mine as well. Which means, if we need an army like he offered before, it's a guarantee. Derven lost his last Blood Bond, and he's determined nothing will happen to me, so he's vested in this battle beyond his personal feelings. This is a twist the Senate and the Dark Ring would never see coming."

EIGHT

FINLEY

Leaving the men to do their thing, I took the laptop with all the information I would need from Margaret and headed to my nest. Then inputting the code, the door clicked open, and I entered, ensuring to leave the door ajar so they knew they were welcome to join me whenever. Curling up on my giant bean bag bed, I flipped open the lid. As it booted up, I gazed out the glass wall, taking in the forest beyond. It was soothing to watch the trees wave in the breeze like they were dancing.

A chime sounded from the computer, and a password request popped up. I went with my gut and entered the one I would use for all Organization purposes and was granted access. The desktop was blank but for one folder entitled *Finley*. Feeling that was far too obvious, I checked a few other places as well, finding it empty of all other data. I clicked on the file and found one video file to click on.

Everything inside me was at war. *Do I open it? Could it be another trap?* It's not like they didn't already know my location if they wanted to attack us. What would Margaret gain from this? Maybe there was information I didn't want to know, and it would be better to leave this be. Tossing my fears to the side, I clicked it.

A man's face appeared on the screen, one that looked familiar to me but I couldn't place. He was sitting in an office alone at night if the view out his windows was accurate. He had jet black hair cut short on the sides but longer on top that fell into his face and stared down at his hands. At first, I thought the video wasn't playing, but I could see him breathing, and other faint background noises could be heard. Then he looked up, and I was met with the same-colored cobalt eyes that I have, and I knew this man was my father.

"This is not how I wanted things to happen, Finley," he said, his eyes sad as he spoke. "I was going to wait until your magic revealed itself, then I was going to help you through it. It was safer for everyone, especially you, not knowing I existed until it couldn't be avoided. I know when you watch this, you'll know what you really are and your magic has been freed. I can feel it through our familial bond. I'm sure you have so many questions, and I want to answer them for you, but knowing the truth might put you in even more danger."

He sighed and ran his hands through his hair before continuing, "Your mother died giving birth to you, and being the creator and leader of the Organization, I couldn't risk having you with me. So many people have tried to kill me to take over the Organization or dismantle it, feeling it's evil and should never have been created. I thought the best thing was to send you to the orphanage, and when you were old enough, I came back for you. Bringing you into the Organization was the only way for me to watch over you without anyone knowing who you were. Hearing this probably doesn't make anything better or make you feel any less abandoned, but you deserve the truth."

I hit the pause button on the video since I saw it went on for another ten minutes and closed my eyes. My father, Ellisor Beinorin, was alive and not only that but created and led the Organization. *Had Margaret told him what happened to me? Did he know she kicked me out since I contacted the alpha of the pack? Is this what she meant when she said all those weeks ago I could have been protected?* Part of me didn't want to finish the video, but I knew I was going to. I'd never allowed myself to think about what life would be like if my parents were alive. If they hadn't wanted me, then what was the point of looking for them? Giving in, I clicked the play button, and my father's deep, even-toned voice started up once more.

"I put together the information on this laptop myself. I created two access points, knowing you would use this password first. At the end of this video, I will give you the second one, which has all the files on each person in the Senate and known Dark Ring members. There is also going to be a file on me filled with whatever information you might want to know about your mother, Tiriana. You take after her in personality more so than me, but oddly enough, for a person with such a big heart, you made one of the best assassins I've ever had in the Organization. Seems that's where you took after me...

"There is another bit of information I want to tell you, but I don't feel like it should be said in a recording, no matter how secure I make it. I leave the choice up to you, but I left you my private contact information because I would really love the chance to speak with you in person. It would be nice to meet you and your mates so I can officially introduce myself. I'm sure you're wondering why now? Why reveal myself to you after all this time? Those that have been after you and me all our lives are the very same you are hunting down. This will make more sense with the last bit of information I have to give you, but that is all I'm holding back. Everything you could possibly need to ensure the destruction of the powers that be is in this laptop. I might not have been there for you as a father growing up, but I would like to be there for you now. This is a dangerous mission, one no one has been willing to take, and you're going to need all the help you can get."

He stared at the camera for a moment as if unsure of what he wanted to say next. His eyes pleaded as if he knew I would be hesitant to believe anything he had to say. "*Cin are in nin emel, nin -iel. Im mel cin alys. N- safe, tul- rad- nin.* The password is, *Mír -o nin emel.* It's what your mother called you while you were still in her womb. It means *jewel of my heart.*"

I logged out, bringing up the request for the password, and reached out to Rath, "*I need your help spelling out a phrase.*"

His curiosity at my request was vibrant in our connection. "*Of course. What is the phrase?*"

"Mír -o nin emel," I answered.

"*Do you know what that means,* nin mel?" Rath asked, his voice hesitant.

Closing my eyes, I leaned back in the bean bag, rubbing my forehead as my own emotions seemed to overwhelm me. "*My father said it means jewel of my heart. He made it the password to the documents I need to get to about the Senate and the Dark Ring.*"

"*Do you want me to come to you? The others are just putting things away in their rooms. I'm more underfoot than anything,*" he offered, aware of how unsettled I was.

"*Okay...*" I answered. "*Rath, he sent me a video to watch.*"

"*You watched it by yourself?*" Rath demanded. "Nin mel, *why would you put yourself through that alone? I'm coming. I'll be there in a moment. Derven is coming too.*"

"*Wait, this room is full of sunshine,*" I warned, but it was too late. They both walked in.

I shot to my feet and ran over to the bookcase Zander had left the remote for the shades. I'd never needed to use it, happy to have the sunlight fill the room, but now I was terrified I was going to harm Derven.

"Sângele meu, it's all right. There is a UV filter on the windows that keeps it from harming me. Seems Zander didn't spare expenses when he built this home," Derven shared as he walked over, taking the remote from my hand. "It seems that after that small amount of blood as well, it's strengthened me even more against sunlight. Who knows, after a true feeding, I might be able to walk this world freely once more." He drew me back to the bean bag where Rath was sitting and urged me to settle in next to my elf.

Derven then sat on the floor, leaning against the bean bag by my legs, so he was still part of the conversation but gave me more space. I didn't realize how a small action like that could mean so much as I was getting used to having him part of the pack. While I felt connected to him and knew he was part of my life from now on, I didn't have the same physical response I did with the others. Maybe it was because he hadn't really fed from me. We'd done enough to initiate the bond but not really connect us.

"Would you like to talk about what your father told you?" Rath asked, pulling me to his chest and tugging me to lie down with him. "Or is it better to leave things alone right now?"

"He is the founder of the Organization," I shared. "When my mother died giving birth to me, he felt it was too dangerous to keep me, so he gave me up."

"Then he came back for you," Rath pointed out.

I hummed my agreement, but the feelings I never gave into as a child started to creep up. "He thought keeping an eye on me as one of his assassins was the best option," I said, burrowing my face against his chest. "He was going to keep silent until my magic came in, and I needed his help, but now he wants to meet. Something about one final detail to tell me, but he wouldn't do it over the video. It had to be in person."

Derven's hand wrapped around the bare skin of my ankle. His thumb gently stroked up and down, giving his own show of support as he asked the question I'd been asking myself, "Do you want to meet him?"

"I really don't know," I answered. "Part of me feels like he doesn't deserve that after all these years hiding in the shadows. He knew what their training was like. He probably helped to create it, then he sent his own daughter to survive it? On the other hand, if I wasn't trained as the skilled fighter I am today, I never would have been able to handle all of this."

I let out a frustrated growl, rolling onto my back and looking up at the ceiling. "Please tell me this is the last of it, that the universe doesn't have any more surprises because I just can't deal with it anymore. All I want is to look at these files, plot out our mission, and end it all. This is what I was trained for, to act rational, cool, detached, and not let things cloud my mind jeopardizing the mission. Yet everything is chaotic, and I don't know how to deal with it."

"Then we will plan," Derven announced. "Rathal and I spent plenty of time with the members of the Dark Ring and the Senate alike. You'd be surprised at how many members cohabitate without even knowing the dark secret hidden in plain sight."

Grabbing the laptop, I handed it to Rath, who quickly typed in the password. The new screen that showed up was filled with files with more names than I could have fathomed. For every single person attached to the Dark Ring or the Senate, it had all the people in their family, mistresses, illegitimate children, and the like. Anyone and everyone attached who I could use for information and leverage. My father had given me more ammunition against these people than I could have dreamed. No wonder there was respect between the Organization and the Senate. With a click of a button, the Organization could destroy any member of the Senate in a political sense.

"That is a massive amount of data," Derven said, having come around the back, leaning in to see the computer.

Having his scent lingering nearby was nice, and it made my wolf happy that he wanted to be around us. My magic didn't really seem to care much at all while Rath was at my back, but if I decided to create a soul bond with Derven, then it might change.

"You're the expert here. Where do we even start," Derven murmured, his eyes taking in the screen.

I clicked the search bar and typed in a name, wondering if a file would pop up, and sure enough, there it was. Tabitha, AKA tango-eight-one-three, the assassin who turned against the Organization and joined the enemy, setting me up to fail. I scrolled through her information, looking to see if there was more that maybe Margaret didn't know, but it was just as she'd said. A year ago, she went to a simple job and never came back. They sent out a team to investigate, seeing as the job was completed, but the assassin didn't return.

"She's the one you thought was your friend," Rath murmured, his lips brushing the skin of my neck. "You told me she was with you on the job where you freed us."

"Come to find out the whole job was meant to put me in a place where they could kidnap me and sell me off like the rest of you. The Dark Ring wanted me gone, but I'm still not sure why the Senate got involved," I shared. "The last job against the Dark Ring was on a lower member, so I'm not sure why they would put in so much effort."

Next, I typed in Delilah's name for her file to pop up. When I opened it, there were tons more information about her than I was given for the job. It showed her connection to her grandfather, who was protecting her right now. That she was part of the team that set up all the social gatherings in secret locations to gain more members for the cause. It would appear Delilah was far more important to the Dark Ring than I'd known. Was this information added after I was taken, or had they always had it?

"This is who you asked Morwyn to acquire," Rath said, sitting up to see past my head.

Derven reached out and clicked on her picture, blowing it up. "Oh, the bitch with King Kong. I've seen her around the parties. They use her to show people just how fun being cruel can be."

"That's how I got bit. I was assigned to take her out, so I got into one of her parties. Everything went wrong, and I killed everyone else but her and her pet monkey," I explained to Derven. "I freed all the supers trapped there, and when I got to Cory, he freaked out and bit me. At the time, I had no idea an omega typically couldn't change someone or that he was Colt's little brother. Cory's last words before he died were to find Colt, and that's how this all happened."

"Hmm, this was before you knew you were an elf, correct?" Derven asked, and I nodded. "Elves are one of the only supernatural creatures I know of who can adapt to any kind of supernatural who transmits a change through a bite, scratch, blood exchange… pretty much anything that isn't a spell. I'm not sure what it is or if it has to do with the magic you possess. I've seen many elf combinations over my many years of life. Of course, they are usually banished from their clan for ruining the purity of their kind, which is why people believe it didn't happen."

"That would explain why everyone was so shocked when I was, without a doubt, changed into an omega," I commented as I connected the dots of all the bits and pieces of information I'd gathered. "Learning to deal with the personality change before my elf magic appeared was rough. Thankfully, now my magic has helped to even out the complexities of being an omega. The more I work with both parts of myself, the more harmony is created between the two."

Derven shifted slightly so he was facing me more than the computer, reaching out to place his hand on my forearm. "While I know Ayla seems to have zero issues with you being a mixed supernatural, you need to understand that many elves won't like it. From what I've seen, your power is the strongest in a long time, even before the war, so there is no denying you are their queen. I just don't want you to be blindsided if their reception of you is less than welcoming."

"Dealing with people like that won't be an issue. I've had plenty of experience. All my life, I've never really had a place in the world. Assassins don't make friends or have long-term lovers or families. The men in this house are the first who have accepted me for who *I* am and not what I can do for them, but I appreciate your concern. It's nice to be looked after and to have people worry about you," I said with a smile.

"I look forward to earning my place in your family. I can't say I've had much of one myself," Derven murmured, leaning in to rest his forehead against mine for a moment, then sat back. "So if Senator Morwyn is bringing us Delilah, then what?"

"Then we get all the information out of her we can," I answered. "That means getting to work on these files to find out what information we already have, what we need, and ensure she's not lying to us. I find most of what comes out of her mouth is pure manipulation."

"Sounds about right for her," Rath muttered. "Don't forget they're supposed to get the gorilla too."

An evil smile tugged at my lips. "Oh, that is purely for revenge and someone we can use against her. While she tries to hide it, I think she actually likes the ape."

"Remind me not to ever make you that mad at me," Derven said, giving me a wary look. "I keep forgetting you're an assassin first and foremost."

"That is most people's biggest mistake," I shared, leaning in, our noses brushing against each other. "They underestimate me."

NINE

FINLEY

E ventually, I moved out into the living room since all my mates wanted to be around me as I buried my head in research. Zander brought up the whiteboard he had as we started to make notes and categorize who were the key players in each group. Clearly, we knew who the senators were, but what we needed to know was who around them held power. Each person we dove into connected back to someone in the Dark Ring or the Senate. Everything about these two groups was intertwined on a level that was frightening.

Someone made sure to provide snacks and drinks and reminded me to eat or drink as I worked. This is where I thrived in my profession—plotting, planning, and dissecting every nuance of the person I was dealing with. Now, this was a much larger scale project with so many moving parts and pieces. We needed to be prepared for whenever Morwyn provided us with Delilah, so as we got the information we needed from her, we could act.

Rath and Derven were amazing, adding bits and pieces about people you wouldn't know unless you spent time around them—what they drank, who they spent time with at parties, did they dabble in one dark, twisted addition or another. Each of these things gave me another way of taking them down. Spike a bottle of their favorite liquor, plant a person to get them right where I needed to take them out. This job wasn't going to be over quickly. I wanted them to know they were being hunted. Start with the people who wouldn't be as noticeable first, but without them there, they were missing a cog in the mechanism. The plan that was taking shape would allow me to attack them at all sides so they couldn't predict where I might strike next.

"Zander, I know you have the jet, but do you have something a little less noticeable?" I asked as I was mapping out some strike points. I would need to get to many states fast without drawing attention to what I was doing or leaving a trail.

He looked at me, confused. "Smaller?"

"Yeah, like a plane that can only fit four people, flies into small private airports, that sort of thing. Your jet is a little more noticeable than a personal plane that a hobbyist can have," I explained.

"No, little dove, I don't have one of those. I got the jet to travel with the band and have more space instead of a tour bus," he said.

I nodded, realizing it would be far too easy for him to have one lying around.

"That doesn't mean I can't buy one," Zander pointed out. "It's not like I can't afford it, and who would think twice about a rock star wanting his own plane?"

I cocked my head to the side, thinking that through. "Can you fly it? We couldn't hire a pilot to do these runs. It would draw too much attention."

"I can," Derven shared, raising his hand. "I mean, it's been a little while, but I flew in the second world war and kept the talent up ever since. I'm sure my affairs have been kept in order while I was trapped with the Dark Ring. It wouldn't be the first time I've disappeared for half a century or so. That's why it's so important to have staff you can trust."

All of us gawked at him as he shared this information with us like it was completely normal. I suppose being someone who never died and lived among humans, you would want a life, hobbies, and things like that, but it would leave a trail behind. Making it slightly more reasonable that he would have people who kept up with making sure his identity was hidden.

"I'll need to call them and let them know I'm re-entering society, but that shouldn't be hard to manage. I'll just need to make a trip to New York to pick up all my current paperwork and whatever name they have me passing as," Derven continued, oblivious to our shock. "Zander, do you think you could lend me the use of your jet to fly there? I wouldn't have any of the documentation they would need for me to fly normally."

Looking down at the list of people, I found a few targets I could take out while we were there. "That works for my plan," I shared. "We just need to use Zander's fame to our advantage so they don't realize it's me who's doing the killing right away."

"Hold on," Lane cut in, waving his arms like a referee. "Sweetheart, I need you to explain to us what your plan is, *all* of it," he warned, giving me a stern look. "Right now, I feel like you have half the plan in your head because you are working way faster than the rest of us. Spell it out like we are a new trainee you are working with."

Handing off the laptop, I walked to the whiteboard and circled a group of names in red. I traced who those people connected to and underlined them. "Think of it like a building. If you want to collapse the whole thing, you need to take out the support. You don't start from the top. You set charges at the base. These people I circled while on their own are insignificant, *but* when you see who they support," I said, tapping on the names underlined. "Things become unstable. What happens when the help they relied on far more than they realized is gone? It leaves them reeling, looking for a way to fill the gap. Meanwhile, other things are going to slip and show me where I need to hit next."

Each of the men were riveted to what I was saying, some nodding along as they understood my train of thought. "When I see the next line of support to remove, it will cause a ripple effect all the way to the top. This whole system is built on no one knowing what the others are doing. That way, if they were ever caught, there's no way for them to betray the group as a whole. Does that make sense?"

"This can all be done without Delilah?" Colt asked. "I thought you said she was going to be the ticket we needed to get in."

"She is, with the top tier of the Dark Ring," I informed them. "When I get to them, I want the ground they stand on to be so shaky when we hit them, there's no coming back. A building that is demolished from the foundation up can't be fixed. It just has to be rebuilt."

"What about the Senate?" Elias questioned. "This will take down the Dark Ring, but I don't see it doing the same thing to the other."

"No, you're right, but what it does do is take away the outside support. There are so many people of both parties dealing with each other back and forth. When you chop off a limb, it slows them down. The connections, dirty secrets, and money they were receiving in exchange for silence or to turn a blind eye are no longer there," I detailed as I marked out all the Dark Ring members on the board, leaving the Senate, which made up only a quarter. "The Senate might have more power in the eyes of the public, but behind the scenes, it was the Dark Ring pulling many of the strings. They became bolder once they knew the Senate couldn't do anything. I believe I was sent to kill Delilah as a signal that the Senate didn't want to be a pawn in their games anymore."

"So, how do we attack the Senate?" Noah asked. "It can't be done the same way. It's not built on a system of blind recruitment. Everyone knows everyone, and many are in each other's pockets with mutually assured destruction between them."

"While the Senate might have control in most of the world regarding supernaturals, the ones they don't control are the humans. The humans have their own government per country as they always have. The United Senate was created to ensure that supers were controlled by their own kind together, creating the rules," I paused, taking in each of my mates, knowing this idea was risky, but it was brilliant if it worked. "My plan is to turn the court of public opinion back on them, leak some of this information, and show the skeletons in the closet. This will draw all the senators' attention allowing us to come in and destroy them one by one."

Mason let out an impressed-sounding whistle. "Damn, snuggles, now I see why you are damn good at your job."

"So, where do we come in?" Ayla asked, scaring everyone as she magically appeared in the living room.

I'd known she was there. Ever since I caught the feel of her magic stalking us at the zoo, I could pick up on it much faster. The reason I didn't say anything is I wanted my men to see her skill and understand how good she was. My reasoning for that was because I wanted her to come with me on these jobs, leaving my men to be the distraction, and they weren't going to like it.

"Holy fuck balls," Mason yelled, almost falling off the couch. "God-dammit, Ayla!"

The others flinched and showed clear signs they were surprised at her appearance, so I knew they hadn't noticed. Rath and Derven were the only two who didn't react, but I wasn't sure if that was more of their trained response or if they could tell she was there.

"Oh goodness, this is far more fun than I thought it would be," Ayla said with a snicker, her eyes crinkling with delight.

Elias slowly stood and approached her, walking around her, sniffing as if he were trying to figure out how she did it. Being my Tracker, it would make sense he would be unsettled by the fact she could get this close to me without him noticing.

"How did you do that?" he asked, his voice full of curiosity and irritation. "Is it your magic that conceals your scent, or do elves simply not have them? Rath has a faint one, but I wasn't sure if there had been something done to him while with the Dark Ring."

Ayla frowned at his question. "I will have you know I bathe quite regularly. I shouldn't have a scent."

Mason snorted at her comment. "That's not what he's talking about, ninja barbie. What he's asking is why you don't have a scent, a smell that is you and unlike no one else. Like how fingerprints are different for every person alive. Werewolves use scent to identify, track, and remember who or what they are. Seems that elves don't carry odor for us to use the way we normally would."

Ayla turned to me. "Is he right? Do I not have a scent? You knew I was here. I could tell even though you didn't tell the others."

"I knew it was you based on your magic, but no, you don't have a scent that can be picked up on," I explained. "Rath doesn't either, so I wouldn't be too worried."

"Wait, you knew she was there, and you didn't say anything?" Zander demanded. "Little dove, I understand she is a friend and is here to help us, but I feel like that is something you should have told us."

I walked over and sat on the ottoman, facing all my men as I prepared to tell them the part of my plan I had left out so far. "Lane asked me to share the whole plan, and the part I was holding back on was to see if you could tell Ayla was here with us. When I go after these people, I want Ayla to be my partner, she is talented in concealment magic, and as you said, she carries no scent. All of these things help me as I hunt these assholes down."

Rath frowned, crossing his arms. "What would we be doing in the meantime?"

"Causing a distraction," I answer. "I saw the invitation to the party in New York a week from today. If we go as a family to this party, then I can slip away and meet Ayla to deal with these men. Together we can hit them fast, quiet, leaving no trace, and I'll be back at the party with none the wiser."

Zander spluttered at this idea. "You had that planned in your head for longer than today, didn't you? There's no way you could come up with something that solid in a day."

"You can when it's all you've ever known," I reasoned. "From the moment I was brought into the Organization, this is exactly what I was trained for. The interesting part is now that I'm the way I am, it makes me even more deadly than when I was a mere human."

Colt rose to his feet and paced behind the couch, running his hands through his hair. "So you go out into the night, kill a bunch of people and come back like it's another average Friday night? Then there's us, just hanging out at a party for some poodle's birthday? I'm not sure I can fly with that little one."

"There needs to be a valid reason for all of us to go to New York City," I argued. "We promised not to split up again, and I'm trying to keep that promise, but nine people with a famous rock star isn't something we can keep on the down low. The party explains why we would be there, and I would go with you, have him introduce me since I'm sure everyone wants to meet Zander's new mate. While we are in town, Derven can get what he needs, and it's a win-win for us all."

"This feels like we are in an *Ocean's Eleven* movie or something," Lane muttered.

"Nah, I think snuggles's plan is way cooler than any of theirs," Mason argued.

Noah rolled his eyes. "That's only because you get to play a part in it."

"Can you blame me for thinking our woman is a total badass? I mean, she came up with this whole thing in less than twenty-four hours," Mason reasoned.

"This plan is nowhere close to being ready," I stated, bringing the conversation back to the matter at hand. "This is the rough outline, and before anything can move forward, I need to know you're all on board. If you hate the idea, then I'll scrap it and try something else that will make you all feel better."

"Little one, no idea you have is going to make us feel better," Colt reasoned. "None of us will like the idea of you going off into the night killing people. As your alphas and your mates, that sounds like the worst possible idea to us. That being said, it needs to be done... you swore an oath to take down the Senate, and the Dark Ring is part of that. If you believe this is the smartest way to see this through, putting you in the least amount of danger, then I'm in."

Lane sighed, his head falling back to rest on the couch. "I'm with Colt. This whole thing is a terrible idea, but we can't avoid seeing it through. That would hurt you far more."

"So I guess I should RSVP then," Zander muttered as he made his way downstairs, where the invitation was lying on the counter.

Derven cleared his throat before speaking, drawing everyone's attention. "I know I haven't earned my place to speak on these matters yet, but would someone fill me in on this oath? I've heard it mentioned a few times, and it has me curious and slightly worried that my Blood Bond has a contract on her life."

"The nitty-gritty version is Zander's mother, Senator Morwyn, wants out of her marriage, out of her place in the Senate, and to be free to live her life with her real mate, who's her bodyguard. They showed up one night and asked Finley to kill her father-in-law, take down the Senate, destroy the Dark Ring, and give her back her freedom," Mason explained. "Apparently, when you make a deal with an elf, and you shake on it, your life is tied to each other to ensure no one goes back on the deal. Morwyn is supposed to get us Delilah and the gorilla, while snuggles does all the hard work."

Derven looked at me, his brow creased, and worry filled his eyes. "*Sângele meu*, is this true? Did you make a contract that you would take down the Senate or die?"

"That and a few other things must be completed as well," I answered. "I understand your worry, but I was going to do this whether I was contracted to or not. They will keep coming after me, and when they can't get to me, they will start to hunt those I care about. Before, I didn't have anyone they could use against me, and now I have more than I ever could have imagined."

None of them had been happy when I made the contract, but it was done and sealed. The mark on my wrist proved it.

"I know you all want to keep me safe and protect me from the monsters that go bump in the night. The thing that you're all forgetting is that I'm one of those monsters. A trained killer who silently moves in the shadows and leaves dead bodies in her wake. I will do this. The Senate and the Dark Ring will be destroyed by my own hand, have no doubts about that," I announced, lifting my chin and holding my head high, pretending to be the queen they kept saying I was.

Ayla came to stand before me, dropping to one knee, a dagger in her hand slicing the flesh of the other. "I vow myself to the queen of the elves. May she find my offering pleasing and use this vessel as she sees fit."

I had no idea what to do, but Rath reached out and whispered how I should respond if I wished to accept her oath. Reaching out, I took the knife and wiped her blood on my palm and called my magic to burn it off my skin, accepting the offering Ayla had given.

"Your queen is pleased with your offering and accepts your vow. Now rise and be at ease until your queen has need of you," I answered, feeling the power in my words.

Ayla wasn't bound to me like a mate but more like a member of my pack, making me her alpha. So started the beginning of my vision to see a blended world where elves and werewolves lived in harmony.

TEN

FINLEY

The next few days passed in a blur of planning, making sure the three new elves, in addition to Ayla, were settled in the pack house. Dealing with the pack as they adjusted to the changes, including the vampire who was now among them, took a bit of work. Many were amazed to find out that elves were still alive and a vampire didn't want to kill them as natural enemies.

I think it also was helpful that the new elven additions to the pack helped in the greenhouse and gardens, teaching those who worked their new tricks. Theodas informed me that just having my magic running through the earth had made a huge difference, but what he was teaching was practical knowledge. He hoped it would be passed down to the next generation who worked to feed our pack and others.

Kolvar was a master craftsman and was more than happy to help anyone who needed it with repairs in their home or build what was needed from scratch. I could understand why he would be a great loss to his clan, but I was more than happy to have him as part of our pack.

Vanya was a healer, quiet, soft-spoken, and tiny compared to the men she arrived with. I even managed to be taller than her, and I was only five-seven, short for an elf, according to Rath. While Vanya had magic to help with her healing abilities, she was also incredibly skilled at holistic medicine as well. That was something I absolutely wanted to learn from her. Having knowledge like that with the war we are about to wage would be invaluable if, for some reason, my magic failed me.

During the day, we spent most of the time with the pack, handling matters and coming clean about who and what I was. With so many things hitting them all at once, I was pleased to see the fact that I was an assassin didn't seem quite so worrisome to them. Derven, on the other hand, was going to have to work much harder to convince people he wasn't going to eat them.

He'd gone with Noah and Rath into town to get some clothes and other things since Rath was also living off hand-me-downs from the guys. Granted, he could use his magic to alter them, but there were other things he needed as well.

Thankfully, every one of my mates was adjusting to having Derven around, and he proved to be quite useful in many areas, having picked up numerous skills in his thousand years. As I wandered around the pack, talking with various members answering questions or getting to know people, I could understand why packs chose to seclude them-selves from the world. This was a family, a massive one, yet every person looked out for each other. Then again, like all families, there was always a problem child, or children in this case, unhappy with everything.

Some of the older members couldn't handle the changes and lashed out at Colt and Lane. They handled it with grace, but ultimately, it came down to whether they were going to stay or go. Some chose to leave, moving to other packs that offered them a place, while many calmed down after a day or two, finally seeing what we were trying to do.

When the sun set and everyone went home to spend the evening with their families was when I got to work. This wasn't something the guys could help me with as easily, but when I did have an opportunity, I always let them. I'd taken over Zander's office, printing out information and creating stacks for each one of the people I was going after while in New York. Ayla, my faithful shadow through the night, kept me company while the guys went to sleep. They needed to be there for the pack right now, which meant being present during the day.

No one could know what I was doing, so working at night made the most sense. A pack expected their omega to be a part of daily life, and I was doing my best to provide that on top of protecting their future. So I worked late into the night and joined them later in the afternoon. That didn't leave much personal time for us, but this wouldn't be long-term. After New York, I would be able to take a breather, watching to see where the cracks started to show in the foundation. Because the best assassins knew when to watch, wait, then act when the time was right.

A knock sounded on the office door causing me to look up and find Derven entering. He closed the door behind him, locked it, then turned to face me. "Everything alright?" I asked.

"Yes... well... ah," Derven stammered as he approached and took a seat across from me. "While I am an old vampire and able to control my urges, I believe going to New York City while hungry might not be the best idea. I've managed just fine off minimal amounts of blood thanks to my time with the Dark Ring, but if I don't need to force myself into that, I'd rather not."

Understanding crashed into me. "Derven, have you been starving yourself to give me time to adjust?"

"I wouldn't say starving. The blood I took from your finger helped to keep the worst of the hunger pains at bay. It certainly packs a punch, so I wouldn't need to take much from you to reach a point where I'll be able to function without problems," Derven explained.

Frowning, I leaned back in my chair. "How much would it take for you to be fully sated?"

"I couldn't ask that of you, not yet," he murmured. "To be fully sated wouldn't just be blood... for vampires to be without hunger, both urges would need to be fed."

"So blood and sex," I stated bluntly. "For a vampire to be truly satisfied, you need to have sex while taking blood from your bond?"

"Yes, that would be the case," he answered, refusing to look at me. "*Sângele mue*, we are still so new to each other, and I know you don't feel the same way about me that you do your other mates. Blood Bonds are more for the vampire. It keeps us from killing the one person we need to feed from, who gives us the most power. As for your side of things, well, I believe you find us unthreatening but nothing more on an emotional level."

I stood, walked around the desk, and perched myself on his lap, making him suck in a surprised breath. He didn't move or even breathe. He simply watched me with wide eyes as if he wasn't sure what I would do next.

"You are correct, I don't feel the instant attachment I did with my other mates, but that doesn't mean I'm not attracted to you. Derven, you are an incredibly handsome man who's been looking after me every night," I paused, seeing his chagrin. "Did you really think I believe Ayla was the one making sure I ate and didn't just live off of coffee? While you might be able to be moving about in the sunlight, you still seem to be more comfortable being up all night and resting during the day."

"I promised Mason I would keep an eye on you, make sure you didn't starve yourself or, as he put it, become a caffeine zombie," he admitted. "Taking care of you is a joy and an honor not only because you are my Blood Bond but because of who you are as a person. The past few days, you've been working yourself to the bone to get this mission planned, then you are out with the pack attending to their needs. I don't think people understand just how amazing you are."

His words warmed my heart and made me bold enough to rest my head on his shoulder as I sat cradled in his lap. Derven wrapped his arms around me and nuzzled his cheek against my hair. We sat like this for a moment, just enjoying each other's presence, and I realized that with all the work I was doing, my wolf wasn't getting the cuddles she needed as an omega.

Lifting my head, I looked into his eyes. They were so full of hope yet hesitant to make the first move. I lifted a hand, cupping his jaw, and leaned in, pressing a kiss to his lips, the scent of sandalwood and copper flooding my nose. It made me groan at how delightful the strange combination was, but it told me my wolf also found him pleasing. His mouth moved under mine, drawing me into him deeper, his tongue flicking out to taste my lips. When I opened up to him, I felt his fangs scrape along the soft flesh of the inside of my bottom lip. It wasn't hard enough to make me bleed, but the desire was there, and it made me shiver with anticipation. Clearly, my body remembered what he'd done to me with only sucking on my finger.

"Finley, we need to stop if you don't wish me to feed from you directly. I am only so strong when it comes to the woman who holds the most delectable blood I've ever tasted," Derven whispered against my lips, refusing to pull back farther than he needed to.

My body begged for him to do just that, but part of me was still hesitant to offer up that much vulnerability to a man who was going to be taking life right out of me. I knew he wouldn't hurt me. That wasn't what I feared. It was more the fear I might become addicted to this. Leaning back, I pushed against him, forcing space between us, then stood. Derven seemed to sag in his seat, realizing I wasn't going to let him drink from me. I walked over to the black leather sofa Zander had moved in here for me to nap on if I needed to. As I went, I slipped my shirt over my head, dropped it to the floor, then looked over my shoulder.

Derven was on his feet watching me as I removed my bra next, letting that fall. My hair was down to my butt now, meaning it covered my breasts, so he couldn't see them clearly yet. I paused before the couch and started to shimmy out of the sweats I'd been wearing, but Derven appeared before me in a flash.

"Let me," he ordered, settling his hand on my hips. "You realize if you let me do this once, drinking from any other source but your vein won't be an option anymore, right?"

"I'm well aware of what I'm doing, Ven," I answered using the nickname I'd heard Rath use. "We are bonded together for life, and that makes you one of my mates. How can I treat you any differently than them? I hardly knew any of them before my first heat forced their hands, claiming me, but I wouldn't change a thing. Rath and I stumbled upon each other in the worst situation and made it work. You appearing in my life the way you did is just how the universe decided it should be, and who am I to argue?"

Derven grabbed my throat and pulled me into a harsh kiss of teeth and blood, and this time, he didn't hold back from biting. I moaned as he licked along my chin, cleaning up what had leaked from the corner of my mouth, then sucked harshly on my ravaged bottom lip. Each pull felt like he was between my legs, sucking on my clit, and my legs began to shake, threatening to drop me. Derven, however, was prepared for this and wrapped his hand that wasn't around my throat against my hips, slamming them into his pelvis. I could feel him in his jeans bulging against the fabric, begging to be released.

My hands slid down his chest until they met the top of his jeans, and I grabbed his shirt, pulling it out of my way as I fumbled to free his cock. I paused as he nipped at my throat just under my jaw. "So needy, sângele meu, there is no rush. We have all the time in the world, you and I." He purred.

He released his hold on me and gripped the back of his shirt, yanking it over his head, revealing a lean, sculpted chest. Derven was not as sturdy as my werewolf mates nor the effortlessly fluid build of my elf. No, this vampire before me was like a marble statue, all muscle that rippled under his skin without an ounce of fat on him. One would think it would make him look emaciated, but instead, it showed off every part of his psyche.

My hands reached out of their own accord, tracing every corded muscle of his abs until I was once more at his waist. I used both hands to follow the dip of his hips leading right to where I wanted to see next. With the button already loose, I pulled both sides of his jeans apart, the sound of the zipper loud in the silence accompanied by our panting breaths. Then, using my supernatural strength, I yanked down his pants, revealing a pair of blood-red silk boxers tented by his rock-hard cock.

"Now it's my turn," Derven announced as he hooked his thumbs around the band of my pants and, far more slowly than I, lowered them.

Dropping to his knees, he took in my body that was now bare to him since I hadn't bothered to put on underwear. Secretly I'd been hoping one of my other mates would have grown tired of waiting and sought me out. Then again, one of them had, and here he was staring at me with hunger wild in his eyes.

"Perfect, absolutely perfect," he whispered, letting his hands run up my legs until he hooked a hand behind my left knee and pulled it to rest over his shoulder. "As an assassin, I'm sure you know where all the major arteries are, but this one has always been a favorite," Derven said as he placed a kiss on my inner thigh. "Though I don't get to enjoy it often since it's quite intimate, don't you agree?"

My hand in his hair tightened at the kiss, trying to hold myself upright while on one leg. Derven reached around and cupped my ass, pulling me closer to his face as he kissed the top of my pussy just above my clit. "Did you know that there's another vein here? While it isn't a major artery, it certainly is fun to drink from."

Teasing me, he pressed a kiss to my clit, then pulled back, dipping his head, and licked me from ass to clit, making me scream as his fangs sank into my flesh on either side. As he sucked, I thought I was going to pass out from the feeling of him drinking as he licked my clit at the same time. The only thing keeping me standing was him, and I couldn't do anything but trust he wouldn't drop me—not that I would care as long as he didn't stop.

A few more gulps, and he released me, stood, picked me up, and laid me on the couch. "Sângele meu, I will show you things you never thought were possible, but for our first time, I want to be inside you as you give me the gift of life through your blood."

"What does that mean? Sângele meu," I asked.

Derven nuzzled into my neck, placing a kiss on my pulse. "It means *my blood*," he answered. "To my people, it means more than the blood that runs through your veins. It means life, purpose, and a reason for being. All things you provide to me as my bond, but Finley... you are becoming so much more than that to me. The fates knew I needed someone to give me a higher purpose for my life, something that gave living this long a meaning. You, my beautiful mate, because that is what you are. You make me want everything out of life and I thought I lost that feeling long ago."

Reaching up, I grabbed his face and pulled him down to me, letting my emotions be said with actions and allowing him in my thoughts, knowing they would express my feelings best. I felt him shuffle about for a moment, then the blunt head of his cock pressed at my entrance.

"Are you ready to be fucked by your first and only vampire?" Derven rumbled in my ear, his teeth nipping before moving to my jaw, where he nibbled affectionately as I moaned my agreement. "It's one hell of a ride, so I'd hold on tightly," he warned right before slamming into my pussy.

A shout of surprise burst from me that was quickly changed to whimpering as Derven pounded into me harder and faster than anyone ever had before. If I weren't a super, he would have split me in half, but I still would have been thanking him for it. My fingers dug into his back, my nails biting into his skin, making him hiss and his eyes roll back in pleasure.

"Fuck, yes, mark me, claim me, so everyone knows I'm owned by you." He growled along my neck before he licked up the column of flesh. "I know the truth, Finley. You might be an omega, an assassin for hire, but no one owns you. It's quite the opposite, isn't it? You, my beloved *sângele meu,* you own us all," Derven said with a roar before his fangs pierced my skin, sending me instantly over the cliff headlong into an orgasm.

"God, *yes*," I screamed, back arching as I thrust myself down on him as he slammed into me. It felt as if he were going to reach all the way up my stomach with how deep and powerfully he fucked the ever-living shit out of me.

Derven flipped us, so I was on top riding him, my hands splayed on his chest. I could feel the trickle of blood running down my neck, but Derven sat up and used his tongue to clean up his mess. My pussy took all of him, so my clit was rubbing on his pelvis as I ground and swirled my hips, leaning forward to get the best angle. Derven latched onto one of my tits, teeth scraping my nipple, making me groan at the shocks it sent through my body.

"Ride me, ride me well, take what you want from my body as I take from yours," Derven taunted before he bit my breast in perfect placement to torture me with every swallow he sucked on my nipple. This caused another climax to carry me away as my body acted on autopilot.

Panting breaths, the tang of copper in the air from my blood, and the sound of slapping skin as I worked my hips assaulted my senses, making it so nothing else in the world mattered but what was happening right now.

"I'm going to come," Derven grunted as he grabbed my hips and held me still so he could fuck me how he needed.

It wasn't long before I felt his cum shooting into me, something I wasn't sure could happen, but it sure as hell did. As if his cum held the same magic as his bites, I joined him in release, dropping to his chest and clinging to him as each spurt sent shockwaves up my spine.

"Holy shit," I gasped, sweat slicking our bodies as we held each other. "You weren't lying about the wild ride."

Derven chuckled as he pressed a kiss to my head. "We're not quite finished. I haven't gotten to taste my favorite spot yet."

"You need more blood?" I asked, feeling like three bites were a lot.

Sitting us up only to lay me down on my back, he showered my face with kisses. "*Sângele meu*, those were what we call love bites, purely done to induce an orgasm. I wanted to save the real meal for last now that one of my hungers has been filled. This way, it ensures I don't take too much from you." He shared, crawling back down my body to lay with his face right at my pussy. "Normally, it wouldn't take this much, and it won't unless I'm severely wounded. As I mentioned, I've been practically starved for fifty years, and your blood packs a punch which is helpful to speed up my recovery."

I let my fingers comb through his hair, feeling relaxed and well fucked. "Take what you need, my mate. I will ensure you never go hungry again."

Derven took me at my word as he latched onto the artery running along the inside of my thigh. My body exploded with pleasure, almost as if a bomb detonated inside me. Now I understood why they outlawed vampires drinking from the vein. This was better than any drug a human could create.

When he'd taken his fill, Derven scooped me up and carried me out of the office and into his bedroom. He tucked me in against his chest, wrapping me up in his arms, humming a song I didn't know but lulled me to sleep almost instantly.

ELEVEN

ZANDER

"**D**o we really need to do this?" Finley asked from the dressing room.

We'd just landed in New York City two hours ago, and I'd had this appointment set with my personal shopper for days. As soon as I knew they were all coming with me to this party, I prepared everything to ensure they would look like they belonged.

"Little dove, we talked about this. The party we are going to is meant only for the elite in the industry. Grim Times got their first platinum album, and they are celebrating it with a select group that just so happens to include me. I'm not going to let anyone have one negative thing to say about me bringing all of you. So yes, we do, in fact, need to do this," I explained for the fifth time.

For the most part, Finley had been great about it all. Back in Tennessee, I had her go for a spa day where they trimmed her hair, gave her a facial, and anything that needed to be waxed, trimmed, or adjusted was also taken care of. I'm sure there wasn't much that needed to be done since Finley had to be the most stunning woman I'd ever met, but I was also biased.

The guys were another story. Well, except for the twins. They loved every second of it, never having experienced a spa day. Each of them got haircuts, beards trimmed, and Derven talked them all into getting pedicures which made me laugh, but when they saw how much Finley was enjoying the time together, they sucked it up.

Now here we were in the heartbeat of New York City, getting the guys fitted with tuxedos and Finley in an evening gown. The party was being held on a rooftop venue with lots of security and reporters lurking to get the best shots of those who showed up. Unlike most people, we wanted these reporters to take our picture, chat us up and prove to the world we were enjoying a party with three hundred other people as witnesses. So that meant everyone needed to look the part, and I was ensuring that happened.

The curtain pulled back, and when Finley stepped out, my jaw hit the floor. There, standing in a dress that hugged every curve of her delicious body in a color matching the cobalt of her eyes, was my mate. The dress looked like it was poured onto her the way it clung to her until it reached just above the knees and flared out. Slowly, she did a spin, showing off the exposed back and how the dress dipped right at the curve of her ass, then the silky fabric cascaded down the perfect roundness making my mouth water.

"Little dove, I want to bend you over and fuck the shit out of you right now. Part of me wants to tell you that you can't come because I will kill any motherfucker who thinks they can even look at you," I growled to her through our connection.

Her eyes filled with heat, and her breath quickened. Finley's spicy scent of cardamom and clove permeated the air, telling me just how much she liked that idea. My dick pressed against my jeans, begging for me to do exactly what I said.

Who would stop me? I'd rented out the shop while we picked out things. I could slip into the dressing room and show my mate just how much I like that dress.

"Holy fuck," Colt said as he walked out of another dressing room in a black tux, a frown clouding his face. "There's no fucking way she can wear that to the party. Everyone will be staring at her."

"I believe that's exactly what we want, isn't it?" she challenged, glancing over at Colt.

"Not if we don't want us all to end up in jail," he muttered, tugging at his jacket sleeves.

Mason walked out next in a deep purple tux that no one but him could make look good. Noah joined us wearing the exact same thing, grinning at his brother. "Damn, we look good," he said before they gave each other high fives.

Fussing with his bowtie, Lane stepped out wearing a gray tux that worked well for him. It was odd to see him without his baseball cap, but he managed to clean up nicely. "Who's going to jail?" he asked, then finally looked up and saw our woman. "Oh... never mind, I know the answer. We are."

"Did you two pick the same tux just to mess with people?" Finley asked as she walked over to them, making us all salivate as the fabric let us know that she was not wearing anything under that dress.

The twins nodded. "We thought it would be fun to fuck with people. They'll never know which one of us is which," Mason shared, a giant shit-eating grin on his face. "The more confusion we cause, the less they will notice you, or that was the idea. Now I'm not sure anyone is going to realize there is life at the party besides you and that perfect ass walking around."

Rath and Derven finally joined us, having taken longer to pick out what they wanted to wear. Having been to many parties with the

Dark Ring, they already understood the drill but struggled to find something they *wanted* to wear versus being forced to wear. The way these two men carried themselves after years of torment and torture from the Dark Ring amazed me. It was only in situations like this that I even remembered they had indeed suffered from PTSD. They just showed it in their own subtle way.

Rath's tux was avant-garde but fitted him perfectly. It was an amazing deep green with stitched patterns on one shoulder and the cuff of the opposite arm. It had a vest like usual, but the jacket was the difference. One side was normal, the other draped down and was held closed by a wooden toggle. It fit him as an elf and as a person, but more than that, he looked comfortable and confident in it.

Derven decided to take advantage of the fact that Finley had made him look completely human and dressed like you'd imagine a vampire would—crushed velvet smoking jacket style tux, with a black shirt, black pants, and to top it off, a black pocket square fluffed perfectly. The most amazing part of all this was after he fed off Finley and was able to restore himself to full strength, he was immune to the sun. It seemed Finley's blood did more than curb his hunger, and he was living it up to his full advantage.

While the bloodsucker was growing on me, I couldn't help but clash with him on certain things. He was of the mind that Finley should be able to freely move about assassinating people without us trying to stop her at every turn. I understood his point that she was a trained professional and was more dangerous than most of us, but I couldn't wrap my head around letting her put herself in a position to get hurt. One thing, it only took one thing to go wrong, and she would be hurt or wind up dead. None of us knew how to help her besides Ayla, and to me, that elf was a loose cannon filled with rage—willing to do whatever it took to get her revenge on the Dark Ring.

I trusted Finley to make smart choices and handle herself, but that didn't mean I liked doing it. She was my mate, and I'm an alpha. My sole purpose in life was to protect her and provide for her. This whole mess my mother put us in went against both of those things, so I tried to do my best not to let my fears cause more trouble.

"*Nin mel*, you look radiant," Rath praised as he took her hand, twirling her about. "Like the queen you are, simply perfect."

"You look rather handsome yourself in that color... sets off that long blond hair women would kill for," she teased, pressing a quick kiss to his lips when he frowned. "No scowling, we're meant to be having fun at this event, or so *someone* keeps telling me."

I cocked a brow at her as her gaze drifted over to me, letting me know she was referring to me. "There will be more fun if you aren't in a dress that makes men want to abandon all reason. How will you be able to sneak out of the party wearing that?"

"Easy, once I'm out of this dress, no one will recognize me with my hair up looking like the waitstaff," she pointed out. "They will be looking for the shockingly stunning woman in the blue dress."

"Remind me what we're supposed to say if someone asks where you went? There's no way that someone won't notice you're gone, or they haven't had the chance to meet you yet," I stated, crossing my arms.

Finley walked up to me and placed her hand on my chest, leaning in close as if she were going to kiss me but halted just before our lips touched. "Tell them the truth. I had to step out for a moment to meet with a few people nearby for work. Let them know they shouldn't worry. I'll be back soon since I'm incredibly skilled at my job."

I slid my hand up the back of her neck, pressing the back of her head toward me, closing the distance as I feasted on her lips, which had been taunting me as she spoke. This woman of mine was going to drive me mad, but I was going to love every second of it. Slowly, I pulled back and pressed another kiss to her forehead. "Now, what is it that I'm really telling them?"

"The world's most tried and true cop-out for women across the globe. A sudden headache hit me, and I went to our hotel room to rest for a moment. As soon as she's feeling better, I'm sure she will come back, first party in the limelight and all that jazz," she answered, grinning up at me. "But I like the first version better."

"We're getting a hotel room there?" I questioned.

She gave me a bright smile. "Well, it's Ayla's room, but who's to say differently? People wouldn't argue with you, would they?"

"How the hell did you get a room in that hotel a week before the event?" I demanded, amazed at her skills.

With a shrug, she backed away, heading for the dressing room. "Some secrets I'll keep for myself. Who knows when they will come in handy to surprise you." With that, she closed the curtain and ended the conversation.

Or so she thought.

I glanced over at the guys, all checking each other's tuxes, not paying attention to what was happening between Finley and me. Smirking to myself, I slipped into the dressing room just as the silky material fluttered to the ground into a puddle at her feet. Her eyes met mine in the mirror, daring me to do what I'd promised when she first walked out.

Careful not to step on the dress, I grabbed her by the hips, turned her to face the wall without the mirror, and stepped up to cover her with my body. "Little dove, you've been naughty today, teasing your alpha like that," I rumbled in her ear. "I think a punishment might be in order."

Finley shivered against me, a soft sigh escaping her lips at my words. If I had any other doubts about her interest in me continuing down this path, the scent of desire was thick in the air, oozing off of her.

"Now, little dove, you better be quiet as I give you this punishment," I warned. *"While we are the only customers in the store, all the staff are here, and I don't want any of them to know what's happening in this room. They don't get to listen to your moans as I bring you pleasure."*

She nodded, her hands splayed out on the wall as she parted her legs, giving me access to her dripping pussy. This was one benefit of my mate being an omega I never wanted to take for granted. It took so little for Finley to be wet and ready. Pulling her hair away from the back of her neck, exposing my mark, I clamped my mouth and sucked long and hard as if I was trying to give her a hickey. We'd all heard her and Derven the other night and had to deal with the boners we'd all sprung without her. Now was my chance to pay her back a little for that.

I let one of my hands drift down between her legs to start strumming her clit. Using her slick, it helped my fingers glide over that little bud full of nerves, moving quickly as if I were playing a song on my guitar. Her breath came faster, and I could hear shallow whimpers as she fought to keep silent.

"That's a good girl. Keep those beautiful sounds just for me," I praised, then bit down on my mark, not hard enough to break skin but more than I needed to send her catapulting into an orgasm.

Finley's body shuddered in my arms as she gasped sharply when I didn't stop working her clit. I brought my other hand up to wrap around the front of her throat, holding her up as her legs started to shake. "*That's it, my precious little dove, come for me again. I know you can do it. Let yourself fall into the feeling and* come," I ordered.

So she did, her back arching into me as her hips tried to shy away from me as I pressed firmly on her clit. I knew it was sensitive, and the pressure might be overwhelming, but this was a punishment, after all.

"*Please, alpha, fill me. My needy pussy is begging for your knot. I promise to be good if you just stuff me full of your cock,*" Finley begged as she let her head rest against the wall as if it were the only thing holding her up.

I removed my hand from pussy and settled it on her stomach as I pulled her against my chest. "*Thank you for asking so prettily, my little dove,*" I remarked, moving us backward so I could sit in the chair placed in the corner of the room. "*If you want it that badly, take it.*"

She stood a little unsteady on her feet, swaying as she looked down at my crotch as I splayed my legs wide. Dropping to her knees between my legs, Finley swiftly undid my jeans and freed my pulsing cock from its confines. Taking me in her mouth, she bobbed her head once, twice, three times before standing and turning her back to me. With her hands on my thighs, she started to insert my dick to, my surprise, her asshole.

"*I know you loved how it looked in that dress. Your mind was filled with images of ravaging my pretty little ass, so I'm making your dreams come true,*" Finley announced just before she dropped her hips roughly, so her ass cheeks slapped against my thighs.

Now I was the one fighting back making noise. The feel of her taking me so deeply, had me seeing stars. The way she clenched, trying to squeeze the life out of my cock was mind-blowing. Resting my hands on her hips, I gave her support, but I let her run the show as she bounced up and down on my dick.

"Do you like to watch my ass as I fuck you?" Finley asked, peeking at me over her shoulder.

A growl burst from me as I shot to my feet, slamming her down on my cock. At this height, she was standing on her tiptoes as I turned the tables on her, using my hold to control how she fucked me, no longer giving up control.

"Little dove, I thought you said you'd be a good girl if I fucked you. Now all I'm getting is sass," I bit out as I pushed her forward so her hands were on the mirror and she could watch me fucking her.

I thrust fast and deep, pounding into her ass, no longer caring if anyone heard what was going on in here. Finley had challenged me, knowing it would get this reaction, so I gave it to her tenfold. Her hair fell in her face blocking her view to watch. Pausing a moment, I widened my stance so she could stand, and I wrapped her hair around my hand and pulled back, arching her back as I started to fuck her again.

"Is this what you wanted, little dove? Did you want your alpha to fuck you like he owns you?" I demanded in a harsh whisper, my wolf pushing at me to show our mate who was in charge.

"Yes," she moaned, her eyes rolling back in her head. "I wanted what you showed me... to be bent over and ravaged just like this."

If that was what my mate wanted, that's what she would get. I let my wolf have more control, my eyes glowing with his presence reflecting back at me in the mirror. A wicked grin crossed my face as I picked Finley up, brought us both to our knees, shoved her face to the floor, and owned her ass. The sound of my balls slapping her pussy echoed in the space, giving away exactly what was happening in here, not that we were quiet anymore.

"Yes, Zander, fuck me just like that," Finley cried out, her nails digging into the carpet to hold herself still.

"You want me to own your ass, fill it with my cum?" I taunted as I felt my knot starting to expand. "Speak up, little dove. I can't hear you?"

"Knot me, alpha, please," she yelled, thrusting back as she felt it growing, refusing to let me deny her my knot.

Soon I was locked in, and the tightness of it sent me over the edge. She slowly rocked herself, using my knot to give herself another orgasm. We came together, her whimpers drowning in my roar as I filled her with my seed. Each pulse of my knot sent shockwaves of pleasure through my body until I couldn't do anything but hold Finley close and ride the wave. Toppling to our sides, I turned her face to me and caught her lips. I wanted to lose myself in her in every way possible. This woman was everything to me, and as much as I loved it, at the same time, it scared the shit out of me.

"I love you, Finley," I whispered between kisses. "More than you will ever understand. It's why I'm such an asshole when you try to put yourself in danger."

She nuzzled into me and wiggled her ass which sent both of us gasping as we were too sensitive for that. To keep her out of trouble, I wrapped myself around her like an anaconda. "Be good," I warned with a growl.

"I love you too," she murmured back, kissing me on the cheek. "But being good is overrated."

"I feel like I suddenly got a brat on my hands," I grumbled. "You're lucky I find this sassy side of you just as endearing as the submissive.

She just chuckled and settled in to let me hold her until my knot calmed down. Not my smartest move, but I was a rock star. Who was going tell me no?

TWELVE

FINLEY

The night had finally come. We were all packed into the limo and on our way to the hotel where the party was being held. Zander's record label had a penthouse we were staying in during our time in the city, so we had more privacy. This is why I needed Ayla at the hotel because she had all the supplies I would need for the job. I could steal away, change, gather my weapons, and sneak out none the wiser. I'd made sure to get a room closer to the exit, so taking the stairs in and out wouldn't be a problem. Not to mention I didn't need the hotel having that much footage of me in an elevator.

I smoothed my hands over my dress rhythmically as I went over the plan again in my head. We'd go to the party and spend an hour or so rubbing elbows with people before I slipped out. Once I was free, I'd meet up with Ayla, gather my things, and the mission would be a go. It would be radio silent between all of us while out dealing with matters. If something went wrong, I couldn't risk them distracting me or tying them to these murders. This was the first time I'd ever had to worry about the blowback from a job. The Organization could never be traced back to, but my men absolutely could be tied to me.

A hand slipped into mine, and I opened my eyes to look at Lane who was sitting next to me. "Sweetheart, it's going to be alright. This is a solid plan, and we've gone over every inch of it. I'm not sure how you could have any trouble."

I leaned into him, needing his optimism and stability right now as my wolf was freaking out at what was about to go down. While being an omega didn't stop me from doing things like this anymore, it didn't mean there weren't any side effects to it either. My anxiety was higher than it had ever been before a job, but this was also the first time I had so much to lose. I knew this was the best way to handle the situation, but my heart and my head were at odds.

"There isn't another option, Lane," I whispered, dropping my gaze to my hands. "This has to go right, or I won't come back at all until it's done."

Lane removed his hand from mine and gripped my chin, forcing me to look him in the eyes. "Don't you ever say shit like that again, Finley," he ordered. "No matter what happens, we will survive this together as a pack and as a family. There will never be a moment where we let you walk away from us ever again. You promised, remember, so don't make yourself a liar."

The weight of his alpha power was beating against me, so I knew he was trying to make it an order. He wasn't strong enough to force me to listen against my will, but I allowed the words to wash over me, letting his command stick. "I hear you, alpha," I answered, leaning forward until our foreheads touched. "I'll keep my promise."

"Good, because I don't even want to tell you the hell we will rain down on this world if we find you gone," Lane said with a growl in his voice. "You belong to us, and we belong together, always, no matter what."

"She trying to pull some self-sacrificing bullshit again?" Zander demanded from where he sat across from us.

Earlier in the day, we'd talked about if something went wrong at the party, and I'd told them to blame me. I'd forced them into helping me so I would take the fall, and they could be free to return home as a manhunt started for me. I'd tried to cover every situation and have a plan if everything failed, but none of them liked that suggestion at all.

"No, she's not because she promised me she wouldn't ever leave us again," Elias interjected, the finality in his words making me shiver. If I broke that promise to him, there would be no chance of saving him from turning completely feral like he almost had after the loss of his family.

"*Sângele meu*, there will be many of my people near the areas you two are hitting tonight. They will keep an eye on the situation and only intercede if there is a problem. On top of that, I have them ensuring that any law enforcement is kept away from you as you take care of business," Derven reminded me.

After we had our adventure getting clothes for the event, Derven and I went together to the law office that handled his affairs. I quickly learned he owned the law firm and even had a private entrance so he could access the top office without ever letting the staff know he existed. It led straight to an office he could use for personal reasons at any time. From there, he called the man who was now in charge of his identity. Chester Banks III was his name, and he was delighted to meet Derven.

"It is such an honor, sir. It's been about sixty years since you've reached out to us. My late grandfather told me so much about you," he gushed as they shook hands. "Please, tell me anything you need, and I will make it happen."

Derven took the whole meeting graciously and made a list of everything he would need right away and other things to be looked into. He also made sure I was added to everything he owned or had the right to, meaning I had many documents to sign.

"Mr. Derven, will we need to be managing her information as we do yours?" Chester asked.

Ven looked at me with a questioning brow. "What would you like to do, *sângele meu*? Do you have someone you trust to deal with matters such as this, or would you like to use my staff? Even as an elf, without being my Blood Bond, you would live to be seven hundred years old at least. It would be wise to ensure that matters are dealt with."

"What all is involved in that?" I asked Chester.

"Give me one moment. I'm going to need the binder," he said and scurried out the door, excitement oozing off him.

"I find they either get all the work or none of it depending on where I'm at in my life," Derven commented as he reclined in his office chair. "Seems he will have all the privilege of informing his offspring that he got to set up the accounts for my wife."

My head snapped to the side, looking at him with wide eyes. "I'm sorry, what did you just call me?"

"Wife?" Derven asked, flashing a fanged smile at me. "Liked that, did you? Well, I figured Blood Bond, bond, or mate didn't quite seem to fit what we are to each other. Yes, that is what connected us originally, but you can't tell me that our connection after that night in the office hasn't taken a turn into something far more serious."

He wasn't wrong. I'm not sure if whatever bond we had solidified itself between us once I let him truly drink from me, but something had changed. Without even needing to use my magic, he was added to the bond I had already with the others when we woke up the next morning. My ability to sense his emotions, thoughts, and even knowledge of his hunger level was made clear to me. It was odd, yet in a way, I was relieved to no longer doubt we were meant for each other, that it hadn't been a mistake because I accidentally cut my finger.

"Just seems odd to me that you call me your wife when you haven't even asked," I murmured, letting my attention wander about the office.

"Hmm," Derven hummed. "You make a valid point, *sângele meu*. Even if I've added you to all my earthly possessions, that doesn't bind us together by human law, now does it? It seems I will need to address that matter... once I've spoken to the others, of course. No need to rile things up when they are going so well."

Chester returned, and we got down to business, ensuring he had all the knowledge of my assets. Both men were amazed at my skills in hiding my money, and Chester decided he wouldn't need to mess with many things. Since I didn't have many pieces of property other than the locations I used to hide my backup stashes, there wasn't much that needed to be looked after.

Unlike the old days when Derven started this, banks and other such establishments understood that many of their patrons lived far longer lives, so unless we needed to wipe our slates clean, it just needed to be managed.

While we were at it, I ensured that Derven was added to all my main accounts, just to be sure everything was fair since the others were added when I was in Florida. Now both of us were equally richer, and I was now both a queen and a princess if Derven ever decided to take up his title back in Romania beside his father. As soon as we finished, we headed back to the penthouse to spend the evening going over the plan one more time.

As the limo pulled up to the hotel, I was pulled out of my daydreaming. Closing my eyes, I took a deep breath letting the familiar detached persona I used for all my jobs. We were trained early to develop a headspace where we no longer focused on anything else but the job before us. Flicking my eyes open, all my men had exited the limo, and Zander stood by the door, holding out a hand for me to take. Reaching out, I laid my hand gently on his and maneuvered myself out of the limo, using all my supernatural abilities to appear as fluid and effortless as possible.

Tonight, I was with Zander Vaughan, the rock star, and I was his mate, superior to all other women who dared to think they would have ever had a chance with him. Head high, shoulders back, and a slight smile on my face to keep it soft as I looked at my mate. His eyes wandered over my frame as the silk rippled and moved against my body. Flashes of light burst into action as photographers tried to capture the moment as Zander kissed the back of my hand before tucking it through his elbow and not letting it go. The others fell in behind us, knowing we would be drawing the most attention, and I knew Colt wanted nothing to do with the reporters yelling and screaming to get our attention.

"Zander, who have you brought with you tonight?"

"Has the rock god finally found his mate? Women of the world will be weeping tonight."

"Zander, do you have a comment on the review written in *Rolling Stone*?"

"Ma'am, tell us your name!"

"Are you his mate? Who are the other men with you? Do you have an open relationship?"

"Zander, are you bisexual?"

The energy and emotions coming off all these people were frantic and desperate. Even having shut that part of me off, it was almost as if they were so intense I couldn't help but take notice of them. We'd agreed we would answer some questions but to leave it up to Zander to choose who we talked to. He knew the ones to avoid and who it would benefit to answer. The more in the limelight we could be, the harder it would be for the Senate or the Dark Ring to retaliate. It wasn't like after this, they could take me out without someone noticing.

"Zander, one comment for old times' sake," an older male reporter called out, waving his notepad.

Zander smiled and steered us over to the man. "Franklin, are you still working for that deadbeat gossip rag? You're way too good for them. I've told you that time and time again."

"Seems you *can* teach an old dog new tricks, working for *Pitchfork* now," Franklin answered, giving Zander a wink before he turned to me. "Now, who is this stunning woman who is clearly out of your league?"

Reaching out a hand, I introduced myself, "Finley, Finley Beinorin, Zander's mate. It's nice to meet you, Franklin."

"Why did you just give him your father's name?" Rath demanded, his words cutting into my mind through my walls. *"Do you know how foolish that was? What if it brings even more danger upon you than there already is?"*

Using my magic, I slammed the door he'd barged through in my mind. I would deal with his concerns later but now was not the time.

"Finley, such a unique name for an equally unique woman," Franklin replied. "Now, do you mind me asking who those other men are?"

"Not at all. Those men are also my mates. We all live together as one big happy family on our pack lands," I shared.

Next was the part none of them were going to be prepared for or like, but Ayla and I agreed it was time. The elves needed to stop hiding from the world and take their place as they rightly deserved to. If they wanted to call me their queen, then I was going to lead them out of the darkness and into the light. They had every right to be a part of society, no longer fearing the world around them.

"I'm not an expert or anything on supernaturals, but isn't it unusual for a werewolf to have more than one mate?" Franklin questioned. All the other reporters around him fell silent as they listened, each wanting to know what I'd say next.

Zander's grip on my hand tightened as if warning me not to do what I was about to. "Yes, for a normal werewolf, it would be, but since I'm actually a Light Elf, it changes things."

That had the reporters exploding with questions shoving recording devices into my face begging for my attention. Unfortunately for them, I only had eyes for the man who was staring slack-jawed at me, his pencil slipping through his fingers to the ground. Using my magic, I whisked the pencil up and caught it to hand back over.

"Here you are. I have a feeling you're going to need that," I said, then turned to Zander. "Shall we head up? The light from these cameras is going to give me a headache if we stay out here much longer."

The rage in Zander's eyes burned as he nodded bruskly, drawing me away from the wall of reporters. Silently we entered the elevator, and one of them hit the button for the top floor. Rath snapped his hand at the camera in the corner, and it frosted over.

"What the fuck, Finley." Colt snarled. "Why the hell did you just tell them that? Do you know what you've just done? Holy this... this is awful," he spluttered, running his hands through his hair, messing up how perfectly it had been styled. "There's no way we can go to this party. There will be people after her in seconds after word spreads about what you just admitted to."

I grabbed his arms and pulled them down until I could slide my hands into his. "Colt, please let me explain. This wasn't a spur-of-the-moment decision or something I was doing to cause trouble. The elves need to stop hiding. If we are going to win this fight, they need to fight alongside me." I turned to look at Rath. "You call me a queen of our people, but if no one knows our people exist, who do I lead? I used my last name because all my life, I never even knew I had one. The Organization stripped it from me. My parents are elves, which means my last name is elvish too, giving me every right to use it."

Rath looked slightly taken aback by my words, and I could feel regret from him in how he had lashed out. "You're absolutely right, *nin mel.* You do have every right to use your last name now that you know it. My protectiveness and need to keep you safe had me reacting before I understood your reasoning. You are our queen, and while I might not agree with you on how you chose to draw out our people, I will stand behind you as your mate and Guide. All I ask is that as that person in your life, I not be blindsided like that again."

The elevator came to a halt with a ding as the doors opened, revealing the rooftop. Noah reached out and hit the close door button giving us a few more moments before we had to put this aside.

"That was unfair to you, but I was worried you would stop me, and I didn't see a better moment to speak the truth. If anything like that should occur again, I will make sure you know," I agreed. "Now we need to set this aside because tonight we have bigger things to worry about."

As the door opened again, Zander laced our fingers together as he led me out. I could tell from the tension in his body he was not happy with me, but right now, I couldn't do much but not make it worse.

"Zander!" a black man in an all-white suit boomed, throwing his arms wide as he spotted us. "Fuck, man, it's been forever since I've seen you at one of these things. Looks like getting wifed- up has kept you a homebody."

Zander released my hand to share a bro-hug with the other man. "Clarence, how the hell are you, man?"

"Doing a whole lot better now that I know someone with a brain is gonna be here," Clarence chuckled, then turned to me. "This must be the lucky lady. How do you do, Clarence Parker, jazz master of the decade," he shared, introducing himself with a bow. "I know better than to be touching another man's lady, especially when that man's a werewolf."

Zander laughed, shaking his head. "Don't try that suave bullshit on her. She'll chew you up and spit you out before you even know what happened." Turning to me with laughter in his eyes, he gestured to Clarence. "The man gets furry himself. Clarence is a werecat, panther to be exact."

My brows shot up at this information. "How are you two friends?"

"Oh, baby girl, that is a myth. Just because we turn into cats and dogs doesn't mean we fight like them. Nah, we made a fast friendship when I pulled his drunk ass out of a bar in New Orleans. Man can't handle the brews those vampire bartenders make," Clarence informed me and nodded over to Derven. "Ask your man if you don't believe me. They do something that can get any super blackout drunk."

"Oh, God, don't remind me," Zander groaned. "It was hell to do a show the next day. I thought my brain was going to explode, it pounded so badly."

"Told you to go to the witches. They would have fixed you right up," Clarence teased, punching Zander in the shoulder. "Now, I won't take up too much of your time. I know you got a crowd to work. I'll find you later when you remember why you stopped showing up to these shit shows." With a wink and a smile, Clarence was off to the bar.

THIRTEEN

FINLEY

Zander and I wandered around the party, sipping champagne and chatting with people I didn't even care to remember their names. Now I understood what Clarence was saying about people without a brain. Some I could tell were drugged out of their minds enjoying the party to the fullest, while others downed drinks from the open bar like it was water. For brief moments, I felt like I could find common ground with someone until it all came crashing down when they found out I was a supernatural being.

"Kathleen, this is Finley, my mate," Zander shared, introducing me to a woman who was wearing heels that might kill her with how she swayed. "Kathleen is the manager for the band we're celebrating tonight. She's been with them since the beginning."

"That's amazing," I gushed, knowing that was the response she was going to be expecting. "You must be so proud of them. It's really an accomplishment for you, too, isn't it? After all the hard work you've put in."

Kathleen teetered forward as she narrowed her eyes to look at me. "Sorry, there are two of you, and I'm not sure which one is the real one," she slurred. "I'm so glad that someone finally recognized I'm the one who got them to where they are. Yeah, they have good music, but no one would listen to them until I made them keep their mouths shut about being supernaturals. Who wants to root for people who feed off sex? I mean, really, that's just fucked up... am I right?"

"Does she not realize we are supernaturals?" I asked Zander.

He glanced at me out of the corner of his eye. *"Do you see how drunk she is? I'm not sure she knows where she's at, let alone who she's talking to."*

"Did you know they were incubi? They are so rare, and she's saying there are five of them together hiding in plain sight?"

"Many supers live that way. Even if the world knows they exist, that doesn't mean they want to live among them or support them," Zander reminded me. *"Why do you think I take so much time to educate?"*

"Wait... oh shit, you're Zander the werewolf," Kathleen gasped. "Please don't eat me for what I said. I promise I'm not a bigot. I just don't think living off having sex with people is right. Oh, God, I think I'm going to hurl."

Darting out of her way, I watched her tumble headlong over a couch, scattering a group of people who'd been sitting there. Then the sound of someone retching let me know she had indeed hurled.

"Well, I would say that is my cue to slip out while everyone is looking after the poor thing," I said under my breath, knowing Zander would hear me.

He pressed a kiss to my cheek. "Please be safe, little dove. I love you."

"I love you too, Zander. I'll be back before you know it. Don't have too much fun without me," I said, pressing a quick kiss to his lips before slipping into the crowd.

The upheaval of Kathleen's disaster was so perfect it was almost as if I'd planned it myself. No one was paying attention to who was coming and going. Instead, they wanted pictures and videos of what was going on to share later on social media.

"I'm off. I promise to check in once things are done," I said, reaching out to all my men before locking my connections down so they couldn't interrupt me.

Once in the small lobby area where the bathrooms were, along with the stair access, I double- checked to ensure no one saw me and slipped through the door. Then, hiking up my skirt, I yanked off my shoes and jogged quickly down to the tenth floor from the fifteenth. Back in the hall, I slowed to an easy amble as I made a show of rubbing a hand over my forehead like I had a headache. Reaching the room Ayla was in, I tapped on the door, which immediately opened, and entered.

"How's the party?" she asked, perched on the edge of the king bed. "I bet it's a glorious disaster like the ones I've watched on TV."

"This is one of those times where I believe they've undersold the reality of it," I shared as I turned to have her unzip me. "Things in the bathroom?"

"Yup, just as you packed them," she answered. "I have to say, I do love your taste in knives. I've never thought of making them black so they can't be seen."

I left the door cracked, so we could still talk while I got ready. Being naked in front of my mates was one thing, but in front of others, I wasn't quite there yet. "That's a trick I picked up from a vampire hunter I encountered on one of my jobs. He told me even with perfect night vision, it was hard for them to see the blade. Been using them ever since, and it's saved me more times than I can count."

Stepping into the catsuit, I shimmied it up my hips and settled into the rest of it before gliding the zipper, hiding every ounce of my skin from the base of my neck to my ankles. The first stop of the night required me to wear a waiter's uniform for a well-known French restaurant, so I donned the black dress pants and white button-down shirt with a black tie. Hair placed in a high pony, I'd purposely kept my makeup light so I could transition right into this persona.

Taking one last glance at the full-length mirror in the bathroom to ensure you couldn't see any of my weapons, I was ready. Using my magic like Rath had taught me, I changed my hair color to a sandy blonde, making it even harder for anyone to recognize me. My skill wasn't high enough for me to use something like this on a job, but it would get me out of the hotel before I lost my hold on it. Learning how to keep something active in the back of my mind was proving harder than anticipated. Rath had told me it was because I was too controlling, and I needed to just trust it would work.

Ayla was incredibly gifted with illusions and had managed to change her whole appearance as we walked out of the hotel. No longer did she have the tattoos of her clan on her face or anywhere else on her body. Her eyes were a more normal shade of blue, and her hair was black instead of navy blue. She would have passed for anyone of Asian descent, never once considering her to be anything but human. She promised to work with me on it, but for this mission, I was going to have to make do with the old-school way of diverting attention.

Once we exited the hotel, she went left, and I went right, each of us with two targets we needed to take care of. I had one at the restaurant, then the other was going to be slightly harder but proved to be far more interesting than slipping a drug in a drink.

The bus was on time, showing up ten minutes later than it should have, just like normal. Hopping on, I swiped my pass and sat near the front, looking out the window. It was much harder to trace someone using public transportation than it was a cab, so it was my default. Four stops later, I got off and *accidentally* bumped into a man with a brown paper bag in his hands.

"Watch where you're going bitch," the man snapped, shoving me away from him.

"I'm so sorry, sir," I apologized as I twisted out of the way, holding the brown bag instead of him. "Have a good rest of your night," I called as the bus door closed.

Spinning on my heel, I headed off down the alley to the back entrance of the restaurant. I removed the brown bag and looked at the bottle of Hennessy Paradis—a rare cognac that happened to be the biggest weakness for my target. This restaurant normally carried a bottle just for him to enjoy, but no matter where they tried to order it, they just didn't seem to have any in stock. Word had gone out to the staff that if anyone knew a connection, they would be well rewarded for being able to acquire a bottle.

I banged on the back door as hard as I could without actually denting it. A few moments later, a busboy opened the door. "What do you want? We don't feed beggars, so scram."

"Do I look like a beggar?" I asked, flashing the bottle. "Word on the street is your boss is looking to make a trade for this."

"Holy shit," the busboy blurted, shoving the door open. "Hell, yeah, he's been looking for that. The guest who drinks it is even here tonight. Come on. I'll take you to the boss."

Easy as taking candy from a baby.

Passing through the kitchen, I found myself in an office with a portly balding man mopping sweat on his brow as he looked at his computer screen.

"Dennis, I got a lady here with something you need," the busboy called, then motioned with my head to go in. "You better play the lotto tonight with how lucky you are," he called as he walked away.

Dennis looked at me with panic-filled eyes. "What? What could you possibly have that I need other than a great ass?"

"If that's how you're going to treat someone with a bottle of Paradis, then I'm out of here," I snapped, turning to leave.

"*Wait*," Dennis blurted. "Show it to me. I'm not some schmuck you can just rip off with a pretty bottle and fancy label you printed off the internet."

Handing over the bottle, the longer he looked at it, the wider his eyes got. "Thank fuck. This is the real deal. Oh, God, I thought I was going to have to sell my soul to get a bottle of this."

"How much you paying?" I asked, crossing my arms. "That shit ain't cheap."

Dennis glared at me. "Like you paid for it, you probably stole it from wherever you work."

"What does it matter where I got it? You now have it, and the busboy mentioned he's here. Maybe I need to take the bottle to him and ask him to buy it off me so he can drink it and take it home afterward," I threatened.

"You know what, yeah, why don't you do that," Dennis said with a cruel smile on his face. "I'd love to see you haggle with Mr. Trevorsy. That bastard will eat you up and spit you out if you think you can pull one over on him." Dennis slammed the bottle on his desk. "Go on. I'll be sure to call an ambulance when he's done with you."

Swiping the bottle off his desk, I stormed out. Then, once I was out of sight, I couldn't help but grin. My contact here was right. Dennis was an idiot who deserved to lose the one client who was floating this restaurant. I grabbed a tray, snifter glass, and put two ice cubes in it just as he liked, along with four drops of a slow-acting poison.

Entering the dining room, I found my mark and headed over. "Good evening, Mr. Trevorsy. I've brought your cognac."

"About damn time. I'm almost done with my meal and was about ready to light my cigar," Trevorsy grumbled.

I set the glass by him and opened the bottle, pouring in the two fingers he liked. "Oh, and Dennis wanted to thank you for your patronage by letting you take the rest of the bottle home with you as a gift," I shared, leaving the bottle on the table. With a small bow, I started to step back.

"Wait," he ordered, then handed over a folded-up hundred-dollar bill. "Remember who takes care of you around here, hmm..." Trevorsy said, giving me a lecherous look.

"You're too kind," I murmured and slipped the money into my pocket before heading back toward the kitchen.

When I knew Trevorsy wasn't paying attention and had taken a gulp of his drink, I handed off the tray to another server and exited right out the front door. Part one complete. Now it was time to deal with the second mark of the evening. This one would take more skill and less manipulation, but I was excited about it.

I'd always wanted to see a Broadway show but never found the time. Guess I wouldn't really see much of it tonight either, but such is the job.

Studying the map of the theater had been the hardest part of this job. With so many entrances, exits, pathways, tunnels, and trap doors, it was the easiest and the hardest job to do. There were so many ways to enter or exit, making it easy if something went wrong. The hard part was dealing with the people who might appear via these various methods, that had me worried. Stagehands were like mice running about behind the scenes fixing things, adjusting for issues to keep everything moving seamlessly.

My next target was in a box tucked away from eyesight because he had a penchant for things that should not be done in public. It was against the law in many places and viewed as vulgar and unseemly, and his kink was to do it in public. The world wouldn't miss Mortimer Drugal and his deep love for shifter women of all kinds in their alternate forms. He would find a woman who indulged him and would play the part of a pretty pet, but when he got bored, he'd kill them and move on to the next animal he *had* to have.

The only time he left his home filled with his wife, seven children, and six pets was to go to the theater once a month with his favorite pet at the time. This one, to my surprise, was actually male. He must be looking to try something new. I'd made sure to include a syringe full of enough tranquilizer to neutralize the *pet* if needed. My hope was that he would realize what I was doing and let me be. With Mortimer gone, he would be free to return to his life before this man had captured him in the name of the Dark Ring.

The show was well underway as I moved through the back halls the staff used. Stashing my waitstaff clothes away in the alley behind the theater, I'd cut the power to this part, so I was in pitch black darkness, and using my wolf's night vision, it was easy to navigate.

I reached the door that brought me back into the main area, just before the entrance to the section of private boxes. Cracking the door, I found it completely empty. It might have been due to the person who was screaming about someone stealing their purse while in the bathroom, but I needed a distraction, and she was the fool who set it on the floor.

Mortimer always took the last box since it offered the most privacy, making my job just a tad harder, but I wasn't one to back away from a challenge. Keeping my back to the wall, I watched the curtains of the other two boxes. There should be an attendant checking on them if they needed anything, but I couldn't see them. They must be in one of the boxes or off getting whatever someone needed. Darting to the end of the row using all my enhanced speed, I almost crashed into the wall, not expecting to be quite so quick. With my sharp werewolf hearing, I could make out the sound of someone's soft moans and the tell-tale *guck, guck* of a blow job.

Using my knife, I separated the curtains enough to get a feel for who was sitting where and who might be on their knees. Mortimer's shaggy head leaned back in his seat, eyes closed, leading me to believe who he was with was the one on their knees. Gliding through the curtain, I stepped off to the side, placing my back in the corner so I could see the whole space before acting. Sure enough, a young man was on his knees, pants around his ankles, going down on Mortimer.

Now I was left with the question of whether I should settle this while Mortimer was distracted or get the young man's attention first. I knew the answer that was the smarter choice but now, having brought more emotions into my life, I was second-guessing things I would never have before. Shaking myself out of this turmoil, I stepped up right behind Mortimer, grabbed the bottom of his chin with my gloved left hand, yanking his head back, then sliced with the knife in my right hand.

Blood shot out from the artery spraying the ceiling as the final gurgles of Mortimer's last breath could be heard. I kept a hold on him until he stopped moving and the blood was seeping out of his neck instead of shooting. The young man gasped and fell back, eyes wide in fear, mouth open as if to shout.

"Don't," I warned. "If you want to live, then run, get the hell out of here and never look back. Staying here will only make them think you're the one who killed him. You're free now, so pull up your pants and get the fuck out of here and start over somewhere else."

The young man nodded, looking at me curiously. "Why do I know you?"

"You don't," I snapped, wiped my blade on Mortimer's shirt, and tucked it back into my sheath.

"Wait, you... you were at one of Delilah's parties. The one where everyone was killed, and we ran," he blurted. "Are you trying to take down the Dark Ring on your own?"

I glanced at him tilting my head slightly as I considered him. "If I say yes, are you going to tell them I'm hunting them down?"

"They already know that. They've sent out warnings with your image on it to let our masters know if we see you," he answered. "But I'm not going to. Those bastards can rot in hell for all I care."

"Do you mind me asking what kind of shifter you are?" I asked.

"A lynx," he shared.

"Do you have any place to go?"

The young man shook his head. "No, that's how I ended up here. I didn't know what else to do."

Groaning internally, I made a gut choice and gestured to his clothes. "Pull yourself together. You're coming with me. I'll make sure you get somewhere safe. What's your name since it seems we're going to be spending some time together?"

"Benjamin, Ben is what I prefer," Ben answered.

"Let's get a move on, Ben. The last thing we need is to get caught with the dead body." I sighed, moving aside the curtain for him once he buttoned up his pants. A bonus in bringing him back to the party, he was already dressed for the occasion in a suit so he wouldn't stick out.

I grabbed him by the arm and pulled him along with me as I sprinted out of the main hall into the still-dark staff area. "I'm assuming you have good night vision being a cat, so stick close and don't make a sound."

This would never have worked with another normal person, but a feline shifter was anything but a clumsy human. We made it out of the theater, into the back alley, down the street, and into the subway station. When we reached the turnstile, I stopped and turned Ben to look at me.

"Do you know where the Prism Hotel is?" I questioned.

"Yeah, that place is super swanky," he answered.

Nodding, I handed him my transit card. "I'll meet you there, and we will find you someplace safe to be, okay?" He looked at me with awe as he bobbed his head in answer. "Go, be smart, don't draw attention, and we'll make it through this alright."

Giving him a final squeeze, I released him and headed back up the steps to head back a different way once I changed back into my server clothes. It would be far more noticeable, looking like I was heading to some leather underground sex club in my catsuit alone.

"The jobs are done. I'm on my way back... with a stray," I shared with all my men.

My connection was stronger, so I could talk to them at almost any distance, but they didn't have as far of a range to answer. Ducking into the alley I hid my clothes in, I hurriedly put them on and hailed a cab a few blocks up from the theater. Let's hope Ayla has been as successful as I had.

FOURTEEN

FINLEY

When I was closer to the hotel, I reached out to Zander privately, *"Hey, can you meet me somewhere with Clarence? I have a stray cat who needs a home unless you don't think he would help."*

"Oh, he'll help all right. He hates the Dark Ring as much as any of us do. Would it be too risky to meet in Ayla's room?" he answered right away.

"Give me a chance to loop the cameras for ten minutes, and that should be fine. Last thing we need is for people to think you're cheating on me with him," I pointed out.

I'd already had this setup in case there was a situation. Plan for the worst, hope for the best, as the saying goes, and I was all about backup plans. Sneaking my way into the janitor's area of the hotel, I'd tapped into the feed since they had backup security footage being routed there. I ensured there was nothing that would cause suspicion and set the loop to run for thirty minutes and reset to normal.

"All clear, Zander. I'm gonna find the kid now, and I'll bring him up." I stepped back into the lobby to find Ben sitting in one of the armchairs reading a magazine. It seemed this kid had some survival skills, after all.

"Ben, follow me," I whispered as I passed by.

After a moment, he closed the magazine, looked at his watch, then got up and headed to the elevator. He joined me, and I tried to do the trick that Rath did, but instead of frosting over the camera, I shattered it. Guess it does the same thing in the end, just not as smooth as Rath made it seem.

"What were you before the Dark Ring took you?" I asked in a low voice so the microphone wouldn't pick up if it were still active. "You move far too easily like you've been trained."

"I was nothing before the Dark Ring, and I'm still nothing. You watch one too many *James Bond* movies, and you pick up a few things that might actually work, I guess," he commented, not moving his head to look at me.

"Why are you lying?" I demanded, my voice just slightly too loud.

Ben didn't answer right away. Then he glanced at me out of the corner of his eye. "Ever wonder what might happen to the kids in training who don't make the cut? When they do those tests every year, pushing you to the max, forcing every trick you learned to be used, or you die?"

He was talking about the Organization!

I sucked in a sharp breath as the realization hit me. I hadn't ever wondered what happened to them because it just meant fewer people I was competing against.

"Depending on how far along they are in training, they die, get removed from the program and returned to a foster home, or end up unknowingly in the hands of the Dark Ring. What better way to make the perfect pet than to groom them from the beginning?" Ben bit out his words, filled with disgust. "I didn't have what it took to be you, so I ended up being a useless victim of the system."

Guilt I'd never felt before churned in my stomach. How had I never wondered what happened to those who got cut from the program? They pushed us to the point of breaking, and if you snapped, you were done, gone, erased like you had never been. It seemed I would need to have that meeting with my father because I'd love to know his answer to a situation like Ben's that I'm sure happened far too often.

I put a pin in that to deal with once this night was over. First, I needed to ensure Ben was safe and secure someplace where the Dark Ring couldn't snatch him up again. I owed him that, whether he knew it or not. It was the least I could do for a system my family created.

When we reached the room, I knocked. When there wasn't an answer, I pulled the keycard out of my catsuit and inserted it. One of the guys had a card, too. I'm not sure who they decided on, but we wanted to make sure they had access if needed. Just as the door closed, there was a knock, then the sound of a keycard being used. I grabbed Ben and pulled him behind me needing to get him out of the way if I had to move into action.

Zander entered the room first, with Clarence behind him along with all my other mates and Ayla bringing up the rear. The room was a good size, but with all of us in here together, it felt a little snug for my liking. I caught Ayla's gaze first, cocking a questioning brow.

"Everything went as planned, four less rotten bastards for the world to fear. Seems you, on the other hand, had a surprise tag along," she commented as her illusion dropped. "Are we adopting cats now?"

"No," I answered, turning to Clarence. "I was hoping you might be able to find a place for him. He's been with the Dark Ring long enough. I think it's time for him to have a real home, don't you?"

He looked at me, crossing his arms. "What makes you think I'd help?"

"One, because Zander said you shared a mutual hate for the Dark Ring, and secondly, let's call it elven intuition. I can tell you're a good person, and you have well-meaning intentions. If you can help someone, you try," I shared, stepping aside so he could see Ben. "For him, I know you're going to try. The man who claimed to own Ben is not going to be an issue. I know for a fact no one in his family will try to look for him either, so there is no fear of backlash. There isn't another reason I can think of unless you have something against lynxes, but I'm guessing that's not the case."

Clarence looked at me with a shocked expression, then glanced at Zander, who tossed up his hands. "Don't look at me. I didn't tell her anything other than there was no love lost between you and the Dark Ring."

Clarence took a deep breath. "I'll help the boy. I know a pride out in Connecticut that is a safe haven for those fleeing from bad situations. They will look after him as they try and find a more permanent pride to settle him into where his skills will be useful. I was getting tired of the party anyway, so I'll take him with me tonight and get out of the city while the gettin's good."

"Thank you, Clarence. I know you didn't have to do this, but I'm glad there are people like you in the world willing to step up. When I'm done with the mission I've been sent on, we'll need lots more like you to help as the world changes," I shared, reaching out a hand to him. "I'm assuming you know how to reach Zander. You need anything, just ask."

Clarence shook my hand and motioned for Ben to follow him before placing a hand on Zander's chest. "You got yourself one hell of a woman right there. Don't let your family or your past fuck this up for you. It's time you stood on your own, and I know you can with her right beside you."

The two men looked at each other for a moment as they came to an understanding, then Clarence wrapped an arm around Ben's shoulders. "Come on, kid, let's get you the hell out of here and someplace you can really thrive."

Ben glanced back at me with a sad smile and a wave before the door closed behind them. I truly wished him the best and hoped he could start over. He might not have been good enough for the Organization, but that didn't make him worthless like he believed.

Noah walked over to me and pulled me into a hug, tucking my head under his chin as he just held me. "You did the right thing, Finley, bringing him here and saving him. I know it goes against everything you were taught, but maybe it's time the rules were rewritten?"

"He was at Delilah's ranch," I whispered. "All I kept thinking is how I couldn't help save Cory, but I had a chance to save him. They are even about the same age. Then just before we came up here, I found out he was recruited by the Organization, but he didn't make the cut. Never once have I wondered what happens to those people. Now it's all I can think about," I admitted.

"So, what does that mean for you?" Noah inquired as he rested his cheek on the top of my head, nuzzling me.

I took a deep breath pulling in his chocolaty scent mixed with hazelnuts. Everything about it was warm and inviting, making you think of cocoa by the fire snuggled up in a blanket. My wolf let out her own heavy sigh as our Companion soothed our emotions. "It means I need to meet my father. I have too many questions and not enough answers that make sense, so the only way to fix that is to make him explain himself."

"Then that's what we'll do," Noah agreed, pulling me back from him to cup my face. He kissed me, letting me know just how much he loved me in the simple gesture. "Now here's the real question… do we need to go back to the party, or can we go back to the penthouse instead?"

"That depends on how you left it when you came down here?" I asked, stepping away from him to see the others.

Mason shrugged. "I just walked away from the dude who was trying to get Noah and me to start a magic act or something equally ridiculous. He thought the whole idea of us being identical had to be put to good use."

"Then I think it would be best if all of us head back up and say our goodbyes. Then there is no question about seeing me at the party after these events have occurred," I reasoned. "It doesn't have to be long, thirty minutes tops, then we can head back to the penthouse and call it a night."

"So are you saying call it a night like you're too tired and want to snuggle and go to bed, or like, maybe willing to be talked into some extracurricular activities?" Mason asked as he followed me into the bathroom where my dress was hanging. "Because I'm not gonna lie, hearing Zander getting lucky in the dressing room has had me all kinds of rock solid since."

"Let's get through this first, and we'll see how it goes. I desperately need a shower. I'm pretty sure I got blood on me somewhere," I explained and pulled the blue dress back on. "Can you smell blood on me? I don't know what other kinds of supers there are at the party, and having a vampire come after me would not be good."

Mason pulled open the bathroom door and leaned out. "Hey, Derven, come sniff snuggles for blood." He turned to look at me with an odd expression. "Can't say I ever thought I'd be saying something like that in my life."

Derven appeared in the bathroom, hands tucked in his pants pockets as he walked up to me, then stopped. "Mason, could you remove the catsuit? I'm not sure if the tang of blood is coming from that or *sângele meu*."

Mason looked at the pile of black leather, then spotted a trash bag and used it to collect my garment. Once it was tied shut, he walked out, leaving me to be checked over by my vampire.

Derven pulled his hands free and settled them on my hips as he leaned in. "The perfume of blood and death on you is quite intoxicating, I must say." Using his grip on me, he slowly turned me in a circle, stopping me with my back to him. He grabbed my hair, pulled it up, and licked the back of my neck. Adjusting the angle, he licked up another part, then released me. "You're free and clear with only my scent on you to cover up the droplets left behind."

"I thought you couldn't drink anyone else's blood?" I questioned as I faced him, stepping into his personal space so my chest brushed his. "Isn't that the whole point of us being bonded?"

Derven smiled, his fangs showing as he wrapped his arms around me and let his nose brush up my neck along the artery. "Do I smell jealousy, *sângele meu*? If it is, that is a rather intoxicating aroma that might just need to be caused more often."

Leaning into him, I let my lips brush the shell of his ear. "You do that, and I'll see how much damage you can take before it starts to affect me." I placed a kiss on his cheek and stepped back.

Derven didn't look the slightest deterred. If anything, it had made him even more excited that I'd threatened him. "As for the answer to your question. I can still drink blood from others, but it does nothing to feed me. It's like eating celery for you. The calories burned negate the calories earned through eating it."

"Did it taste good?" I asked as I trailed a hand down his chest before stepping past him.

He grabbed my hand and pulled me back, causing me to crash into him. "It tasted vile, like acid burning on my tongue." His mouth moved to my neck, and I felt the scrape of one of his fangs before he licked it off. "There is nothing in this world that will taste more intoxicating than you, Finley. That being said, I never want you to doubt that you mean more to me than the blood that flows in your veins which gives me life. You are everything." With a kiss to my neck, he let me go, and we joined the others.

Back up on the roof, it was worse than when I'd left. I wasn't sure there were more than a handful of people who weren't totally wasted on something. The DJ was playing, and most of the people were on the dance floor, grinding on one another with zero shame. They might as well just take their clothes off and fuck while they're at it. Not like there was much separating them from each other.

That's when I noticed a man standing at the opposite end of the party, leaning back on the railing with a glass of something in his hand. He was watching me with a hesitant expression, and when my brain finally caught up and realized who he was, I froze.

"Little one, what is it?" Colt asked, settling a hand on my low back.

I blinked a few times, hoping that what I was seeing wasn't actually there. It had to be a trick, an illusion of some sort. But why would they choose that person out of millions of people to choose from?

"That's my father," I said, my voice sounding as hollow to me as I'm sure it did to them. Colt's head snapped up and followed my line of sight. "Do you see him standing there in the tan suit?"

"Yeah, I see him alright." Colt snarled as he started to charge away from me in his direction.

I grabbed him and pulled him to a stop. "Wait, please, don't do this here. Let me speak to him for a moment. Then I'll decide whether to feed him to the wolves or not."

"Oh, she's got jokes," Mason commented as he came to stand on my other side. "You're not going over there alone. One of us or all of us are coming with you."

"If we all go over there, then it will draw attention." I sighed, then looked over my shoulder at Zander. "Do you recognize him? Why would he be here?"

"Holy fuck, that's Eli Beinorin, owner of Starling Music. His wife was an amazing singer before she died..." Zander started to share, then looked at me. "They said the baby died too."

"Wait, hold the fucking phone," Noah demanded. "Your father is the founder of the infamous Organization and has a record label on top of it? How the hell has he been able to keep the fact that he's an elf a secret for so long?"

"There are many supernatural creators who live well beyond human years. He could easily let people assume he was one of those," Derven pointed out. "I have to say I'm quite impressed with my father-in-law, even if I want to rip out his heart for abandoning Finley."

"For once, I'm on the vampire's side," Elias muttered. "That man has no idea how lucky he is to be alive right now."

Turning my back on the man who biologically was my father, I looked at the others. "Zander, it would make the most sense for you to accompany me as I talk to him, but will you be able to control your temper?"

"Yes," he bit out through a clenched jaw. I gave him a skeptical look, but he held out his arm to me, and I took it. "All I will promise you is that he will leave here alive tonight. Other than that, it would be a lie."

"At least you're being honest with yourself," I said, patting his arm. "Anything else I should know about Eli?"

"He never, ever... I mean, it's a known fact everyone accepts and knows he doesn't come to parties like this. I bet my life he came to meet you," Zander shared under his breath. "He also seems to think it might keep him safe from us lashing out against him. That would be a mistake on his part."

We stopped with a foot or so between us, just staring at each other. There was so much of myself I could see in him, and part of me wanted to hate him, to close off any chance of there being any kind of relationship between us. Yet the moment he spoke, tears pricked at my eyes, having never thought I would hear those words in my lifetime.

"Hello, daughter," Eli greeted with a slight nod. "You look absolutely beautiful, so much like your mother in how you carry yourself. When you first walked out, I thought I was seeing my beautiful Tiriana once more. She would be incredibly proud of you, Finley. I know that I am."

Zander scoffed, shaking his head. "Don't stand there and talk like you know anything about her. You might have seen her from a distance, but that doesn't entitle you to speak like you've been a part of her life all this time. Hell, when she was bit and reached out when the job went south, you just cut your losses and wiped your hands of her. Some father you are."

Instead of being upset like I assumed, Eli just smiled at Zander warmly. "You have chosen well for yourself, although the vampire was a bit of a surprise, but I guess it shouldn't have been. Nothing about you or your birth was what we expected."

Zander took a breath, gearing up to let the man have another tongue-lashing, but I squeezed his arm and shook my head. When I was sure he was going to keep his mouth shut, I returned my attention to Eli. "I hope this isn't too rude, but what are you doing here? In the video, you said you were going to leave the choice of meeting each other up to me."

"Would you believe me if that was my intention, but when I found out you were planning to be at this party, I couldn't keep myself from taking the chance. I knew it could go badly, but with no risk, there is no reward," he answered with a shrug.

I looked the man over as I reached out with my magic and empathic abilities, just trying to gather as much information about him as I could. Emanating from him was a deep longing mixed with sadness that was old and deep in his heart. He mourned the loss of my mother to this day, and seeing me look so much like her was a mix of good and bad emotions. The deeper I looked, the more I found he was holding nothing back. It wasn't that I had the skill to bypass his mental barrier. He was welcoming me in, arms open wide, giving me whatever I wanted to know.

"Did you find what you were looking for?" Eli asked. "I'm more than happy to tell you anything, but I understand if you don't trust me. There's no reason you should."

"Not here," I answered. "Do you have time to meet tomorrow? There are things I wish to speak with you about."

He frowned as I talked. "Clearly, not all of them are good things, but I am willing to be fully transparent with you, Finley. Whatever it takes for you to believe I'm on your side and I always have been, whether you feel like I have been or not. You name the time and place of your choosing, and I will be there."

"I have your number. When I have those details, I'll reach out," I said and turned to look up at Zander. "I believe it's time for us to head back, don't you?"

"Yes, I think we've had enough of this party," Zander agreed. Without acknowledging my father at all, he led me back to the others. "We're going."

They all headed for the elevators with us trailing behind. My hands were sweating, and I felt like I might be going into shock after speaking to Eli. Having parents hadn't ever been something I allowed myself to think about or dwell on at any point in my life. What good did it do me when I had to survive, and surviving was what I did best. Somehow, now having met the man face to face, there was no denying he was real. Before, he was the man on the other end of the video keeping enough distance between us. Now, that distance was shattered.

FIFTEEN

FINLEY

"Are you alright?" Lane asked once we were all in the elevator heading down.

"You know, for once, I think I'm going to be honest with myself and say no. No, I'm not okay," I answered, my hands shaking. "But I'm going to hold it together and make it back to the penthouse where I can safely have my meltdown."

"How about when we get back, I draw you a nice hot bath, you can soak, relax, and just be for a moment. Things have been so crazy since the zoo, it would do you good. All those late nights and work on this mission, it's taking a toll," Noah reasoned as he ran a hand up and down my back.

"You're right," I said, looking at him with a quivering smile. "A bath sounds incredible, and I wouldn't mind sharing it with anyone who can fit in along with me."

They all looked at Zander since he's stayed at the penthouse before. "Just to be clear, I've never had the need to figure this out, but someone told me there were four of them in the tub. So three of us plus Finley should be a safe bet."

"Well, it's not gonna be you since you got your knot wrung yester-day," Mason pointed out, then quickly turned to me. "Not that I am expecting you to do anything you're not feeling up for. I know I asked earlier in the night, but that would make me an ass after what's happened. You need some good cuddles tonight, not someone poking you... unless that's what you want," Mason babbled on like he was worried he'd make me upset.

I just reached out a hand and placed it on his arm. "It's fine, Mason. I know what you meant. Let's just get back, and we'll figure everything else out once I'm not on display anymore."

The elevator doors opened, and we all filtered out. They kept me in the middle with Lane's arm around me as we passed through the crowd of reporters still outside. The limo was waiting, and I ducked inside first, taking a seat. Elias had other plans, though, as he scooped me up and settled us in the corner. He wrapped his jacket that he'd taken off before entering around my shoulders, tucked me close against him, and held me tight. He didn't say a word, just cradled me in his arms, allowing me to soak in his presence.

"Thank you," I whispered.

He didn't answer, just kissed my temple, and tucked my head under his chin. All of my men had suffered loss or hardship when it came to family in one way or another. It allowed them to understand how I was feeling without me having to say a thing. While it was slightly different from having a parent you believe didn't exist appear in your life, it came with its own hurricane of emotions to sort through.

When we reached the building where the penthouse was, Elias refused to put me down and instead handed me over to Noah, my Companion. Seeing a *nos* functioning as a perfect unit, I didn't understand why more people didn't see the value. Granted, this was slightly different due to the fact they were innately wired to act in this capacity, and my magic knew it, which was why it chose them. Still, to have a man in your life who took care of you on an emotional level was invaluable, but Noah was one cog in the *nos* that kept things turning.

Noah paused just inside the door and nodded to my feet. "Go ahead and kick them off. I know you've been dying to get rid of them all night."

"Seriously, though, who likes to wear high heels? They are like torture devices," I complained as I toed them off, and they plopped to the floor.

"I don't have an answer for you, babe. I, myself, have never worn them," he teased as he headed into the back bedroom with the master bathroom.

Mason was already at the tub with the water filling, adding the bath soak they'd provided us. It had a lovely scent of roses, already making me relax as Noah set me down on my feet. His hands on my waist held me steady for a moment until I got my bearings, then he unzipped me, sliding the dress down my body. Naked and ready to relax, I climbed into the bath and moaned. The hot water felt so good on my body as I slipped in. Then, spreading out and taking up the whole space of the tub, I just let myself shut my brain off from anything I didn't need to focus on right away. The job had gone well. I'd saved a life and managed to light the fuse in the destruction of the Dark Ring.

I heard someone enter, and I cracked an eye to find Derven holding a glass of something red in his hands. "I don't know if you enjoy wine, but I always found it helped me relax when I wasn't having the best of days."

"To be honest, I haven't had much experience with drinking since it wasn't something they recommended for assassins," I shared, sitting up. "Meaning to say, I don't know if it will help, but I'm happy to try something you find comforting."

He handed over the glass and crouched by the tub, resting his arms on the edge. "Have I or Rathal ever told you anything about my father?"

I shook my head as I lifted the glass and took a small sip testing the wine. It was sweet but not so much that it was like dessert, more so fruity. I liked it. "No, you've never talked about your father, and I didn't want to pry, so I figured if you wanted me to know, you'd tell me."

"He's a bastard, and if he weren't my maker, I would have washed my hands of him long ago, but there are some ties that bind you in ways I never expected. My father was a decent man when he was human, but when he was bitten by one of the first vampires created from dark magic and God knows what else, he morphed into something I couldn't recognize. He became paranoid that someone was going to kill him, like he had his maker, to steal his power and wealth. The madman's plan was to change his own children because there was no way they could turn on him. He was their father, and they loved him, but when your father hides away in a castle surrounded by guards believing anyone at any time could be after him, it changes things.

"After a hundred years of being proverbially trapped in his castle, manipulated by his words, I decided I wanted to see the world, live life to the fullest like he'd promised. So that's exactly what I did for about twenty years, then I returned home to check in and see how things were going. When I arrived, I didn't get the welcome I assumed I would receive and was thrown in jail for betraying the king. My father had taken me leaving as a personal offense, so I was being punished like the child he still believed I was. It took me thirty years to get him to understand that I wasn't trying to take the throne from him. After that, I stayed for another hundred years working on a plan to get him to put himself in hiding, leaving others to run things for him. He would direct the way the covens he ruled over through a proxy. Which is still how he does it to this day," Derven finished with a sigh, resting his head on his arms. "The day he was turned, I lost my father. The man who calls himself that isn't even a shadow of who he once was. It makes me sad, but we make the best out of what we are dealt."

I rested my head next to his, on his arm. "How did you get to the point where you can do as you please now?"

"I had four older siblings, and none of them survived the changes in the world as easily as I did. They couldn't adjust to a different way of thinking every hundred years—the evolution of technology or the enlightenment of people's minds. They were like my father, choosing to believe the world was out to get them. Now, in some cases, that was true, witch hunts, the Spanish Inquisition, and not to mention, thanks to those vampires who told our secrets, monster hunters. Each of my siblings died in a different way, but for the same reason, now I am the only one left besides my father. So I run the American branch of our coven and report back to him when I need to, but being his only living son, I'm his heir. Everything that is his will be mine if the time comes someone manages to find and kill him," Derven explained. "Cheerful story, isn't it?" he added with a deprecating chuckle.

"Seems that no family is perfect," I reasoned, lifting my head to take another sip of wine. "This stuff is really good."

"Be careful how fast you drink it. I put a few drops of my blood in it. Doing that can give you the same high feeling as when I drink from you," Derven warned. "It's how vampires spike drinks to help get supers drunk or feeling like they are."

"Does it affect me the same way, being your Blood Bond?" I questioned, looking at the glass differently.

"I suppose we will find out, won't we?" he questioned, kissing me on the cheek and standing. "I'll leave you to it unless you'd like me to send someone in?"

Taking a moment, I paused to consider that, checking in with my wolf to ensure we were good. When she voiced her request, I agreed completely. "Would you mind asking Elias to join me?"

"Not at all, *sângele meu,*" Derven assured as he headed out to find him.

Cautiously, I took another sip of the wine and hummed with delight as it slid down my throat. *I wonder if I would like it as much if it didn't have the blood or if that's why I like it.*

"My heart, is everything okay?" Elias asked, walking in.

He looked much more relaxed in pajama pants and a T-shirt, his curly hair once again wild and free from the product holding it in place.

"It would be better if you joined me," I answered.

A slow smile tugged at his lips as he grabbed the back of his shirt and yanked it off. Quickly he shucked off his pants and climbed in without any other encouragement. He sat across from me, but I didn't like that at all, so I got on my knees and made my way over to him.

Straddling his hips, I sat facing him, my ass planted firmly on his thighs. "That's better. You were too far away."

"My apologies. I didn't mean to be so distant." He placed his hand on my hips and slid me forcefully forward until I was right up against his chest, his hardening cock between us. "There, I think that's better."

This action had my wolf perking up, incredibly aroused by his act of dominance. Even though I was enjoying my glass of wine, I set it on the ledge where it wouldn't get knocked over, feeling like I was going to need both hands.

Letting one hand trail down his chest, I gripped his cock in my hand, leaned in, and nuzzled under his jaw, an act of submission between wolves. "Has my Sentinel finally decided to claim his mate?" I purred.

"My heart, I claimed you that day you leaped into my arms. Never in my life had someone been so completely unafraid of me, trusting I would catch them as you were with me," Elias responded, running his nose along the shell of my ear. "But to answer your question... yes, if you are ready for it, then I desperately wish to claim you officially as mine. I know we are mated through the soul bond you created, but my wolf almost tore out every man's throat for looking at what's ours. I'm thinking it might soothe him some to know our mark is on you, so if I do act out, they knew it was coming."

Shivers of delight rippled through my body hearing him speak like that. It fulfilled every wish my wolf had to be claimed, protected, and loved by her mates. Wanting to show him how much I loved the idea, I started to kiss up his neck until I reached his ear. Then I sucked in the lobe, biting it with my teeth, just this side of being too much but didn't break the skin.

Elias hissed, and his fingers dug into my skin, making me smile at the thought of having his marks all over my body. I soothed the bite with a lick and pulled back enough to see his face. His hazel eyes glittered with hunger, a hunger that only I could fulfill for him, and I grinned back at him.

"You are not going to be a good girl, are you?" he asked, cocking his head "I think that's exactly how I want it, though. Unlike Zander, I *enjoy* when you push back and stand up for yourself. There is something so incredibly sexy about a woman who can choose to submit herself to someone but also be an equal partner as well."

Not feeling the need to respond to his comments, I lowered myself enough to seal our lips together. Right now, I wanted action, not words, and that was always Elias's strength. We battled with tongue, teeth, and our hands to get the upper hand—groping to distract, then moaning when he or I found that perfect spot that sent tingles up your spine.

Water sloshed out of the tub, but neither of us cared as our bodies moved, gliding against each other. Elias thrust two fingers into me, causing my head to fall back as I let out a groan of satisfaction. Finally, something was inside me, working my needy flesh that had been begging to be fucked.

"You like that?" Elias taunted as he curled his fingers over my G-spot. "Is my omega feeling needy? Does she need her mate to fuck her, mark her, and fill her with my cum?"

My breathing was coming in quickly, shallow pants with how incredibly turned on I was right now. "Yes, oh God, please! I want all of that." I whimpered as he finger fucked me hard, creating waves in the water around us, but I needed more. "Please fill me with your cock. I *need* more." A whine slipped out as I begged, but I wasn't ashamed of showing my men just how badly I wanted them.

Elias slipped his fingers from me and stood, pulling me with him. He turned me to face the massive window that looked out over the city and bent me forward with my hands planted on the glass, ass up in the air.

"I want the world to be able to see as I claim what's mine. Then everyone will know to keep their goddamn hands and eyes off you." He ended that statement, slamming into me so hard that I almost smashed my face into the window. Thankfully, I wasn't human and could catch myself before it happened.

Now that Elias was fully seated inside me, he draped himself over my body and wrapped his arms around my front, each hand cupping a breast. A cry left my mouth as his teeth gently scraped over the skin of my neck, taunting me with the promise of a bite. It wasn't the same as when Derven did, but it was just as intoxicating.

"You feel so good inside me, Elias," I whispered, my breath airy as I spoke. "I've been waiting, knowing you would find the right time for us to become one."

Elias gave a shallow thrust with his hips, almost as if he couldn't stop himself from moving. "I know the others don't mind sharing their time with you. After tonight, I won't either, but this moment is just for us. Some might call it selfish, but I wanted your full attention as we become mates for life. No other woman will ever be enough to draw me away from you. Finley, you hold me, mind, body, and spirit in the palm of your hand. Which is why I wanted this to be *our* moment."

"Then take what you need from me, my love. I give it all to you freely," I vowed, releasing any thoughts I had of controlling what happened tonight between us. This moment was for us, and right now, he needed me to surrender, which I would gladly do.

With how direct and forceful he'd been up until this point, I assumed he was going to take what he'd been longing for, but instead, he did the opposite. Staying draped over my back, he clung to me as he slowly moved his hips. Elias was going for the long game, and no one was going to rush him as he enjoyed my body, and I reveled in the feeling.

His hot breath ran along my neck as he nuzzled me, whispering all the things he loved about me into my ear.

"My heart, the world doesn't deserve you," he confessed. "If I could keep the evil from ever getting its claws on you, I would, but you're too good for that. Tonight, you saved a life even though you went on this mission to take them."

Slowly, he stood, pulling me with him, and one hand shifted from my chest to wrap around my neck as he pressed it back to rest on his shoulder. His thrusts got quicker and had more force behind them, pulling moans from me with every movement. The hand not around my neck drifted between my legs and started to swirl around my clit, adding even more stimulation to the situation.

"I'm going to come, and I'm going to fill that pussy of yours up until it overflows. Then I'm going to wash you from head to toe in the shower and do it again. Once I mark you with my teeth, I plan to mark you with my seed every day until you give me a child," he informed me. "Do you want that, Finley? Do you want to give me a baby created by our love for each other?"

While my body and wolf loved the hell out of that idea, my brain wasn't convinced. None of us had talked about kids, and I didn't know how things worked for elves, but I knew it wouldn't be an option until I was done fulfilling this contract between Morwyn and me.

"Someday, my love, someday I would love to give you that joy," I answered.

Elias growled with excitement. "Then, until that time, I better practice so I'm ready when you choose to open your body to my seed."

With a few more thrusts, we both came, screaming our climaxes as the slow build brought with it more intensity. My legs shook as Elias gave a few more short thrusts, ensuring his cum was good and deep inside me. Together, we sank back into the water that had cooled to being more lukewarm, but with how hot and sweaty my body was, I didn't mind at all.

Elias refused to pull out of me, letting his dick shrink naturally, keeping us connected for as long as possible. He gripped my jaw and pushed my face back as far as it would go. Confused, I let him do what he wanted, knowing he'd never hurt me. When he got me the way he wanted me, I gasped as he bit down on my chin. His sharp wolf teeth sliced through the front and underside of my face, bringing our wolf bond to life. I was now officially claimed by werewolf standards as Elias's mate. Pulling back, he started to clean it as he licked away the blood, humming to himself almost as an alpha would purr.

"You had to pick a spot no one would miss, didn't you," I groaned as each swipe of his tongue felt like he was licking my pussy, making me twitch.

"Didn't I tell you that I was a jealous man when it came to those outside our pack?" Elias countered. "No matter what, everyone will know you are already taken." Moving from my chin, he captured my lips and kissed me senseless.

When we decided it was time to get out of the tub, he lifted me out, placing me to stand on the bathmat. I paused for a moment, feeling his cum leaking out of me, running down my leg. Elias appeared behind me and slipped his finger through my legs from the back, smearing it all over my pussy, shoving some back inside.

If I had any doubts about him making good on his promise to clean me up only to dirty me again, I no longer had them. The sight of me

dripping with his cum had him rock hard and jumping with excitement to do it again, and we did. I almost didn't make it to the bed
before he was back inside me, rutting into me like a crazed wolf. He
laid on top of me, holding my shoulder in his mouth as he rammed
into me, wild and desperate.

The others tried to join us, but Elias was having none of it and snarled,
hiding me away from them. The moment they left, he was back inside
me, laying his claim any way he could. He fucked my ass, pussy, and
mouth throughout the night, not letting me clean up in between.
Instead, he rubbed it into my skin, sniffing me all over as if searching
for a place I didn't have his scent. Finally, when morning broke, he fell
into a deep sleep, almost to the point I was worried he'd gone into a
coma.

Taking advantage of the moment, I showered, then crawled into bed
with the twins, who wrapped themselves around me and fell right back
to sleep. The others would have asked questions or needed to check in
on me. Right now, all I wanted was uninterrupted sleep and no one
trying to poke me with their dick. That's why the twins were perfect.
They hated to wake up and would sleep until noon every day if we'd
let them. They were my nap buddies, and I trusted them not to take
advantage of the fact I was only wearing a T-shirt.

Now to get sleep before having to deal with my father.

SIXTEEN

RATH

"Are you sure he's okay?" I questioned as I looked over the passed-out wolf.

I didn't have healing magic like Finley did, but I could check someone over for anomalies to see if they needed a healer. The beta in question seemed fine, if a little dehydrated, but by the sounds we heard all night, I wasn't surprised.

"Trust me, after a rut like that, he'll be sleeping for a good long while," Colt assured me as we left the bedroom.

I cocked my head at the term. "Rut?"

"It's when a male werewolf goes into their own version of a heat, and they become mindless sex fiends," Mason answered with a yawn as he entered the living room. "I'm not surprised it happened to him. In the eight years I've known him, he's never let a woman get close enough to him that sex could happen. All that built-up testosterone just exploded once he blew the first load."

"Gross, don't ever say that again," Lane said, scrunching up his face in disgust. "She still sleeping?"

"Yeah, all curled up next to Noah, but I couldn't lay there anymore and not want to start something. Pretty sure if I tried, she might shrink my dick or something equally horrible."

"Wise choice, my friend," Derven agreed. "I just made a fresh pot of coffee, knowing all of us were going to need it after last night."

Barely having been with us for a week, Derven seemed to be fitting in with the pack easily. Then again, he'd always been like that. With the flash of a smile and sweet words, he could charm just about anyone. It was how he survived so long with what I knew about his father.

His gaze met mine with a questioning look, probably wondering why I was staring at him so oddly. Shaking my head, I wandered to the kitchen and pulled open the refrigerator, looking for something to eat.

"Something the matter?" Derven asked in a low voice behind me.

I should have known he wouldn't leave things be. He was a fixer and hated to have a situation unresolved. Between us, there were many things unresolved or unspoken when it came to telling Finley anything about what our friendship had really been like.

"It's nothing, just got lost in thought and didn't realize I was staring at you," I answered with a sigh, closing the refrigerator, not seeing anything I wanted.

Derven narrowed his eyes as he looked me up and down like he could spot the problem if he searched hard enough. "Are you upset about the wolf keeping Finley to himself?"

"What? No, if I had the chance to do that, I would take it, so I can hardly begrudge the man for doing it himself," I said, moving to the coffee maker.

I'd really never seen the appeal to coffee, preferring tea, and they'd been gracious enough to now have an electric kettle at home for me to use. It made things much easier, and I truly appreciated the effort to include me in normal life things like that.

"You're doing that thing where you tell me things are fine, but really you're upset and don't want to talk about it," Derven challenged. "I've seen it before, and trust me, I hated it when you were mad at me about something. Thankfully, I know it's not me you're upset with, or you'd be sealing my mouth with magic so I couldn't irritate you."

I slammed the mug I'd just grabbed down on the counter much harder than I planned to as I glared at him. "Stop talking like that."

"Like what?" Derven asked, confused. "Oh, you mean stop talking like we weren't together for five years as more than just friends before we were separated?"

"Yes," I snapped. "I haven't told Finley anything about it, and I want her to hear it from me first, not to stumble into a conversation and feel like I was lying to her."

"About that..." Derven said, pointing at something behind me.

Spinning on my heel, I found Finley standing in the kitchen, rubbing the sleep out of her one eye with the heel of her hand. Her hair was wild, and I could tell she was exhausted, not just from lack of sleep but everything else on top of it. Planning for this mission had pushed her to the max. Last night had been a good idea in theory, but the sexcapades might not have had the best timing.

"Good morning," I blurted, unsure if she actually heard what I had just said or not. "Coffee?"

"Can I just have the whole pot?" she mumbled as she walked forward right up to me and let her head land on my chest. "I feel like I still haven't gotten any sleep, but it's already the middle of the afternoon. How is that possible?"

"*Nin mel*, you have taxed yourself well beyond just last night's adventures," I pointed out. "The week up to this point, you were sleeping a few hours just to get things right."

"Ugh," she groaned, wrapping her arms around me. "You're making too much sense before I have coffee."

"Here you go, *sângele meu*," Ven said, handing over a mug just the way she liked it, teeth achingly sweet.

She didn't have many vices but allowing herself some sugary treats throughout the day was one of them. "Can we have pancakes or French toast for lunch? I really want breakfast, but I know it's well past that time of day."

"How about both? They are easy enough to whip up," Ven suggested as he pushed off the counter he was leaning on to gather the ingredients.

The person who organized the penthouse for us asked what we would want, so we gave them a list and ensured to have all of Finley's favorites just in case we needed to do something special. Now I'm glad we made that call after having run into her father last night.

Finley took a seat at the island while Ven worked, and I made a cup of tea, letting the moment fall into a comfortable silence.

"So, what did you want to tell me before I accidentally overheard it?" Finley asked just as I was taking a sip of tea and nearly choked on it.

My gaze instantly went to Ven since what I was going to say had as much to do with him as it did me.

"Go on, tell her," he directed, waving his whisk at me. "I have zero shame about our past. That's all you."

Clearing my throat, I gave Finley my full attention. "When I told you that Ven and I didn't know each other well, that wasn't the truth of the matter. Ven and I became best friends, and after a year, we became *more* than best friends, in an intimate nature."

Ven sighed and looked over at Finley. "We were fuck buddies that then became lovers until we were separated because Rathal was sold to a new master. My old master was a sick and twisted bastard who liked to use whatever he could to cause me pain, so he took Rathal away."

I grimaced at how bluntly he put it. We'd cared deeply for each other, and some might call it love. I might have called it love until I found Finley, the difference between being with your mate and a person you have strong feelings for are completely different. To this day, I still love Ven, but not in the same way I love and belong to Finley. Being able to have them both in my life was something I never thought could happen, and I was thankful for it. Yet Ven and I would be nothing more than best friends who know each other inside and out.

"Are you two still wanting to be together?" Finley asked, looking at us both with curiosity. "For the record, I would never stand in the way of people's love if that's what you both want."

Just when I didn't think I could love that woman any more, she said things like that. "While it means everything you would say that, *nin mel,* but the time for us is passed. Now we both have you, we can be best friends with each other. As an elf, once you are bonded to your mate, there is no one else for you. I love Derven, but in a way you would a brother. He is family and having him back in my life is something I never thought I was going to get."

Ven quietly flipped the pancakes he was cooking and didn't respond right away, making me nervous. He wasn't one to hold back how he felt about things, and if he told Finley he loved me in the way we used to be together, I didn't know how I would feel about that. My gut reaction was guilt and sadness for not being able to love him that way, but it was impossible. With the way elves were, once we have our mate, we are incapable of feeling intimate love with another like I could before. Everything in me wanted Ven to be happy, and I thought things were going well, but maybe that had been wishful thinking.

"Rathal is right," Ven said when he finally spoke. "We used to love each other, and I think when I first found him again, I had hoped we might rekindle something." He paused to look at Finley. "That changed once you and I solidified our connection. It showed me I hadn't *loved* Rathal the way I'm falling for you, *sângele meu*. As he said, to have him back in my life is amazing, and to be able to share you with him so he can have the same joy I have is everything to me."

"I'm sorry if you feel like we kept something from you, but I felt like I needed to figure out how I felt before I could explain it to you," I said, reaching across the counter to wrap my hands around hers. "You know, as an elf, I cannot lie, but a way to work around that is just avoid it, and that's what I was doing."

Finley smiled and kissed my lips softly. "That is something I understand completely. Many times I need to sort through things myself before I share them with others. I'm not upset with either of you, so put your minds at ease."

"You are the world's most perfect mate, you know that, right?" I whispered before giving her another kiss and pulling back.

"Couldn't have said it better myself," Ven agreed as he slid a plate over to her. "Hope you don't mind. I snuck some chocolate chips in there."

A delighted smile beamed on her face. "Who would ever be upset about that?"

"Do I smell pancakes?" Noah asked as he walked into the kitchen. "Oh, hell, yeah, with chocolate chips too!" Then he paused and looked at Ven. "Are you cooking for everyone, or is this for Finley special?"

"No, I planned to make enough for everyone. She just got the first batch since no one else was here. Seems her wolf doesn't get as upset when none of you are in the same room when I serve her first," Ven explained.

Noah nodded and sat next to Finley, cutting a chunk out of her pancake and stuffing it into his mouth. I shot over to him and smacked the back of his head, making him almost choke on the bite he was eating.

"None of that," I snapped. "There will be plenty of food. Do not steal off her plate. Why do you and Mason always do that?"

Noah shrugged. "We've always done that to people we are close with. I guess we are used to sharing everything all the time that we assume everyone else feels the same way. Obviously, we aren't as bold with the alphas, but we've snatched a fry or two off their plates before."

I suppose that made sense, but I still didn't like it when they did it to Finley. We had a hard enough time getting her to eat as much as she should without them making it harder.

"Did you decide if we are gonna meet your dad?" Noah asked, nudging Finley with his elbow.

She didn't answer right away. Instead, she ate in silence for a bit, and none of us felt the need to press her for an answer. As the smell of food filled the penthouse, the rest of the pack found their way to the kitchen.

"Alright, everyone out," Ven ordered. "I need space to make the food you hungry beasts want. Now scram and take what I've made with you. Don't forget plates this time," he added, pointing his spatula at Mason.

"Man chooses to eat a slice of pizza not over a plate, and the old man never lets you live it down," Mason teased as he grabbed a stack of plates for the table. "Let's go, elf. I'm sure he'll be chasing you out soon enough."

I chuckled as I shook my head at this odd group of men who just seemed to make sense when put together. Having known I would be part of a *nos*, I'd been prepared to share life with a few men. Most elven women these days had three men, but here I was with seven of them. I brought the pot over and refilled Finley's cup before taking her plate.

"Hey, I wasn't done with that," she grumbled.

I looked at her over my shoulder. "I'm aware, but you're going to join us at the table and not hide here while you wrestle with the answer of meeting your father or not."

"You know, having people in my head all the time isn't so much fun," she shared as she followed after me.

"*Nin mel,* I didn't have to read your thoughts to know what you were doing. It's written all over your face," I informed her. "Now sit, eat, and try not to worry yourself into a hole when you could talk to us about it as well."

The rest of the table pretended like they weren't at all interested in our conversation, but with supernatural hearing, I knew they'd heard us. It was incredibly hard to keep any secrets with supers around but add in the fact we could sense each other's emotions and some wayward thoughts. It was a courtesy to ignore it unless addressed.

"There are so many things I want to ask him, but the problem is..." She paused to stab at her French toast with her fork. "Do I really want to know the answers? What if everything he tells me just reveals more lies or dirty secrets that should have been left alone? Ignorance is bliss, right?"

Colt leaned back in his chair, sipping on his coffee. "Did you want the truth or the answer you want?"

My eyes widened at his candor with Finley. Most of the time, they all tried to keep in mind that she was an omega, and words hit deeper and harder. Although I think they were finally realizing she wasn't the same anymore now that her elf magic had come into play.

"The truth," she stated, locking eyes with her alpha.

"You need to talk to him regardless of what you learn because you will always wonder what would have happened if you don't. Who knows, you might find out what you thought he was going to say isn't even close to the truth," Colt said with a shrug. "It's better to know the devil than let him sneak up on you unprepared."

He had a point. I would much rather know now if we had another person we needed to watch out for. With danger coming at all fronts, a sneak attack could kill us.

"You're right. We need to know what we are dealing with. If the truth is that he is working closer to the Dark Ring, then we know that will be important. I might be able to handle myself one-on-one with another assassin trained by them, but an army?" She let out a heavy sigh. "I'm not sure anyone could win against that."

"Then it's settled. We'll meet up with the bastard, get the hell out of here, and go back home," Zander agreed, slapping his hand to the table. "Now we just need sleeping beauty to wake his ass up."

"Or we could leave him here? Serves the bastard right after doing that to us last night," Mason muttered, causing everyone at the table to laugh.

SEVENTEEN

FINLEY

After getting ready to head out and meet at the restaurant Zander suggested with a private room for us to use, I caught my reflection, and it stopped me in my tracks. I didn't know how long I stood there in front of the mirror, looking at myself. There on my chin was a healed scar from Elias's mate mark. To me, it was beautiful. It made me feel special, and I loved being able to see it there. Then I started to look at the rest of me and how it might be viewed by other people.

My mahogany-colored hair fell in a shiny, smooth sheet from my head to the middle of my back. It had been down to my butt before I'd had it cut for the event. My skin was still pale as it's always been but had more of a luster since my elf nature came out fully. Just like my chin, you could see the faint marks on my neck where most of my other mates had bitten me. Only one of them had chosen to pick a place only he could get to on my breast. There were even two puncture marks from the first time Derven bit me deeply on the neck like his own claim on me.

While I looked human to everyone else wandering around the world, I was anything but. As a trained assassin, werewolf, and elf, I might actually be one of the deadliest supers out there. Skill, speed, strength, and magic? Who else could compete with that? It seemed fitting that I would be the one tasked with removing evil from this world, but what if I found out I was created by evil? My father seemed to be a man of mystery, and I was terrified to find out what else he could be hiding from the world.

"Sweetheart, are you ready?" Lane asked as he stepped up behind me.

I smiled at him in the mirror and leaned into him. "That's the million-dollar question now, isn't it?"

"No matter what Colt said, if you don't want to do this, we can leave right now. Get on that plane and fly the hell out of here and get back home," Lane assured me.

Tilting my head back, I looked up at him. "I love you."

He cupped my cheek and kissed me long and slow, filled with all the love he had for me as well. "I love you too, Finley, but that doesn't answer my question."

"Colt's right, I need to ask my questions, or I'm going to go crazy thinking what-if? It will be better to get this over with and never have to see the man again if I don't want to," I reasoned. "Just know that if things don't go well, I'm going to need a hell of a lot of cuddles and ice cream."

Lane laughed softly. "Can we do that even if things don't go wrong?"

"Yeah, I think we can, but you'll have to convince Zander if I'm not a hot mess. He doesn't argue when it's to cheer me up," I pointed out.

"Hmm," he paused, rubbing his chin with a hand. "Could you pretend?"

"Sorry, elves can't lie. You're on your own," I quipped.

"I don't believe that at all, by the way. How can you pull off jobs like you did last night without telling a lie?" Lane argued as he turned me toward the door and pushed me forward. "You had to con that restaurant owner into getting you to serve that bastard."

"It seems there is some gray area when I'm playing a character, but I didn't lie to him completely. That bottle of cognac did cost us a pretty penny, and I knew I could see it to my target if I wanted to, but I didn't need to. When the restaurant owner challenged me, all he said was for him to buy the bottle from me. I got a hundred dollars out of it," I shared, walking him through the entire process.

Lane gave me a wary look. "Your interpretation of what is the truth kind of scares me."

Feeling it was better to leave that subject alone, I grabbed his hand and pulled him out into the living area where the others were. "Everyone ready for dinner with the in-law?"

No one seemed to feel that was amusing so I shrugged and headed for the door. We had a driver coming to pick us up, another perk of being here with the record label. They didn't like having Zander take ride-shares or public transportation, so they gave us what we needed instead. The restaurant had been thrilled to host Zander and his pack as we were now being called. Amazingly enough, the news that I was an elf hadn't shown up anywhere, but the fact I was with all my men was plastered all over the place. There was speculation if there were more intermingled relationships as well between the men.

We all tried to pretend none of this was an issue and things would die down once we got back to our pack lands. Of course, I knew that wouldn't be the case at all, especially not after Zander had a two-hour conversation with his team that we were not doing interviews. Maybe once things were done, I might be open to it, but the last thing we needed was people learning too much about us. Let them speculate all they want and spread misinformation, but I wasn't going to help it along.

Everyone piled into the SUV, and we were off. The restaurant was Italian, and I was excited about having some amazing alfredo. It had been far too long since I'd gone out for dinner in New York City, and having all my men with me made it even better. The guys allowed Elias to sit next to me after he begged for my forgiveness for how he'd treated me during his rut. While I wasn't looking to have sex in the next couple of days, I didn't think he did anything wrong.

Rut was a normal fact of being a werewolf. It could have happened to any of them. He was still a little clingy and didn't love the others touching me, but he was doing his best to keep his reaction in check.

He did bring up a good point, though, with everyone else. "How do we make sure we don't get Finley pregnant right now?"

Of course, that question immediately went to Rath as the only one among us who might have the answer. The elf cleared his throat and folded his hand in his lap, telling me he was slightly uncomfortable with this conversation.

"When it comes to female elves, they have the innate ability to decide when it's the best time for that to happen. Now I'm not sure how the werewolf part of this comes into play, but I believe that until Finley wants it to happen, it won't," Rath offered.

Hearing him say it made me nod in agreement as I listened. Instinctively, I knew that even though Elias had tried his best last night to get me to bear his child, it wouldn't happen. I didn't want it to and wasn't in heat, so there was no concern.

"How many times does an omega go into heat?" I asked.

"Once or twice a year, and it's the only time they are fertile," Colt informed me. "That's one reason children from an omega are so rare. You only have two shots a year to make it happen, and if it doesn't, then you have to wait six months to a year to try again."

I looked over at Elias. "So it would be safe to say that you can carry on with your practicing unless I'm in heat. Then we're gonna need to figure something else out until I'm ready."

"That would be anal," Mason volunteered. "Can't get you preggers that way."

"Guess we'll just have to wait and see when the next one rolls around if you're still feeling that way," Lane reasoned.

Learning that had me breathing a sigh of relief because I didn't think I could handle being pregnant during all this. But, slowly, the guys were making the idea more appealing, especially when Elias seemed so excited about sharing that experience with me. We would have to see how I felt after talking with my father if the idea of children is still somewhat appealing.

The restaurant was one that had accommodations for the rich and famous who didn't want to be noticed. We got dropped off at a side entrance that led to a set of stairs into a separate dining section for those who didn't want to be with *normal* people. Zander had request-ed an even more private setting in a banquet room for us all to enjoy our meal. When we entered the room, my father was already there, seated at one end of the table.

The moment he saw us, he stood and came over to greet us. "I wasn't sure if you were really going to reach out to me or not, but I'm really glad you did."

We stared at each other for a moment, then I decided to break the silence and try to start this off on the right foot. "Let me introduce you to the guys. You already know who Zander is since, apparently, you work in the same industry. Next to him are Colt and Lane. They are the founders and alphas of our pack in Tennessee. Their betas are Elias, my Sentinel. Noah, my Companion, his twin, Mason, who is my Hunter and also a Companion. Rathal, my elven mate, who is my Guide, then Derven, my Blood Bond and vampire mate."

"I know this is an extremely unorthodox *nos*, but I do believe my daughter has chosen well with you men. In the spirit of full transparency, I've done research on all of you with the contacts I have. Not that there would have been much I could do to prevent you from mating with my daughter, but I felt better knowing you were good men," Eli shared, taking a moment to look at each of my men as he spoke. "Shall we have dinner and get to know one another better?"

"What's the point if you know everything about us already," Mason muttered under his breath.

Eli smiled and nodded. "I suppose that's fair, but just because I know the facts about you, it doesn't tell me who you are as a person. I can make assumptions, but I'd like for us to one day be more invested in each other's lives."

No one said much to that, at least out loud.

"That's up to you, little one. If you want him in your life, we will support you. On the other hand, if you choose that he's not worth it, we'll never speak of him again," Colt assured me as we took our seats.

"You don't think he can tell we are doing this like the vampire can, do you?" Mason asked.

Derven sighed. "*I do have a name, you know.*"

"*What? It's a loving nickname. I could have settled on fang boy, but it didn't seem to fit. You're too posh,*" Mason countered.

I couldn't help but snort at the look of horror that crossed Derven's face when he found out he'd almost been dubbed fang boy.

"*Vampire is fine as long as you don't mind me calling you pup,*" Derven commented with a smirk. "*You are a werewolf and so much younger than myself. I think it fits nicely.*"

"*Don't start a fight you can't finish. I'm sure I could come up with something worse than fang boy,*" Mason countered.

Derven gave him a wide smile showing off his fangs. "*Do your worst, pup.*"

"Enough," Rath snapped. "*I understand you are trying to help, but we need answers, so keep it down.*"

"*Ooo, you got in trouble from daddy elf,*" Noah teased.

Everyone tried to cover up their laughter at the banter going on in our heads. While Rath was right that we needed to stay on task, I couldn't be more thankful for them lightening the mood.

"Finley," Eli said, grabbing my attention.

I turned to look at him sitting next to me, his eyes wide with shock. "Did you create a true soul bond with your men? All of them?"

Cocking my head, I reached out to his emotions, getting amazement and a hint of fear from him. "Something tells me, by your reaction, I shouldn't have been able to do that, but yes, I am mated to them as an elf and however my mates' species requires."

"That's impossible. There's no way that should have been able to happen," Eli rambled as he combed his fingers through his hair. "Your mother tried to do that and failed."

"What?" I demanded. "Why would my mother need to create a soul bond when you are an elf?"

"Like you, your mother had a mixed *nos* as well. There were only three of us compared to your eight, which by the way, is impressive any way you look at it. Maybe that was the problem. Your mother's magic wasn't strong enough to make the bond," Eli mused, his eyes losing focus as if he was looking into the past.

I reached out and placed a hand on his arm and immediately got sucked into what he was thinking. There stood a woman who I knew had to be my mother. When he said I was the spitting image of her, he hadn't been lying. Other than the eye color which I got from him, I looked just like her.

She was lying in a field of flowers with a tiger as her pillow and another man with his head on her legs, hand resting on her pregnant belly. I couldn't tell what he was, but I didn't get the sense that he was a shifter. Assuming I was looking at this from Eli's point of view, this must be an outing all of them had gone on together. There was so much pain and sadness emanating off Eli that it nearly choked me.

Were the other men still alive? The feelings of sadness ran so deep it led me to believe they were gone as well. Why is it that she had drawn others to her when she was purely elven? It made sense to me that I did, being a werewolf, but what if the same thing would have happened if I wasn't?

Removing myself from his memory, I opened my eyes to see my father looking at me with a tear running down his cheek. "That was the last time we were all together before you were born. Liam, the weretiger, killed himself after your mother died. He couldn't bear to live without his mate and ended it on his own terms. James disappeared. I don't know where he went, but he wanted nothing to do with me or you. He couldn't even look at you without seeing the reason his wife was dead."

He slowly reached out and cupped my cheek. "We were happy, the four of us. We had sixty beautiful years together as a family before we lost your mother. I hope you will see how they were in that moment because that is what our life was like, not what you see now. We loved each other as brothers, and your mother hung the moon in our eyes. To lose her shattered everything. I suppose it's good we weren't soul bound, or you would have been left with no one in the world to look after you."

"What is he talking about?" I asked Rath.

"There are some who believe that when you form a soul bond, when one person dies, the others die with them since their souls are connected," Rath explained. *"Many bond with their mates, but few create the soul bond. For all of us to be connected as a unit, it was the only way for that to happen."*

"So there is a chance that if one of us dies, we're dead?" I demanded.

Silence was my answer. Now I understood why he was so upset with me for making the contract with Morwyn. If I couldn't do this or died trying, then I took everyone with me. Taking a deep calming breath and letting it out slowly, I centered myself. That was a problem for another day, there were things I still needed to understand, and it seemed my father knew more than anyone.

"How did she die? I understand it was during childbirth, but how could that happen for an elf?" I asked.

Eli dropped his gaze to his hands, where he picked at the cloth napkin wrapped around the silverware. "Your mother was cursed by a witch whose husband she killed while on a mission. She thought the home was empty like it should have been, but the wife came home early from her trip. A security ward we didn't realize was there trapped your mother from getting out. James was working on breaking the spell but couldn't do it in time to get her out before the wife returned. The curse was to ensure that Tiriana wouldn't get to the future of her line, that she would die the moment she saw her child's face."

"Why would she even risk having me?" I gasped. "That makes no sense?"

Eli gave me a wavering smile as he took both my hands in his. "She wanted nothing more than to be a mother. Tiriana was a warrior like you, but deep down, she wanted to have seven children and be a homemaker caring for her family, but the world wasn't safe for that. James believed he had broken the curse, and the first thing she did was tell us she was ready to have a baby. Two months later, you started to grow in her belly, making her the happiest I'd ever seen. When it was the last few weeks, there was complication after complication making me believe the curse hadn't been broken.

"Your mother didn't care. She was determined to have you no matter what. Before you were born, you were everything to her. So when the time came, it was a struggle, but she gave birth, and you entered the world silent as a whisper staring up at me with those big blue eyes of yours. Liam tried to take you out of the room right away, refusing to let Tiriana see you in fear it would kill her. She begged and pleaded for us to let her hold you, but none of us were willing to risk her life, no matter what. James finally came up with the idea of blindfolding your mother so she could hold you, and that's what we did. She fed you, cuddled you, whispered secrets in your ear that to this day, I don't know what they were. We relaxed and most of us fell asleep after having been up with her all night. When we woke, there she was dead, cradling you in her arms with a beaming smile as she looked down at you," Eli shared, his voice cracking with emotion at the last part.

My mother, knowing the risks, wanted so desperately to see me that she ignored all the dangers just to get a glimpse of my face. "How could she give up everything just for one look at me?"

"That is the strength of a mother's love, Finley," Eli stated. "She picked your name, by the way, it means courageous one, and I believe you've lived up to it quite well."

"How long did you keep me before giving me to the orphanage?" I asked, pulling my hands from his.

"Two weeks, then the attacks started to happen," he answered. "I don't have any proof, but I believe they were James trying to kill you. He became convinced he'd broken the curse but that you had somehow absorbed it, so it killed her. To be clear, I never thought that for a second and honestly assumed he never was able to break a dark magic curse that's powered by the caster's own death. James couldn't live with himself, so after I caught him trying to smother you with a pillow, I cast him out and never saw him again."

"So, what made you come back for me? If I was in so much danger from one of my own fathers, why would you bring me into the Organization?" I challenged.

A hand rested on my leg as Noah offered his support, sensing I was getting upset.

We were interrupted as the waiter arrived and started taking drink and food orders for the table. Thankfully, I already knew what I wanted, having looked at the menu beforehand. When the waiter left, there was a lull with an uncomfortable silence before my father took a sip of his water and answered.

EIGHTEEN

FINLEY

"That is a hard question to answer and one that will make me sound incredibly selfish. Were you safer being in the orphanage in another state where no one would ever be able to find you? Yes. Did I feel the need as your biological father to keep a close eye on you? Also, yes. Did seeing how much you looked like your mother push me into the choice to bring you into the fold so I could protect you and watch over you personally? One hundred percent yes," Eli admitted.

"Had the attacks stopped?" Colt asked, leaning forward to get a better look at my father as he answered.

Eli nodded. "After they realized I'd hidden her away, they stopped, telling me it was more about her than me. The Organization started with the four of us as a unit using the cover as a music mogul while we built the foundation as a four-person team. The others decided they wanted to back out of it after what happened to Tiriana, but I soldiered on alone, creating the version of the Organization you know now. The practice of pulling children out of orphanages and foster homes started when I knew I wanted to bring you home.

"So I made the youngest age we would pull children five so it gave me four years of it becoming the normal, so when I came to get you, no one would bat an eye. Like I told you the other night, you were the epitome of perfection at becoming an assassin with your lineage. When we'd done one of the blood draws on you, I ran your DNA, and you are absolutely an elf, but you are also a blend of your other fathers as well. Not enough to change you being an elf, but I believe it might have made you predisposed to being transformed when you got bit by the omega."

He was hitting me with so much information I needed to move, my brain was overloading, and if I didn't get some fresh air, I would explode. Rath was at my side in an instant, holding out a hand to me. Desperately I took it, and he had me out the door, down the stairs, and out into the city's open air.

Bending over, I rested my hands on my knees as I took deep, gasping breaths, now that the walls were no longer closing in around me. It was too much. Everything he was saying was too much. I went from having no idea about my family to wishing I'd left it all alone.

Rath pulled me into his arms, hugging me tightly as he softly sang to me in elven, combing his finger through my hair. "Just breathe, *nin mel*, it will pass," he murmured. "This is a lot to take in for anyone, don't feel ashamed for reacting this way. So much has happened in the past few months since you became an omega. No one expects you to take each hit without repercussions."

"I killed my mother, and one of my fathers wants me dead." I heaved as I tried to get the words out. "What if he knows who I am and where I am? This means you're all in more danger than I'd already put you in."

"Stop," Rath ordered. "Don't you dare put this on yourself. You were but a babe growing in your mother, being born into a situation you didn't create. They had choices in how they chose to respond to what happened, and each of them made poor decisions. That man upstairs is broken and wounded, but he did the best he could to do right by you. Were all his choices good ones? No, but I applaud the man for not abandoning you completely."

I buried my face in his shirt, hugging him as tightly as I could, needing someone to hold me together right now. Another body came up behind me and wrapped himself around my back, sandwiching me between them.

"*Sângele mue*, my precious mate," Derven whispered in my ear as he pressed a kiss to my temple. "Strength is not shying away from the feelings you have or the things that scare you. It's facing them head-on and accepting that there are times when weakness and vulnerability are powerful in their own way. Don't let his words change anything you believe about yourself."

We stood there together until I'd calmed down and returned to the room just in time for the food to arrive. We sat down and enjoyed our meal, deciding to talk about our lives instead of delving deeper into my past. The guys were amazing, carrying the conversation as I lost myself in the best fettuccine alfredo I'd ever had.

"So you are working on an emergency medical response unit specifically for supernaturals. That's rather a massive undertaking," Eli commented as Lane explained their company.

"I realize that, but I believe training normal EMTs and having our own unit to respond will keep what happened to me from happening to others. Colt didn't mean to hurt me or change me. He was wounded and in pain. As someone whose first response is to act, I did so without taking into consideration he might not be a normal human," Lane explained. "We have a team of supernaturals who've been removed from their job in hospitals and other medical professions who we've trained for trauma response, plus having a research team to make medication more effective."

"Truly impressive, and I applaud you for doing it on top of also running the largest pack in Tennessee," Eli praised as he then turned to Derven. "Now, I have to say you were the hardest person to get any information on. Whoever you have dealing with your previous identities and information is incredibly good at their job."

"Thank you, I founded the company and keep it running to this day. Finley just hired our services as well, although she's done an impressive job of hiding away everything she already has. It helps that laws are changing to deal with the fact there are now those of us in the world who live well past a hundred years old," Derven expounded. "Tell me, how does one juggle running a music empire and the world's most feared group of assassins? While I know the Organization is whispered all around the world for its talents, it's surprising to find out it's the work of one elf."

"There are two people under me who run the day-to-day aspect of the Organization while I handle the more delicate details," he admitted.

"Like dumping those who don't pass training back into a foster home where the Dark Ring picks them up?" I said, the disgust clear in my tone.

Eli's eyes went wide at the attack, slowly setting his silverware down. "I'm sorry, Finley. I don't know what you're referring to. Those who don't meet the requirements for being an assassin are given jobs else-where in the Organization. We would never release them back out into the world when they know so much. Children are given a full education at our private school until they graduate high school. If they wish to go to college to learn a trade that will benefit the Organization, then it's paid for until they graduate. Others choose to work in other opportunities or go through an apprenticeship. I would never allow the Dark Ring to get their hands on my people."

I scoffed, shaking my head as anger burned in my stomach. "You say that but was I the one who was sent to deal with Delilah? She is one of the top social coordinators of the Dark Ring, and that mission landed me getting bit, turned into a werewolf, and considered dead to the only life I knew."

"I never *knew*," Eli snarled, slamming his fist on the table.

This had my wolves rumbling warning growls.

Eli sat back, closing his eyes as he calmed himself down before reopening them and meeting my gaze. "When that whole thing went down, I was out of the country dealing with an issue that needed to be handled in person. Upon returning, you were already gone and with your new pack. If Margaret hadn't ensured the report made it to my hands, it would have taken me far longer to investigate what happened."

"So?" I snapped, crossing my arms. "What did happen?"

"Someone from the Senate did contact us, but it's not the normal person we work with. They specifically asked for you to take the job and said they had everything set. They just needed a person to infiltrate and take the target out. Nothing was done how it normally is when we do favors for the Senate, which for the record, is fairly often. The thing is, I don't accept all of them. If I feel they are an abuse of power or there's no cause for them to be killed, I'll tell them no. They will have to deal with the dirty work on their own if they want it done. I would never have allowed you to be pulled into that mission. It was doomed from the start." Eli's eyes pleaded for me to believe him as he spoke. "The fact you survived proves just how amazingly skilled you are, Finley. Everything was planned to happen while I was gone, they knew you were my favorite, and I kept an eye on you. Of course, they assumed it was because you were our best assassin, but they didn't like how I played favorites."

"Who are these people?" Derven demanded. "If they are undermining you while you're away, then I'm sure they've done other things. Possibly like supplying the Dark Ring with supernaturals who fail out of your system?"

"No, it's not possible," Eli shot back. "I keep a close eye on what happens to everyone I bring in."

I shifted so I was facing him fully. "Then what happened to the lynx shifter named Benjamin who failed his assassin testing? He prefers to go by Ben if that helps narrow it down, probably around twenty-ish years old."

"He died," Eli answered, his brow creased. "He was sent on his graduating mission at eighteen and was killed. I remember every single name of the people we've lost."

"Really, because he's as dead as I am to the Organization. He washed up in training earlier than that and was landed in a foster home where the Dark Ring picked him up. Funny enough, he was one of the *pets* Delilah had in her home. He managed to get away but landed back in their clutches until last night when I got him out for good," I explained, my anger burning white hot in my chest.

Hand's settled on my shoulder. "*Nin mel*, you need to calm down. Magic is responding to your anger, and I'm afraid it might hurt others in the building by accident."

With Rath's touch on me, I was able to slowly take a deep breath through my nose until I couldn't take in any more air at all. Then when

I released that same breath, I focused on pulling my magic back into the well where it sprang from. Doing this made me realize just how far my magic had spread through the building without me knowing it. Thankfully, I couldn't decipher it doing anything malicious to anyone it came in contact with. Once it was back where it belonged inside me, I relaxed, letting my anger cool.

I'd been able to easily track Eli's emotions through the interaction, and he truly had no idea about Ben. It didn't make me any less upset knowing he wasn't aware of what went on in his business, but I didn't believe he was a monster either. Reaching up, I placed a hand over Rath's to keep him where he was. My emotions right now were so volatile I needed him to help ground me.

"Finley, that was all you?" Eli asked, a hint of fear in his voice. "I assumed it was a combination of you and your alphas creating that much power."

"That wasn't even half of her power," Rath informed Eli. "She controls the whole of the Great Smoky Mountains area with her power. The forest there has accepted her and her magic, absorbing it, starting the foundation our people desperately need."

Eli shot to his feet, knocking the chair to the ground as he yelled. "*No, she cannot be the new queen. There is no fucking way my child will be put in that role.*"

"That isn't up to you," Rath stated, his tone icy with rage. "Our people have decided, and they are already flocking to her. At this moment, there are four who have left other communes and joined the pack as a blended community. One of them is a warrior, and the others are craftsmen who will begin to build a new home where we will no longer need to hide from the world."

"Do you know what that means for her?" Eli spat. "Her mother was the previous queen, and they rejected her because of her *nos* being impure."

"Mom was that powerful?" I asked, not having gotten that sense from her in his memory.

"At one point, she was, but then the elders rejected her as queen, and her power began to fade. If she'd retained her magic, she might have been able to break the curse on her, but with how weak she was, there never was hope." Eli came over to me and dropped to his knees. "Finley, I know I have no right to ask this of you but don't do this. You might be chosen to be their queen, but that doesn't mean you *have* to accept it."

I looked at the man who helped to create my life but other than seeing a shadow of similarities in us, I felt no connection. He claimed to have tried to keep me safe, watching over me as I grew up, but if he didn't do that for every person in the Organization, then I wanted nothing to do with him. What I saw kneeling before me was a man who was scared. Fear was driving him in every choice. He didn't want me to be in danger or to lose my magic, but I already knew it was too late.

"No, Eli," I answered. "There is no other option but for me to accept what I am. If the elders reject me, then so be it, but that won't stop me from doing what I know must be done." Pulling up my sleeve, I showed him the mark. "The Senate and the Dark Ring will be destroyed, and it will be me leading the charge. My fate has already been sealed."

Eli tentatively reached out and took my hand, brushing a finger over the mark. "Who?"

"That doesn't matter. What's done is done," I said simply, removing my hand from his grasp. "I believe it's best for us to be getting back to our pack now. If I have any more questions, I'll reach out, but I suggest you take a good long hard look at your people. I have a feeling you've been too trusting to let others control something as powerful as the Organization. Right now, you are not the one in charge."

Rath pulled my seat back for me, and we left Eli still kneeling there on the floor, tears falling from his eyes. "No matter what you think of me, Finley, you will always be my daughter, and I will do right by you," he whispered.

I wasn't sure if he meant for me to hear that or not, but I continued like I hadn't. The chance for us to be a family had passed when he gave me to the Organization. Now I had my real family—the men who would do anything for me as I would do the same for them. While I'd learned about my past, it didn't change who I was now.

NINETEEN

FINLEY

Two weeks had gone by since our trip to New York. Life fell into a routine of working with the pack and planning our next move as Ayla and I watched the cracks begin to form in the Dark Ring. Zander's office was covered in maps, flow charts of how people were connected, and a list of names with four crossed out. It was our hub of operations and where they would find me if I weren't out working with the pack.

After dinner, while the guys were relaxing watching television, reading, or Derven's newest hobby—whittling, I slipped away to get some work done since we had a rule I wasn't allowed to work all night anymore. Nine o'clock was my cut-off, then I was locked out of the office and attached to one of my men for the rest of the evening.

A knock sounded before Zander entered, an odd look on his face, his cell phone in his hand. "It's my mother."

Slowly I stood and walked over to him, taking the offered phone and raising it to my ear. "Morwyn."

"I have her. I'm sending people I trust to pick you up and only you to deal with this matter. No matter what they say, my son is not allowed to come to this exchange. Do you understand me?" Morwyn ordered.

My brows shot up at her tone and the snark of her words. "Morwyn, I understand you perfectly well, but let me explain one thing to you. While you might be used to people falling over themselves to do your bidding, I am not that person. We are in this together, you and I. If you fuck me over, you kill us both, simple as that. I will share your request with my mate, but I guarantee it's not going to fly. There will be one or two of them who will come with me, or I'm not coming at all."

Silence echoed from the other end of the line, but I could still hear breathing, so I knew she didn't hang up. "Two, you can bring two as long as one of them is not my son. He is already beginning to hate me, and I won't give him more fuel to fan that fame."

"Now, those are terms that I can work with," I said. "Who should I be expecting to pick me up?"

"Peter and one other, a woman named Tabitha," Morwyn responded.

My blood ran cold hearing that name. "How long has Tabitha been working with you?"

"Since they betrayed her and made her sell you out to the Dark Ring," Morwyn explained. "When the end of that mission went all to hell, she fled. Somehow she found out you and I are working together and threw in her lot with me."

Nothing about this sat right in my brain, but I knew how skilled Tabitha was and if she wanted to play double agent, she sure as hell could. Who knows, maybe she could have been a double agent all this time. "How soon should I be expecting them?"

"In about an hour. If you have more questions, ask Peter." With that ending remark, she hung up the phone.

Dropping the phone from my ear, I saw she called from a number within the Senate building. Was it secure? Did anyone listen to what she'd just told me? Could everything about this be another trap? No, not with the contract we had together. It assured she couldn't act against me or change her mind about the deal we made. If that were to happen, it would kill us both, and I was still very much alive.

"What the hell was that, little dove?" Zander demanded.

Buying myself some time, I wandered out of the office and up to the second-floor living room. *"Could everyone gather for a moment? I have some news."*

"Why aren't you answering me, Finley?" Zander barked, his irritation and fear swirling in him like a vortex.

I took his hand and interlaced our fingers, squeezing it. "It's going to be fine. I just don't want to have to explain this twice when I can just do it once."

The other alphas and the twins were already in the living room watching basketball, so we just had to wait for the other three to wander in. It didn't take long as they all sat on the couch, watching me with warry expressions.

"Morwyn called to let me know she has Delilah," I announced.

This information had everyone talking over each other, trying to get a word in until I let out a shrill whistle. "Stop."

I'd been trying to respect them better and not use my magic to end the squabbles that seemed to pop up every so often as we adjusted to living together with nine people in the house. Eventually, they quieted down, and I could explain what I knew, which wasn't all that much.

"In about an hour, Peter is coming to pick me up. I'm allowed to bring two of you with me to this secret location where she has them. The one and only stipulation that she would not budge on was..." I paused to look at Zander. "You can't come."

"The fuck kind of rule is that?" he demanded. "If I want to go with you, I damn well will. Who does she think she is telling you not to *allow* me to go?"

"She's your mother, Zander, and what she wants most in the world right now is to be able to still look you in the face. Your mother is convinced you will turn against her the deeper into this mess you get, and she doesn't want to risk that," I reasoned, knowing he wasn't going to hear me, not yet. After he had some time to cool off, he would, but not right away.

Zander shoved off the couch to his feet and started to pace. "So, who are you going to take since I'm clearly not invited."

"My plan was to take Derven and Rath. They know the system the best. If she's lying to us, they will be able to tell. No one else has that kind of inside information, and Delilah is a conniving bitch who knows just how to manipulate people," I shared, trying to explain my logic the best I could so they wouldn't be upset with me.

None of them looked thrilled while Derven and Rath looked equally unsettled by the idea. "I won't force you to go if that's not what you want to do."

The two men looked at each other, then turned to me. "*Nin mel*, of course, we will go with you, but you have to understand that if she tells you anything about the men we were in their clutches... it's not the men you are mated to. There were many things we did to survive and not one I am proud of," Rath expressed, wringing his hands, refusing to look at me.

Sitting on the ottoman before him, I placed my hands on his knees. "Rath, there is *nothing* you could say to me that I won't understand. I'm an assassin. I kill people for a living. Did they deserve to die? I don't know, but I was given a file and sent on my way to do my job. What you and Derven survived, though, no one would blame you for doing what was needed. I've seen the other side of this and watched what they forced you to do for the sake of entertainment. All I care about is your health and well-being now. Don't force yourself to do this if you're not up for it." I turned to Derven, who was sitting next to Rath. "Either of you, just say the word, and I'll make a new plan."

"Give me a moment to think it over," Rath requested.

Derven gripped Rath's thigh in a reassuring gesture. "I will go with you. That way, at least you have one of us if Rath chooses not to be involved in this."

My gaze then landed on Elias. "If Rath stays, will you come?"

"Without hesitation, my heart," Elias answered. "I will be more than happy to help you do what is necessary to get the information we need."

"That settles it then, Rath will stay, and Elias will go. Unless by the time we are ready to leave, you make the choice to come, but I feel like it might be best for you to leave this to others," I suggested. "I'm going to change and gather a few things I might need."

Jogging up the stairs to my shared room with Zander and whoever else landed in the bed at night with us, I changed out of my comfortable house clothes and slipped on black jeans and a black T-shirt. It was the best color to avoid showing blood stains, and I felt like that would be a concern. Punching in the code for the safe we'd installed for my weapons, I grabbed my case of syringes and two knives.

Delilah was human, and we really wanted to get information from her, so I didn't think a gun would be needed. Besides, these weapons weren't for her. They were for Tabitha. I wasn't going anywhere with that bitch until I knew the truth. Screw me once, shame on you, screw me twice, shame on me, because there would be a third time.

I exited the room and found Rath sitting on the end of the bed, looking forlorn. Walking over to him, I climbed into his lap, straddling his legs as I wrapped my arms around his neck. "Whatever it is that has you feeling this shame, there is no need for it," I murmured.

"*Nin mel*, how I wish I could tell myself that and believe it." He sighed. "Every day, I try to remind myself I am free and will never have to live like that again now I have my family. I've never told you this before, but the nights I don't spend in your bed, I have nightmares. Flashes of the past torment me, and I don't know how to get them to stop."

Hearing the brokenness in his voice had me gripping him tighter. "I'm so sorry you have to deal with this kind of torment. It breaks my heart to know it still haunts you, and no matter what, if it becomes too much, you come find me, and you will always have a place to sleep in peace."

"There are no words for how blessed I feel to have you as my mate, Finley. I love you more than words could ever express, and I'm beyond grateful you do not see this as a weakness in me for not being able to face Delilah." Rath breathed into my neck, where he rested his head.

The sound of a vehicle pulling up caught our attention. It seemed they were closer than Morwyn assumed, or this really was a trap. I held Rath's face in my hands and kissed him deeply, letting all my love for him overwhelm his senses so he had no doubt how I felt about him. "I will be back with answers, and you will be sleeping right next to me tonight. Something tells me you won't get any rest otherwise." Another quick kiss and I was flying down the stairs to deal with a certain someone.

I didn't go to the front door. Instead, I raced out to the second-floor balcony and climbed up onto the roof that overhung the front entrance. I crouched low in the darkness, the branches of one of the trees lowering to offer me cover. Learning the perks of having a forest listen to your request was surprising and always came in the moments I didn't know I needed them. Peering over the edge of the roof, I saw Tabitha get out of the vehicle's passenger side door. Drawing a dagger out of the sheath on my low back, I pounced.

As I hit Tabitha knocking her to the ground, she reacted instantly, the problem was she was still human. I twisted out of the way as she kicked out and rolled into my tackle. The moment she paused to figure out who or what was attacking her, I was on her again. Knocking out her feet, she dropped to the ground, and I flipped her on her stomach, wrenching her arm up behind her, making her scream in pain.

"Hello, Tabitha," I whispered in her ear. "I'm going to take a quick peek inside your head for just a moment. The less you resist, the easier it is on you and me."

Replacing my knife, I placed my free hand on the side of her head and closed my eyes as my magic flooded into her. Ignoring what's happened most recently, I moved into the older memories back to when she would have left the Organization. Everything came to a screeching halt when I saw her talking to someone who looked vaguely familiar, but I couldn't place why. So I decided to listen in to what this person had to say in case that might help me place them.

"Tabitha, did you get the information I need?"

Tabitha handed over a file, and I caught a glimpse of the name on the tab. It was mine. "Tell me again why you need this information? She was found in an orphanage just like the rest of us."

The man waved her off. "You're not being paid to understand why I'm doing this. All I need from you is to make sure that you keep an eye on her. They have you doing this next mission together, right? Find out if she's as good as they say she is."

"None of this makes sense," Tabitha challenged. "You don't need her. You have me."

The man whirled on her, grabbing her by the neck, flashing his fangs. "You have no idea what I need, human. Now go do what I told you to do before I decide you'll be a better meal than my mole. That bastard Ellisor won't know what hit him when I steal the only thing he's cared more about than Tiriana. He put that goddamn baby in her arms, not me!" The vampire spluttered, spit splashing on Tabitha's face before he tossed her away. "That bastard stole everything from me. Now it's time to return the favor. He has no idea I've been manipulating the whole business right under his nose for years. I can't believe he'd think I'd let him thrive when I've become a monster."

Then it hit me—I knew exactly who this man was... James. The last of my mother's *nos* who was still living and apparently trying to ruin my father and me. This certainly made things more interesting. I moved forward in her memory, watching as James was the one who manipulated the system to send me after Delilah. It seems the Senate really did want her dealt with, but he was the one who ensured I was the one sent on the mission. It was clear Tabitha believed James was working for the Senate, but when the mission with Vicky and Blakely went down, she learned differently. Vicky was a true Senate lackey, whereas Blakely was a double agent for the Dark Ring.

Now Tabitha chose to work with Morwyn, knowing she was trying to take down the whole system. It would seem Margaret told her when Tabitha tried to come back into the fold but was turned away. I was surprised about that, but at the same time, not since she'd been MIA for so long. There was no way they could trust her.

Backing out of her mind, I got off her and reached out a hand to help her up. "You have terrible judgment," I announced.

"That's the understatement of the century," Tabitha agreed, letting me help her to her feet.

"Would someone like to tell me what the fuck is going on and why your woman just leaped off a roof to take out Tabitha?" Peter demanded, glaring at my men who'd gathered at the bottom of the steps.

Mason let out a bark of laughter. "What makes you think we know? Finley is her own person, and if that's the Tabitha I think it is, she had her reasons."

Peter turned his angry gaze at me. "Care to enlighten the rest of us?"

"Not particularly," I answered with a shrug. Peter's jaw dropped at my response, clearly not used to someone disregarding his orders. "There is no reason for you to know what's going on since it doesn't pertain to Morwyn. Even if I told you, none of it would make sense, and I don't have time to explain it all to you. Now, is there anything else before we get going?"

This seemed to bring Peter back to the situation at hand. "No, who-ever's going who isn't Zander, get in the fucking car."

I could see how hard Zander was trying not to explode at this, but he kept silent as I kissed each of them before getting into the SUV. Zander made sure I was buckled and gave me one more kiss before shutting the door. He stood there watching as the vehicle drove away, furious at his mother and Peter for doing this to him.

In an effort to distract him, I sent all of them an image of James from the memory I saw in Tabitha's mind. *"Seems my other father has been keeping tabs on me as well and ended up becoming a vampire of all things."*

"Finley, I've met this man before," Elias informed me. *"The night the attack happened, he came looking for you. He kept demanding that we hand you over, but I believe at that point, you'd already fled the tunnels. Why would he be looking for you?"*

"I don't have all the information on that yet, but Tabitha was working with him. She believed he was part of the Senate but later learned he wasn't. I'm hoping to ask her more about it later when we don't have Peter around," I explained.

"Please be careful," Zander pleaded. *"I trust my mother, but I don't trust Peter. Maybe it's because he's always tried to be a father to me, but I just never felt he was safe."*

"Don't worry, we will keep our woman safe," Elias assured the others. *"This whole thing reeks of a trap, but we need the information that Delilah will give us too badly not to chance it."*

Elias was right. The plan I had worked for only so long until they learned what I was doing. The closer I got to the top of the pyramid, the more they would close ranks, making it harder for me to get to them. These people had all the money and power in the world to hide and hide well. I could get one or two more attacks in before they started to be concerned and figured out they were being attacked strategically. Right now, it was so random, and the people weren't that valued. It was slipping through the cracks.

To bring down the Dark Ring, I would need to hit hard and fast when the time was right. The information to do that lay with Delilah. Part of me was looking forward to this, knowing that I would keep my promise and end her, but I'd get some retribution as well.

The drive took about a half hour, and we ended up in an abandoned barn on the property, well off the beaten path. No one would find us here unless they knew just where to look. Even the screams I'm sure Delilah would be letting out wouldn't be heard by anything but the trees. Thankfully, their loyalty was to me, so I wasn't worried at all. Two men dressed all in black tactical gear stood outside the barn doors giving me pause.

"What's with the mercenaries?" I asked as Peter brought the car to a stop.

He looked at me in the rearview. "You didn't think we were just going to leave her here with that gorilla alone, did you? The senator has her own personal security we've built up over time for situations like this. They can be trusted to keep their mouths shut, or I'll kill them."

"That'll do it," Derven quipped. "Nothing like the fear of death to keep you in line. Works every time I've done it, but it becomes a gray area when it's applied to other vampires... seeing as we're already dead and all."

Peter turned in his chair to look at Derven, then me. "When did you add the bloodsucker to your group of fuck boys?"

Elias snarled, and Derven hissed at the implications. I sent them each a subtle warning to calm down and responded to Peter's venom, "Why?" I questioned, cocking my head. "Are you afraid Morwyn might like the idea of having more than one man in her life?"

Peter's face started to turn red as he fought to keep his anger from exploding on me. I wasn't concerned. Peter might be head of security, but I could tell he was a lazy fighter used to having people to order about.

"I'd be careful, bitch. Omega or not, I'll teach you your place in the pack," he bit out.

I shoved open my door and stepped out only to glance back at him. "If you can get past them, I'd love to see you try and lay a finger on me. Out of respect for Morwyn, I'd try not to hurt you too badly, but it seems you have no respect for those who are deadlier than you. That might cause your life expectancy to shrink considerably one of these days."

Derven and Elias flanked me as I strode across the grass to the barn, Tabitha leading the way. She'd remained silent the whole time, and I couldn't tell if she was upset with me or not. Even when I tried to feel her emotions, she'd buried them so deeply, I couldn't get any sense of them. Was this what it was like for Rath when we first bonded? No wonder he was so upset.

The two guards looked at the three of us with curiosity but didn't say a word as Tabitha brushed past them and entered the barn. There, under two gas-powered flood lights, Delilah and her pet gorilla were expertly tied to chairs, looking worse for the wear. Delilah looked up at our entrance and met my gaze with wide, shocked eyes.

"Hello there, long time no see," I greeted.

TWENTY

ELIAS

The woman Finley greeted so warmly paled as recognition hit her. While my mate had never gone into detail about what happened at this woman's party, I knew the reputation she had. While I understood why she wanted both Rath and Derven to be at this meeting, I knew I was the better option. I wasn't sure what kind of stomach the elf had. The vampire I wasn't worried about. You don't live to be a thousand years old without spilling blood. When it came down to the dirty part of this job, I knew he'd be able to handle it.

The hulking giant of a man in the other chair had to be the gorilla, and I wanted to pummel the shit out of him. He attacked Finley, and that was never going to stand. Even though he was going to die at the end of this, he still needed to pay for that infraction before I ripped his heart out in front of the woman he loved in his own sick and twisted way.

"You," Delilah spat. "You're the reason I got kidnapped and dragged all the way out to a fucking barn? Do you know who I am? Who my family is? We will have your head for this, you *bitch*."

I darted forward, grabbing her throat, and snarled. "You will *not* speak to her like that, you cunt. I'd take a good look at where you are and who's really in charge right now because it isn't *you*."

"Get your hands off me, you mutant mutt," Delilah screeched, trying to yank herself out of my grasp.

I leaned in and whispered in her ear. "Is that what you say to your gorilla when he fucks you up the ass? I'm sure you just love it when he uses you like the dirty whore you are."

Delilah's response to this was to start screaming her head off, making my ears ring, but it did little else. A hand settled on my back, and I knew it was Finley. I'd know her touch anywhere. I released the bitch and wrapped an arm around Finley's waist, drawing her to my side, feeling the need to shield her back.

"Would you like to know why you are here?" Finley asked once the screaming stopped.

"You're going to kill me, aren't you, just like you did everyone else at that party. So just get it over with already," Delilah responded, her eyes going wild as she spat at Finley.

Before the spit could leave her mouth, Derven appeared and slammed his hand over her mouth so hard the chair teetered, almost falling back before he stopped it.

"That is absolutely no way for a young lady of your status to act. Spitting on people, your parents would be ashamed." Adding insult to injury, he wiped his hand off all over her face before getting the last of it off on her pants.

Delilah gasped, looking at him. "I know you!"

"Yes, I suppose you would, which is why you're here," he commented, pulling a bottle of hand sanitizer out of her purse that was sitting by the chair. "We need some information, and you're going to give it to us."

"Why would I do that? I'm not going to get out of this alive if *she's* here," Delilah shot back, gesturing with her chin at me. "I know what you are, *assassin*. They know you're coming for them, and they're just waiting for you to make your move."

Clearly, they had no idea what Finley had already made a move weeks ago. I wasn't sure if that was a good or bad thing they hadn't noticed. My gaze drifted over to the gorilla, whose mouth was taped shut and was bound with silver chains. We'd need Tabitha to deal with those since none of us could touch them. His eyes bore into mine with the desire to murder my mate loud and clear in that look.

"That's good, Delilah, so then you also know it's futile to try and hold anything back from me," Finley commented as she pulled a slim zippered case out of her back pocket. "This is going to help you feel more comfortable as I ask you questions."

Delilah's eyes went wide with terror. "No, no, not that, please don't do that. I'll talk, please, no drugs. They always use drugs on me."

Finley paused and cocked her head slightly. "Who uses drugs on you?"

"My parents... they... they drugged me and let those filthy bastards use me until I was too old for their liking. One of them decided he wasn't going to let me go and inducted me to the Dark Ring early, telling me that I would one day rule all of it if I listened to him. Now here I am strapped to a chair going to die by the hands of an animal that we hunt for sport," Delilah raged.

Squatting down so she was more eye level with Delilah, she rested a hand on her leg. "Who?"

"Gareth Vaughan," she spat.

"The senator's mate?" I blurted, completely shocked by this turn of events.

Tears filled Delilah's eyes. "I didn't know he was a werewolf until he threatened to bite me when I turned seventeen. He wanted to keep me because his frigid bitch of a wife was just a sham who had her own side piece."

None of this made sense. Why the fuck would Morwyn's husband be working with the Dark Ring? He already had power over the Senate since Morwyn, as we discovered, was a figurehead for them. What was the purpose of having created the Dark Ring as well?

"Why are you lying to me?" Finley questioned. "That story is true, but it isn't about Gareth. Who was it really?"

Delilah dropped the crying act and turned to stone. "I don't know what you're talking about. You asked, and I gave you the answer."

"No, you didn't, not completely. There is something you are leaving out, and that is the most important part that I need to know," Finley challenged. "Tell me who it is that took you under their wing?"

"You won't get to him," she taunted. "I know why you want to know, but you won't be able to take him down. He's far too guarded, and there are hundreds of people who will die for him."

Finley took a deep breath and started to open the case once more and draw out a syringe. "If you won't tell me what I want to know, then I'll make you."

The threat was clear by the icy tone in Finley's voice. She'd once more shut herself off, allowing her assassin persona to take over. It was an odd feeling, being cut off from her in this way now that we'd been soul bonded.

"Do what you have to do," Delilah taunted. "If the waterworks didn't make your frigid heart question your motives, then what's the point in keeping up the act?"

That had been an act? Damn, this woman was more twisted than I expected. Clearly, whatever happened to her fucked her in the head royally. Finley ensured the syringe was ready to use as Derven secured Delilah's head to the side, making it easier to hit the vein. With quick assured movements, Finley administered the drug and stepped back.

"Let's have a chat with our friend while we let that take effect," Finley commented as she walked over and ripped the tape off his mouth. "We meet again, but this time you're the one tied to a chair instead of me. Oh, how the tables do turn."

"I have nothing to say to you," Bakos said with a growl.

Finley nodded her head right before slamming her fist into his face. "That's good because I don't want any information from you. The only reason you were brought here alive is because I wanted to kill you myself."

Having never seen Finley in action as an assassin, it was shocking to see her so brutal. Avoiding the silver, Finley landed another few shots to his face, chest, and groin, making the bastard groan in pain.

"I know how you treated those around you who did fall in line. Always the biggest and the strongest, right? Well, not tonight," Finley snarled, her nails turning into claws as she sliced across his face. "How many of our kind did you serve to your masters on a silver platter? You betray all of us, loving a real monster in sheep's clothing. Is she that good of a lay that you'll fuck her any way she wants you to? Has she ever put *you* up on one of those stages to be fucked and bled like a living juice box for a vampire?"

The whole warehouse started to pulse with her anger as her magic rose, responding to her emotions. Rath wasn't here to stop her, so I prayed we could manage whatever happened without him here.

"Like you're any better than me?" Bakos roared. "You kill humans and supers alike for the money. Now all of a sudden, you've grown a conscience? Don't make me laugh. You're a stone-cold bitch who could kill anyone without batting an eye."

"If you believe that, then what's left for you?" she countered. "Why fight? Isn't it better to know you've lost and take it like a man?"

He bared his teeth at her trying to lunge forward, but the chains stopped him. "You know *nothing*."

Finley took a step back and waved her hand at him dismissively. The scratches she gave him healed, and he almost seemed to shrink in size, losing the bulk of his muscle. "I know they turned you into what you were, and now, I've *undone* it. How does it feel to be human again?"

The look of horror on his face was enough to tell me that Finley had taken everything from him. "No, that can't happen. There's no way you would be able to do that to me. I was finally what she wanted. Now I'm nothing."

He was talking about Delilah. She wouldn't want just a normal human following her around. A batshit crazy woman like her would need to have something that made people fear her. Being turned into a gorilla shifter meant he was her brute power. If my mate had really made him human again... that was a fate worse than death.

"You tell me," Finley countered. "Do the chains hurt? Does the metal burn, or is it just something that is holding you down?"

"*No*," Bakos bellowed, thrashing about in his chair until he toppled to the ground, face in the dirt.

I made a move to at least flip him over so he wasn't choking, but Finley stopped me. "Leave the worthless human where he lies."

Doing as she said, I left him, but I hoped she had a plan because I wasn't so sure about this side of Finley. I'd been prepared to be the evil one in this situation, not her. Clearly, I hadn't been paying attention when she said working for the Organization stripped everything from her.

"Stop, please don't hurt him. I'll tell you whatever you want to know," Delilah begged, tears streaming down her face. "He was forced onto this, they ruined him forever, but I still loved him anyway."

This time I could tell the crying was real—the snot dripping from her nose, the tears gushing out of her eyes, and the heaving breaths. It was an ugly cry, one you could only do if you were absolutely devastated about something. It seemed that Finley had known this would be a trigger for Delilah all along.

"You want me to help him? Then tell me what I want to know," Finley demanded. "He's once more fully human, not a speck of supernatural to him. Bakos can once again be the perfect man you loved before they, as you said, ruined him."

"What do you want to know?" She sobbed. "I'll tell you, please just don't let him die. He doesn't deserve it."

That was debatable but clearly, whatever Finley had given her worked. Now let's see what the witch had to tell us.

TWENTY-ONE

FINLEY

"Tell me the best time and place to be if I want to take out everyone important to the Dark Ring. I want to shatter the whole thing into a billion pieces so they can never recover from it," I said, staring down at the sobbing woman.

The drug I gave her appeared to be having a stronger effect than normal. I was getting the response I wanted, but it seemed a little more extreme of a response. Delilah was an impressive actor. I'd almost believed her the first time around. The thing was, that story was true, and it had happened to someone. I'm just not sure it was her. You could fool a polygraph by telling the truth, but it might not be *your* truth. Whatever you said well and truly happened but maybe not to you. It was clever and whoever taught her did it well.

This reaction to Bakos, however, was true, the most authentic I'd seen her act this whole time. Delilah absolutely loved that man in her own way, and me torturing him had brought the effects of the drug out tenfold. Now to see if she would actually tell me what I wanted to know or if the lies continued. The side effect of this drug was it made everything feel ten times more. Pain was far worse than it would normally be, so a paper cut feels like I just stabbed you. The downside, the drug only lasted a half hour. If I didn't get what I needed by then, I didn't have another dose. The Organization had given it to me. I just squirreled it away if I didn't use it for a rainy day like today.

"The Coexist Gala, it's the biggest event the Dark Ring and the Senate attend together, even if they don't realize it. There used to be a separation of the two units, but as the years have gone on, both are so blended now it might as well be one. That night, they party into the night, celebrating the fact that humans and supernaturals alike live together in harmony, thanks to the United Senate. Bunch of bullshit if you ask me, they are the ones who are destroying the world. Polluting our bloodlines with their monsters... soon there won't be any humans left. They'll all become like *you*," Delilah spewed her rage.

I glanced over at Derven, who seemed irritated. "Have you ever gone to the gala?"

"No, it was one even for only the important people to attend. No slaves, servants, pets, or bedwarmers were allowed. If your name wasn't on the list, you weren't getting in no matter who you are," he explained. "If you want to go to that gala, you have to be the right kind of people, and none of us are. I'm not sure even Delilah would be able to go."

She gave him a wide smile. "Oh, I can go. You said you knew who my family was. Well, my grandfather likes to take me along with him, so he's not alone at these events. I might not warm his bed any longer... that honor has gone to my sister, but he still has a special place for me at his side."

So the story was hers but also her sisters. Did that mean her grandfather was the founder of the Dark Ring?

"Your grandfather is an important person, but he's getting old. He must worry that someone will come in to usurp him," I commented.

Delilah shook her head dramatically. "Nope," she said, popping the P. "He has a person already lined up to do it, and I'm supposed to marry the bastard, so we keep family alliances and all. He's so much older than me, though, and I hate him."

"Tell me who he is, and I'll get rid of him," I offered, hoping this would get her to spill her guts.

She gave me a funny look as if she was surprised. "You don't know, do you? I thought you just wanted confirmation, but you really have no idea."

"Then this should be a crowning moment for you that you get to tell me something that will apparently rock my world," I taunted as I started to circle her chair. "The great Delilah has knowledge I want, and by your tone, it's something that will hurt me to learn. What's keeping you silent? Go for the shot, take me down a peg, and make it good." I paused before her as I said this last part, cocking a brow at her.

"That's the thing, though. I don't think it will hurt not if you don't know the truth," Delilah explained. "The person you are looking for is closer to you than you think. He's been a shadow in your life lurking, waiting for the right moment to pounce, but somehow you keep slipping through his fingers. It's almost as if fate knows you're supposed to ruin us just like you want to."

Elias growled, losing his patience, and backhanded her across the face. He, of course, had no idea that would hurt a million times more than it should as she screamed bloody murder. It worked in my favor, though, as I pulled him back.

"Answer me, Delilah, or I'll let him do more than backhand you. This drug makes everything worse. Better yet, why don't I do the same thing to Bakos and torture him since you don't care about him as much as you say. You won't do the one thing that can save him, so what happens next is your fault," I warned.

"*James,*" she screamed. "His name is James. He's your father."

I froze, not expecting that answer at all. "What?"

"See, you don't even know who he is or the danger you've been in," she carried on. "He blames you for killing your mother and joined the Dark Ring for the sole purpose of using it to torment you for the rest of your ridiculously long life as an elf."

"He's a vampire. How could he possibly take over the Dark Ring? Their whole purpose is to prove that humans are still higher on the food chain then. Why the hell would your grandfather let him take over or marry you?" Derven argued.

Delilah looked over at him. "So you do know who he is." She nodded her head a moment, lost in thought, before answering. "Vampires have amazing powers to manipulate people's minds. Add to it that he was also a witch before he was changed, making him even more dangerous. My grandfather is old and losing his mind, but he was fine before *he* showed up. Back then, he was just a witch, and many people feel that witches are human because they have to cast spells to use magic. They don't have it living inside them like you elves do.

"There was an accident at one of the parties, and during a hunt, a vampire who lost their mind to hunger drank James dry, but the bastard had a spell on him to keep him alive. Just didn't realize that mixing it with vampire venom in his blood changed him into one. Technically he is still *alive.* As for the marriage thing, that was a contract made before he turned fangy, and there's no way out of it unless one of us dies," she finished with a shrug. "Looks like both of us are gonna die anyway."

An incredibly small part of me felt bad for Delilah. It seemed like she didn't have a chance to grow up as anything but this cruel, heartless woman. She had so much going wrong in her life and had only been surrounded by people who wanted to destroy each other. Maybe killing her would finally set her free. She wouldn't have to be in pain anymore.

"I told you if you gave me the information I wanted to know, I'd do something about it. I'll tell you so you know this whole thing is going to crash, burn, and be ground into the dirt under my heel." I shared squatting to look her in the eyes. "The Dark Ring and the Senate will end by my hand, same with the bastard who claimed to once love my mother because he's damn well no father of mine. I'll even send the man you really love along with you, so maybe you'll be able to find each other in the afterlife."

Delilah's eyes welled up with tears. "Thank you, I've been too much of a little bitch to do it myself, and Bakos would never allow me to leave him behind."

Shoving to my feet, I stepped behind her and pulled out another syringe with fast-acting poison. I wouldn't need the whole thing to kill her, so I could use the rest on him. They'd even share the same needle in their death. How romantic is that? Holding her head gently, I acted as quickly as I could to ensure it wasn't cruel. I might not want either of them to live, but I wasn't going to stoop to their level either. Done with her, I moved over to Basko and kneeled beside him.

He lay there, tears leaking out of his eyes, turning the dirt to mud. "Is she dead?"

"Yes, but you will be right behind her," I answered as I pressed the plunger the rest of the way.

Staying there a moment, I waited for his last breath, needing to ensure this bastard was well and truly dead, not coming for me anymore. Task completed, I put the syringe back in the holder to be disposed of later where it wouldn't ever be tied back to me or anyone else.

"*Sângele meu*," Derven said, offering me a hand and pulling me to my feet.

He searched my face, probably assuming I would be flustered by the turn of events we had just learned, but I felt nothing. Not anger, sadness, betrayal, or even satisfaction that we got the information we needed. I was numb, and I wished to stay that way for a while. I'd let myself process what happened but for now, being hollow was better. Besides, I had a phone call to make, and it wasn't going to be a pleasant conversation.

Without a word to anyone, I got back into the SUV and pulled out my cell phone. I typed in the number I had memorized and listened to it ring twice.

"Daughter?" Eli answered. "I didn't ever expect to hear from you again."

"Can you get me into the Coexist Gala?" I asked.

There was a pause on the other end. "Why would you need to go to that?"

"That wasn't the question," I countered. "It's a simple yes or no."

Something akin to a growl came from Eli. "That's not how this is going to work. You can't just call and demand things from me. While I might not have raised you, I am still your father, and I will be treated with respect."

I scoffed, shaking my head. "No matter who you are, respect is earned."

"Then my answer is no, and I'm going to hang up if you don't give me a reason to say yes," he threatened.

"Ah, now there is the man I would believe runs the Organization. Did you look into your underlings yet? They are the ones who have been working for James funneling information through unsuspecting operatives like Tabitha. Your fellow brother has been working to take you down and me along with you since Mother died," I shared. "Interesting fact is that he has been incredibly close to pulling it off a few times, but it seems fate has other ideas."

"There is no possible way you can know all that for a fact," Eli snapped.

"Can't I? You're the one who trained me, the best of the best, right? Who's to say what I can and can't do now that I'm at full power," I challenged. "Trust me when I say I got it from some incredibly reliable sources, direct from the mind, if you will."

This shut him up quickly, no longer willing to argue that I didn't have the right information. The mind might play tricks on you, but I don't think it was that good to fool me watching memories.

"If you are willing to come out and publicly declare you are my daughter, then I can get you into the gala," Eli answered. "Of course, also making your declaration publicly that you are the elven queen will also do it but might be less risky to admit you're related to me."

"What if I do both?" I asked. "If I make myself public enough, then it will be far more difficult for them to come after me."

"If you choose to bring down that world of hurt on yourself, then so be it. Making that announcement will bring the Elders to your doorstep far quicker. Do you really want to risk losing your magic before this fight?" Eli demanded.

"That isn't for you to worry about. I'll handle whatever comes my way. I might look like my mother, but we are not the same person. I won't let anyone take from me what is mine," I announced just as the others joined me in the car.

They must have sensed I needed some time to myself and held Peter and Tabitha off. For that, I will be forever grateful. While I would have had the conversation with them in the car, I was glad they didn't need to witness my argument with the man who demanded to be claimed as my father.

"Set it up so I can go with you to the gala. I'm sure Zander can do the same with his connection to his mother. Am I allowed to bring a plus one or seven?" I asked.

There was a heavy sigh on the other end of the line. "They allow you to bring your partner, but since you will be accompanying me, that doesn't apply. If you somehow get an invite, then I'm sure you could make them accommodate your men."

"Then it seems I have a press release to work on, now doesn't it," I shared before hanging up.

"Fun having parents, isn't it?" Derven commenced, giving me a cheeky smile. "Now you get to join the shitty dad's club."

Slipping my arm around his, I took his hand in mine, taking the strength from him he was trying to give. Then I turned my attention to Tabitha. "I need you to tell me everything you know about James."

"That's going to take longer than a thirty-minute drive," she informed me.

Figured this couldn't be easy.

"Fair point, then start with how you met him and got you to play both sides?" I inquired, giving a little more direction.

She shifted slightly in her seat, and for Tabitha, that was a big sign that whatever she had to say wasn't going to be what I expected. "He's my dad... I'm two years younger than you. He got my mother pregnant but only because he wanted a weapon. He paid her to carry his child, then gave up all rights to me so he could put me in the foster system for the Organization to take me. Everything was planned before either of us knew he existed. James didn't tell me who he was until after everything went wrong on the Sutton job, and I walked away."

Out of all the things she could have said, that hadn't been it. "Did you know him growing up? Is that how you trusted him so easily when they trained that out of us so early?"

"He worked with Judge Slesinger, Delilah's grandfather, so when he told me he worked with the Senate, I believed him. Then his requests got more and more odd and focused on things the Senate would never need or want. He'd ask to look at case files he shouldn't have known I had, but I assumed the Senate was who asked for the job to be done. Everything started to get worse when he zeroed in on you after we worked that mission together. Something caught his attention, and he was desperate to find out more about you," Tabitha said, twisting in her seat to look at me.

"I never would have left the Organization, but he told me they thought I was a mole and the Senate was going to protect me, so I had to go dark. When I came to find you that night with Vicky and Blakely, my orders were given to me from another source inside the Senate. We were still listening to your coms when Blakely attacked you, so we both heard his threat about the Senate and the Dark Ring. We knew you would go to ground, hiding out, and needed to figure out what the hell was going on. The first person I went to was Senator Morwyn because word was she wanted out. That was the kind of person I needed, so now we help each other so we can both get out of this alive," Tabitha finished.

Elias leaned his head back and groaned. "We are so fucked, aren't we? Everything is so intertwined there's no way we can unravel it all at once. It's going to take years to clean all this mess up, isn't it?"

Leaning into him, I rested my head on his shoulder. "Then we cut off the head of the snake to stop the thing from growing. It makes it easier to chop up the rest of it when you're not worried about getting bitten."

"Why does that make perfect sense?" he asked, pressing a kiss to my head. "It's like you just know how to handle this already, and we're still playing catch up."

Tabitha let out a huff of laughter. "Welcome to what the rest of us had to live up to. She held the gold standard of what each assassin should be like. Growing up, we hated her, but she was so good, all we wanted was to be close to her. Not that they ever encouraged making friends."

"Interestingly enough, I never saw it that way myself," I mused. "Each time someone tried to get close, I assumed it was a test and refused to engage. That being said, I did count you as a friend, Tabitha. We functioned the same, and when we worked together, it was like we could read each other's minds."

"Then taking down the Dark Ring and the Senate should be a piece of cake," she said with a grin. "I'll be on the senator's security team at the gala."

"Doesn't that work out well?" I laughed under my breath. "Anyone have the best idea for me to announce to the world that elves are still alive, and I'm their queen? Seems to be the fastest way for me to get a ticket to the party."

Peter slammed on the brakes, nearly sending me through the car's windshield, but Derven had a hold on me, yanking me to his lap. "Didn't anyone tell you when you ride in the death seat, you really should wear your seat belt?"

The driver's side door shoved open, and Peter got out of the car and yanked open Derven's, trying to grab for me. Before he could even get close enough, Derven was out of the car with me on his hip like you would carry a child and his other hand around Peter's throat. "I would seriously advise against touching my mate if you wish to live. Now, if you're willing to explain yourself, I'll set you down, but if not, I'll just let your own body weight choke you out."

"Ven," I said, trying to calm the situation, seeing the flash of red in his eyes. "How do you expect him to answer if he can't speak?"

"He can tap my hand three times if he promises to be a good doggie," Derven said in a dramatic baby-talk voice.

Peter wisely did as instructed and was dropped to the ground in a heap. He grasped his throat as he coughed, trying to get his breath back. "Fucking crazy blood-sucking monster. You're cut from the same cloth as your father, aren't you?"

"Oh, I'm sorry, have you had the pleasure of meeting my father? I thought you didn't know who I was?" Derven questioned, setting me down as he loomed over the werewolf.

"When I heard her say your name, I did some research, figured out who you were. It was easy since you've been in the Dark Ring system for so long," Peter snarked.

Derven made a move to attack Peter, but I stopped him, grabbing hold of his arm. "Would you like to share why we are on the side of the road with you having a meltdown?"

"Are you really an elf?" Peter demanded.

I looked at him, perplexed. "Morwyn didn't tell you? It's the whole reason I have so many mates. I assumed she told you everything."

"Not that she didn't, probably because I'd ask if you can fix her," Peter said, getting to his feet. "When that bastard who calls himself her mate had her miscarry, he also ensured it couldn't happen again. If you're really an elf, you could heal her, make her whole, so she can someday have our baby once this is all over."

There was nothing more I wanted than to say I could, but I wasn't sure. I didn't want to promise him something I wasn't sure I could do. "I'd have to see. It depends on what they did to her. If she'll let me look her over, I'll do what I can. Now can we please get out of the road?"

"Right, time to get you home so we can settle things here and get back to Washington D.C.," Peter agreed and trudged back to the car.

Derven and I exchanged a look of confusion and climbed into our seats. This time, I made sure to put on my seat belt.

TWENTY-TWO

FINLEY

All my men stared at me in shocked silence as I told them what I had learned from Delilah and Tabitha. The moment we got back to the house, they demanded to know everything that happened, but I made them wait for me to take a quick shower. It was a ritual I needed to cleanse myself from the mission I'd been on and bring me back to dealing with normal life.

"You want to tell the whole world that elves are real and you're their queen?" Zander questioned. "I'm just asking because I wasn't sure if I'd lost my mind and ended up in some alternate reality where my mate wanted to bring down the wrath of all her enemies all in one fell swoop."

I shouldn't be shocked at his response. It did seem like a horrible idea at face value. "Does that change anything? The way I look at it, they have been after me since I was born. James even ensured he had a child he could use to infiltrate the Organization. They know where I am. They've attacked the pack, and Peggy gave them all our secrets. Safety is an illusion they are choosing to let me believe in right now. What I want to do is call them out and force them to act before they are ready."

Zander just groaned and put his head in his hands in response. Lane looked thoughtful while Colt looked pissed, and the twins seemed to be still absorbing everything I'd said. Rath was pacing behind the couch, chewing on his thumbnail, more agitated than I'd ever seen him. Derven watched his friend with a concerned expression but let him be, telling me I should leave him alone for now as well.

"Have you been to this gala before?" I asked Zander.

He shook his head. "No, but I tried to avoid all those things like the plague. It was all about making friends in the right places to get you what you wanted. There was nothing I needed or was willing to offer to make anything happen. Mother needed to be there, and Father ate that shit up like candy. He loved being able to barter his soul away to get the power he wanted."

"Look, I know this isn't what you guys signed up for, so if you don't want to do this with me, I'm more than capable of doing this on my own," I offered, knowing what I was planning put all of them in a gray area most people weren't comfortable with. "I'm the trained assassin who's already got more blood on her hands than anyone should. You don't have to join me in this just because we are mates. If you want to keep clear of the fallout, I get it and won't hold it against you."

Lane got to his feet, took my hands in his, and kissed them. "These hands hold the future of our world as we know it, and I'm honored to be at your side, making the world a better place for all of us. That might sound cheesy, but it's the God's honest truth, Finley. Tell us what you need, and we will do everything we can to help and keep you safe. We are a team as well as a family. We won't abandon you just because we might get a little dirty."

A tear rolled down my cheek at his words. I know I said I wouldn't be upset but to know they would stand behind me was more powerful than anything else they could have done or said. These men loved me and believed in the future we could build together if we managed to pull this mission off.

"Okay, then let's make this happen," I said, my voice cracking a little as I spoke. Looking past Lane to meet Zander's gaze, I took a deep breath and made my first request. "Any chance you can call your reporter connections and get us a press conference?"

"Yeah, little dove, I can make that happen," he answered. "How soon do you want to set it up?"

"I'm thinking the sooner, the better, but let's shoot for two days from now so I have time to talk to the pack and the elves under my protection. I don't want anyone caught off guard about this," I reasoned.

The twins got up from the couch and pulled me from Lane to make me the center of a twin hug. They wrapped me up so tightly I wasn't sure I could breathe, but it was comforting to have their reassurance. "We will win this fight, snuggles," Mason stated. "We have an army of vampires, magical elves, and werewolves who have more than enough hatred of the Senate to take a stand if they need to."

"There will be more elves," Rath interjected. "The elders will come and so will more of our people. Soon we will have a whole new city of elves teaming in these woods. Our people have been waiting for someone to pull them out of the shadows, but those in power feared what might happen. Anytime we were discovered, they kidnapped, tortured, or enslaved us, causing them to fear life outside the safety of our communes. All that will change now."

Colt ran his hands through his hair as if he were struggling with something. I tapped on Noah's arm to let me free, and he instantly stepped back. When I kneeled in front of Colt, I could feel his fear and sadness. "Talk to me," I whispered.

"Why does it have to be you?" he asked. "It's almost like this whole thing has been set in motion since the beginning, and I just can't wrap my head around it. I lost one of the most important people in my life, but at the same time, he gave me you, who's become my whole world." Dropping his hands, he pulled me up onto his lap, wrapping me in a tight hug as he nuzzled his face in my neck. "Why do I have to keep watching those I love get put into dangerous situations? I know you're not Cory, and you are strong, trained, and brilliant, but that doesn't stop me from imagining the worst outcome."

"Anytime we love someone, we give them the power to hurt us, but we also have the ability to heal as well," I shared, combing my fingers through his hair. "All of you saved my life when I didn't know I was dying inside. This might not help make you feel any better about this, but I know this is what I was meant to do. The reason I was born and put on this earth was to come to this point and overturn everything so we could start again."

"I know," he agreed. "You say that, and I know in my mind it's the truth, but it doesn't stop my heart from fearing it might break. Because if I lose you, there won't be any of me left."

"Then I suppose it's a good thing we are soul bonded, and no matter what, we won't have to live a life without each other," I said, pressing a kiss to his neck. "If anything happened to any one of you, it would shatter me beyond repair. Nothing else would matter, so in a way, I hope what they say about soul bonds are true. Let's just take this one day at a time, hmm? Make the most of each moment."

Colt's response to that was to start purring and slide a hand behind my hair, letting his thumb rub across his mate mark on the side of my neck, making me gasp. "I think that sounds like a brilliant idea," he murmured. "We've been so busy we haven't been tending to our omega the way we should. I believe it only makes sense to take advantage of the here and now, don't you?"

"You never know what the next day might hold," Elias agreed, coming up behind me, slipping his hands under my shirt. "I also know for a fact you didn't bother to put on a bra or panties after your shower. Such a little tease."

I arched into his touch as his hands slid up my ribs, bunching the shirt up as he went. Colt dropped his arms, giving Elias the space to yank the shirt off me in one swift movement. The second my chest was bare to Colt, he descended upon my breasts with his mouth and hands, continuing to purr, sending vibrations throughout my body, adding to his touch. My head fell back as I let out a soft whimper of pleasure.

"Louder," Elias encouraged, grabbing my hair and making me look at him as he spoke. "We all want to hear how good he's making you feel. There's no need to keep it quiet here in our home."

As if they had planned this moment beforehand, Colt bit down on my nipple, making me scream as my sleep shorts were flooded with my slick. Elias captured my mouth, tongue fucking it as Colt slipped his hand not supporting me into my shorts, circling my clit. I let them own my body, relaxing as they laid me out on the large, padded ottoman. Colt tugged off my shorts, then cupped my ass, dragging me to the edge so he could get between my legs easier as he devoured my pussy.

"You taste so good, little one, spicy and sweet. I could stay here all day," he shared, licking his lips dramatically.

Noah walked over, undoing his sleep pants, kicking them off before he kneeled by my hand. Then, taking my hand, he wrapped it around his cock.

"Don't forget about me," Mason teased as he did the same thing with my other hand. "Twins get jealous if you don't pay attention to us both."

"Alphas feel the same way, too," Zander informed me as he cupped my chin and had me lean my head all the way back so I could take his dick in my mouth easier.

There I was in the middle of the night, after having tortured and killed two people, getting gangbanged. Could my life be any more perfect?

"That's a good girl," Zander encouraged. "Let's see just how little of a gag reflex you really have."

With that as my only warning, Zander used my mouth as his personal fuck toy. While I didn't gag, getting railed down the throat still made my eyes water as he shoved it all the way until his balls hit my forehead. I'd swallow a few times, making him snarl at the sensation before pulling out and letting me breathe. It was hard to remember to keep stroking the twins, but they weren't bothered as they would thrust into my fist to remind me.

"I want her ass," Derven announced. "Let me slide under there out of the way, and you can continue on as you were."

Zander and the twins backed off, letting Derven pick me up and set me on his lap. He made sure to drag his cock through my slick before sliding into my ass.

"Oh, fuck me, that feels so good," I whimpered.

Derven nipped at my ear. "That is exactly what I plan on doing, *sângele meu*, and I won't even make you beg for it. You want to know what I will make you beg for?"

"What?" I croaked as Colt started to push inside my pussy.

Derven let his teeth scrape gently down the column of my neck. "My bite."

My breathing was now coming in heavy pants as I was filled in both holes, with Derven teasing my neck. God, I wanted his bite so fucking bad. He'd fed from me two days ago, but we didn't get to enjoy it how we wanted to, feeding from my wrist as he quickly finger fucked me. Derven knew how much that had been a tease for me, and he was using it to his advantage.

"Please, Ven, I want you to bite me," I pleaded.

With a nip, he pulled away. "You have to make Zander come in your mouth first while Colt and I fuck you, filling up all your holes at once."

Fucking hell, that sounded like the best idea anyone had ever come up with. I let my head fall back, rounding with Derven's shoulder opening my mouth wide, waiting for Zander to fill it with his cock.

"What a good girl, opening up like that for me," Zander purred as he stroked my cheek. "Do you think you can handle all of me this time?"

Unsure of what he was talking about since I've already been able to take him balls deep, I nodded my head.

He flashed me a wide smile as he slipped his dick between my lips. "Let's see just how good of a girl you really are."

Derven wrapped his hands around my waist as he and Colt found their rhythm. At first, they started off alternating, but then Derven kicked it up a notch. None of the others had used their full supernatural strength or speed when it came to sex. They all veered on the side of being cautious not to hurt me. My vampire had no such qualms.

Instead, he loved the fact he could rail into me as hard and fast as he wanted.

"Holy *fuck*," Zander swore. "He's fucking her so fast it looks like a blur."

While I closed my eyes to lose myself in all the sensations, I could still feel them as they moved in closer to see what was happening. Taking his cue from Derven, Colt started to pound into me harder and deeper, making me scream around Zander's cock.

"Fuck, fuck, fuck, if you keep doing shit like that, I'm going to come way too fast," Zander warned, but to me, that was more of a challenge. If he wanted to know how good I could take him, then I was going to take all of him. Lifting my hands, I grabbed Zander's ass and shoved him deeper and faster down my throat.

"Fuck me like you own me, Zander," I taunted. *"The others are taking what they want, so why not take yours?"*

Zander let out a growl at me and grabbed my jaw, holding my face still until he was using all his supernatural abilities to fuck the living hell out of me. I started to feel his knot swelling and wasn't sure what he was planning on doing at that point. He didn't make me wait long as he pulled me down on his cock, getting his knot past my teeth, so it filled my mouth as his cum shot down my throat. I swallowed it, licking what I could of his knot in my mouth, making it spurt even more.

"Goddamn, little dove," Zander snarled. "I fucking own your mouth right now."

He most certainly did, seeing as his knot locked him down deep in my throat. It was too much for me to simply open my mouth wider to remove him. I was knotted the fuck up. Derven slammed up into me slowly as he started to come as well, with Colt right behind him. I was now knotted in my pussy and mouth, trapped just as Derven wanted me as he bit me.

My whole body vibrated with the orgasm he gave me, then each pull from my neck had echoes rocketing through me, making my eyes roll back in my head as I arched, trying to get away from the overwhelming pleasure I was experiencing. The trouble was, there was no way I was going anywhere with an alpha attached to me at each end.

Eventually, Derven took pity on me and sealed up the bite with a bit of his blood and nuzzled into me. "I realized I couldn't make you beg with a cock stuck in your mouth, so we'll save that for another time."

"Ah... do we like put on a movie or something while we wait for the knots to go down?" Mason asked, peering down at me. "You okay, snuggles? Give us a thumbs up since you can't really answer." I rolled my eyes and gave him a thumbs up. "Great, good to hear it. We'll see what we can do to make you more comfortable."

I could tell he was trying not to laugh at my situation, but he was failing as he coughed to cover it up. Derven wriggled his way out from under me, then helped to get me on the couch with Colt lying next to me and my face in Zander's lap. Wrung out from pleasure, I dozed off and didn't really notice when I was carried to bed.

A few hours later, I was awoken by the twins eating out my pussy and ass. Once I was awake and fully receptive to the idea, they made another Oreo out of me as I was sandwiched between the two of them. As rough and fast as things were earlier, the twins made love to me. Hand's touching everywhere, lips caressing each other's skin as the soft echo of our breaths filled the room. This was what I loved most about my twins. They could care for me in a way I didn't know I needed.

Right now, I needed to feel loved and cherished, to reassure myself that they would still love me after what I'd done tonight. As we all came together, our moans making the others stir in their sleep, we nestled under the blankets and slept well into the morning.

⸺◆○◆⸺

"How do you want to address this with the pack?" I asked as Colt, Lane, Zander, and I walked down the road to the main pack area.

I'd asked for us to take the stroll, wanting to spend time in the forest but also deal with the situation at hand. These men were the leaders of this pack, and no matter what I became to the elves, this would be a joint decision.

"We already had another pack meal set up for tonight, so we can go over things there. Theodas, Vanya, and Kolvar were planning on being there. They seemed excited by the idea," Lane said. "Is Ayla back from visiting that other commune of elves?"

Ayla had become an ambassador of sorts going to the elven communes that she knew of or Rath told her about. She was spreading the word about me and looking for those who would stand against the Dark Ring. I made her promise that no one would be forced into being a part of this fight.

"The interview is tomorrow, and she promised to be back in time for that," I answered.

Yesterday after I'd slept in and taken a lazy day with the twins, Zander and I got down to business setting up the press conference. The alphas had decided they weren't going to tell the pack too far in advance to keep from the possibilities of information getting out before we wanted it to. Yes, we planned for the world to know about elves, but I wanted to control the narrative.

"I'm sure they will take things just fine," Zander assured me. "They are more than aware elves are still alive and part of this world. What would they have to be upset about?"

Shrugging, I kicked at a rock. "I just know that some of the pack members still work in the surrounding area, and I don't want them to feel like they're getting attacked. They chose to be part of a wolf pack, not some social experiment to see how elves and wolves coexist."

"They are werewolves, little one," Colt reminded me. "They are already a social experiment to everyone who's human. Those who choose to be part of the human world understand the risks and still choose to do it."

Nodding, I grasped his hand, swinging it between us. "How are you doing?"

He stopped and turned to look at me. "I know I didn't take things well the other night and had a bit of a meltdown, but I'm fine. After I've had some time to process and go over the plan with you, I feel better about things. It would be worse if you cut me out, and I didn't have all the information. Then I think I would just go completely crazy with worry." He brushed a hand down my cheek. "Knowing helps more than I thought it would."

Leaning in, I pressed a kiss to his lips. "Okay, I trust you to tell me if that changes."

"Promise," he answered with another quick kiss, then resumed our walk.

"Zander, did your mother get you an invite?" I asked, knowing the conversation between them hadn't gone great.

He just grunted and nodded. So I left it alone, feeling how much he didn't want to talk about it on top of his body language. "Then our backup plan is in play. I have an invite with my father and you with Morwyn. Having the two of us inside makes the whole plan work."

"I have to admit, it all seems too simple," Lane commented. "Then again, they did it to themselves, only allowing people who should be there into the gala. It will be much easier not to worry about innocents that way."

"Sometimes the best plan is the most obvious because no one thinks you'll do it," I explained. "Who in their right mind would storm the gala with an army of vampires, werewolves, and elves? It's ludicrous to think anyone would do something so basic and direct. The way to kill this snake is to take off the head, and that's who will be there."

We fell into a comfortable silence as we each dealt with the reality of what we were going to do in the next week. The basic plan had already been etched out, but now it came down to Ayla and me doing one last mission to break the rest of the foundation and ensure security would be tightened. So far, no one has commented on the fact that Delilah and Bakos had disappeared, but it had only been forty-eight hours.

"Oh, thank God you're here," Katie called when she spotted us.

I'd been surprised when Peggy's sister decided to stay with the pack, but they understood what their sister did was wrong and deserved to be cast out. With the spell cast on Peggy, she'd become increasingly volatile, and when we tried to relocate her, she ended up killing herself two days later. The sisters mourned for their sister, but to them, she was gone the moment the witch fucked with her brain.

"What's wrong?" Colt asked, sensing her distress.

"There's a man here saying that he's Finley's father. I mean, they sure do look a lot alike, but I remember her telling me she didn't have any family. There was nothing I could do to make him leave. He insisted that I come find you," Katie gushed, her hands waving everywhere as she talked.

I tensed, knowing that it could be Eli, but then again, it could be James. Then I remembered James was a vampire, and he couldn't be out in the sun, and it was the middle of the day. "Where is he?" I asked.

"Ah, sitting at the kitchen counter in the elves' house," she shared. "Said something about that being where he belonged. Wait, is he an elf? He doesn't look at all like the other four, but it's so damn hard to tell since none of them carry much of a scent. Maybe that's how I should figure out what they are by the lack of scent instead of looking for one."

When Katie was nervous, she tended to ramble, and right now, she was coming unglued. I reached out and took her hand, allowing a flow of calming energy to fill her, settling her nerves. "Everything's going to be alright, Katie. By the sound of it, that man is my biological father, even if I don't consider him my dad."

"Oh, I know how that works," Katie huffed. "My old man walked out on us when I was three. The bastard and I might share DNA, but that doesn't mean he means anything more to me."

I smiled and nodded. "Yeah, it's something similar to that. Leave it to me. I'll deal with things. Thanks for looking out, though."

"Of course, Finley, you're part of the pack, and we look after each other. Besides, since you've been here and getting to know everyone, it feels like people are bonding more. Then with the other elves joining us, the pack has had new life breathed into it," Katie said, gripping my hand in comradery. "Good luck with the sperm donor, and come find me if you need anything."

She walked away, and I turned to look at the others. "What could he possibly want?"

"Maybe he knows about the press conference and wants to talk you out of it again," Zander offered.

That could be, but something told me he wouldn't risk coming here just for that. He knew I didn't want to see him or be around him if I didn't need to. This had to be something that could only be talked about in person. Now, I just had to go find out what that was.

TWENTY-THREE

FINLEY

There, sitting at the counter sipping on a cup of coffee was Eli. Vanya must have made it for him since she was watching him warily from the corner nearest the back door exit. Why he felt he could come in here and order her about, I wasn't sure, but I didn't like it one bit. I was the person in charge of the elves here, not him, and if he didn't want to acknowledge that, he could get the hell off my land.

"It seems I've done something to make you angry, daughter," Eli commented, then sipped his coffee. "Your magic is whipping its tail like an angry cat."

"Why are you here?" I demanded.

He looked at me out of the corner of his eye. "Here in this house or on your pack lands? You're going to need to be more specific, so I can apologize for the correct offense."

"How dare you come here to my home and act like such an asshole," I growled out, stepping closer to him. "I understand you don't like the choices I'm making and you're under the delusion that I give a fuck about what you think. My whole life, I grew up without anyone to look after me. *I* took care of me, no matter what it is you think. So you watched over me, who gives a shit. I was beaten, drowned, trapped in small spaces, taught to remove my emotions, all in the name of training. Tell me, what kind of parent would ever wish that for their child?"

Lane came up behind me and wrapped his arms around my waist, pulling me back against his chest. "*I'm not trying to stop you, sweetheart, but I do think it's best if you tone down the magic. It knows you're upset with Eli, and I don't want it to do something you'll regret later when you're not so mad.*"

He made a good point, so as I waited for Eli's answer to my question, I took a few deep breaths trying to bring down my anger level.

"I deserve that," Eli sighed, setting down his mug and turning to face me. "I'm taking my anger out on you, and you're the last person who deserves it. After you told me what you found out about James and him having more control over the Organization than I realized, I took a deep dive into things I've been avoiding and found you were entirely correct. I'd been so lost in my own problems that I wasn't seeing what was right in front of me."

Hearing him admit he was wrong cooled my anger some, but I knew it wouldn't take much to fan the flames again. "What are you going to do about it?"

"I've already personally dealt with the two men who've been pulling the strings and helping James. I even found there were two more recruits James planted to help him in case Tabitha turned on him," Eli shook his head. "James has been controlling the Organization almost from its inception. Of course, he was one of the original founders, but when he left, I assumed that meant he left everything. It seems I was foolish to believe such a thing when James has always had a vindictive streak."

"Is that what you came all the way here to tell me? Couldn't you have done this over the phone?" I questioned, leaning back into Lane as my anger churned in my chest, just waiting to be let out.

Eli stood and took one step to be right in front of me. "I'm shutting down the Organization. With the Dark Ring and the Senate soon to meet their end, there will be no need for a company such as mine. It was created to balance the power structure. If they became too big or powerful, then there was a way to stop them. Instead, it has been used to further their agenda, which is the last thing I want and anyone needs."

It took me a moment to process what he'd just said, so I blinked at him a few times before the words came out. "You are shutting it down?"

"Unless you wish to control that as well?" he offered. "All I know is I'm not the right man to do it, and clearly, I've fucked up more than I have helped. Like you said, what kind of father would sit there and watch what they do to train you all without batting an eye? My logic was it would protect you, teach you to be strong, and no matter what came at you, you'd survive."

"If she doesn't want to run it, can I?" Ayla asked as she walked into the house. "I feel like having an elven queen with a team of assassins would come in handy."

Eli's brows rose as he looked at Ayla then looked at me. "You willingly took this abomination in?"

My hand lashed out, and I slapped Eli in the face, grabbed his throat, and jerked him close enough for us to be nose-to-nose. "I would suggest you speak more carefully about those I've adopted into my pack. These people are my family, and I will not let *anyone* speak ill of them."

"That means you don't know what she is," he hissed as I allowed him enough air to speak. "She's a Dark Elf, the reason our people were nearly wiped out."

"What are you talking about?" I demanded.

"Look at her, see the markings that are on her? They are the sign that she is a Dark Elf, using dark magic to manipulate and kill others. She's sold her soul for the magic she now possesses, making her more evil than anything in the world as we know it," Eli raged, spit flying out of his mouth as he talked.

I tossed him away from me. "Get. Out."

"What? I tell you there is a Dark Elf in your pack, and you kick *me* out?" Eli snapped, picking himself up off the floor. "I raised you better than that. You were taught to be able to read people and see their true intentions, not to mention the natural gift you have of breathing thoughts and emotions."

The guys started to move in on him, but I held out a hand, letting them know I had this. "*You* taught me better? That is laughable, I didn't even know who you were until a few weeks ago, and you claim to have any claim on how I turned out as an adult?" I gave a harsh laugh. "Let's go with that for a moment, shall we? If you know I have such great skills at reading people, don't you think there would be a reason I keep her around? I've seen and felt all I need to know about Ayla to trust she has the best intentions, not to mention she's given me a life oath as her queen to protect me and mine."

Eli just stood there looking between Ayla and me like he still didn't believe me. I glanced at her, the shadows of her past clear in her eyes. This was the response she got from many elves who remembered the old days, which was why she tried to find a commune with younger people in it.

"I won't tell your story, Ayla. He doesn't deserve to know," I told her. That had her snapping her gaze to meet mine, eyes wide with fear. "To me, there has never been a reason for us to talk about it, so I've never brought it up. What happened doesn't change who you are, and it never will to me."

The relief and gratitude I felt from her were overwhelming. When she'd given me her oath, and I rested my hand on her, I saw a whirlwind of information. Part of that had been what happened to her.

"Thank you, my queen. I appreciate that more than you know, but I'd like to tell him... to prove that his daughter is a far superior person to him, a man who was mated to the old queen. It's not surprising the elders found her lacking if this is the type of man she called to herself," Ayla expressed, wrinkling her nose in disgust.

"How dare you speak of her like that. Tiriana was pure and good, unlike anything else in this world," Eli defended.

"Clearly not good enough, or the elders never would have stripped her of her magic," Ayla challenged. "As for me, this was not of my own doing. I was captive to the Dark Ring, and they are the ones who turned me into a dark elf. They wanted the power they believed I would possess. The problem was, now that I was powerful, I couldn't be controlled any longer. In an effort to keep me tame, they used my mate-to-be, but they went too far and killed him. Then there was nothing holding me back. Now I serve at the pleasure of the queen, and I will assist her in anything she asks of me."

Eli deflated at this story, dropping back into the chair he'd been sitting in when we arrived. "How could the Dark Ring know that magic?"

"James," Ayla answered. "He was a witch before he was turned and having had an elven mate and fellow brother in the *nos* who knew all there was about that time in our lives. It wasn't hard for him to gather what he needed and force me to sign the contract to offer up my soul for magic."

"How can you control it when so many others couldn't?" he pressed, still trying to understand what was going on.

Ayla shrugged and gave him a wide, carefree smile she used so often as a shield. "Guess I'm just too stubborn to let the magic control me like that." Then she looked back at me. "So, back to my original question… if you don't want the assassin business from Daddy, can I have it?"

"You know, I think that sounds like a brilliant idea," I shared, returning her smile. "Like you said, a queen who has an army of assassins she controls, well, that's just smart. Soon I'll have an army of vampires, elves, werewolves, and assassins. I don't think anyone is going to be messing with me anytime soon once we topple the system as we know it."

The rest of my men had filtered in through this interaction, and now they all stood flanking me. It was blistering to know that no matter what or who I was up against, they would always be there right at my back. "Now, is there anything else you would like to embarrass yourself over before you leave?"

Eli opened his mouth, taking a moment, then spoke, "It is clear to me that my efforts to step in as your father are not wanted or needed. You're right. You did raise yourself, and I've been deluding myself into thinking what I did was for you instead of just acting selfishly. As I said before, I will always be there for you, however you might need my help. I know you have a press conference tomorrow. Would you allow me to be there and add some additional press that will ensure the correct story gets out into the world?"

My attention went to Zander, trusting him to make the right call since this was more his expertise than mine.

"You may join us, but you will not speak unless you tell me exactly what you're going to say. We have planned out how we want this to go, and I'm not going to let your skewed ideals fuck it up," Zander ordered.

"That's fair," Eli answered. "I've gotten myself a hotel room in town, so I will head back there. What time is the event set for?"

"Noon," I answered. "Be here by ten thirty."

Eli nodded in understanding and got up from his seat. "I am sorry, Finley, for not being the father you deserved, but I'm thankful that whenever you choose to have children, they will have many wonderful role models to look up to." With that said, he headed out, got into the rental car parked out front, and drove off.

"Every day is so exciting here," Ayla announced, hopping up to sit on the counter. "So much better than living in one of the communes trying to hide from the world."

"Would you care to share with us how visiting the communes went?" Rath asked.

Ayla waved him off, pouring herself some coffee. "Give a girl a minute. I get back, and there is a knockout drag-out fight between father and daughter in the kitchen. That is *not* something you see every day."

"Ayla," Elias warned.

It was becoming clear to me Ayla was the sister none of my men wanted but were lucky enough to receive.

"*Fine*," she huffed, sliding off the counter. "The three that Rath told me to check out were much larger than he remembered but still in the same place. I would expect there to be about fifty total elves who might show up."

"From all of them?" Rath confirmed. "That's better than I expected."

"Oh, no, sorry," Ayla cut in. "That's *per* commune. So more like a hundred and fifty or more since some were still on the fence. We are going to have our first clan village up and running in no time. I made sure they knew they'd have to help build homes and are aware this isn't a free ride."

My jaw nearly hit the floor as she talked. *A hundred and fifty elves would be showing up here in our pack over the next few days?* That would be a third of the wolves that live here already.

"Where are we going to put them all?" I asked, looking at the others like they would have the answer.

"Oh, did I forget to mention that all elves living in a commune have a go bag and supplies to live on the run, aka, tents?" Ayla added.

"Tents, we're going to have a whole clan of elves living in tents around our woods," Noah mused. "That is going to make scouting work much harder."

"That's the thing, though. Elves live in a community much like yours. They understand it will be expected for them to work and pull their weight. It's only going to help the pack, trust me, because these are not all fighters. You're getting more craftsmen, green thumbs, and healers as well," Ayla explained. "There is an expectation they will be the founding group of people and will have to help create the village from scratch because Kolvar can't be doing it all by himself. That's impossible."

Understanding this part of the situation had me breathing easier. These fugitives wouldn't be coming here expecting us to have everything ready for them. They would help create what was needed. Really they were the lucky ones since they got to decide how things were set up, creating the foundation of this village.

"We have a lot to cover tonight," Colt grumbled as he kissed me on the cheek and headed out.

Glancing at the clock, I noticed it was later in the day than I expected, and they would need to start setting up for the pack meal. We'd been doing them twice a month now instead of one a quarter. It helped the whole pack integrate with the new members who weren't werewolves. It made my thoughts drift to Ben, and I hoped he was able to find a home like this for himself. He needed a break after all he'd been through, and I hoped I was able to give it to him.

"You gonna be alright while we take care of things?" Lane asked, squeezing my hand.

I planted a quick kiss on his lips and waved him off. "Go, or Colt's going to lose his mind when someone doesn't start the charcoal correctly." Lane laughed and jogged out the door after Colt.

Turning, I looked at the others with my hands on my hips. "Don't you have things to do as well? I'm going to be fine, I promise, now scat," I added, shooing them away with my hands.

"Yeah, sometimes women just need time to themselves or, I don't know, with another woman for a change," Ayla called after them as they filed out of the house. Once they were gone, she walked over to me and rested her arm on my shoulder. "We got rid of the men... now what?"

"Wanna help me out with something?" I asked.

Ayla grinned. "Anything you need, my queen. I'm more than happy to help. Please tell me it's taking out more Dark Ring people."

"Yes, it's taking out two more people to set the wheels in motion," I answered. "The guys already know about it, but I'm deciding to pull this off sooner since this press event is going to be so much bigger than I planned now with Eli involved. After that goes live, I won't be able to sneak around. Thankfully, one of our targets is in Nashville and the other in Charlotte. Both are about an hour away by plane."

"Good thing I also got my pilot's license so that when Derven's busy, I can help out." Ayla cheered, clapping her hands together. "Are we doing this now?"

"After the dinner, I want us all to be here for the announcement," I explained. "But I think we should go over the plan. Grab what you'll need for tonight and meet me back at my house. I'm gonna shift for a bit and run back."

Ayla saluted me and headed upstairs. I hated that I was sending her all over the map now that she could fly the plane Zander bought for us to use. She seemed to love it, though, appreciating being busy, and it kept her out of trouble. Ayla was an elf who left idle for too long, seemed to find ways to keep herself busy but not always in ways people would appreciate.

The other day I had one of the pack members come find me because she was teaching the children how to fight with knives. Then one of the younger boys took it upon himself to deal with a bully in the group, and I had to heal them. Ayla's intentions were always good, but the follow-through was missing the mark just a little.

Stepping out of the house, I pulled off my clothes, folded them up so I could carry them, and shifted. My wolf was thrilled to be out and feeling the spring breeze on her coat. I didn't shift as often as I should to make things more comfortable for her. With my elf magic now present, I didn't feel the *need* to shift like others did, but when I took the time, I felt more grounded. Snatching up my clothes, I trotted off into the woods letting my magic seep into the earth as I went. After the interaction with my father, I knew it was building up inside, and it was better to release it instead of allowing it to fester.

Everything was calm and peaceful until the forest told me a group of wolves it didn't know were now on our land. I stopped in my tracks and let the forest show me what was happening through the eyes of an eagle flying overhead. Fifteen wolves were running as fast as they could in our direction. Another bird showed me where they'd parked their SUVs and their clothes scattered on the ground. I had a feeling they weren't here looking for a safe haven.

"Guys, we've got incoming. Fifteen werewolves heading at us from the northwest," I alerted my men.

I checked back in with the hawk who was following them and noticed something hanging off one of the wolves. Giving in to my request, the hawk dove lower, and I could make out a machine gun hanging around the wolf's neck. It wasn't just one of them either. All of them had a gun of various kinds.

Fuck me. I can't believe they are coming at us armed.

"Alert the pack and get them into hiding. They're armed with guns," I yelled.

Reaching out to my pack connection to Ayla, I tugged on it, forcing her to find me. Dropping my clothes, I bolted off deeper into the woods, sending out my magic to help bolster the forest as I made my request to slow them down. Anything it could do to misdirect them away from the pack out toward the mountains was what would help us right now.

"Finley, don't you dare come here," Elias snapped. *"We will handle this. They are here for you. It's the only thing that makes sense. They don't want the press conference to happen."*

"You know I can't just sit back and watch. What if one of you gets hurt? I'm the best option we have to keep everyone alive," I argued as I kept moving.

With how fast the group of wolves were moving toward us, it didn't take long before our scouts and my men were upon them. The hawk flew off, knowing it was no longer needed, but this left me blind to what was happening. Thankfully, Ayla appeared at my side, waiting for instruction, so I sent her ahead of me. I understood why the guys didn't want me to make myself a target, and I would be smart about approaching the situation stealthier, but I was going to be there no matter what.

The sounds of a wolf fight were incredibly distinctive. Snarls filled the air, followed by whimpers or yelps as their attacks hit home. We had the element of surprise on our hands with them not realizing we knew they were coming. Slinking along the underbrush in the shadows, using my dark-colored fur to my advantage, I made sure no one was slipping through the cracks. Then I saw a naked man trying to climb up one of the trees, his rifle strapped to his back.

Reaching out to the forest, I shared my desire for the tree to trap this man or knock him off and back to the ground. The tree was more than happy to get the thing crawling on him off and used some branches to smack him off. Once the naked man fell to the ground, I pounced, baring my teeth as I snarled. The man froze his eyes wide as I shifted back but left my hands tipped with claws.

"What are you doing here?" I demanded.

When the naked man saw who I was, he started to fight. Slashing him across the chest with my claws, he screamed and writhed on the ground. I used them to cut the strap to his gun and tossed it away from him.

"I'll ask you again, what the fuck are you doing here?" I snapped, slamming the man down on the ground roughly. "I can make this an easy death or a slow one, your choice."

"I'm not scared of an omega bitch like you," he spat, his spit landing on my cheek.

Ignoring the nasty feel of it sliding off my face, I settled my hand over his neck and carved my claws into his skin. He gushed blood everywhere as I cut the artery in his arm.

"You should be terrified of me," I whispered. "Do you want to know why?"

The man didn't answer as he started to gag on his own blood, the acceptance of his death in his eyes. Too bad for him I wasn't going to let that happen any time soon—flooding him with my magic healing the damage I'd done, bringing him back to life, then doing it again.

"See, I can kill you and heal you forever, with no end in sight of when I might choose to let you die for real," I taunted. "Tell me what I want to know, and I'll actually kill you."

"Fucking bitch," he spluttered, taking in deep breaths of air now that his lungs worked. "I'll never tell you anything."

"We'll see about that," I warned as I started to inflict as much pain as I could in the most tender of places. It wasn't until I'd healed him two more times that he caved, just as I was about to test the theory of if I could regrow body parts starting with his dick.

"Stop," he screamed. "I'll talk. Please just don't do that. I'll tell you what you want to know."

"I'm listening," I said, holding his dick in my hand.

"The Senate sent us. We are soldiers of the Senate here to kill you for inciting fear within the community. You can't hold that press conference tomorrow. If we don't stop you, then they will send others. We aren't the last of it. In fact, we are just a distraction," the man said with an evil grin on his face.

Fear raced through me as I reached out to the forest to see if he was telling the truth. In response, the forest around me started to shake as the roots of all the trees rumbled under the ground sending out a warning to the far-reaching parts of my land. Soon I would know if there was anyone in the five hundred thousand acres I controlled. The farther out from here, the magic was weaker, meaning the forest was as sentient, but it would respond to the call of its brothers.

Having gathered all the information I needed from this man, I ripped out his throat and tossed it aside. When I turned around, I was faced with one of my own pack members with a shotgun in his hands. "I'm sorry, Finley, but they have my family, and I'll do anything to save them."

Knowing what was coming because I couldn't move fast enough to dodge it all, I twisted, ensuring that the most vital organs were turned away as the blast went off. The pain that bloomed in my side and back had me screaming in agony. It felt like hot lava was being drilled into my body, burning its way through me.

They'd used lead and silver in their shotgun shells for maximum impact, and I dropped to the ground in a heap.

"*Finley!*" Colt bellowed, his voice echoing through the woods as I gasped for air.

TWENTY-FOUR

COLT

Just when I thought we'd made it through this fight without anyone getting majorly wounded, I heard the gun go off. Whipping my head around, I saw Finley turn away from the blast. The scattershot caught her in the back and side. Her naked body was littered with blooming spots of blood. Her scream had me moving faster than my brain could keep up as I shifted and tackled my own pack mate, who'd pulled the trigger. Ripping out his throat, I switched back to my human body and crawled over to Finley.

"Little one, look at me, come on, open your eyes," I begged, brushing her hair out of her face. Every shift of her body had her crying out in pain, so I tried to be as careful as possible. "*Rath.*" I roared, praying he would be able to do something.

The elf appeared at my side in a moment. "What the fuck happened? We'd gotten them all. Who the hell shot her?"

I nodded my head to the man behind me, someone I'd counted as a friend for three years. Now he'd done the one thing I couldn't forgive—he attacked my mate.

"But he's one of ours?" Rath argued.

I snarled at the elf. "Don't you think I know that? Fuck the bastard and why he did it. Finley needs our help right now, not him."

Rath reached out and placed a hand on Finley's shoulder, where it was free of damage and closed his eyes. In a second, they snapped back open. "The shell was filled with silver and iron pellets. We need to get her back to the house so we can remove them before I can do anything to heal her. If we wait too long, the iron could cause permanent damage. It's fatal to elves. My hope is that being a werewolf, too, will help to lessen that effect."

Derven suddenly appeared behind Rath, biting into his wrist, then bending down and letting the blood drip into Finley's mouth. "My blood should help to strengthen her. We are weak against silver too, but it might help slow down the iron poisoning."

"Who's the fastest out of us?" I asked. "We need to get her to Vanya so she can start removing them as fast as possible."

Derven scooped her up, which pulled a strangled scream out of her. Then she fainted, her head lolling back almost as if she was dead, but I could hear her heart beating still. I met his gaze and nodded. "Get the fuck out of here, *now*."

That was all he needed before he blinked away. Elias let out a howl that sounded like a war cry telling me he was not in a good place. It was followed up by the twins and the other two alphas as they tore off after Derven. Rath and I stood there for a moment as I looked at the guns scattered around.

"We need to get these locked away somewhere. They can't just be left," I muttered, my heart desperate to go after Finley but knowing this needed to be dealt with so we didn't have more incidents.

Rath grabbed my shoulder. "Grab as many as you can carry. I'll take what's left, and we'll store them in the hidden shed where the cells are for now. It's right by the pack house, so we'll be heading in the right direction."

Nodding, I grabbed the shotgun and many other weapons they had brought with the intention of murdering my pack. They'd known to put silver and iron into the ammo, ensuring it would have maximum impact no matter what they were fighting against. Rath and I ran back to the pack house as fast as we could. I was slower on two feet, but I pushed my body to the limit.

The bond I had with Finley was quiet, but I knew she was still alive. I could feel the faint tug of it still being grounded in her magic. Today was not the day we were going to find out if the soul bond meant we all died or not because Finley still had to save the world. There's no way she would have survived through everything up until this point, only to die at the hands of one of our own people.

How many others could there be? Did the Senate truly get in and infiltrate my pack without me realizing it? We haven't had any new members in over a year. How could they possibly turn them against me? Seems the pack dinner was going to take on an entirely new tone tonight.

Back at the pack house, I chucked the guns into the cell Rath picked and locked it so no one could get to them. With my anxiety thick in my throat, I raced up the steps and slammed open the door. There, on the dining room table, laid on a sheet, was Finley. As Noah held the flashlight, Vanya was crouched over her with tweezers picking out pellets. The others stood around the table or paced, trying to keep themselves under control. Elias was still in his wolf form, lying under the table, his hazel eyes glittering with rage as they looked at me.

If Finley died and we didn't follow her into the afterlife, no one would survive Elias's rage. He would murder everyone in our pack in retribution for what they'd done to our mate.

When we'd found him and brought him to the pack, he was almost feral at that point. It took lots of work to bring him back. I don't think there'd be any coming back from this for him.

Rath stood at the end, his hands wrapped around Finley's ankles, his hands glowing green, telling me he was using his magic for something.

"He's keeping her asleep and dull to the pain," Noah answered my internal question, meeting my gaze. *"Things are moving slowly since her body wants to heal around the silver. The lead is just sinking through her flesh like it's acid. Before Rath took over her mind, she was screaming silently. I could feel it in our bond when I touched her."*

A growl rumbled in my throat as white-hot rage exploded in my body. I wasn't going to sit here and let this stand, not when my mate was lying there, losing her mind in pain. Stalking to the spare room we kept extra clothes for shifters who needed them, I yanked on a pair of jeans and marched outside.

"Pack emergency meeting, now,*"* I ordered through my pack link, using my alpha energy to force the command. They would all be here within moments. *"Rath, I don't mean to distract you but can either Theodas or Kolvar spot lies like you and Finley can?"*

"Theodas's nature only responds to those of pure intention. He can see that in others as well," Rath answered before he slammed the door in our connection. I couldn't blame him. I wouldn't want to be distracted either if I were keeping Finley from losing her mind to the pain she was withstanding.

There, I waited on the steps to the pack house I had built, imagining one day I'd have a mate and children to fill it. Now it was a refuge to elves who were taking a stand and announcing to the world they were still here. They were part of my pack as much as these wolves were.

Each of them worked hard in the service of the greater good of our pack. I'd truly thought my wolves understood that with Finley as my mate, also being an elf. These new additions were family. If they were mad enough about the changes to let the Senate worm their way into this pack, then we are on shakier ground than I expected.

It didn't take long for the majority of the members to arrive. I could tell there were some who had been sent out to scout the perimeter after we got word of the attack to ensure we weren't getting hit from multiple sides. What I didn't count on was them attacking from within. If that was their plan all along, then they'd done well. It was a shock and one I didn't see coming in the slightest. Our attention had been outward attacks, and looking inward seemed so pointless.

"Alpha, is it true we were attacked?" Lisa asked, wringing her hands. She'd always been a worrier, and this wasn't going to help her nerves.

"I'll explain everything in just a moment. I'm waiting for the scouts to come in," I assured her.

Katie rushed up to the front. "Did I hear Finley got shot?"

"Katie, please be patient with me," I asked. "I only want to have to say this once."

She nodded and backed up to her sister, Milly, wrapping her arms around her. The same sort of tension was radiating through the rest of the pack as well. I knew the attack would cause turmoil since I had everyone retreat to their homes, but we also did drills to ensure the new plan worked how we wanted it to.

Within another few minutes, all the members of my pack were present, along with the two elves. They chatted amongst themselves, curious about what the hell was going on. I signaled to Theodas to come join me, and he did a little hesitantly.

"Yes, alpha?" he asked.

"Rath said you can tell the true intentions behind people's words. Is that accurate?" I asked.

Theodas's eyes grew wide. "Yes... but can't our queen do that far better than I can?"

"She isn't available right now, and this needs to be handled," I explained. "While I'm talking, I need you to pick up on anyone who feels guilty, rage, or any other malicious intentions and remember who they are."

Zander stepped out of the house and walked up to me. "He can point them out to me, and I'll do what needs to be done."

I nodded and turned back to face my pack, the people I had been providing for the past eight years. "Today, we were attacked," I announced, ensuring my voice carried so everyone could hear me. "They came with the intent to hurt us, going so far as to bring guns along with them. Just as the fight was ending, which we had the upper hand in thanks to Finley's warning, she was shot." The whole pack gasped. "It wasn't one of the interlopers. It was, in fact, one of our own. Drew Miller picked up a shotgun, aimed it at my mate, and shot her. The shells were filled with lead and silver, ensuring they did maximum damage."

I paused to let that information sink in as the women reacted, clinging to their men or each other. As I let them process, I watched, looking for those who weren't reacting at all or weren't reacting in the appropriate manner. There were a few I took note of just in case Zander didn't round them up after.

"Finley is fighting for her life as we speak with the help of Vanya and Rath. Thankfully, they both have healing magic and will do all they can to save her. My assumption is that the news of our upcoming press conference got back to the Senate, and they sent these men to ensure it didn't happen," I shared, taking a good long look at my people, then decided it was time to set the tone of how things would be going forward.

"News of this press event was going to be announced to all of you at the dinner tonight, along with the fact that about a hundred and fifty more elves will be migrating here from other communes. As one of your leaders, we've tried to be as transparent with you as possible, but when it comes down to it, we are the alphas, and you are our pack. I've never wanted to be the kind of alpha who forces their members to fall in line, but it seems in doing so, we've given the impression this is a democracy. Let me be clear... it's *not*. Lane, Zander, and I are the ones who make the choices for what's best while you follow them. Don't like it, then get the fuck out of this pack," I ordered, pointing down the road that led out of the pack lands.

Many gasped and whispered quietly to one another. Zander stepped forward, his arms crossed over his chest, making sure his alpha energy could be felt by all. I'd always been a strong alpha, but when Zander let his strength loose, it was intense, even for me.

"That wasn't a suggestion," he bit out. "The handholding and acceptance of those who don't follow orders will no longer be tolerated as they once were. That tolerance might cost us our mate, and *that* is unacceptable." He snarled, lashing out with his energy.

Many lower pack members dropped to their knees, baring their necks in submission, while others staggered. Some had murderous looks on their faces, and those were the first ones I was going to deal with.

"You get one chance. Pack up and leave in the next thirty minutes if you're unhappy with how things are going because we will not be hearing any grievances from any of you," I ordered.

"I challenge," someone yelled from the back of the group.

The crowd split, and there stood a man I'd never seen before. He was shorter than I was, but his bulk was impressive, yet it didn't mean shit.

"Who the fuck are you?" I demanded. "Only a member of this pack can challenge the alpha."

"Yeah, but I'm not challenging you," he stated. "I'm challenging one of your betas which anyone is allowed to do."

"*No one knows that rule,*" Zander said. "*He has to be a plant, but it doesn't make sense. Why would he be challenging?*"

"*It's a distraction,*" Finley's voice whispered to us. "*Before he died, he told me there were more coming.*"

"*Alright, little one, we'll handle it. You just rest,*" I coaxed. Then I reached back out to Rath, "*I thought you were keeping her under?*"

"*I can only do so much when she's this powerful,*" he snapped back.

Elias stalked out of the house and leaped down the steps to sit in front of the man who called the challenge. Seeing him, the rest of the pack made room for them, knowing Elias wasn't someone they wanted to get into a fight with.

"You wanted to fight a beta. Here is one of our top three betas who holds a leadership role," I said, motioning him to continue. "Are you going to fight him as a human or wolf?"

Before the man could act, Derven was ripping his head from his shoulders and tossing it away. "Anybody have a match? I find it's always better to burn evil witches once you've killed them. They have a nasty habit of coming back if they have a body to return to."

I gawked at him, trying to understand what just happened. "He was a witch?" I asked as I walked over to examine the man closer.

"Yup, it sure was," Derven said, wiping his hands on his jeans. "Elias gave me a heads up, and I figured it was best to deal with it quickly before he could cast some spell. Dark magic witches like to make werewolves their slaves." He looked up at me with concern in his gaze. "What's going on here today?"

"We're under attack, and the Senate is using all its tricks before they can't stop her anymore. Once she goes public, the world will know the truth, and that will make her someone far too noticeable to go missing," Zander pointed out.

"Then we need to make this happen fast," I blurted, my brain coming up with a plan. "Call everyone who was supposed to be there tomorrow and find out who can be here now. Fuck it, call Eli and make him figure out a way to get her on the air before we have more people attacking us."

"What about them?" Zander asked, nodding to the four hundred people before me.

"I got this. You do what you need to," I assured him.

He started to go but paused. "She's in no condition to do this."

"That's exactly why it needs to happen like this. If we can show the world what it looks like to piss the Senate off, then the world will start to turn against them. Once that happens, they'll have to do whatever they can to save face. What they want most is to ensure she doesn't talk. After that, they're fucked," I explained.

With a grunt, Zander headed back into the house, and I motioned Theodas over. "Who do I need to address?"

The elf pointed over at a group of men standing off to the side. "They all have ill intentions toward you and your mate."

"Derven, Elias, care to ensure our friends don't leave till we've had a chat?" I requested.

Derven flashed me a smile as he appeared next to the group, placed his hand on two of their shoulders, and whispered something that had them going pale. The rest of the pack shifted nervously as they watched everything going on, but none dared to leave or speak after watching a man get his head ripped off.

"As you can see, things are at work here, not of our doing. The Senate claims to be there to protect us. Well, how's that going right now? They send people here to kill my mate and blackmail you into helping. What good have they ever done for us, really? My brother was taken and my pack slaughtered. Where was the Senate then? The Dark Ring is stealing more and more of our kind for sick and twisted desires. Interestingly enough, the Senate is doing *nothing* to stop it. In fact, you could say they are so interlinked they are one and the same. My mate has been charged with bringing them down, and they will do whatever it takes to silence her, but we won't go quietly," I roared, thrusting my fist up in the air. "We demand a government that has our best interest in mind and not one that destroys others who might threaten them. Who's sick and tired of looking over their shoulder wondering when they're going to be next?"

A thundering sound of agreement answered me. I grinned, glad to see my people wouldn't be the ones who hid from the fight, that they would put their actions into play.

"This pack has always promised to be a safe haven for those who needed it. Right now, that promise is being put to the test, and I, for one, am not going to back down. We will fight to keep this pack whole. I refuse to let the Senate, the Dark Ring, or even our own prejudices keep us from doing what we know is right. As I said, if you don't want to fight for that, then leave, but know that if you come back wishing harm on me or mine, I will destroy you," I warned. "Now, women and children, head back home, keep the little ones inside and take what precautions you want to keep yourselves safe. Men who are able-bodied and willing to stand for our pack, we need feet on the ground watching our borders for those who might be sneaking in. Now *go.*"

TWENTY-FIVE

FINLEY

My mind filtered in and out of consciousness as Rath tried to keep me from feeling the worst of the pain as Vanya worked. She was moving quickly, removing what she could as swiftly as possible, but the lead pellets seemed the worst as they burned through my body. Clenching my jaw, I tried to concentrate on anything besides what was happening.

I was catching snippets of what the others were saying when they talked through our bond, but I wasn't following. Suddenly, Derven was gone from where he'd been holding my hand, and Lane filled the spot immediately. I clenched onto his hand, using it as a lifeline to stay grounded in my body when all I wanted was to float away from the pain.

Outside there was screaming and yelling from hundreds of people. I felt Colt talking to the others and listened in, catching that someone was challenging for the beta spot. Before I could figure out what caused the screaming, I heard Derven warning the others that the man was a witch.

"It's a distraction," I called out, begging them to hear me. *"Before he died, he told me there were more coming..."*

Hot angry tears rolled down my cheeks as my brain clouded in pain. This should have never happened. If I'd listened to my men, then I wouldn't have been there and gotten shot. Then again, it was by one of our own, so it still could've happened and been even worse. He could have killed me if I wasn't already on the defensive. Now I had to fight to make it through this. I wasn't going to let the Senate take me out before I had the chance to fix this. My death would take everyone I loved from the world, and that wasn't how this should go.

A hand smoothed away the hair that fell in my face, then wiped away my tears. "You're doing amazing, sweetheart," Lane whispered. "I know this is painful, but you're strong, and we are right here with you. Vanya says she'd gotten all the silver pellets. Now it's just the last few lead ones."

I took a shaky breath and squeezed his hand so he knew I heard him.

"We got you, babe. I promise this will be over soon," Noah encouraged, letting his hand run through my hair. My wolf let out a whine when he didn't continue petting me. Right now, I would take any comfort I could get. "Alright, I won't stop as long as you keep breathing through this."

True to his word, he continued as I made the best effort I could to keep breathing. *If only I could use my own magic on myself. Then I could heal the damage and push the pellets out of me or at least stop them from burning through my flesh... Wait, why couldn't I do that?*

Turning my attention inward, I sank into myself until I reached my well of magic. It was leaking everywhere, and my wolf lay beside it, breathing shallow as she tried to drink up some of the magic flowing out of us. The damage to my body was affecting everything else in turn. Maybe if I could repair this, it might help everything else. *Was this what lead poison looked like internally? Did it erode at my magic, then kill me once it was through that?* Anything was worth a try. I knew Derven's blood helped for a bit, but with how much blood I was losing, I doubt adding more of his was a good idea. The last thing I needed to do was add another supernatural species to my list.

Kneeling in front of the fountain of magic, I placed my palms over the largest crack. In my mind, I imagined the crack sealing itself, stemming the loss of magic. Pain roared through my body as I slowly, inch by inch, filled in the fissure. My breathing was coming hard and fast, sweat breaking out on my forehead as I gritted my teeth and kept pushing.

"*Finley, what are you doing?*" Rath asked as he appeared next to me.

I couldn't deviate my attention to answer him, afraid I would lose whatever momentum I'd found.

"*Nin mel, whatever you are doing is taking too much of a toll on your body,*" he tried again. "*Please, talk to me, tell me how I can help?*"

My body gave out, and I collapsed against the fountain, but when I looked, the crack was half the size it was before. "*I need to fix it. If I can stop the magic from leaking out, I can slow the lead poisoning.*"

"*That's crazy, Finley. No one has been able to combat the damage done by lead. It's the one thing we can't heal,*" he challenged.

I looked at him over my shoulder. "*Are you really going to stand there and tell me to just give up? To make this my fate? You and the others keep telling me there isn't a limit, that I can be* more. *Well, right now, all I want is to be whole. Is that really too much to ask for?*"

"*No, nin mel, it's not too much,*" he said as he kneeled beside me. "*I will do what I can to assist you, lend you whatever magic I have to offer.*"

Stealing myself for the pain I was going to endure, I placed my hands higher on the crack. With everything I had within me, I focused on mending the fracture. It was the largest damaged area, and if I could heal this part of me, well, then the others would be easier, or so I hoped. Rath placed his hands on my shoulder, and the cool feeling of his magic entered me. Then as if he'd become the conduit, I felt my connection to all my mates and to the forest around me. The magic I poured into it every day for the last few months was sitting there waiting for me.

I could have wept as I funneled all I could into this wound, keeping my mind's eye on the image of it being fully restored. My mind went to the first time I found it, seeing it shooting so high in the air, filled with so much power I had to let some of it go. This is what I wanted it to be like once again, brimming with magic to the point I would need to release it back into the world or explode.

"That's enough, Finley," Rath warned. *"You can't take in any more magic, give back what you've taken, or else you'll shatter your source this time."*

Opening my eyes, I looked around to see he was right. My center glowed a soft blue light with little darts of energy that reminded me of fireflies. Next to me, tongue lolling, was my wolf healed and eyes glowing with a power I'd never seen before. She nudged my arms, pushing them off the fountain that was repaired, not just repaired but shining with silver glint. Like I'd taken what was left in me and coated my magic in a protective force.

My wolf nipped at me with a whine, shaking her body as if she was uncomfortable. She was holding power, trying to keep it from overwhelming me, but now it was becoming too much for her to hold onto. I reached out and wrapped my arms around her fluffy neck, hiding my face in her fur. "Thank you," I whispered, knowing she was being so brave in protecting me like this.

She licked my face reassuringly and sneezed loudly like she was ready for me to get to work. I slowly drew the magic out of her and sat back, turning to Rath. *"I need you to take me outside. There's no way I can dispel all of this without having direct contact with my forest."*

"Will you be alright if I leave you?" he questioned.

Reaching out, I cupped his face with my hand and pulled him into a kiss, returning the magic he'd given me and then some. *"You never leave me. We're connected for life."*

He returned my kiss fiercely, then vanished from my side just as suddenly as he had appeared. I looked back at my wolf and gave her a wink. *"Don't worry. I'll take care of this. You've done your part."* She sat down, her tail wagging as I let myself return to the world around me.

"What do you mean take her outside? We can't do that," Mason argued. "She literally almost died, and you want us to put her in the dirt with her wounds?"

"Don't argue with me. She's the one who told me to do it," Rath countered. "Finley pulled all the magic she could from the forest, and it's going to hurt her if she doesn't let go of it. She said that she needs to be directly connected to it for that to happen."

An arm slid under my legs and behind my back. While I was no longer in danger of dying, the damage the shotgun blast did to me was still incredibly slow to heal and hurt like a bitch.

"Listen to her. You're hurting her," Noah snarled.

Groaning, I managed to crack open my eyes to see the twins blocking Rath's way. "Stop... let him go..." I rasped.

Their eyes snapped to me. "Snuggles, you don't know how bad your injuries are. We shouldn't move you."

"Magic will kill me... have to let it back out..." I tried to explain, but I was so incredibly tired.

"I'm not going to lose her," Rath said, his voice booming like thunder. "Now, get out of my way."

The two backed away, but the moment we passed them, they were right on his heels.

"What's happening?" Zander asked as he appeared in my vision.

"She needs to be in the forest," Rath answered.

"Like fuck she does," Zander spat. "Colt, Derven, and Elias are dealing with the traitors, and the last thing that needs to happen right now is Finley being out in the open."

"You're not going to win this argument. She needs to release the magic she gathered, or she'll die. Trust me when I say that as she's doing this, I don't think anyone, not even us, will be able to touch her," Rath shot back and shoved past him.

Moments later, my broken and battered body was placed in the soft grass. The earth around me welcomed me, softening, so it was more comfortable for me to lay there. I took a deep, ragged breath before letting it out, allowing my magic to flow with it. I remembered the first time I did this, awakening the forest around me. Now, as I gave back what I borrowed, it funneled out to the areas that needed it the most.

"The fuck is going on?" I heard Colt's demanding voice. "I feel like my hair is standing on end as if I've been shocked."

"It's Finley," Noah answered. "How is she doing this?"

"That young wolf is the power of the queen of elves," a stranger answered, his voice accented from a dialect I couldn't pick out. "What has happened that she required such a massive amount of magic?"

"Don't answer that, Rath. First, these guys are going to tell us who they are." Elias snarled.

"Your Sentinel is right. We should introduce ourselves, but I believe now is not the right time. When our queen is done blessing the forest, we will speak properly. Until then, we will commune with the land while she works," another new voice spoke, his tone nasally and far too proper.

Tuning all that out, knowing I was safe for now, I concentrated on the task at hand. My magic flooded the earth around me, entering into the deep network of roots traveling out into the wide reaches of the forest until it reached the mountains. Then it spread wide, encompassing all the forests of the Smoky Mountains. As it circled back to feed the remaining power to the forest closest to the pack, I found an encampment of men. Using the eyes of animals around the area, I found it was more werewolves armed to the teeth and far too close for my liking.

"Have you heard anything from the point team?" a man asked, poking at the fire they'd made.

Another shook his head, looking at the radio next to him. "It's a mixed bag, isn't it? They could be dead, or they could still be radio silent. No way to know until we hit them later tonight."

"Either way, they'll assume that was the attack and never suspect the real fight hasn't even begun," the first man said with a laugh. "Bitch will be dead before she ever gets the chance to say a word to the press. Problem solved quickly and cleanly like Alpha Vaughan wanted. Can't believe that cunt of a wife betrayed us."

Rage filled me as I listened to these men talking so carelessly about the innocent lives they were going to take. That wasn't going to happen, not in my woods. These bastards were going to die before they ever had a chance to step foot near my pack. The ground opened up and swallowed the fire, leaving them in the dim light of dusk, unable to see the vines and tree branches coming for them.

The forest was just as enraged at the treatment of these men chopping off branches to burn and killing animals that were young and healthy. Before they had any chance to realize what was happening, the first man was run through with branches as another was strangled with vines. The sounds of their screaming filled the night air scaring away all the animals. I trusted the forest to do what was needed and bury all evidence of them ever being there.

Satisfied that the forest was free of danger, I withdrew back to my body, confident we would be safe for the evening. When I opened my eyes, I was surrounded by three ancient-looking men in flowing green robes sitting cross-legged and hands palm up resting on their knees. Looking down at my body, I was dressed in a simple sky-blue dress that was light as air but covered my battered body.

"*Eithel govannen nin rís*," one of them greeted, bowing his head. "It is an honor to meet the one who will lead us out of the darkness back into the light, your majesty."

FINLEY

Staring at the men for a moment, I then looked behind to see all my men standing guard, none too pleased with the situation. Returning my gaze to the three men, I cocked my head to the side, looking at them curiously. "Are you the elders I've heard about who are going to potentially reject me like they did my mother and steal my magic?"

One of them chuckled and shook his head. "Goddess, no, we don't have the power to do that. We can reject a queen, but that has nothing to do with her magic. That is all based on the person's own worthiness. If the fates don't agree with their actions, they can remove the gift they've given them. It is one thing we look for when we meet the potential queen."

"You, my young child, have been blessed well beyond anything we have seen in millennia. Then again, I suppose desperate times call for desperate measures," another commented. "With the battle you must face soon, I understand its need, but as you've experienced yourself, there is only so much magic one can control at a time before it could kill them."

Taking in everything they were telling me, I just nodded dumbly, watching them speak. My body ached, and I knew it would take more than a day to recover from what I went through. Glancing down at myself, I could see the wounds were sealed, but they weren't even close to being fully healed under the skin. I wasn't in danger of dying, but it would take a few days until I was back in fighting form.

"Your Guide told us you were able to heal the damage from the lead poisoning. Is this true?" the voice I remembered being irritatingly formal inquired.

Just by his voice alone, I knew I wouldn't like this elder. I'd had my fill of pompous people like him, and most of the time, they were my targets. Interesting how that worked out. It seemed no one liked a know-it-all. The sound of gravel crunching under tires could be heard as a vehicle flew down the road and skidded to a halt.

Eli burst out of the car and raced over to my men. "Where is she? Is she alright?"

Mason just pointed over to where I was sitting amid the elders. Eli's eyes went wide with horror as he recognized who they were. "Get the fuck away from my daughter. You bastards already took my wife from me. I'm not going to let you take her too."

My brows shot up at the venom in his tone as he spoke to the elders. While I might not enjoy the one man, the others seemed fine for a bunch of old men. Then there was the fact they couldn't have done anything to Mother's magic, and since they were elves, I knew they couldn't lie.

"Ellisor, it has been a long time," one stood and greeted. "I'm sorry to hear of your mate's passing and the nature of what caused it. While we might have rejected her as queen, we didn't reject her as an elf, and we mourn the loss of all our kind taken from us too soon."

The snooty elder stood and shook out his robe. "Don't bother, Druindar. He's blackened his heart toward his own people. He won't believe a word you have to say."

"Purtham, it is our duty as elders to nurture those who are lost. Ellisor is still grieving the loss of his family. We must offer grace in times of mourning," Druindar countered, then looked down at me, offering a hand. "I hope you don't think of us as the boogie man like your father does. Unfortunately, we haven't had the chance to meet under welcoming circumstances."

I allowed him to help me to my feet, but I almost crashed back down with how my muscles screamed at me. Derven appeared, scooping me up into a bridal hold. "I've got you, *sângele mue.*"

"It's absolutely fascinating how you and your mother have called such diverse mates. One might think it's a sign for us old doddering fools to realize as the world changes, so must we," the third elder admitted.

"Couldn't have said it better myself, Mirthal," Druindar added with a nod.

"Yes, that we should be overjoyed at the fact we soon won't have any pure Light Elves on the earth," Purtham muttered. "Who listens to me? I'm just the oldest elder of the group."

"*Who pissed in his Cheerios?*" Mason asked. I had to try as hard as I could not to snort at his comment.

When the sound of many vehicles making their way up the drive caught my attention, I froze. I reached out to the forest, trying to assess what was coming but couldn't sense any danger from the nature around me. Then I saw the first van with a national news station name written on the side.

"Derven, what the hell is going on?" I demanded in a low whisper.

He glanced down at me with a guilty expression. "Ah, about that… Colt decided that tonight was going to be better for the press conference. That way, we could ensure the Senate won't come after you anymore. Well, for now, that is, until they make a smarter plan."

"We would have been fine for the night. I already took out the group of werewolves that Zander's father sent after us," I explained.

Derven narrowed his eyes. "What did you just say? How the hell did that happen if you never left our sight?"

"Perks of needing to dispel so much magic," I answered with a shrug. "The forest took care of them and made sure all the evidence was gone as well."

Derven let out an impressed whistle. "Just when I didn't think you could get scarier." He pressed a kiss to my forehead. "I have to admit, though, I absolutely love the fact that the most terrifying woman is also in my bed. That's a thrill of the likes no one will ever know but us."

I couldn't help but laugh at that, letting my head fall to his shoulder as he carried me over to the others.

"What's so funny?" Noah asked as he ran a hand down my leg before gently gripping my ankle. "It's not nice to keep secrets from your mates."

"Trust me, it's not a secret, but I'll have to tell you later when we don't have so many prying ears," I assured him. "Someone care to tell me what the plan is?"

Colt walked over to me, grabbed my face, and kissed the hell out of me. "Little one, don't you dare scare me like that. You're gonna give me gray hair far too early, and we haven't even had kids yet."

Smiling at him, I returned his kiss and nuzzled my nose against his. "I think you'd look dashing with salt and pepper hair."

He growled in response. "Don't even think about trying to pull shit, so it happens."

Biting my lip, I nodded and relaxed into Derven's arms, trying not to push him too far after today's events. "So I'm going live tonight?"

"No sense in waiting for them to try something else to keep you silent. Figured it would be better to beat them to the punch," Colt answered. "Come on. They're being directed to the living room of the pack house. I want this to take place in the center of everything and where it all started."

"Thank God the elders clothed me or else these reporters would be getting an eyeful." I chuckled.

"No, they'd all be dead," Zander grumbled.

With that announcement, we all entered the house, and I was placed in the middle of the loveseat while my mates surrounded me. The twins sat on the floor, one on either side of me, as the rest made a semi-circle behind the couch.

Eli seemed to have put himself in charge of wrangling the reporters, and he did a good job of it. The staff of one of the news stations came over and tried to put makeup on me, but none of my men let her get close.

"She needs something on her, or she'll look like death on camera. Everyone knows they do nothing helpful for people's images," she argued.

Eli stepped up and drew her away. "Why don't we see how it looks in the test shot? Elves tend to have the ability to shine no matter how they are viewed. I think we'll be fine."

Within twenty minutes, the whole room was filled with lights, cameras, and so many strangers it was overwhelming. Still hurt, my wolf wasn't at all feeling like this was a safe experience for us. All she wanted to do was slink back to our nest and sleep for the next two days. I promised her we would do just that when this was finished.

The main person interviewing me, Abby Riley, took her seat in an armchair across from me, looking at all my mates with a wary expression. I suppose I couldn't blame her with how grumpy they'd been when anyone got too close. It wasn't their fault they didn't know I'd almost died a few hours ago. The elders and Eli stood off to the side since they were to be added to the interview after they'd gotten my story.

"Now, this isn't going to be live since it's past the seven o'clock news, but we'll be sharing this everywhere tomorrow at each major news hour. Your father has made it clear this needs to be front and center, shared with the world... would you care to tell us why that is?" Abby asked.

I nodded, keeping a light smile on my face knowing I tended to come across as cold most of the time. "That story is why you are here tonight instead of waiting to do this tomorrow as we had planned. You see, three hours ago, the United Senate sent their soldiers to come and kill me before I could speak the truth to the world."

Abby sat up straighter, her expression surprised. "What truth would that be?"

"Elves are still alive and in hiding because there is a group called the Dark Ring hunting them down along with other supernaturals, and the Senate isn't doing a damn thing to stop it," I stated bluntly.

"Excuse me?" Abby blurted, then just as quickly collected herself. "Those are some heavy allegations there. What proof do you have about all of this?"

"For one, I, myself, am an elf, the queen of the Light Elves, to be exact. I'm also an assassin who had been hired to help take out the Dark Ring. It's where I first learned of the underground criminal empire that thrives on the abuse and mistreatment of supernaturals. I've managed to rescue many of their prisoners, two of which happen to be my mates." I paused to let that information sink in before continuing. "As for the Senate's part in this, that is harder to prove, but as an assassin, I do my ground work, and I've been investigating the Dark Ring, and time and time again, I come back to a connection to the Senate."

I could see the thrill of the hunt in Abby's eyes as she realized what had just landed in her lap. "Queen of the Light Elves, so that must mean your father, Ellisor Beinorin, is one as well. Wait a moment, are you the child who supposedly died in childbirth along with his wife?"

Nodding my head, I glanced over at Eli, but there was nothing in his expression to reveal how he was feeling. When I looked deeper, reaching for his emotions, it became clear he was nervous but also relieved that the truth would be coming out. This gave me what I was looking for since I wasn't sure how much to tell.

"Tell me, Abby, what do you know about elves?" I asked, folding my hands in my lap.

"I suppose just the general information about the war and that they sacrificed themselves for all of humankind when they destroyed the Dark Elves," she answered.

"There is a lot to explain, but I'm only going to touch on the important parts that tie into the problem that is going on currently," I said, taking a deep breath and launching into what a *nos* was, how it worked and clearing up how I had so many men as mates.

Abby asked so many questions, and occasionally, I would have to bring her back on track. The elders and Eli were brought in to explain about James, though we left out his name. Altogether, the tale of my parents was a sad one and hit hard when you saw the man left behind shed tears for his lost mate. I couldn't help but reach out and take his hand. When we ventured back into the topic of the Senate, I had to tread carefully to make sure I didn't out Morwyn, leading them to believe a senator was giving me information. By the time we were done, it was midnight, and I was barely able to stay awake.

"This was amazing," Abby gushed, shaking my hand. "We will do our best to make sure this information gets out there. Who knew the Senate could be so corrupt, lying to our faces about things? It's just wrong. It's stories like this why I became a reporter, holding big government accountable for its actions."

From our contact, I knew she was telling the truth. This was going to be her big break, so she wasn't going to fuck it up. I'd just handed her a golden ticket to a promotion and possibly more, depending on if this made the waves she thought it would.

Once they all left the pack lands, I melted into the couch completely and utterly wiped. There was no more fighting the fatigue, and I was more than happy to surrender to the rest my body was crying out for. "Please tell me there isn't anything more I need to do?" I pleaded.

"No, sweetheart, you've done more than enough today. Sleep now," Lane murmured, cupping my cheek and kissing me on the forehead. "We'll handle everything from here. You just rest."

With that assurance, I trusted my mates to do as they promised and slept.

FINLEY

After two days of straight sleep and three more days of keeping things low-key as we watched the world around us implode with the news blasting my story all over the place, I was almost back to full strength. Rath and the elders helped speed along my healing with their magic, but there was only so much they could do since my shifter side was taking its time to recover from the silver.

Now we had a day to perfect our plans before we brought this whole thing to a close. The invite to the Coexist Gala was on my doorstep a day after the story went live. The Senate had been doing damage control, making a show of cracking down on crime against supernaturals, but it was all surface-level bullshit. While I was out, Ayla and Derven went and dealt with the two targets I'd picked out, and it caused the collapse that I'd hoped for.

The Dark Ring now knew I was coming for them, and they closed ranks just as I hoped it would. They all had bodyguards with them at all times and changed their routines in as many ways as they could think. The interesting part was there was always something they would never give up on, and that's where I decided to leave little presents for them. With the help of the army I was building, I had supers all over the world helping me deliver my little gifts, that on face level, didn't have any connection with me.

The gift was an invitation to witness my coronation happening the day after the Coexist Gala. The truth of the matter was no such event was planned or needed, but it was my way to remind them *I* was the one hunting them down, and I could still get to them no matter what they did. Watching the chaos it created was how I hoped the news would be taken. The more they panicked, the easier it made my job. They would strip down the list to those who had to be at the gala or lose face, making it all the easier to take out the biggest players.

In this whole cat-and-mouse game, the only person I ignored completely was James. I had him under watch and knew every move he was making, but I wasn't going to give him the satisfaction of knowing I cared. He was one person I wanted enraged, frothing at the mouth with anger because then it would make it so simple to get him to walk into my trap. No matter what his skill with magic was or how powerful he was with mental manipulation, like Delilah seemed to think, I was stronger. The thing that brought down my mother's one-time mate was his confidence and ego. James would never see me coming until it was too late, and that was the beauty of it all.

What I was worried about was Morwyn. Zander hadn't been able to get ahold of her or Peter. I'd shared with him what I'd overheard the werewolves say, but there was no way for us to check on any of it unless we made it obvious we were working together. I knew she was alive because I was, but it was always lingering in the back of my mind if I might just drop dead at any moment. While we all tried to ignore that possibility, it wasn't as far from our minds as we'd like to believe.

Finally, I decided it was time to bring in reinforcements, so I called Eli. We hadn't really spoken to each other after the interview since he didn't stick around for me to wake up. Even if he weren't someone I wanted to rely on all the time, he held the keys to the Organization, and they could get the information I needed without drawing attention. Since the press release, I could no longer go anywhere without someone recognizing me, which was what I wanted, but I was quickly learning it had its drawbacks.

"Daughter, it's good to hear from you," Eli greeted. "Have you recovered already from your injuries?" he asked, sounding surprised.

"I'm nearly back to full strength, still have some stiffness, but I'm working through that," I answered, allowing the small talk.

"I'm incredibly glad to hear it. Now, while I'd hoped this was a social call, something tells me it isn't," he commented. "How can I help?"

"Can you get information on Morwyn?" I asked. "During the attack, I heard it might have been found out that she was betraying the Senate and trying to leave. Zander hasn't been able to get a hold of her or her bodyguard, Peter. I know Tabitha has been working with them as well, but I don't know how to reach her."

"Hmm, I'll put out my feelers and see what intel I can gather, but I'll be honest, one of the hardest people to spy on is Gareth. That wolf has eyes in the back of his head. I've lost one too many of my good people to him, and I'm not looking to add to that number," Eli warned.

"I understand, but with the contract between us, her life does affect mine," I reminded him. "I need to know if plans need to change. Can I wait two days, or do I need to act faster?"

"Give me a few hours, and I'll get what I can for you," Eli stated and hung up the phone. Clearly, my dear father didn't like to be reminded that my fate was tied to hers. There was nothing I could do to change that now. I had to make the best out of the situation I was in.

Getting up from the couch, I headed downstairs to the kitchen and pulled open the refrigerator door. My stomach was rumbling, and I didn't know what the guys were up to. I glanced at the clock seeing it was late afternoon, so they were probably out coordinating things with the new elves who started to arrive yesterday. I'd wanted to go out and greet them, but I was under house arrest until my men deemed I was well enough to resume normal activities. This included any sexual interaction, which I was not pleased about.

"Snuggles, whatcha doing?" Mason asked as his face appeared next to mine.

"Looking for something to eat," I shared, snagging a bowl of fruit from breakfast. It was cut up and easy to eat because I did not have the energy to make an effort for more.

Turning, I crashed into Noah, who'd been behind me. "Babe, that's not going to cut it. You need real food... meat to help you recover."

This had been an argument between us for the past two days. "Noah, I've been eating meat with every meal the past two days. I just want something light and fresh."

"That isn't going to help you get better, though," Mason countered. "Look, you're already exhausted, and all you did was work on some stretches and a little hand-to-hand fighting with Elias."

My lower lip popped out in a pout as I looked down at the fruit. "Can't I eat this while you make whatever meat you decide I need to eat?"

Noah let out a heavy sigh and pointed to one of the chairs at the counter. "Sit, eat your damn fruit while I make you something."

Smiling, I popped up on my tiptoes and kissed him. "You're wonderful. You know that."

Playfully, he smacked my ass as I walked by, making me laugh. "Sit your fine ass down before I do something else with it."

My wolf and I perked up at the flirting, but Mason gave me a stern look that told me absolutely nothing was going to come from it. With my pout back out, I sat and picked at the fruit. "Just so you know, this whole treating me like I'm an invalid isn't fun, and I'm sick of it."

"You just have to suck it up, Sally, and deal with it until after this shit show of a gala. We can't have you getting hurt, overtaxing yourself, or anything else that might affect how things go down. Remember, we're going up against the two most powerful groups of people in our world," Mason stated, crossing his arms as if he were preparing for me to argue with him.

Instead, I just popped another grape in my mouth, trying to tell him I was well aware that what we were up against wasn't going to get me anywhere. I just needed to get through the next day full of primping and final adjustments to my dress. The biggest perk of the announcement that I was queen of the elves meant I had companies reaching out to me to wear their dresses. They came to the house so I could try them on and did the fittings. Later today, the seamstress was coming with the dress to make sure it was perfect.

The same thing happened with jewelry, shoes, and purses. You name it, they were calling like crazy. Zander seemed to think I was more famous than him now and needed my own manager. I knew they wouldn't want anything to do with me once we destroyed the government of the supernaturals as we knew it. It's not in good taste to glorify someone who slaughtered two hundred people at a party, even if they were the scum of the earth.

"Here you are, chicken stir fry. You wanted something lighter, so that's what I came up with... protein and veggies," Noah announced.

Just as I put the fork up to my mouth, there was a knock at the door. I looked up at the other two, pleading for them to ignore it so I could eat because if I had to be dressed up like a doll and gushed over, I'd stab someone with this fork.

"Eat," Mason ordered, pointing at my plate like I didn't know what he was saying, and went to answer the door.

"I'm here with the dress..."

The moment I heard it was Tabitha, I dropped my fork and raced to the door. There she stood, indeed holding the dress with another lady next to her, cowering like she was going to be attacked.

I looked at her and smiled. "Thank you so much for ensuring my dress got to me, but I think I'll take it from here."

"Yes... of course... I'll just go now," she stuttered as she backed away and bustled off to the car she'd driven up in.

Grabbing Tabitha's arm, I yanked her into the house, and Mason shut the door after her. "What's happened?" I demanded.

"Gareth, he figured out that Morwyn was trying to get out," Tabitha answered, passing off the dress to Mason. "He has no idea she's working with you or that she's plotting to kill him as well, but he's keeping her under lock and key until the gala. I'm sorry I couldn't get to you sooner. I've been stuck in limbo without any direction. I was trying to get here, but I didn't have a valid reason that wouldn't draw attention. Then, out of nowhere, there was an order being sent to me that you needed a bodyguard for the gala, and that was me."

"Seems Dear Old Dad figured out a way to get me the information I needed without having to get near Gareth," I mused as I returned to the kitchen and shoveled food in my face. "Tell me everything you know about what's happening with her. Wait, let me see if Zander wants to be here for this."

Tabitha gave me a funny look as I silently reached out to him. "*Tabitha is here with news about your mother.*"

"*I'll be right there,*" he answered, and I could feel him shift heading in our direction.

"He'll be here in a moment," I shared and slid over the bowl of fruit. "Hungry? Didn't want to be rude and eat in front of you without offering."

"No, no, we are not just going to glaze past the fact you just talked to one of your men with your mind," Tabitha shot back. "Is that an elf thing?"

"It's a mate thing. I can only do it with them because we are soul bonded," I answered. "Apparently, it's not something many elves can do, especially when it comes to cross species," I explained.

"Woman, you are full of weird tricks," Tabitha muttered. "No wonder you were always so much better at things than I was. You've always been a super."

Before I could even get into that argument with her, Zander showed up, adjusting a pair of sweatpants he's slipped on before entering. Not that Tabitha would have cared that he was naked, but I might have clawed her eyes out. My wolf might not get upset about much, but that was one thing she couldn't stand for.

Zander walked up to me, placed a gentle kiss on my lips before standing behind me, and wrapped his arms around my waist so I could still eat. Tabitha cocked a brow at me but didn't comment, which I was thankful for. I knew our natural PDA wasn't common to humans, but it was for us.

"You have news about my mother?" Zander asked.

"Your father found out she was trying to leave the Senate for real and partnering with someone to make it happen. He doesn't know who it is, but to make sure she doesn't do anything stupid, he has her locked in her room. She's only allowed to be escorted by his people, and Peter is in a cell undergoing torture to get the information they want out of him. He'll die before he talks, but I'm glad we don't have long before the gala to pull this off," Tabitha informed us.

Zander's arms tightened around my waist, and I could feel his fear growing. His father wasn't a man who knew the meaning of mercy and forgiveness. We both knew his mother was just a puppet for them in the Senate. Gareth controlled every choice she made, never allowing her autonomy. Her one and only role was to be the figurehead who was clean of the dirty deeds they all did to honor Senate's wishes or ensure no other pack could become big enough to threaten them. Our pack was now both since the elves started to join us, and many were more than willing to fight at my side.

"They will still be attending the gala, correct?" I inquired.

Tabitha nodded. "This isn't an event they can miss with all the press you've now created. This is their big push to mend the damage you've done. They hope by showing that the Senate welcomes you into their midst, you're not a threat to them at all. If one of the senators were missing, there would be a flurry of gossip going about. The Senate can't risk that."

Looking up at Zander, I leaned back. "We'll save your mother, I promise, and not just because of our contract but because she is family to you. That means she's family to me."

"You know, I thought I would feel sad knowing my father is going to die in a day at the hands of my mate, but now I just want the bastard dead. He's done nothing in his life but create pain and heartache for everyone who comes in contact with him," Zander seethed.

I nuzzled my cheek against his bare chest, offering him what reassurance I could. He started to purr and buried his nose in my hair.

"Should I go..." Tabitha asked.

"Don't mind them. This is normal for werewolves," Noah said. "Come on, let me show you the office where she has all the plans laid out. I'm sure that will be far more interesting for you."

A smile tugged at my lips as I watched Tabitha sag with relief. It made me think about how stiff and cold I must have been when my mates first met me. Shifting so I could look Zander in the face, I settled my hands on his hips. "You okay?" I asked.

"I will be once this is over. Right now, it feels like we are waiting for the world to end, and I wish it were just happening already," he answered, pulling me into a hug. "There has been so much build-up to this plan, and in some ways, it seems so simple, but if one thing goes wrong, it could be a slaughter of us instead of them."

"This is something I had to deal with a lot during missions. There was so much work getting to the finish line that I felt like it should have been a lot harder than it was. The benefit of putting in all the work is that plans go smoothly, and unexpected bumps in the road don't derail everything. They can be managed with minimal damage," I explained. "When things are easy, it means we did it right."

"You realize how backward that sounds, right?" he argued.

Nodding, I slipped off my seat. "Yes, yes, I do. Now I'm going to go over everything one more time with a fine-tooth comb now that I have Tabitha to catch any mistake I might have made."

"Terrifying and beautiful, that is what you are, my mate," Zander commented as he watched me head into the office.

Tabitha and I spent the rest of the day going over the plan time and time again, making backup plans to back up plans trying to account for any and all situations that could possibly go wrong. This reminded me of working on other missions with her and how alike our brains worked, yet we saw different details as well, ensuring we didn't overlook something.

That night I made up a bed for her in my nest on a luxury air mattress Zander had for some unknown reason, while the rest of us created a puppy pile in the master bedroom like we had since I'd been shot. Having them all close helped me relax and sleep better, knowing where they all were if I woke up. That was the only trauma I'd developed from the whole event, and it was mostly driven by my wolf. It was getting better every day, but with everything happening tomorrow, I didn't want to risk any reason why I wouldn't be fully rested.

FINLEY

The morning flew by literally and figuratively. We all agreed that flying in the morning of the gala would be the safest bet, giving fewer chances of someone trying to kill any of us before the event. Plan for the worst and hope for the best was the name of the game until we started the real plan into action.

Tabitha came with me since she was my Senate-assigned bodyguard. I didn't reach back out to Eli just on the odd chance he wasn't the one who made that happen. Either way, I would be seeing him in a few short hours.

The gala arrivals started at six o'clock, but it was more of a time for photos and chatting up reporters covering the event. We planned to be there around seven-thirty when the sun was setting. Since our plan involved vampires, it only made sense to arrive when there was less time between their ability to help and the sun still high in the sky. Elves and werewolves would be in the area led by Ayla and a few hand-picked men from the pack.

Chewing on my thumbnail I'd just painted at the salon a few hours ago in the hotel, I paced, unable to sit still. I knew I was driving the others crazy as they tried everything to get me to calm down, but I needed to get the jitters out before I locked everything down to play the role of a lifetime. Tonight I would come face to face with the devil himself and his faithful pet vampire, who at one point was family to me.

"My heart," Elias pleaded with me. "Tell me what I can do to help you. I'll do anything... we'll do anything. Please just let us do something."

I paused to look at him, dropping my arms to my side. "Do you really mean that? Anything?"

"Yes." He growled in frustration. "Name it."

"Bend me over this table and fuck me," I ordered, calling his bluff.

The guys had been firm in their 'no sex' because they were afraid of hurting me, but my body needed a release *badly*.

Elias's eyes flashed bright as his wolf pushed forward at my challenge. "Well, I did promise anything."

"Not alone, you're not, beta," Lane snarled. "I played nice the last time, but I'm fucking my mate whether you like it or not, Elias."

Elias grinned at Lane. "Sounds to me like she needs a good hard fuck, and I'm thinking it will take both of us to satisfy her."

My skin grew hot, and my slick started to pool between my legs in anticipation. I was more than ready for them. "One rule," I said, halting them both. "No foreplay, just get down to fucking business."

They growled their agreement, and we started shedding clothes, tossing them carelessly aside. Lane reached me first, picked me up, and impaled me on his cock right where he stood. I groaned out my pleasure as my body accepted him easily. I'd been so needy there was no way my body wasn't waiting with open arms to welcome him.

"Finally," I sighed, resting my head on his shoulder. "Thank fuck you gave up this stupid no-sex rule."

"Oh, we aren't done with you yet, omega," Elias said, his only warning as he worked his cock into my asshole.

In minutes I went from no cocks to two cocks at once, and I couldn't be happier. Pressed between them, their bodies the only thing supporting me, they fucked me hard, and I let them know just how happy I was to be taking it.

"Fuck, yes," I gasped. "Just like that, fuck me as deep as you can get it," I begged.

Lane pressed me back against Elias so he could wrap his lips around one of my nipples, his teeth teasing the tip, making me scream.

"Shit, man, whatever you're doing is making her clench down on me so tight, I might not make it too much longer," Elias groaned.

Lane just chuckled as he continued his work, driving me wild with all the sensations assaulting my body in the best way. Elias's hold on my hips tightened as he only managed to last a few minutes longer before shooting off in my ass.

"Goddamn, woman, you're wringing me dry," Elias rasped, his lips brushing along my skin, making me squirm.

"Step aside and let someone else who can handle her take a shot," Rath ordered.

Elias chuckled. "Alright, elf, let's see what you got. I'll tell you right now, it's almost like she's in heat the way she's responding."

I knew I wasn't, but he was right that I was desperate for more and happy to allow any of my mates quality time if they wanted it. Rath gripped my hair, pulling it away from my neck, and yanked it to the side so he could nibble on it. My breath came in quick pants as he slammed into me, shoving me deeper onto Lane's cock. "Oh, God, *yes*," I cried out.

The feel of Rath's cock changed to feel far more ribbed than it had ever before. I knew my elf had magical tricks up his sleeve and whatever he was doing was fucking amazing. Every counterstroke to Lane's movement rippled through my body as I could feel every ridge and dip of his rock-hard dick.

"You like that, *nin mel*? Didn't you say you wanted to get fucked hard? Well, does this feel *hard* enough for you?" Rath taunted as he worked his hips in and out of me with ruthless abandon.

"Yes, yes, this is everything I needed," I praised, shoving against them to manage as much as I could.

Lane started to shorten his strokes as his knot swelled. "Whatever you did, I hope it doesn't do any damage as I fill her perfect pussy up with my knot."

"Oh, she'll be able to take it just fine," Rath whispered in my ear.

That comment sent me hurtling over the edge of an orgasm, which they both fucked me through. I had no idea what I was saying as my mind went blank with pleasure, eyes rolling into the back of my head. Lane's knot swelled, locking me to him, but that didn't stop him from using his knot to rub my sensitive channel against the texture of Rath's cock. Within seconds, another climax slammed into me, making it impossible for me to control my body, and I slumped limply in their arms.

I whimpered as they let their hands caress my skin and kissed any flesh they could get their lips on. Once I stopped twitching at every move, Rath slowly pulled out, his dick back to normal, leaving me wrapped around Lane like an anaconda. He carried me over to the couch, and we lay there together.

"Now, I want you to take a nap," Lane instructed, kissing me deeply. "We have three hours before you need to get ready, so close your eyes and rest."

"Yes, alpha," I sighed, lulled by his purr into the rest they all so desperately wanted me to have.

Dressed like the queen I was, I looked out the window of the limo as we drove to the gala. We ended up later than planned, but it didn't affect anything other than having less time to force myself to chat and mingle with people I hated and would soon see dead. Here I was the dichotomy of natures—an elf who was a trained ruthless assassin, yet the tender-hearted omega who could feel every emotion known to man. Somehow, though, they blended to become a perfect balance of light and dark, yin and yang, working in harmony to create the only person who could actually pull off this mission.

As the limo stopped, we did the same routine as we did for Zander's party, leaving me for last. My golden dress sparkled like the sun as the flash from all the reports glinted off it. This was never something I would have chosen, but it fit in a way I hadn't expected.

The dress was actually three parts—a corset and a full ball gown skirt with pants underneath. It was meant so when I wanted to dance, or after all the pictures were taken, I could drop the hundred pounds of tulle that made up the dress.

People were screaming my name, begging me to answer questions, but I simply waved and smiled. This wasn't the time or the place for me to indulge their need for gossip. I had Zander on one side and Rath on the other, walking me down the path to the entrance. Three of my mates went ahead and the other three behind to ensure I wasn't in any danger. The crown on my head felt ridiculous, but everyone agreed that in the human world, they would expect me to be wearing one if I was a queen.

When we made it to the entrance, they had me bypass the metal detector since my dress was covered in rhinestones attached with metal and was haphazardly patted down by a woman. It was hilarious to me that this was happening since the scariest people in the world were all going to be here drinking champagne and dancing the night away. Once cleared, I rejoined my men, and we were escorted into the ballroom set up in an old historic building in downtown Washington D.C.

"Any trouble?" Rath asked as he took my hand once more.

"Not at all," I murmured, a slight smile resting on my lips as we entered the area filled with tables that had place cards on them.

We found our table near the front, and since there were nine of us, we had the table to ourselves. I set my purse down and removed the gloves I'd worn for pictures. Now we just needed to mingle and wait for the speeches to start at nine. It was so much easier to kill people when they were seated and watching someone blather on about how our worlds are united and we keep the world from turning on each other. A load of utter bullshit is what it was.

"Queen Finley," a gentleman greeted, coming over to me. "Allow me to introduce myself. I'm Edward Crain."

"Senator, it's an honor to meet you," I addressed him, taking his offered hand. I assumed he was going to shake it, but instead, he kissed the back of it. I could feel my mates tensing, not at all appreciating this warlock touching me.

As if he could sense his mistake, he released my hand and took a half step back. "I do apologize. I forget that shifters are more sensitive to touch from others when it comes to their mates."

"That's a fucking lie if I've ever heard one. He literally works with shifters every day. The rat bastard knew exactly what he was doing." Elias snarled through our minds.

I gifted the Senator with a reassuring smile. "It's alright. We sometimes forget that warlocks are even considered part of the supernatural community. I'm afraid I don't know any of your customs or rules myself, so you'll have to forgive me if I cause any offense."

The anger and indignation that came off this man told me I'd pissed him off. Seeing that had been my intention, the smile on my face was genuine. If these people thought I was just going to roll over and be a good little elf queen because I got invited to the party, they would quickly realize that wasn't the case. Granted, they wouldn't be alive much longer, but what's the harm in having some fun with them before they died? As their lives ended, I wanted them to know who'd done it and why. This queen wasn't going to shrink away from the truth.

"That is one of the wonderful things about this gala. It brings so many of us together so we might be able to grow in our knowledge of other types of supernaturals," Senator Edward explained. "I hope you enjoy the rest of your evening, and if you'd ever like to learn more about warlocks, I could offer you some books to expand your knowledge."

"I would offer you the same about elves, but it seems that the Senate has taken all our texts and put them under lock and key. Do you know by chance who I could talk to about getting those? I feel it's only right for us to have them back," I commented, flashing him a bright smile so he would never be sure if I meant it as an insult or not.

Edward's jaw clenched, and his hands flexed as if he wished he was strangling me with them. "You might want to talk to Senator Morwyn. She is the one in charge of our historical texts and other documents."

"Bless you," I said, placing my hand on his arm gently. "I truly appreciate that you've taken the time to speak with me when I know others are vying for your attention."

The senator's chest puffed up as I stroked his fragile little ego. "Yes, well, it seems you somehow got the wrong impression of us, and I wanted to ensure we didn't reinforce it. Enjoy the rest of the gala. Make sure to check out the finger food. It's all divine."

"How much longer do we need to keep up this act like we give a fuck?" Mason asked, yawning as he looked around the event space.

I glanced at him out of the corner of my eye and shook my head. "Why don't we do as he suggested and check out the food?"

"We need to make certain the important people are here," I reminded them. *"James should be arriving soon now that it's dark out, but I haven't seen the judge yet. Zander, have you seen your mother?"*

"Yes, she's sitting at their table next to my father with a bodyguard right behind her. I've never seen her look as miserable as she does now. He

must be doing something awful to cause that kind of expression," Zander shared.

"Oh, look, darling, your mother, we must go say hello," I said aloud so others would hear, and there would be no question as to why we were talking to her. "Besides, I haven't had the chance to meet your father yet," I added.

Zander gave me a tight smile as he took my hand and led me over. *"No matter what that man says, don't believe a single word of it. He is a master manipulator and gets anyone to give in and do what he wants. He's also an incredibly strong alpha, so be aware if he tries to pull that shit on you."*

"Is he stronger than you?" I questioned.

He didn't answer right away, almost as if he hadn't really thought about it. *"No, I'm stronger than he is when it comes to that. He is ruthless in a fight, always looking for your weakness, but sheer alpha energy, I could take him."*

"Then I'll be just fine," I assured him. *"If I can ignore your orders, I think I'll be alright to brush his off as well."*

Our conversation halted as we stopped in front of a table where Morwyn was seated, wearing a regal emerald-green dress with her husband next to her, dressed just as smartly with a matching tie.

"Mother, Father, it's good to see you," Zander greeted, kissing his mother on her cheek and nodding to his father. "I'm sorry it's been so long since I've come home, but I suppose that happens when you meet your mate so suddenly."

Placing a hand on my lower back, Zander had me step just slightly in front of him, putting me closer to his mother. "Morwyn, it's lovely to see you again. I must say that dress is stunning on you."

Gareth snarled at me as I reached out to place a hand on her shoulder. With the contact, I was able to get snippets of what's been happening to her, and none of it was good. The fact she could sit here right now and not show just how cruel he'd been to her was a miracle.

"That's Senator Vaughan to you, *omega,*" Gareth barked, trying to throw his weight around.

My smile was plastered on my face as I cocked my head. "I'm so sorry, did you not hear? I thought with it being all over the news and wearing this silly thing on my head you might have caught on... it's *queen* to you," I stated, letting my tone hold all the disgust I had for him out in that last bit. "I'm not one of your wolves you can order around no matter what my rank is. Elf first, wolf second, leaving you with no power over me whatsoever."

Gareth shot to his feet and got right up in my face. "Listen, you little elf bitch—"

"Say one more word, and I will cause a scene the likes of which you have never experienced before," Zander threatened. "I will not allow you to speak to my mate with such disrespect. Now, *back off.*"

With Zander right behind me and feeling him putting all his alpha energy behind his words, the only thing that kept me standing was his touch. It was almost as if he were grounding me from the effect, but his father was forced back a step. Gareth's eyes widened as he realized what had just happened. Zander had out alpha 'ed him.

"Boy," he bit out. "You don't know what you're doing, but if you don't back down, I will end you, son or no son. I won't let you threaten me."

"No, I think the one who doesn't know what he's doing is you," Zander shot back. He reached out a hand to his mother, his expression softening slightly. "Come, Mother, I think you will find sitting at our table will be more enjoyable."

The bodyguard started to follow, but Tabitha cut him off and shook her head. "As one of Senator Vaughan's personal bodyguards, I'll take it from here. You can go."

The beta bared his teeth at her, but Zander cut him off. "Did you not hear her? She said for you to go."

When the order slammed into the shifter, he whimpered, spinning on his feet and hurrying off.

"You're playing with fire, Zander," his father called after us. "Don't come running to me when you get burned."

I paused, looked back at him over my shoulder, and talked in a low voice, knowing he could hear me. "Same goes for you. There will be no mercy found with us."

TWENTY-NINE

FINLEY

"Could everyone please find their seats? The awards and speeches are about to start," a woman announced from the podium on the stage they'd set up at the front of the room.

There was a flurry of movement as people grabbed their fill of finger foods and drinks before they took their seats. Not feeling the need to indulge in either of those, I wandered back to the table with Mason on my arm and watched as Zander and his mother had their heads close, whispering angrily at each other. I'd tried to give them space once we freed her from her husband's clutches, but that didn't seem to be going over so well.

"*What do you think she's chewing his ass out about?*" Mason asked as he slowed our progress. "*She looks pissed.*"

"*I imagine it has something to do with us pulling a stunt like this so publicly. She has no idea what our plan is, and I doubt Zander is filling her in,*" I commented. "*Everything ready?*"

Mason and Noah were the two in charge of making sure people were in their place at the gala. We'd managed to place elves throughout the staff since many of them could apply a glamour that could make them resemble other people. The catering staff had been through many checks, so we decided to replace them the day of, so we didn't have to battle with those details.

"Yup, everything is as it should be. You sure fifty of them is enough with how many staff they have running about this building?" Mason questioned.

I glanced at him and patted his hand. *"We just need them to deal with the humans. That tactic won't work with the supers. It will cut down the number of people we have to manage at once. Speaking of humans, have you seen the esteemed judge?"*

"Yes, he arrived about ten minutes ago with James right behind him. Those two are attached at the hip," Noah answered as I took my seat between Colt and Lane.

"How long until it takes effect?" Lane asked as he placed his hand over mine.

Turning to him, I kissed his cheek. *"Once you see it happening, you won't have any doubts as to if the plan is working or not."*

"Why does that worry me even more?" he commented.

"Thank you all for coming tonight and celebrating the hard work the United Senate has put into making our world a better place allowing all the supernaturals of the world to coexist together," the MC for the night said from the podium. "I'm Tatiana Burges, and I will be leading the events tonight."

The room filled with polite clapping as was expected from that announcement, but I didn't know who she was, so that meant it was no one important.

"Now, to start things off, let's hear a few words from Senator Sebastian Ragar," Tatiana announced, clapping her hands.

The senator for the vampires stood from his table and stepped up on the stage. "Welcome, all of you. It is good to spend time with the people of our world who are determined to make the changes that are needed. Before the United Senate was created, the world was in chaos after the loss of the Light Elves. There was a void in leadership, and many of you stepped up and decided to make the best of a terrible loss." He paused for a moment to look down at the note cards he had in his hands, then set them aside. "Tonight, not only are we here to celebrate the work we have done together, but we have something else unprecedented happening here."

A spotlight then landed on me at our table.

"The queen of the Light Elves has come out of hiding and is taking ownership of her role, bringing the Light Elves back out into the world they've been hiding from," Senator Ragar cheered, clapping. "Please come join me, Queen Finley. We'd love to have a few words from you."

I had expected something like this might happen, knowing they wouldn't invite me and not do something to call me out. I'd caused too much of a stir with my press announcement for them not to punish me in some way. It would appear the way they wanted to do it was public humiliation. Too bad for them, this wasn't going to work the way they wanted.

Gracefully, I rose from my seat, and Colt escorted me to the stage but let me walk up alone. He didn't move from that spot, ready in case something should happen, but I wasn't a helpless damsel.

Senator Ragar took my hand, bowed over it, and kissed the back of it lightly. "It is an honor to meet you. Please, we would all love to hear what it is you have planned for your people and if you have aspirations of joining us as a member of the United Senate."

I gave him a warm smile before I turned to face the worst of the worst our world had to offer the world. "Thank you, Senator Ragar, for the chance to allow me to have a voice here tonight. I know I might not have come across as being supportive of the Senate in my press conference earlier." I paused as the room tittered with laughter and other whispered conversation. "I would like to formally apologize for the way I handled that and prepared a little something for the night. Would you please pass out the champagne?" I called, signaling the staff.

Soon the room was flooded with servers passing out flutes of the simmering gold liquid.

"This isn't just any champagne. This is elven champagne, something only we know how to make and produce. Even the supernaturals here will get a slight buzz off the stuff," I added with a wink.

Waiting for everyone to have a glass, I lifted mine high into the air. "To the United Senate and all those we work with for the good of supernaturals all over the world. May we all learn from you today, tomorrow, and in the future," I toasted.

Everyone cheered and clinked their glasses before they guzzled them down. I waited a few beats before continuing to talk as everyone made delighted noises about the beverage, draining the last of it from their glasses.

"I might be queen of the elves, but I am so incredibly young to many of you, and I hope there will be much that I will glean from your vast experience. The Light Elves are no longer taking a back seat and watching the world go by. We are here to stay and hope to make an impact on the world once more," I declared, raising my voice so it could be clearly heard even without the microphone.

That seemed to get people's attention, and the clapping was far more hesitant, as if unsure what I was meaning. Then in the back of the room, someone screamed and fell out of their chair, trying to get away from someone else. "Help, please, we need a doctor," they yelled.

Another person stood from their table, grabbed their stomach, then puked blood everywhere. Hysteria ensued throughout the room with people screaming and crying, trying to get away from those who were vomiting blood everywhere as it also leaked out of their eyes, nose, and ears.

A hand grabbed my arm and yanked me to face him. His blood-red eyes, typical for a vampire, glowed with rage. "What have you *done*?" Senator Ragar demanded, baring his fangs at me.

"I said we were going to make an impact on the world, and the first step in doing that is bringing down the United Senate and the Dark Ring in one fell swoop," I explained, flashing him a predatory smile. "Or weren't you listening to my speech?"

He roared at me and lunged, but Colt was there yanking him away from me, his hand turning into claws as he ripped the vampire's heart out of his chest, dropped it to the ground, then removed his head. "Hurry, Finley," Colt demanded.

I grasped the hooks holding my skirt to my corset top and yanked it away, letting the tulle fall to the floor. Once it was gone, I was able to get to my weapons, but I didn't draw my knives yet. Scanning the room, I looked for Gareth, knowing I needed to deal with him quickly. I couldn't let him get away. Then I found him making his way toward Morwyn with murderous rage written on his face. Zander's first job was to get his mother out of the gala with Tabitha, who would get her to a safehouse Eli had provided for us.

Running from the stage, I leaped off, using my magic to freeze the werewolf. He was strong, and I could tell he had some kind of magic on him, making it hard for me to hold him still. He wasn't looking for me to be the one to attack him, so when I bowled into him, bringing us both crashing to the floor, surprise flooded his face.

"*You*," he snarled. "You've been the one working with the bitch this whole time."

"Guilty as charged," I admitted. "Now it's time for me to hold up my end of the deal and end your disgusting life. I won't let you ruin more lives just to ensure you get to stay at the top of the pack. Your days of ruling are over."

Gareth got his legs between us and kicked me off him. I let him do it, putting space between us as I crouched low, pulling a knife from my lower back sheath. Zander warned me he fought dirty and would do whatever it took to win. Knowing that, I watched him and everything around him he could possibly use against me. Even if the poison in the champagne wasn't enough to kill a super, it should have at least slowed him down a little.

I watched as his hands shifted to claws and his teeth sharpened into points. If either got a hold of me, I was fucked, but my faith in my abilities and knowing I was faster than him set me at ease. Striking out with a hand, I blocked it with my blade, then used the other to swipe at his stomach. The blade bit into his skin but not enough for it to do much damage. He hissed, realizing they were silver, and his eyes flashed with his wolf. Before I knew what was happening, he burst out of his clothes, and a giant gray wolf was standing on top of me. A pendant of some sort was hanging from his neck, and the power I felt from it told me it was the reason my magic had little effect. A witch had made him a talisman.

Grabbing for the necklace, I screamed as it burned into my flesh with a sensation I knew all too well when my hand touched it. It was made of fucking iron. Yanking my hand back, I swung with my elbow and smashed it into his skull right below his eye, where the bone wasn't as strong. I heard the crack, and he yelped, stumbling off me. Using his daze, I plunged the knife into his side, knowing it wasn't a killing blow, but it would really fucking hurt. Blood gushed from the wound, and I got my feet under me. Just as I was going to land another strike, a body slammed into me, tossing me across the room and crashing through a wall.

"Hello, daughter," James spat. "So nice of you to join us tonight. Seems you might have some of me in you, after all, slaughtering all those people in one fell swoop without even batting an eye."

I lay in the rubble of drywall, trying to get my lungs to start working again as I looked into the haunting eyes of the man who'd been trying to kill me since the day I was born.

"Aren't I just a lucky girl," I bit out as I slid my legs under me so I could kneel. "The poor orphan girl actually has two dads. One wanted to make her into a killer, and the other just wanted to kill her himself. Lucky me, right?"

"Shut the fuck up, you demon spawn," James snarled, spit hitting my face as he spoke.

Using my arm, I wiped the spit off and looked up at him. "What are you waiting for? Isn't this what you wanted? To kill me, rule the Dark Ring to torture and murder even more of your kind? Out of the two of us, I'd be calling you the demon, not me."

James pulled a small glass bottle from his jacket and tossed it at me. I deflected it with my blade, but another slammed right into my chest.

When it shattered on impact, the dust filled my nose, and I realized it was iron pulverized into powder. My mouth, throat, and lungs burned as the small particles scarred my flesh, and I screamed.

"Look at you, so tough yet brought down by such an important invaluable puff of dust," James taunted.

Rage flooded my body, and I shifted into my wolf, clothes bursting from my skin as my teeth sank into the flesh of his stomach. James roared in pain as I thrashed my head back and forth, spilling his guts to the floor. As a vampire, it would hurt like a son of a bitch, but it wouldn't kill him. He dropped to the floor, and I pounced again, ripping his throat out. Again, not a killing blow but fuck, it felt good to give him back some of the pain he'd put me through. A pulse of magic slammed into me from him, but I was far stronger than he'd ever be no matter what devil he sold his soul to.

Shifting back to my human body, my magic blocked his attack, and I shoved mine into him. This time I put my full intent behind it, and my magic was more than happy to do just as I asked, knowing it would inflict the maximum damage we could. I watched as James's eyes drained of the red coloring and returned to his natural brown color. His fangs receded into his gums, and within moments, he was human once more, but none of the damage I'd done so far was healed.

"I'm going to leave you to die like this, your guts on the floor, unable to cry for help, and no magic to save you," I rasped, my voice raw from the iron. James gurgled his protest, fear bright in his eyes before they started to dim at the blood pulsing out of his body. "Oh, and just because I know this will hurt you even more... Mother didn't lose her magic because of the elders. Her magic left her because she wasn't worthy of it because she never wanted to be queen. I was never the one who killed her. She chose to leave you," I divulged, watching as he gaped like a fish at me, trying to speak but couldn't.

Standing, I looked at the man who, at one point, could have been a father to me but chose to turn against me instead.

"Is that true?" Eli asked, his eyes wide, the pain in them so vivid it made me flinch.

"I don't know about the last part, but I do know the elders never did anything to cause her to lose her powers. The magic itself decides if you are worthy of it, and if it doesn't agree, it abandons you," I answered. "That last part I said because I knew it would hurt him the most."

Eli looked down at James and nodded numbly before snapping out of it. "Quickly, the battle in the other room is still going strong, and I saw Gareth trying to sneak out." He reached out to give me a hand. When I was back on my feet, he handed me his jacket. "Can you alter that with your magic, or can I do it for you?"

I motioned for him to go ahead, my throat burning like it was set on fire from the iron. It seemed with how fine it was, it wasn't going to continue to do more damage, but it fucking sucked, and I would probably have damage from it permanently. Soon with Eli's help, I was in a simple black jumpsuit that I could easily move in. Snatching up my knives, I smiled my thanks and took off into the other room.

It was chaos. Bodies strewed the floor, blood seeping from them while vampires, werewolves, elves, and other supernaturals fought tooth and nail to survive. I knew this fight was going to be brutal. These people didn't last sitting at the top without being able to back it up. My people had more to lose than they did, and it showed with how viciously they fought.

Moving through the battle, I took out those I could along the way as I searched for Gareth. Then Edward appeared in front of me, his hands sparking with power. "You dare to challenge us," he roared. "I'll show you what it looks like to take on a warlock who's five hundred years old."

Before I had time to react, a hand was shoved through his chest, holding his heart. "Child's play for someone a thousand years old," Derven hissed, dropping the heart and pulling his arm back the way it entered the body, slumping to the floor. My vampire looked me over before meeting my eyes. "You alright?"

"James is dead, but not before he left his mark," I croaked, my voice harsh even to my ears.

Derven's eyes flared with concern only to flick over my shoulder and pull me out of the way as a bobcat flew through the air, its head cocked at an angle that told me it was dead. Derven grabbed my neck with both hands as if he could fix it with his touch alone, but I just saw sadness in his gaze. "We will find a way to cure this," he said, dropping his hands and leaving a bloody handprint behind if the wetness on my skin was any indication.

"Let's end this. I need to find Gareth," I explained.

Derven nodded, and we waded into battle, slashing, clawing, and ripping limb from limb. I shoved out the back entrance and found Gareth and Zander locked in battle, both in wolf form. Blood was covering Zander's white fur, but I couldn't tell if it was his or from his father. Morwyn was getting yanked out of the car Tabitha was supposed to be driving her away in. I found my friend on the ground bleeding from her head, but I could still see her chest rising and falling, albeit incredibly shallow.

Knowing I needed to ensure she was safe, I bolted over to the car and took out one of the brutes trying to take Morwyn as Derven took care of the other. "Derven, get her the hell out of here," I ordered as I settled Tabitha in the back seat. I shoved enough power into her that she wasn't going to die, but I didn't want to drain myself being so far from my forest that held my backup magic.

"If you think I'm leaving you, you've lost your mind, *sângele mue*," Derven answered.

I grabbed his arm and looked him dead in the eyes. "If anything happens to her before this is over, I'm dead. Saving her is saving me. Now get her the fuck out of here and to the safe house."

Derven snarled, but he knew I was right. Giving me a searing kiss, he slipped into the car and peeled out the back alley. Relief flooded me as I knew she was going to be safe, and I didn't need to fear that part going wrong. Flipping my knives in my hands, I looked at the fight between father and son, trying to determine if I should involve myself or not. By the looks of pure loathing in Zander's eyes, I felt it was best to leave it to him but knowing his father was a bastard, I stayed to watch. I would intervene if I needed to or be able to heal Zander right away when it was done.

The two wolves were merciless, teeth tearing, claws slicing through fur and skin. The sound of impact when they crashed into each other was brutal. The wound I gave Gareth earlier was still bleeding, thanks to my knives being pure silver slowing him down slightly. The older werewolf knew how to fight and wasn't afraid to use what he needed to gain the advantage. He spotted me watching, flashing me a teeth-filled smile as he slammed Zander into the SUV his men were supposed to get Morwyn into.

The blow stunned Zander, so when his father came charging at me, he wasn't there to stop him. What this old bastard didn't realize about me is that I wasn't the wilting flower of your average omega, and I noticed in the fight his iron pendant was missing. As he launched himself at me, I didn't flinch. Instead, I took hold of my magic and caught him in midair with the ivy that was crawling all over the side of the building and tightened it. He struggled to get free, the ivy twining around his throat, causing his eyes to bug out at the lack of air.

"I told you I wasn't just a damn omega," I snapped, stepping up to him as the realization that he wasn't going to get out of this alive hit him. Glancing over at Zander, I saw him shaking himself, trying to get his balance back as he padded over to me, standing at my side.

Looking the alpha dead in the eyes, I decided to share with him what the final act of my contract was with Morwyn. "You were right. I am the person your wife was working with to free herself from you and everything you've forced on her. Do you know what it means to make a contract with an elf? Right, sorry you can't answer, so I'm just going to assume you don't."

I paced around him knowing each moment was killing him slowly, but being a werewolf, it wouldn't kill him... at least, I didn't think so.

"It's an agreement of terms that I'm then bound to, and if I don't fulfill them or try to stop whatever the agreement is, I will perish, and so will the other members of the contract," I shared, flashing him the mark on my wrist. "Would you like to know the last thing on my list?"

There was a strangled growl as he thrashed harder.

"Something tells me you probably know it's your life," I mused, then pressed my blade to his chest. "The question is do I kill you fast or slow?"

"Little dove," Zander called out to me, drawing my attention. *"Do not stoop to that bastard's level. Kill the man, and let's be done with this night. There will be much more that we need to handle."*

"Your son wants a quick death, and I believe he's right. While you deserve to be cut into tiny pieces while you're still living, what you don't deserve is that much attention from me. Nothing about you is worth my time," I admitted as I slit his throat, then followed it up by plunging my knife into his heart. "Die knowing that everything you strove for is going to be shattered into pieces, and you will be forgotten, wiped from memory, forever."

I watched as the light dimmed in his eyes, then extinguished into nothingness. One of the worst members of our kind was dead, and so were the other alphas of his pack who sat with him at his table. They were on our master list to ensure they never made it out of that room alive.

Cleaning my knives off on my pants, I settled them into one hand as I plunged the other into Zander's fur. "How badly are you hurt?" I asked, kneeling beside him, letting my forehead rest on his.

My magic trickled into his body, healing even the smallest of scratches it found along the way. There was a massive gouge in his side and a deep bite on his back leg that were the worst of things. Once he was fully healed, I used my magic to cleanse the blood from him, so his white coat was gleaming once more.

"Thank you, little dove, this is now finally over, and I no longer have to fear that man or what he might do to anyone else," Zander said, licking my neck where he'd left his mate mark, sending tingles through my body. Completely the wrong time for that kind of thinking but more of a promise for what was to come later.

"Let's go end this once and for all." I sighed but paused as the mark on my wrist vanished from my skin. The contract had been fulfilled, and my fate was no longer tied to Morwyn. I was free to do as I pleased once more. I couldn't help but smile, knowing this whole ordeal was over, but the battle had just begun.

THIRTY

FINLEY

The police showed up as one would expect when there was a massacre at a public function. My men and I sat on the edge of the stage, waiting for them to arrive. I'd sent everyone else into hiding. They didn't need to be held accountable for this. I did. The only reason they'd been involved in the first place was because I asked for their help. As queen to my people and the mate to alphas who led a well-respected pack, I would shoulder the blame for all of it.

When the police stormed in dressed in riot gear, guns at the ready, to find the floor littered with the dead, they froze. There was no point in making things look better when it was what it was, and I wasn't going to deny any of it.

"You won't need your guns," I announced. "None of us wish you any harm."

The man in the lead scoffed, looking around the space. "Like any of us believe that?"

"I'm an elf, officer. We cannot lie," I answered with a shrug. "Ask whatever you want to know, and I will tell you."

And so began the hours and hours of questioning. We called in lawyers that Derven had on retainer, along with Morwyn and Eli speaking on our behalf. It wasn't until the wee hours of the morning that we were allowed to leave the precinct with the knowledge we wouldn't be going to jail. With Morwyn being the only living member of the United Senate, she made it clear I was hired to take out the members I did. Then with the amount of evidence I had on the Dark Ring members, it wasn't hard to show they were dirty. Granted, they wouldn't approve of killing, being the way this should be handled, but no one was willing to press charges.

The biggest question on everyone's lips was... what now? The United Senate was dismantled, and Morwyn proclaimed it was dissolved and the leaders of each supernatural species should choose their next leader. There would no longer be a united front. Each would tend to their own, creating a council of three members to govern. It was how things should have been all along.

Our lives were chaotic for months after the gala—news reporters sneaking onto the land, or should I say, tried to. The forest wasn't having any of it and would keep them from interfering. The pack grew in more ways than one as elves created the first village within the Smoky Mountains forest.

There was a good fifty miles between the pack and the village, but they did truly coexist, helping each other out, learning new skills, and improving old ones. It was just how I envisioned things would be.

The elders came to live in the village, teaching those who wanted to learn all about elves. The texts and scrolls the Senate had kept locked away were given back to us, and a records hall was built. All were welcome to visit the village if they had pure intentions, and if they didn't, well... the forest had a knack of making sure they never arrived and ended up in some other odd location. It didn't matter how many times people tried, they'd find themselves in a different state if they weren't careful.

It took about six months for the world to start returning to some semblance of normal. It was easier for us since we hardly had to leave the pack lands for anything. Now the holidays were upon us, and the guys wanted to make a huge deal out of it. I'd never been one to put much stock into the whole festivities, but this year, it was different since I now had a family to spend it with.

The twins wanted to bring their mom out, Morwyn was coming to stay for a few days with Peter, and Eli was even going to join us for the weekend over Christmas.

Eli and I didn't have a father-daughter relationship, but I accepted he was part of my life and allowed him to be part of it. We stayed in contact through email or occasional phone calls. If he were in the area, he'd stop by, or if we were in New York for something to do with Zander, we would do the same. It was odd learning how to be family to someone who knew all about you, and you knew nothing about them. We disagreed on more than we agreed but soon learned how to agree to disagree. He was of an older mindset, and I had more experience in the world. We came from different perspectives.

Begrudgingly, he sold the Organization to Tabitha and Ayla, who ran things vastly different and used it to hunt down the remaining members of the Dark Ring. They were like sisters to me, and they would be joining us as well for Christmas. The pack house was now the guest house since we didn't have any room in Zander's house to keep anyone else there. We'd talked about adding onto the property, maybe another wing or adding a guest house off to the side for when people came to visit.

Most people thought it was odd that my guys had their own room, even if they hardly slept in it. We'd had to upgrade and get another king-size bed and put it in the master suite, so we had more room.

Every night, the guys climbed into bed like a massive puppy pile with me in the middle. If there was ever a night I wanted to be on my own, I could stay in my nest... not that that's ever happened. Occasionally, if one or two of the guys wanted *alone* time with me, then I'd stay in their room with them, but most of the time, we slept together. None of them had any shame and would either join in or roll over if they caught us fucking.

⸻ ◆ ⸻

For the most part, our days were so busy dealing with the influx of people in our pack and the funding that Colt and Lane got for their business. So, in an effort to get them all in one place before all our guests arrived, I mandated a family dinner they all had to attend, or I was going to kick them out of the bed for a week. If any threat would do it, it would be the one that worked.

I still wasn't all that skilled in cooking, even though the others had been trying to teach me, elves and wolves alike, but it was not a skill I possessed. Thankfully, this wasn't something the guys needed from me since Zander, Derven, and Noah could handle it, and the rest could make passable food when needed.

So for this dinner, I had Katie helping, more like I chopped things up, and she did the cooking. It was just about finished when they guys started to file into the house. They all came and greeted me with a kiss, then headed up to shower or change.

"Katie, I can't thank you enough for helping me do this. I didn't feel like it was right for me to ask them to come to dinner, then make them make it." I laughed, my voice raspy from the permanent damage the iron left behind.

She smiled and gave me a tight hug. "What is a pack for other than to help out when needed? I couldn't let my alphas starve or be forced to eat Kraft Mac and Cheese, now could I?"

"That only happened once," I muttered, rolling my eyes as she blew me a kiss.

"All you have to do is take the bread out of the oven when the timer goes off, and the rest is just keeping warm," Katie instructed as she gathered her things. "Call me if anything goes horribly wrong, but I think you're safe for now."

After Katie left, I let out a heavy sigh and pulled the apron off, hanging it up on the pantry door. Someone stepped up behind me and settled his hand on my hips. "You know, snuggles, I don't think there is anything sexier than a woman with an apron on."

"You mean when it's the only thing she has on," I teased.

Mason made a noncommittal grunt. "Bra and panties could be hot too…"

"Oh really, is that so?" I asked, turning in his grasp to wrap my arms around his neck. "Are you telling me that's what you want for your birthday, or is there another reason you're bringing it up?"

Avoiding answering the question, he caught my lips in a searing kiss that had me moaning as I got backed into the pantry door. The harsh sound of the buzzer had me shoving him away and racing over to the stove.

"Where's the fire, babe?" Noah asked, his brows raised in concern.

Yanking open the oven, I pulled out the bread that was perfectly toasted, and the cheese melted just the right amount. "No fire and trying to keep it that way," I answered, slipping it onto the cutting board.

"Little one, that only happened once. You're gonna need to give your-self a break already. All of us have burned a pizza once or twice in our lifetime," Colt reminded me as he wrapped his arms around my waist, kissing my neck. "You are amazing at so many things. It's perfectly alright if cooking isn't one of them."

"While I appreciate that, I just want to make sure all of Katie's hard work doesn't go to waste," I rebutted as I cut the bread into chunks. "Can you take this into the dining room?" I asked Colt, changing the subject.

"The dining room, hmm?" Zander asked as he arrived in the kitchen. "Something special happening?"

I shrugged. "Just wanted us to have a special night just for us before all the family comes into town. We've all been so busy, and I miss us having this kind of quality time."

Zander stopped me and cupped my cheek. "Little dove, I told you if you don't want me doing the Asian tour, I won't. It's going to be four weeks out of the country, and I know you can't leave for that long."

"It's not that at all," I assured him. "I was honest when I told you I would be fine. When you do a US tour again, I'll come along for however long I can. Just because you now have a mate, I don't want you to give up something you love. You fought hard to get back to doing this after everything that happened. It will be an amazing way for you to start the new year."

He gave me a skeptical look but took my word for it being an elf and all. The guys helped me carry in all the food and set them on the table, and I looked around the room, seeing all my wolves but not Derven or Rath. "Where are the other two? I saw them come in?"

"Derven got a video call from his dad, and Rath was keeping him from throwing the computer through the office window," Lane shared, popping a crouton from the salad into his mouth. "This looks amazing, sweetheart. I'm glad you decided to do this."

I smiled at him and blew him a kiss. "I'm gonna go rescue him. His father loves me for some strange reason."

Heading to the office we all used now for our various roles, we had to add two more desks, so there were more surfaces to cover with papers. Sitting behind the one that Derven used mostly, he was speaking to his father heatedly in Romanian. Rath was leaning against one of the bookshelves out of sight but close enough to intervene. When he saw me, he smirked at me as I walked over.

"*Coming to rescue your vampire from his evil father?*" Rath teased.

I shot him a look. "*Oh, and you're just standing there to keep him company? Or are you tired of fixing windows when he chucks the laptop out the window?*"

"*Touché, nin mel, touché.*" He laughed, reaching out a hand to me, pulling me into a hug, kissing me slowly before he allowed me to go rescue Derven.

I stepped behind Derven and leaned closer to the computer. "*Buna ziua,* Remus," I greeted with a small wave.

"*Fiică,*" Remus announced excitedly. "It's so good to see you. Matei, when are you going to bring your beautiful bride home for me to meet? I keep asking and asking, and you keep telling me no, this is not good."

"Remus, you know how it is to be a ruler," I countered. "Things are just getting off the ground, and I need to be there for my people. I've promised that once things settle down, I will make him take me to see you," I promised once again.

"Ah, such a lovely woman you found yourself, Matei," Remus gushed.

Derven looked up at me, his love shining bright in them. "Yes, I am beyond lucky to have her in my life."

"Now I know how hard it is for you two to connect, but we are just about to sit down to dinner, and I made them promise they would all be there," I shared, knowing how Remus was about keeping his word.

The ancient vampire might be paranoid and crazy, but he was a man of principle and believed in a man's word being unbreakable. "Yes, yes, go be with your family. One day we will all meet and have dinner together... one giant happy family," Remus announced, then ended the call.

Without warning, Derven pulled me into his lap and nipped at my neck. "You are too good to me. You know that?" he whispered into my ear. "What would I do without you?"

"Be stuck on the phone with your father for five hours and starve to death," I answered, giving him a cheeky smile.

"Evil woman, no one sees your true colors, but I do," he muttered as he stood, tossing me over his shoulder and slapping my ass. "Come on, Rathal, let's go enjoy the meal our woman has prepared for us."

"Are you even going to eat it?" Rath asked.

"Maybe, depends on if someone is going to be my snack later," Derven teased, groping my ass. "I know of a big juicy rump I don't mind taking a bit out of." They both laughed at the terrible pun he made.

When we reached the dining room, Derven set me down at the head of the table and pulled out the chair for me. I took my seat, and the others all settled into theirs. We dished up the food and dug in, talking about our days and things going on in the pack or with work.

I loved how this just felt so perfect, and I couldn't even begin to know where to thank them for becoming my family and teaching me what it meant to love someone. As we drew to the end of the meal and the guys relaxed, Zander got up and poured everyone a drink. Then I got up, grabbed eight small boxes, and placed them in front of each.

"My heart, you know that Christmas is next week, right?" Elias asked, looking at the box with curiosity.

I nodded but gestured to have them open the box. They did slowly and picked up the object and started to unwrap the item from the tissue paper. Mason got his free first and looked at the coffee mug in confusion, reading the words over and over again on it before understanding hit him. His eyes snapped up to mine, and his jaw dropped.

Elias was the next one, and he shot up from his seat, backing away from the thing like it bit him. "Are you serious?" he demanded, his gaze blazing with passion. "You better not be joking about this because if you are, I'm going to beat your ass."

I couldn't help but laugh at his threat. "Is that any way to treat the woman who is going to be the future mother to your children?"

"Wait, does this mean you're already..." Lane asked but couldn't finish his question.

"No, it means that with your help someday soon, those mugs won't be correct. I'll have to replace them since *Soon To Be Dad* will be wrong, and it will need to be *Number One Dad* or something equally silly," I explained.

Colt cleared his throat and looked at me with hope in his eyes. "I'm going to need you to say it out loud, please, little one."

Standing, I looked each of them in the eyes as I spoke. "Will you, my mates, help me be a mother someday in the near future?"

Noah whooped as he leaped out of his chair, charged over to me, scooped me up, and raced up the stairs. "Last one naked doesn't get her pussy," he hollered to the others.

That had them all racing, tossing clothes off themselves and me left and right, as they sped to the master bedroom. Colt snatched me out of Noah's arms and thrust into me as he landed on the bed, rutting into me as he whispered all the dirty things he wanted to do to me.

"I'm going to fill your pussy with so much cum, you won't be able to hold anyone else's." I groaned at his words, his hot breath on my skin pushing me to the limit.

My men made quick work out of spending the entire night filling me again and again until I was a sticky mess of their seed dripping out from between my legs. Elias kept trying to shove it back up inside me until I scolded him strongly enough, he left me alone.

"I don't care which of us gets your belly round first because no matter what, that kid will be ours just as you are," he murmured against my stomach as he kissed it. "God, I don't think I'll be able to let you go a moment without one of us shooting our seed into you."

Running my fingers through his hair, I smiled. "Can't say I'm opposed to that, just so long as I can still get my work done."

"Sounds like us betas might get more of a shot then since we don't have to be stuck to you for a half hour," Mason pointed out the smugness in his voice.

Zander chucked a pillow at his face. "I'll just fuck her while she's sitting on my lap, then she can do work at the same time while I ensure my cum won't leak out before it's had time to knock that womb up."

"Fuck," I swore. "Why is that one of the hottest things you've ever said?"

He grinned at me. "We alphas can come up with many ways to keep you knotted up good and still doing life. Just you wait and see."

"Best early Christmas present ever," Colt added.

Rath chucked. "Now it makes sense why you didn't want to do that with the family around."

Everyone laughed and snuggled around me closer until I was smothered by their bodies and their love.

"Not so tight, Derven," Mason chided. "What if she's already pregnant, and you're squishing the baby?"

Derven snorted. "I don't care what kind of supernatural you are. There is no way it works that fast. We've got a few weeks yet before we know if it worked."

"Now, I definitely am not going on tour," Zander shared. "Tour or knocking my mate up? Yeah, I know which one I like the sound of more. It can wait."

I drifted off to sleep smiling, knowing that this family of mine was more perfect than I ever could have dreamed of. The way it came about wasn't the best of circumstances, but fate had a funny way of making things happen just the way they should.

Now, we just had to wait and see what the future had in store for us.

The End

ABOUT AUTHOR

Elizabeth is an International Best Seller, originally from Illinois but now living in sunny Phoenix, AZ. Elizabeth has been writing for nine years and started out in YA Fiction but recently found herself loving the Reverse Harem genre. Like her favorite books, Elizabeth loves to write about strong women of all varieties. Not all strength is flashy or apparent at first glance—some lies just under the surface.

Don't Miss Out!

Be the first to know what is coming next by following Elizabeth's social media! You never know when or what will be coming next!

Website: ElizabethKnightBooks.com

Facebook: Elizabeth Knight's Unicorn Queens

Instagram: elizabethknightauthor

TikTok: elizabethknightauthor

Newsletter: sign up here

ALSO BY

Knot All Omegaverse

Knot All Is Lost: Part 1 & Part 2 (Complete)

Knot All Is Lost: The Complete Duet Omnibus

Knot All Is Ruined: Part 1 & Part 2 (Complete)

Knot All Is Ruined: The Complete Duet Omnibus

Caprioni Queen

Book 1 – Glitter & Guns

Book 2 – Blood & Heartache

Book 3 – Revenge & Truth (June 2023)

Standalone Books

Nicolette: Ladies of the MC

Lying Lainey: Underground Omega Syndicate (May 2023)

<u>Hidden Empire Series – Complete series</u>

Book 1 - Two Tricks

Book 2 - Three Tricks

Book 3 - Four Tricks

Book 4 - More Tricks

Book 5 - Our Tricks

<u>Hidden Empire Novel</u>

Harper's Renegades

<u>Omega Assassin - Complete series</u>

Book 1 - Dual Nature

Book 2 - Hidden Nature

Book 3 - Perfect Nature